By BEN ARONIN

AMERICANA — PLAYS AND PAGEANTS

FRONTIERS OF FREEDOM
(1950)

SONG OF MID-AMERICA
(1951)

ADAM TO ATOM
(1952)

OTHER LITERARY WORKS

THE LOST TRIBE
(1934)

THE MOOR'S GOLD
(1935)

DEAR SHOSHANNA
(1938)

THE ABRAMIAD
(1941)

CAVERN OF DESTINY
(1943)

BOOKS FOR CHILDREN

BIBLE TALES IN RHYME

A CHILD'S BOOK OF PRAYER

THE NEW MOTHER GOOSE RHYMES

MOTHER GOOSE AND FATHER GANDER

JOLLY JINGLES

FINIAN HIMSELF

Walt Whitman's Secret

FIRST EDITION

DEDICATION

*To Frieda—my wife and dearest friend in
this world's magic and its loneliness.*

*"Not till the sun excludes you do
I exclude you"*—

WALT WHITMAN

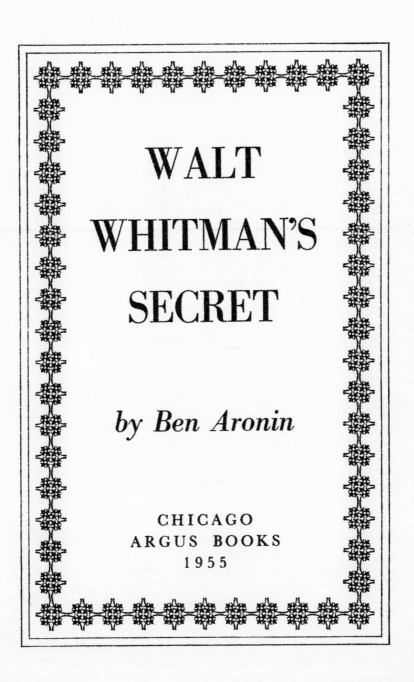

WALT WHITMAN'S SECRET

by Ben Aronin

CHICAGO
ARGUS BOOKS
1955

Part One

NEW ORLEANS SOJOURN

THE TERRIFIED KITTEN SHIED away from the stone.

"Hi! Yi! Missed him!"

The grinning convict tossed a heavier rock. Now even the white guards were amused. They did not order the Negro chain gang to "Get to it!"—but watched with condescending detached interest, their rifles held loosely in the bend of their arms.

There was a shower of rocks as the kitten wriggled away—and then a piteous whine and blood dropping in big red drops from its mouth.

A squat white guard with flabby rolling flesh ambled over to the wee bit of whimpering fur.

"Might as well put it out of its misery."

He placed the long dark barrel of the rifle against the tiny head.

"Come, kitty!"

The kitten looked up, licking the gun barrel with its pink tongue and caressing it gently with its paw as though at last it had found a friend.

The flame was purple and yellow as it leaped from the musket's mouth—and on the glaring white rock was —blood and fur and twisted gray green entrails.

Walt shook his head and sighed. He pulled the brim of his hat over his eyes and stifled a longing to weep. He stared at the chain gang and listened to their laughter.

1

They had forgotten the kitten and were swinging the heavy sledge hammers in cadence.

"M'allé couri dan dèser—"

The guard who had fired the bullet shuffled closer to Walt and sat down on a rail of the fence.

"I hate Yanks!" he said to no one in particular. His eyes wandered from the prisoners to his fellow guards and then came to sombre rest on "the Yank." From there they did not move.

"I said I hate Yanks."

Walt ignored him and watched the shackled, sweat-drenched men labor among the glaring white rocks.

The air was heavy with sunlight. Finally the guard spoke again.

"What you starin' at, Mister?"

Loose of bone and limb, with the rifle now held across his knees, he was not openly hostile. He seemed merely curious. Walt nodded his head towards the ankle-shackled prisoners, and said: "That."

"Hm — niggers working? What's strange about that?"

The festering sore where the iron ring bit into the ankle anchored and held his eyes.

Where should he start explaining? Children squawk their way alike into living, and then—some wield the whip and others feel it.

"It's hard for them to move with those things on."

The drowsy air seemed suddenly charged with menace.

"That's the general idea, mister. Any objections?"

This is your moment, Moses, and these are the task-masters. Speak out!

"A few."

"Hey, Sam." The flabby fleshed guard arose to his feet and called out peremptorily to another warden at the far side of the ditch.

Why should he take it all upon himself? He should have choked the impulse before it flowered into speech.

The men stood together and talked, glaring ominously and scowling from time to time in Walt's direction. Walt inwardly squirmed and looked away. He thought, "Hate frightens more than the blow."

Finally the guard who had been called Sam ambled over. "You're McClure's friend, aren't you?" Walt nodded. "You work for him?" Walt nodded again, breathing with greater ease.

Sam eyed him curiously. "McClure's all right. Ain't got no quarrel with McClure. Don't know much about you, though. You looking for trouble? Why don't you hunt yourself a squattin' place somewhere else? Now don't go beatin' your jaws, Mister. Git!"

He turned abruptly and walked off. Walt did not move. A warm flood of relief suffused him. He would stay. He felt his dignity demanded that he stay. Besides, there had been no out and out threat—merely an expression of annoyance.

Walt Whitman had come to New Orleans to write for the Crescent. He liked the languid half-dream life about him—drank it in like a glass of sweet port. He loved every spot of the old city—the mild and gentle flowing grounds of the Ursuline Convent, the ornate pompous Opera House on Orleans Street, the sedate and stately homes on Esplanade Avenue dreaming in the sun in pleasant senility, the noisy and turbulent levee and the intimately narrow streets of the Vieux Carré!

The soft cozy mud had a pleasant odor in the warm afternoon sun. He leaned his great body snugly against the log-built fence, fitted the small of his back contentedly against the top rail and listened.

They sing with all their bellies and laugh from their kidneys.

Do *I* feel the misery *they* do not feel?

3

> *"M'allé couri dan déser*
> *M'allé marché dan savane."*
> *"I will run into the desert.*
> *I will march through the prairie."*
> *They wrap their wretchedness about them like a*
> *cherished robe, and hug their slavery to their breasts.*

Walt's ears tingled with the brittle rasping voices of the negro convicts who were clearing the ditch. It was strange, clamorous disonance — the clanking of their ankle chains and iron collars; their song, wheezy with breathing, and the monotonous dull sucking blows of the picks as they fell.

One sweating Negro raised his shackled hand and held it up until he was noticed. The warden named Sam cursed deeply in his throat, impatient at the interruption and spat his command through ugly teeth. "All right, nigger, bend down where you're at."

Why trouble to unchain him? Why interrupt the rhythmic beat of shackled flesh?

"Get movin'!" The picks rose and fell. The convicts worked on, in silence.

Walt heard a step and turned his eyes to encompass a loosely-jointed boy of fifteen or sixteen—tall and with the long, thin face of a prophet. "Hi, Jeff!"

The boy did not answer. So slim he was that his bones seemed out of joint. His cheeks were hollow as though he were sucking them in. He stared long and hard at the wardens, who returned his glance in kind.

"Hope Jeff keeps quiet. Why repeat the unpleasantness." Walt wanted no trouble.

"Your feet are soaked through, Jeff. Let's go back to the shop."

Jeff turned darkly away from watching the convicts. His muddy shoes made a gasping noise as he lifted them from the black ooze and buried them again in the slime. His eyes were wide—intense—stern. His long face was

sallow and hollow as though drained by a bowel-gnaw-
ing hunger.

"I don't like New Orleans, Walt. I hate this scummy
damned place!"

"Jeff, you're homesick for Brooklyn. Give this part
of your country a chance."

*Too young! Too young for loneliness. Shouldn't
have taken him! Shouldn't have taken him!*

"This isn't my country. Let's go back, Walt."

The older brother placed his hand gently on Jeff's
shoulder.

"Let's go to the shop, Jeff, and set a column or two
of type."

Jeff shook off the hand impatiently with a twitch of
his arm. "Let me be!"

"What's gnawing in you, Jeff?"

"I don't know, Walt,—or maybe I do. My stomach's
tied into a horsetail knot. My heart's hanging in the
middle of nothing—and I'm so miserable I could die."

Walt looked at his brother's wan despairing features
and pitied him.

"It's like planting yourself in new soil. Give the
roots a chance to take hold."

They turned into Canal Street and walked slowly
past crowded cafes and noisy saloons. Then they cut
over to Iberville Street. Jeff hated with Puritanical zeal,
and yet was inevitably drawn to that street where ladies
leaned from the windows—their lips very red, and held
their kimonos closed with one hand while they waved
at passersby with the other.

"I want to go home, Walt. I've made up my mind.
I want to go home. I'll go by myself, if you want to
stay here. I can't stand it here."

"You haven't made any friends—"

"That wouldn't make any difference."

"Yes, it would. Your feelings about any city depend

a lot on the kind of welcome you get."

"Well, it's been a hell of a welcome then. They bow and scrape to get your coin—polite on the surface—"

"Quit your carping and moaning, Jeff. People are the same the world over. One warm handshake—and you'd have felt differently about New Orleans. You're so busy chewing the cud of your own homesickness that you haven't got eyes for anything else."

"I've got eyes, all right. I saw what you saw." Jeff jerked his thumb back in the direction of the convicts.

"Cruelty isn't peculiar to New Orleans or the South. There's been worse or as bad in New England. Be fair about it, Jeff."

A fleshy cheerful woman called out:

"Come up for a little lovin', papa. Bring your son up."

"Shut your damned mouth!" Jeff yelled back.

Walt grasped his arm "Easy there, Jeff. She gets enough of grief without you adding to it. And besides you're not angry with her; you're angry with yourself for being drawn toward her."

Jeff's too young to reveal himself to himself.

"I'm not drawn toward her. She's fat and ugly."

"And yet she draws you—why don't you admit it— there's a kind of beauty in what you call ugliness."

"There you go again, Walt. Everything's beautiful —everything's good. Put a horse dropping in your button hole and call it a rose."

The dung and the stars—teeming, teeming alike.

Walt merely smiled. "Roses *could* grow from it, — and they do!"

Back at the shop Jeff took off his soggy shoes and stockings. Padding busily about in his bare feet he solemnly began to set type.

He's young and should be playing — laughing — eager. Too much monotony of print and paper in his brain!

Walt felt his heart contract with pity. "You're not well, Jeff. Something is wrong. Why don't you tell me? You were full of life and song on the trip down."

Jeff did not look up. He accused sullenly, bitterly: "You're not doing what you came out to do."

"I told McClure I'd run the Crescent for him, and I'm doing it, Jeff. It's a straight newspaper job. I'm running his paper as I agreed to do."

"Yes, you're doing it all right — like a Prudence Primrose column, showing New Orleans its prettiest streets—glorifying the houseboat, the oysterman—the French market—the Creole flower girl."

Jeff thinks in black or white; no in-between. Where do I fit in such divisions?

Walt regarded his young brother with a whimsical grin. "Well, Isaiah — Jeremiah — Ezekiel — impatient young prophet—what's wrong with showing a city to itself? Take a good look at New Orleans, Jeff. But be fair. There's a lot of beauty here—scattered all over— and the people ought to see it. A city has personality; it's a living thing. It should see itself, and preen itself occasionally; so I hold up a mirror."

Jeff flung himself at his brother with a quick turn of his body. "That's what I'm trying to do to you, Walt. All your talk about beauty in ugliness can't change it. Good is good and bad is bad. Can't you see what's happened to you here? You're showing them their flower girls, not the mud on their souls."

And are souls like white cucumbers and sins like ink spots?

Walt's voice was even — deliberate. "Relax, Jeff. Don't preach. You should be enjoying all this." Jeff kept his face averted. "There's no mud on their souls, Jeff. They're no different from you and from me. They're all human beings. If it's the negroes you mean

7

—be patient. They know it's a bad thing. — The whites know it. A little more time is all they need."

"A little more time and then what? Will they use the auction block as a table for a black and white brotherhood feast? You keep telling me you have a song in your heart and I guess, maybe for a while, I believed you. But Walt, what are you singing? I've always wanted to work for you, Walt, but not on this bilge and molasses water."

I was happier when I was his hero. Now his furious, impatient youth is shaking my deliberate years out of their assurance.

Jeff began to cough in his excitement and his thin face became purplish red and swollen.

"It went down the wrong way," he explained sullenly to Walt, in the midst of his coughing. "It's not a cold. Don't go worrying about me; it's not a cold."

I love him. I love him. How shall I tell him?

Walt's voice was kindly. "Jeff, you're intelligent and very well read for a boy of fifteen. You feel things, but you don't reason things out. This is the South—the land of plantations, hot weather and cotton. If you had been born and raised here, Jeff, you'd take it for natural and ordinary that African slaves are needed to work the plantation."

Jeff avoided Walt's eyes. "You don't sound like you did back home, Walt. You blow hot and cold."

"People have different ideas, Jeff, and you've got to listen to both sides. People change their ideas, too, and they've a right to. The only ones I don't like are the doughfaces that change ideas when it suits their pockets or their politics."

"Buying and selling human beings for so much a pound." Jeff kept his face averted doggedly toward the floor.

Poetic license—but let it be.

"It's bad—and I don't like it. And it'll change the way it did in Europe. It won't do any good for the North to shout 'Blackguard!' That'll only make the South bitter and stubborn. It's easy to be an abolitionist when you live up in Maine—or even in Brooklyn, but when it touches your pocket—" Walt shrugged. "I'd hate to tell you, Jeff, how many slave ships had northern owners and crews."

"You admit that the North and the South are both guilty. Then why do you keep praising this country as though it were the hope of the world?"

"It *is* the hope of the world, Jeff."

Jeff grunted impatiently, "Gambling, drinking, quarreling scum all fighting for the dollar and selling human beings for it, — the dumping ground of the whole world."

"Hold on, Jeff—"

"Hold on to what?"

"The idea."

"What idea?"

"Freedom, Jeff. Freedom to choose where to live and how to live, instead of having it pushed down your throat by centuries of habit and caste. Sure, this is a young blustering country, and it will make a lot of mistakes, but it will grow bigger and better than all the rest. There are plenty of scoundrels here, but for every man that came here looking for gold, there are three or four that came looking for God, and for every man that came here looking for a *living,* there are three or four that came looking for a better *way* of living. If Europe dumps its worst here, then it also sends us its bravest and best." As Walt warmed to his theme he turned and placed his hand on his brother's shoulder. "Wake up, Jeff. This country is the parliament of peoples—the only hope of the federation of the world. It belongs to no one people or religion, it belongs to all peoples and all creeds. No human being is a stranger here."

Jeff spat impatiently on the floor. He jerked his thumb in the direction from which they had come—"The Negroes, too?"

Walt nodded. "It will take a while, Jeff, but the Negroes, too."

Jeff began to cough again, and Walt showed his concern. "That's enough, Jeff. You oughtn't to work on Sunday, anyway. Leave that for pagans like me. I'll finish the column. You go on home."

Jeff wiped his lips slowly with a crumpled handkerchief and looked at Walt for a long time. "Home?"

He picked up his muddy shoes and carried them towards the door. The gleam of his thin white feet made his brother's heart ache with pity.

"Good afternoon, Walt."

Should he send him home alone? Long, long lonesome journey. Should he go home with him?

Give him time—a little more time. A few dollars saved—something to ballast the pocket—and then—

Walt looked after him as the door closed. He slowly surveyed the room—the sombre presses, the grimy cases of type — and then leisurely and thoughtfully approached the desk. He looked down upon the scattered proofs, many of them smeared and wrinkled. He fingered them as though attempting to draw from them a determination to set to work. Then he shook his head violently as though ridding himself of the whole unappetizing mess and went eagerly out into the street. He felt that he walked with the stride of a giant. *Come, life—stare at me—keep your eyes on me, for I'm your special lover.* His eyes explored both sides of the thoroughfare and his nostrils dilated as though he were embarking on a great adventure.

II

He walked north from Rampart Street. This he loved—people, sounds, color, voices—movement—constant restless movement. The slaves had begun to assemble in Congo Square, the women in big dotted calicos and with brazen bright kerchiefs of Madras as their headdress. Mighty women with mighty thighs containing generations in their dark sheltered caverns.

"Buy a lemonade!" roared the Negroes, leaping up and stamping.

Walt always wondered at their joy. *Do they, the slaves, not grieve or weep? Do chains give such security? Are tears only for the free?*

He found himself in a shimmering whirlpool of delighted speech. One group of Negroes was conversing in Spanish, another in French. A visiting easterner was speaking German to his wife and she was answering him in English.

A burly free Negro twirled a heavy oak staff and puffed at his pipe as he stolidly watched the dancers. A heavy gold chain dangled from his bright red vest.

A florid perspiring white man hailed him from a distance—and jogged toward him with heavy feet.

"Hi there, Johnson! My last offer—positively my last. Give ya seven hundred for Lucinda!"

The Negro grinned and shook his head. "I'm not selling her, Mistuh Morgan."

"What's your price?"

"I'm not selling her."

"Johnson—you damned miserly nigger, haven't you got enough black meat?"

The huge Negro fumbled with his heavy watch chain and grinned broadly at the white man. "I'll rent her to ya, but I won't sell her."

The pipe fell from between his teeth and a little

black urchin hastily bent to pick it up for the hope of a coin. Johnson's heavy coal-black chin doubled as he lowered his head. He swung his thick oak staff so that it smacked viciously against the little fellow's bottom. The boy screamed with pain and tumbled forward on the grass. "I wuz only gonna pick it up for ya," he sobbed with rage and tore at the grass with his hands.

Johnson slowly bent his huge bulk and picked up his pipe. He shook with laughter. "Hi-yi! Never knew what hit ya, did ya, black boy?"

Walt waited till the Negro and the white man had moved away and then drew some copper pennies from his pocket and dropped them near the boy's face.

Slowly the sobbing subsided. The boy looked up through his tears and grinned "I'll get a rag and shine 'em for you."

"No, my boy, my boots are all right."

"What did he hit me for? Huh? I was gonna pick up his pipe. Did you see him do it? Did you see him?"

"Yes, I saw him." Walt stopped and picked up the boy. The boy looked suddenly frightened. He stared beyond his benefactor in growing terror, and as Walt followed his glance he saw Morgan's scowling, florid face staring into his own.

"Who the hell do you think you are, — Jesus Christ, or somebody?"

Hate again, — venom in the face. How had he aroused this hate?

Walt couldn't understand at first. He watched the boy scamper away like a frightened woodland creature.

"Let the nigger get up himself, unless you're lookin' for trouble. A kick in the ass isn't gonna hurt him any."

Morgan moved away and lost himself in the crowd.

Walt felt sick with disgust.

Morgan the white man he could, with some difficulty, understand, but Johnson —? Why? Why? Why did he persecute his own? Both black—both the oppressed—

Now the beat of tom-toms became deafening, flooding and overwhelming speech, almost drowning out the sound of the violins, banjos, jawbones and triangles.

One lithe, ebony skinned Negro girl became the object of all eyes. She leaped into the air, her arms and legs twisting and flashing. The speed of her motions excited the spectators and they tossed picaillons and other shining coins into the ring.

With a laughing scream she finally sank down exhausted on the grass, her full lips widely parted as though to drink in the air. A young friend brought her water, while still another girl fanned her. Motion—motion—furious rhythmic beat. The soul like the heart has a pulse. Faster—faster—

Walt delightedly munched a "mulatto's belly," enjoying the spicy little ginger cake as he watched them. Excitement made him hungry. His nostrils twitched with enjoyment. He gulped the frenzied scene ravenously with his eyes. The brown and dark skin, smooth and full, drew from within him a great physical longing —as though if he were to embrace the panting dancer he would hold surging vital powers within his grasp—kindle a greater flame in his own blood;—then the leer—"black meat"—Morgan's twisted face—Johnson, with ebon bulging neck, "I'll rent her to ya." Man! Man! What are you, Man? More than a snorting bull furious to mount? Walt! Walt! And after—the nerve ends weary—what? Will the brown-black skin still invite—and the full lips? No—no—not enough! Not lasting!—Ebb tide of nerve hunger,—then nothing or worse than nothing. Guilt for the thought? What guilt? Pigment or none—what matter? When chaos groaned and flung itself about in the primeval darkness—did white rocks cling to white? And when the last dawn comes—?

Easy, Walt—easy does it. Look about you without tearing yourself apart. Enjoy! Enjoy! Conquer with eyes and ears. Don't let a moment pass untasted.

The drums were beating — steadily, steadily — an urgent, throbbing beat. The women were swaying. Children were leaping, twisting and gyrating in eager imitation of their elders, while the whites looked on as condescendingly aloof, but pleasantly amused, spectators. The handsome bright-vested blades with their tall-crowned top hats and the pretty ladies with their tiny sun parasols drifted casually about in senseless splashes of color. Walt watched them happily. Faces so close— he was not lonely now.

"Good afternoon, Sir!"

"Ah, good afternoon, Colonel Bingaman." Walt liked the pompous yet jolly white-haired aristocrat who had made a fortune from his Mississippi paddle wheelers.

"My carriage will soon be here. We shall be in time for the third race at Metairie. Do you care to join me?"

"I'm sorry. I've made other plans, but I do thank you, Colonel Bingaman."

"Nothing of the sort! You're an obstinate frozen livered Yankee. McClure's right about you. You like people better than horses."

"I'm afraid I do!"

"Put your money on a horse and you get a fair run for it."

"If the jockey rides fair."

"*Now* who's the misanthrope?"

"I like them *with* their weaknesses—just as they are."

"Damned if I don't believe you. Take my card. Anderson's playing the melancholy Dane at the Star Theatre. There's a loge reserved for me. It's yours and your lady's and gladly."

His lady? Perhaps — perhaps, somewhere in the crowd.

Walt smiled and accepted the card. Colonel Bingaman tapped his cane against the brim of his hat as though trying to remember an elusive something. He cleared his throat. Now he had captured it.

"Man delights not me; no nor woman neither, though by your smiling you seem to say so."

Colonel Bingaman spied his carriage and with a hasty bow pushed his way through the dancers.

Walt felt himself thrust this way and that as the multitude pressed forward to catch a glimpse of the slight volatile Frenchwoman who had made a daring balloon ascent the previous Sunday. She posed gracefully against the ropes as she gurgled her delight. There was a ripple of applause and her crisp oft-repeated "Merci, mes amis!"

"Ah, the wine of approval!" mused Walt as he set his legs wide apart and determined to stand like a rock of granite amid swirling human rapids. "Could anyone live without it? Could I?"

There was a rude jostling in the crowd. Someone lurched against him. "Oh, I'm sorry, truly sorry." A sweet fragrance was in his nostrils. A book dropped and fell half open on the moist earth. Walt stooped to pick it up and noticed as he did so that it was a copy of Longfellow's poems. He hesitated and glanced again at the soiled gray-wet stain where the page had touched the earth. Then he raised his eyes. The so pleasantly near young woman, who held a white sun parasol nervously in her hands, was looking at him with an uneasy inquiring smile.

The book—oh, the book! "Forgive me. Here you have it, Miss." Walt thrust the book at her with one hand as he removed his wide-brimmed hat with the other.

"Thank you, sir." Her features relaxed. "I was to blame." Her voice was calm, poised and precise. "Thank you." She turned to go. Her eyes were so restfully mild and dark, her complexion so warm and her features so even.

Walt struggled to say something—anything to restrain her, and suddenly blurted, "It isn't good poetry."

The verbal lariat caught and held.

She seemed startled. "I beg your pardon!"

"The book you're reading—it isn't good poetry."

She gave him a faint puzzled smile. "Do you know of better poetry?"

"Yes. Mine."

She caught her breath, obviously amazed at his effrontery and slightly amused. Then as her lips parted, her even white teeth enthralled him. Walt hurried on, "To make words rhyme and preach a sermon at the same time is not necessarily poetry." Then abruptly— "My name is Walt Whitman. I'm one of the editors of the Crescent. May I—?" He wasn't exactly sure— but he wanted—he wanted—her nearness.

"May you what?"

Walt blinked at her directness. He found himself staring hungrily at the exquisite beauty of her carriage, the soft roundness of her form, the deep mounting calmness in her eyes. There was a secure quality there, a deep, understanding serenity—

"May I walk with you?"

"Yes. Why not?"

A wave of unbelievable joy engulfed his heart. Altogether exquisite—altogether exquisite.

The din of the dancing and the tinny clatter of the drums faded from his ears. They walked in silence down St. Louis Street. She spoke first.

"You were saying that you didn't like my book."

"No, I didn't say that. It's a good book, but it isn't good poetry. Sweet words, sweet phrases, prim morals, regular beat, neatly rhymed——. He's a perfect gentleman, mind you——I'm not denying that."

"You have opinions, haven't you, Mr. Whitman?"

"What did you mean by that?"

"I once read a copy of something you wrote in the Brooklyn Daily Eagle. You see, I do know you, Mr. Whitman."

Behold thou art fair, my love, behold thou art fair.

"The Brooklyn Eagle! That's strange. How did you get a copy out here?"

The young lady disregarded his interruption and continued with an oratorial sing-song which she good-humoredly affected, as though amiably teasing him——

" 'Must runaway slaves be delivered back? They must. There is no remedy but in the state itself.' Am I quoting you correctly, sir?"

Myrrh and cloves with all the chief spices.

"You are not quoting me but only a part of what I said."

"You believe that, don't you——let slavery go on?"

Dove's eyes within thy locks.

"No, no, of course not. All I said is that the slavery in the South is something for the southern states to solve. I don't like slavery, but I'm not abolitionist. I want to keep the North free soil. What the South does is its own business."

"Its own business——even if it's criminal and wrong?"

"I don't mean exactly that. It's just that morality cannot be imposed from the outside. It's got to be a self discipline arising from inner conviction. The South resents the North's 'holier than thou' attitude. I believe that if you let the South alone it will gradually grow out of this evil."

"You're a very patient man, Mr. Whitman." There

was a delicate flavor of irony to her words.

Why must I be talking around my heart—avoiding —skirting?

"On the contrary. I'm impatient with impatience. It took the cave man perhaps a hundred thousand years to lift his knuckles five inches off the ground, and perhaps another hundred thousand to give his narrow forehead another quarter inch of breadth. Nature does not leap—growth is gradual."

"You've been reading that erudite Englishman who voyaged on the Beagle."

"Whom do you mean?"

"Charles Robert Darwin."

"No, I've never heard of him. But I have read Aristotle, Kant, Buffon and Lamarck — and done a little thinking of my own."

A garden enclosed—a garden enclosed—

She was silent. Walt felt he must say something lest the distance grow between them, and he plunged on. "I'm a Free Soiler. That's my stand. Let there be no new slave marts in California and the Southwest. But as for slavery in the Southern states—it's bad for the whites as well as for the Negroes and should gradually disappear."

The young woman turned and stretched out her hand. "Has laissez faire ever solved anything? It's only a short distance to my home. Good day, Mr. Whitman."

Walt ignored her outstretched hand and took her arm instead. "Please let me escort you to your door. Please." He insisted, and then without pause, "Tell me, how did you obtain a copy of the Daily Eagle all the way from Brooklyn?"

"I have a younger brother who lives there. He works for a newspaper, too."

"What is his name? I may know him."

The young lady drew away from him with a

troubled perplexed frown. "John Sedley. But I'm sure you've not met."

"No, I don't think so." Walt scratched his slight beard thoughtfully. "He isn't a reporter, is he?"

"No, he isn't a reporter."

"Then your name is —"

"Anne Sedley."

By this time they had reached an impressive brownstone house not far from the French Quarter. The beautifully patterned iron gate was partly open. A tall dignified woman was seated on the wide porch filling a flower pot with earth. She arose inquiringly as they approached.

"Mother, this is Mr. Walt Whitman, the new editor of the Daily Crescent."

Mrs. Sedley bowed slightly but did not extend her hand. "I am pleased to know Mr. Whitman." Her exquisitely deep voice was vibrant and friendly. "Won't you come in?"

They climbed the steps in silence and followed Mrs. Sedley into the house. Mrs. Sedley regarded him gently for a long while as though carefully appraising him.

"You find my daughter pleasing?"

Walt was startled out of his easy-going manner at the soft-voiced query. He looked from mother to daughter with a bewildered glance. He felt suddenly very ill at ease. Had he heard her correctly?

"Mrs. Sedley —" he tried to choose his words. "Your daughter is one of the most beautiful women I have ever met."

There was a long silence. Anne Sedley, who had been seated on the sofa, her eyes lowered while her mother was speaking, now arose abruptly. "Mother, he doesn't —" She did not finish the sentence but, turning to Walt, her face suffused with a sudden crimson blush, she laughed a jarring forced laughter and continued

rapidly, her words crowding and jostling one another
in their haste.

"Don't let anything ever startle you, Mr. Whitman.
The charming thing about life is that it's so illogical.
It has no pattern, no design. It isn't a dream we dream,
for then it would have some sort of a plot. But —"

"No, Miss Sedley," interrupted Walt gravely. "Life
is very logical. There is nothing complex about it at all.
You in your own person are all the people that live
upon earth. And I am all the people that live upon
earth. And what I feel, you feel."

She seemed anxious for him to go—but Walt was
as determined to stay.

He sat down upon the sofa and dipped his hand
into his large pocket, while mother and daughter
watched him curiously. He was thinking, "I must relieve the tension of this moment. There is something
here I don't quite understand."

Out came first a faded notebook held together by
a few large pins, and then a cracked stub of pencil.
He bent over his work, conscious that mother and
daughter were standing over him. Anne gave voice
to a strange high-pitched laugh as though she welcomed
his attempt to change the subject touched upon by her
mother. "Is this the way your inspirations come?"

"I've got to write them down—or I forget."

"Anne, bring Mr. Whitman a pen."

Walt shook his head without looking up. He must
be casual. "No. No. This pencil will do. Please sit down,
both of you, for just a moment. I think I can write
what I mean if you'll give me —" and then Walt began
to trace the words and read aloud slowly—very slowly,
as he wrote:

"O take my hand, Walt Whitman
Such gliding wonders! such sights and sounds!
Such joined unending links, each hooked to the

next
Each answering all, each sharing the earth with
all
Each of us inevitable
Each of us limitless—each of us with his or her
right upon the earth
Each of us allowed the eternal purports of the
earth
Each of us here as divinely as any is here."

Walt smiled and looked up for their approval. "You see, that's what I believe —"

The notebook almost fell from his hand as he heard her sudden cry. "Oh, you fool! You fool! Go away, go away—please go away!"

Walt winced at the stinging slap of her words and slowly rose to his feet. He felt ashamed, chagrined and hurt. The room swam about him. Abject and apologetic, utterly uncomprehending the cause of her outburst, he restored the notebook and pencil stub to the pocket of his coat.

"What have I said, Miss Sedley? If I've offended in any way —"

He heard Mrs. Sedley call sharply, "Anne, Anne! Mind your manners"—saw Anne Sedley sobbing uncontrollably as he backed out hat in hand, bewildered —bewildered.

III

When Walt, numb and stupefied, found himself in the street, he first examined his garments as though trying to find there something that had given offense. Unconscious of any definite objective he was walking through a blurred fusion of sound towards the Crescent office. Anne Sedley—Anne Sedley—Anne Sedley—and motion. Then as a carriage rattled by splattering him with annoying, infuriating drops of mud he thought of Jeff and turned toward their lodging. What was it all about?

"You find my daughter pleasing?" What had Mrs. Sedley intended by that naked query?

The boarders were already seated noisily together when Walt entered the cramped dining-room. He took his accustomed place at the right side of his brother Jeff and, absorbed in his bewilderment, reached for the beef and potatoes without actually desiring the food. Why did the chairs have to be placed so tightly together? If only he could spread his elbows!

"You naughty, tardy boy. You know you really don't deserve any soup for coming so late."

Coy, prim in her starched dress, and fragrant with perfume, Priscilla Claiborne, the widowed proprietress of the Twin Oaks, performed the motherly role of one who, striving to be severe, could nevertheless not prevent the generous lava of her abundant human kindness from bursting its barriers and coming forth.

Walt must be gracious. A lonely hard-working widow, after all.

"You are truly forgiving, Mrs. Claiborne."

"I can't stand her sugary sweetness," mumbled Jeff.

"She tries to be nice."

"She tries too damned hard. Let's move, Walt. We can get a room at the Fremont and have our meals out."

"Wait. We'll see."

Walt had his soup—while the beef and potatoes thinned and dwindled beneath the victorious assaults of the other boarders. There were five of them—five other guests of the hostelry of Twin Oaks, and each lodger was a unique, distinct, sharply-etched type as though Mrs. Claiborne had selected her boarders as a director of a play casts his characters.

There was Emanuel Caprin, a freckled, pasty-faced

artist whose teeth were too wide apart or he might have
been handsome. His hair, which he kept heavily pom-
aded, curled up at the nape of his neck. He leered when
he spoke, as though he were looking at one's private
parts through the garments that covered them. Indeed,
his favorite dissertation ran as follows: "You talk of
love as though it were divine—but should you marry
one so soft of speech and sweet of soul as to out saint
the saints, and on your wedding night discover that she
lacks a womb—"

There was Paul Griffon, the fencing teacher, whose
black accent-circumflex pointed eyebrows gave him a
Mephistofelian arrogant fierceness. He carried his chin
at a high tilt as though disdaining the world—and his
cupid bow lips gave his accent-tortured speech an
effeminate charm. His conversation ran something like
this: "Mrs. Claiborne, allow me to observe that the
stairs need a new carpet. Should any one trip ascending or descending, he might easily fracture his neck or
his rump and if that someone should be I, I'd strangle
you with your own virginal snood. Don't we pay you
enough for this slop? Can't you afford a carpet?"

There was Earl Chase, the gentle mannered typesetter for the Picayune. He was plump, mild, grave
and generally taciturn. He ate, worked and slept with
the same gravity of expression and there was about him
an air of constant serene resignation to life and all of
its turbulent problems. "Lie down in the afternoon for
ten minutes—and that's enough. Even if you don't
sleep. It'll save you from a coronary".

Then there was Sergeant Terrence Breen, heavy
and perpetually abashed, uncertain in his speech and
almost apologetic in his manner. He was extremely
fat and spoke to one with a side glance of his eyes.
He never looked anyone squarely in the face.

Finally there was James Hewitt, the barber, even

of features, affable of manner and entirely pleased with his self-assumed role of perspicacious commentator on world affairs—with politics as his very special specialty.

"Taylor will be President. There's no doubt of it." Hewitt's voice seemed to express at one and the same time finality and yet the hope of a contradiction on the part of his hearers, so that he might do verbal battle.

"Why?—because he's a good general?" Jeff's query was abrupt and belligerent.

"That seems to me a reasonable qualification, my very young man."

Caprin, the artist, leered tenderly at Jeff, his freshly shaven face looking like a newly peeled stick. "But you and your brother being from the North are already prejudiced against him."

"I don't know about my brother, but you can bet that *I* don't want a slave owner for President."

Griffon leaned back in his chair, a faint sneer twisting his lips. "Being young you lack tact and savoir faire, Mr. Whitman, so we'll forget your insulting remark."

"Youth is no synonym for folly, Mr. Griffon," interrupted Mrs. Claiborne, anxious to avoid the hot retort that surged to Jeff's lips. "There are older people that should know better. I've seen your hot-headed young students anxious to try their swords at the Duelling Oaks—anxious to provoke a quarrel in order to demonstrate their skill—and whose folly is it but yours, Mr. Griffon? It's the sin of violence!"

Griffon laughed, lifting his chin high, his eyes fairly brimming with merriment. "It's the fencing lesson money that finds its way into your prudish purse, dear lady—so lay on Macduff, and may I remind you again of the carpet?"

"Can't you make your living any other way?" Mrs. Claiborne set the cream pitcher down in front of him, blushing furiously. She was, in the adytum of her heart, much drawn to the fencing master and covered her secret feelings with frequent outbursts of petulance.

"The question is personal and offensive—nevertheless I choose to answer. Fencing is the only skill I know—except perhaps dancing, which to me is a kindred skill, an assault upon the lovely feminine to win her favor."

"A new and intriguing definition of dancing!" commented Caprin. "A prelude to assignation."

Again Mrs. Claiborne blushed. "But why didn't you learn some other skill? The Bible says 'not by power and not by the sword' —"

"Why not, indeed? Splash paint exhuberantly on a canvas in childish imitation of nature, like Caprin here? Clip manes and cowlicks like our friend Hewitt? Or pine away like Breen for a ruined Army career because he's too fat to mount a horse? Or perhaps pound out the letters of what other people write—like Mr. Chase—and our young northern friend—who lack the originality —"

"That will do, Mr. Griffon!" Emanuel Caprin had risen quickly from his chair, his eyes narrow and hard with rage.

"What have we here?" murmured Griffon, with his expressive feminine lips. "A challenge, no doubt. I'll tweak your nose, my good man. Your pallette for a shield and your oil-smeared brush as your sword. See?" He walked slowly over to Caprin and pulled his tie loose with a quick tug and then turned mockingly to Mrs. Claiborne. "There's your answer! That's why I chose fencing. Perfect freedom—sense of power—an argument sharp, convincing, and very often final."

Jeff opened his lips to speak, but Griffon made a peremptory gesture with his hand. "Hush up, Yankee boy! Don't protest that 'the pen is mightier than the sword'—for while philosophers yawn and scribble, a man like Zachary Taylor carves out a healthy chunk of Mexican meat to add to our table, and the philosophers and poets eat of it with no protest—like our slender, pious Madame Claiborne accepts my fencing fees to line her fat purse."

"You pay little enough, Mr. Griffon." Mrs. Claiborne's cheeks were a perspiring scarlet.

"More than enough, you threadbare old bag!"

Now Mrs. Claiborne was fighting to hold back her tears.

"You shouldn't call me such names, Mr. Griffon! You've no call to!"

"Why not? You're a hard headed business woman who's bound to collect a man's last dollar and leave him without a penny in his jerkin. If that's not miserly, then I suppose I do owe you an apology."

She raised her voice as though to justify herself before the others. "Is that fair or decent, Mr. Griffon? When you needed drapes for your room, I sewed them. Day and night I sewed. Then you called me 'Priscilla darling.' Now you call me an old bag. There's no goodness or gratefulness in you."

"Forgive me, Priscilla darling! 'Twas a slip of the lip." Griffon laughed and seemed surprised that the others at the table did not join in.

"You are cruel, vulgar and insolent!" Mrs. Claiborne was now thoroughly angry.

"And you, my dear, are old but lovely!" He arose from the table, chucked her under the chin and bowed courteously. "Excuse me, gentlemen. No offense intended—a mild case of spiritual dyspepsia in no way occasioned by Mrs. Claiborne's delightful cooking."

He left the table quickly and for a long while there was no sound except the spiritless clatter of fork and knife. To Walt the whole conversation had seemed like a foggy mist of words beating against his ears but not touching the misty brooding of his own brain. He ate his soup slowly with no regard to its taste. He watched the almost empty meat plate being passed to Jeff. Jeff, still sullen and bitter, speared two pieces with his fork just as Hewitt was reaching for the plate, and tendered these to his brother with a sternly triumphant gesture.

"Hang on to 'em, Walt." Then, with a slight bow, "Sorry for my haste, Mr. Hewitt, but my big brother needs looking after."

Caprin had left the table in a white tightly leashed anger. Chase sat regarding Walt and Jeff with a benevolent gentleness, shaking his head sadly from side to side.

Walt stirred himself. "Jeff, do you know anyone by the name of John Sedley? He's with one of the Brooklyn papers."

"No. Why?"

"Sedley?" volunteered Hewitt. "There used to be a tough brawling bully around here—name of Bill Sedley. Flatboat man he was. Hung around the saloons on Tchoupitaulos Street. Killed two men with a knife in the swamp."

From no such loins did she spring.

"Was he married?" asked Walt.

"No, I don't suppose he was. He disappeared from these parts after the killing and has never been heard of since. He's something of a legend around here."

Hewitt, ignoring his napkin, wiped his mouth deliberately with his handkerchief and continued—"Then there's Ralph Sedley—a grand gentleman—owns three ships—drives a fine carriage—no relative of Bill's, of course. Anyone want the last piece?"

Such lineage far more fitting.

"Where does Ralph Sedley live?"

"He has a big estate on Randolph Point."

"Has he a family?"

"Yes. He has two sons that I know of, Ralph Jr. and Will. One's at West Point and the other is running the shipping company."

"What's up, Walt?" Jeff sat hunched forward in his chair listening to the dialogue. Now he sensed that his brother was animated by more than a desire to make polite table talk.

"Someone I met. A name is mentioned. Naturally one is curious."

"Yes, and you've got your answer. A murdering bully or a grand gentleman. That's the way it is in New Orleans! Walt, let's go home. I can understand Griffon or Caprin liking New Orleans. Swords are popular—and an artist doesn't care much whether he squeezes his paint out of a cockroach or out of a plant as long as it's vivid —"

"Easy there, son." Earl Chase tapped Jeff kindly on the shoulder. "Fall in with the climate and relax a bit."

"You can have your damned climate. Everything grows here. Toadstools, skunks, stinkweeds and poison berries—and I don't mean flora and fauna either."

Chase opened mild blue eyes. "You know, Jeff, for a young lad, you sure can throw words around. I wish I had your knack. But it's like Griffon says. I can only pound out the letters that other people write. Walt, how about you, Jeff and me going down to the levee?"

Jeff edged sullenly over to his brother.

"I'm going to help Walt look for that Sedley fellow. Thanks, Earl, just the same."

Walt felt a romantic urge to make his quest alone. "No, Jeff. You see, this is a personal matter —"

Jeff flinched and drew back.

"All right, Walt. Go ahead. I'll accept your invitation, Mr. Chase, but not to the levee. I've got enough homesickness tearing my guts apart without seeing another paddle wheeler leaving for home."

IV

Walt strode quickly to St. Charles Street. The world blurred beautifully around him. The girl was in his blood and in his brain—possessing him with the tormenting fire of impatience. He searched anxiously for the brownstone house. There it stood cold and bleak in the darkness. No lamp kindled. No life stirring. Hollow with disappointment, he walked slowly to the Crescent office.

Pete Krause, the night watchman, met him at the door. He waved a bony forearm vaguely. "There's a lady in there waiting for you. I told her you might not be back but she said she'd wait anyhow."

A lady—for him!

Walt knew it was she even before he saw her seated at his desk. He stood in the doorway and looked down at her. Oh—healing fountain. Every cell of his body swam in waves of delicious hunger and longing. She had removed her hat. Her dark hair fell in soft curls and ringlets on either side. She looked at him calmly without a sign of greeting as though her being there was by appointment.

His eyes, hungry with yearning, touched her high forehead, her firm chin and the sweet fullness of her lips. Under her loose jacket he sensed the roundness of her breasts.

The room was all light and shadows but she was in the light, while the type cases and the presses, grimly stern and accusing, were swallowed up in the darkness.

Her anger—she couldn't have meant it. He said no word but bent over her, pressing his lips down firmly on lips calmly waiting. She showed no surprise, as though all this were known and understood. He wondered, "Can this strangely beautiful thing be happening to me?"

. Then he heard her say slowly, "Forgive me, please forgive me for the things I said, — and forgive my mother."

"*I would lead thee and bring thee into my mother's house. I would cause thee to drink special wine.*"

Walt felt reality dropping away, leaving him suspended in space—with her, with her. He heard himself answering, "One kiss—blots out—many painful words," and then felt all strangeness dissolve into delicious nearness as she twinkled at him, "Sir, your beard tickles."

They laughed at that and Walt pulled a box heavy with type close to her and sat on the edge of it. This was intimate yet strange—intoxicatingly intimate, yet as distant as the farthest star from earth.

"If you only understood what your being here means to me."

Words, words, words—how their awkward, lumbering hulks get in your way!

"What does it mean to you, Mr. Whitman?"

"Please don't call me Mister—and don't say 'sir.' I dislike all titles because they make a man less, not more. They limit him—and he should be infinite. I'm Walt Whitman."

How like a little boy slapping his chest.

Why keep on talking? Everything is known.

"Who are you *really*, proud man?" Her fingers rested lightly on his hand. Her eyes were gently coaxing—curious.

"Surely *you* know!" His arms were around her and he strained her to him brutally, knowing that he was hurting her with his fierce incredible passion and yet unable for the crazy moment to be considerate. "*You* know," he whispered again and again. "You've been waiting for me and I've been hungering for you. Anne.

Anne!"

There was a vague, uncertain fumbling at the latch. Startled they recoiled from each other as Pete thrust his head in the door. "There's a nigger boy out here asking for Miss Anne Sedley. Be you Miss Anne Sedley?"

"Yes, yes I am." She had leaped wildly to her feet. "There's a message I must give him. I'll be back, Walt. Wait for me here."

Walt frowned and waited in silence. In a brief moment she was back, pretending a joyous eagerness and animation which Walt knew was far from real.

"Go on with your work, Mr. Whitman," she stammered—"Walt. Will it bother you if I just sit here and watch?"

Walt's aching hunger consumed his blood with flame.

"Watch what, Anne? Watch me set type?"

"Yes, let me watch you work."

"My work, Anne? This isn't my work. I'm not a typesetter!" He arose and clenched his hands. "My work is the work of a lover—to kiss and caress a world into life—to touch its most secret parts and say to it, 'Do not blush, for you and I know each other.' "

She trembled and drew away.

"I don't understand what you are saying. You are a strange man. Must you always talk the language of poetry? Can't you just talk?"

"Do you *feel* what I am saying? I'm so full inside I've got to pour it out—and you've got to understand, Anne. It's all poetry—all of life! I'll make you understand."

She placed her soft hand on his clenched fist. "All right then—you're a poet. And, Walt, I *am* trying to understand you. I'm trying to understand your departure from classic forms. You sound wild and rebellious. Have you written any of these things—or do you just say them?"

"Every once in a while the flame leaps out and then I suck it back in again, afraid I'll burn things with it, when I want to light and warm with it. Here's a little book I keep—jotting down a phrase here and a phrase there."

"Yes, I remember your book —"

Anne stared at the hand-stitched pages stained with smudges of printer's ink and thumb marks. She bent close to the kerosene lamp on the desk and read softly:

"We found our own O my soul in the calm and
*   cool of the daybreak*
My voice goes after what my eyes cannot reach
Through me forbidden voices
Voices of sexes and lusts, voices veiled and I remove
*   the veil*
Voices indecent, by me clarified and transfigured.
I do not press my finger across my mouth
I keep as delicate around the bowels as around the
*   head and heart*
Divine am I inside and out, and I make holy what-
*   ever I touch or am touched from*
The scent of these arm pits aroma finer than prayer
This head more than churches, bibles and all the
*   creeds."*

Anne turned the page and read on:

"If I worship one thing more than another it shall
*   be the spread of my own body or any part of it*
Translucent mold of me it shall be you
Shaded ledges and rests it shall be you
Breast that presses against other breasts it shall be
*   you."*

Anne slowly lowered the book. "I'm trying to understand. You love yourself very much," she said haltingly. "You're in love with your own voice. You like the sound of strange wild words."

"No! No! Then you don't understand at all. I must make you understand. I'd smash all words if I could get my thoughts or feelings over without them. Myself is yourself and everyone. I am important but you are as important as I! Anne, sometimes it seems as though there is no 'I' inside of me—just things read or seen, drifting through me—like a child who pretends one minute he's an explorer or a hunter and the next minute he's a soldier leading a charge. No real person—just the many turbulent waters of the sea flowing through a clay pipe. Or flame—a devouring flame needing no wood to feed on. And then at other times I feel as though I am everyone—the whole world—and every heart beats in me—and every pain cries in me —"

"Walt —" and her eyes suddenly blinked with the weight of tears. "You're just singing to hear yourself sing. You can't mean what you're saying! I must go now. Good night, Walt."

"No, let me walk with you. The streets are dark. You mustn't go alone."

"The streets are darker than you think, Walt."

Walt clung to her arm. "I've been frank with you. Why aren't you open with me? Why do you talk in riddles? I show you the soul of me or what I think is me, and you keep yourself hidden. You're beautiful, Anne! You are beautiful!" Then abruptly—"What did your mother mean?"

She seemed startled at his question and looked at him for a long moment wonderingly. He was shaken by her beauty. Trembling he asked again, "What did your mother mean when she asked if you were pleasing to me?"

She half raised her hands as though to ward him off.

"This, Walt, this." Her arms were suddenly around his neck. She was kissing him hungrily, her lips pressing against his beard—against his cheek.

The kerosene lamp stained the chimney with its smoke as it flickered. Anne's head lay pillowed in his lap. He looked down at her and his fingers touched her hair.

V

The French boats were in—a wilderness of masts and funnels seemed to block their approach to the dock. Fashions—the very latest in finery, and French perfumes were their cargo. No wonder the belles of New Orleans chattered and swarmed about.

Walt stumbled over a sleeping tippler and hurried on. He paused abruptly and felt a paralyzing choking anger—a mad, ecstatic, furious jealousy. Two sailors were tipping their hats to Anne. She was smiling and holding her bonnet tightly against the wind. Walt frowned and walked forward grimly. She stretched out her hands to him.

"How did you find me, Walt, in all this bedlam?"

The two sailors, smoothly shaven for their spree ashore, grinned uncomfortably, hesitated for a moment and then, seeing the chill in Walt's features, moved awkwardly away.

"What's wrong, Walt?"

"Nothing."

"But there is—the way you tighten your lips—and no greeting"—she hesitated—"no kiss."

"Perhaps not by me."

There it was out—the cruel gibe he had restrained against his teeth.

She stood wide-eyed as though he had slapped her face, hurt and anger stiffening her form, and her lips trembled as though she were gasping for breath. Then suddenly she began to run from him, sobbing and running between the bales of cotton and the heavy crates, past the exposed piles of rotting fruit swarming with flies and insects.

"Anne! Anne! I'm sorry!" Walt, overwhelmed with remorse, ran after her, caught her by the wrist and tried to draw her to him. She loosened his grasp and pushed him away.

"Stay away from me! Let me alone!"

"Forgive me. Please forgive me. People do foolish things sometimes—say stupid things —"

She leaned against a crated slab of granite and wept silently.

Gently he touched her elbow and urged her to walk by the pleading pressure of his hand.

They walked for a long time in silence.

"I'm no different from the other males of the species. Hurt, vanity, jealousy, exclusiveness—possession."

"I can't blame you, Walt. After all I spoke to them when they spoke to me. They asked the news. They'd been away for almost a year—and so I told them —"

"You don't have to explain."

"Oh yes, I do. You're still wondering, for didn't *we* meet by chance—you and I—and did I repulse you as a lady should?"

"Sailors are a rough lot. They might think you were accepting their attentions."

"Broad daylight and people all around. No, Walt —you weren't worried about *them*. You were worried about *me*. And why shouldn't you? For I was caught red handed."

"Don't, don't! Let's go where we can talk."

"And if we talk will I convince you that—there's no one—no one else? You'll be doubting again—and all you'll have is my word. And I'm afraid."

"Afraid of what?"

"Jealousy — worse than drunkenness — worse than madness — worse than the plague of cholera. In a woman it's spiteful—in a man it's beastly."

"I'm sorry."

"Don't keep saying it. I'm sorry for you. It's a cancer that will eat your heart out —" Anne's hand was on his arm. "When I was a little girl I used to hear my father come home after midnight. He'd start right in shouting — accusing — and mother's mild silence seemed a confession to him."

" 'Bitch!' he called her. 'Whore and bitch!' That was her reward for slaving to keep the house and me spotless. I knew how faithful and loyal she was. Walt, women aren't like men. Women want the security and the anchor of one man to love."

They had reached the promenade of the Charles Hotel. The flower girl thrust herself forward with a dimpled laugh.

"A rose for your lady!"

Walt felt the agony and the tenseness of remorse relax its hold on his heart. The silver coin produced a squeal of delight and he stretched the moist flower out to Anne.

"Darling, I'll learn—or it will destroy me. Just loving you should be enough. Why must I demand to own you in return?"

VI

There was a noisy disturbance near the ornate desk of the Charles Hotel, and Walt recognized the louder voice.

"Plague take you. I asked you a civil question, didn't I? Open your mouth at me again and I'll cut your tongue out." The speaker was Griffon. He was clearly and patently drunk.

The manager took up the quarrel of the frightened clerk. "The lady is not registered here. Please do not make any further disturbance."

Now several of the loungers had arisen to their feet and were crowding the desk in their eagerness to see and hear.

"I demand to see your register." Griffon's voice arose imperiously above the confusion.

"And I must refuse." The manager was white-faced. "The clerk was entirely within his rights in taking the register from you. It is not public property, Mr. Griffon. I must ask you to leave."

"I'll leave with Mrs. Stuart and when it pleases me to leave."

"The clerk told you she is not registered here."

Walt was very close to Griffon, but Griffon was far too angry to notice him—too angry and too wine sotted.

Anne pleaded softly, "Stay out of this, Walt"—and it was at that moment that Griffon saw them both. His thin lips opened in a welcoming smile of recognition.

"Greetings, Mr. Whitman—and the lady with you —won't you present me?"

Walt stood silent and now all eyes were fixed on him. The clerk retreated behind the desk and straightened his cravat with fumbling fingers.

Walt saw all this—and saw Griffon waiting—swaying unsteadily—waiting for the introduction.

"Mr. Whitman, I am most anxious to meet the lovely lady at your side. I have so expressed myself."

Walt could not. He knew what his refusal might lead to. He saw the clouding features of the fencing master—and yet he could not subject Anne or himself to that indignity.

Griffon raised his cane as though it were a sword; he flicked the point of it under Walt's beard and exposed the black tie. Walt did not move.

"I can't duel him," he thought, "but if he raises

that cane again I'll take it from him and break it over
his insolent head. No—No—before I could grasp it his
trained muscles would snatch it away and I—I would
receive a humiliating beating—and what then—what
then?"

Griffon slowly lifted his cane once more—

"Paul!" A woman's clear bell-like soprano echoed
through the lobby. It was the same magnificent voice
that drew the crowds to the Variety Theatre night after
night. The "incomparable Mrs. Stuart"—they called
her. She was a stormy, exquisite vision in shimmering
silk as she swept down the richly carpeted stairs.
"Paul!" She sped towards Griffon in full sail, while
Walt turned and took Anne's arm, breathing normally
again.

"Mr. Whitman!"

Walt turned. Griffon, swaying slightly, was offering
his arm to Mrs. Stuart, and addressing Walt at the
same time. "We shall renew our little discussion at
Twin Oaks."

"He means to make trouble." Anne's voice was
almost a sob. "Who is he? What does he want?"

"He's a fencing master who boards at Twin Oaks
as I do. When he's sobered up he'll forget the whole
incident. But *I* won't forget."

"What do you mean?"

"Anne dear, I've already found out one very disagreeable trait I possess—namely, jealousy—and now I
may find that there's another flaw—equally vile—
cowardice."

"But you were not afraid. You refused to present
him. You were splendid and brave."

"Don't, Anne—please don't! I should have thrashed
him for his trick with the cane—and then, as though
the gods pitied me, came the deus ex machina in the
form of Mrs. Stuart to extricate me from my predica-

ment, else I don't know what I would have done. I don't know."

"Don't quarrel with him, Walt. I beg you."

"It isn't up to me." He bent and kissed her. "Anne —Anne—don't let you and me ever quarrel."

VII

At Twin Oaks Paul Griffon's threat vanished under the impact of an unexpected announcement.

First, Mrs. Claiborne served the wine; then she mincingly drew near to Mr. Chase and slid her hand under his arm. Chase attempted to look dignified and only succeeded in looking discomfited. It was at that moment that Griffon entered, apparently sober after his dinner with Mrs. Stuart.

"What goes on? Qu'on dit de nouveau? Unfaithful one, is it not me that you love?"

"Oh, do behave, Mr. Griffon. It's just that we have something to tell you. Mr. Chase and I are going to be married."

"Luck!" "Good luck!" "The best of luck!" "Congratulations!" Walt joined in the general hullabaloo of well wishing—relieved at the vanished threat of Griffon's petulance—and genuinely happy for Mrs. Claiborne. "So unexpected!" "Great news!"

Chase beamed where he sat at the head of the table. No wonder the few hairs on his pate shone with stiff and pompous splendor. Mr. Hewitt had given him "the works"—the entire gamut of his tonsorial art.

"And all this time you've been envying me my charm with the ladies." Griffon teased. Chase's voice was firm. "I don't envy any one, sir. I wish things for myself, but I don't envy anyone. It's no secret that I've been lonely. The Holy Writ says 'It's not good for a man to live alone'."

"And I agree," laughed Griffon pinching Mrs. Claiborne's cheek. "In that respect I am more than pious."

"I'll do a portrait of the lovers as my wedding gift," volunteered Caprin, then lifting his third glass, "Who says that love belongs only to youth?" He nudged the florid-faced Mr. Chase with his free hand as he drank.

"Oh—I don't know. I'm only forty-six and I take good care of myself. I eat only crackers and coffee for lunch—and a ten minute nap in the afternoon. Just to lie down is enough—the heart must rest, you know. A man should take care of himself."

Griffon turned to Walt. "This deserves a column in the Crescent—and as for the Picayune—Chase can set his own story."

Chase's features shone like burnished copper caldrons—"I've already written something." He fumbled in his pocket—"if you would like to hear it." Griffon glanced at the paper and grimaced, "Oh, the devil! Poetry! Every fool in love must embroider pretty phrases. See you in the morning, mes amis. Congratulations again! Come with me, Sergeant Breen. How about you, Mr. Whitman? I'll buy you both a drink."

Breen, responding slowly to the invitation, walked dully towards him. Walt shook his head.

After they had left there was a long agonizing silence.

"May I hear your verse?" Walt fixed his eyes gently on Chase.

Chase hesitated. "I'm no poet. I'm just a typesetter —but sometimes a person gets to feeling things." He thrust the paper at Walt, "You read it."

Walt studied the neat writing, so like a copper engraving, and slowly read aloud:

"My love is like a garden
That I tend
Each broken twig

> *I cherish and I mend*
> *Each fallen blossom do I weeping, lay away*
> *And to the rest my anxious heart bids 'Stay.'* "

Walt lifted his eyes and looked into the round flushed face of the middle-aged bridegroom—feeling a great affection for this stolid, good man—and a consuming contempt and disgust for Griffon.

VIII

When Jeff did not arise the next morning Walt bent over his bed and felt his forehead. It was clammy and hot. He called Mrs. Claiborne and she was all tenderness. She roused him out of his drowsy stupor to drink fresh orange juice.

"You go to the office, Mr. Whitman. I'll take good care of Jeff. He'll be sound and well for the wedding—won't you, Jeff?"

"Sure, I will. Go on, Walt. I'll be all right. I don't want to be hanging like the albatross around your neck."

All that day Walt worried about Jeff. "I should have paid attention to his misery and loneliness. Now he's sick and I'm to blame."

When Walt returned that evening he found a group of people gathered in solemn groups in front of the broad porch and lofty colonnades. His blood froze. He ran forward, half sobbing. "What's happened?"

"It was sudden—very sudden!"

"No! No! Jeff! Jeff! God forgive me! He wanted to go home—and I kept him here."

"I don't understand you, sir. Calm yourself. We were all fond of Mr. Chase."

"Mr. — Mr. Chase?"

Walt wanted to laugh—and then to weep—Oh flesh ties strong—strong! Poor Mr. Chase. Poor Mr. Chase, and Mrs. Claiborne after her long gray years of loneliness—after her sudden glimpse of joy.

Mrs. Claiborne stood in the doorway austere in her silence. Walt hesitated and stepped towards her. She broke suddenly in his comforting arms. "Oh, Mr. Whitman. Mr. Whitman. He was so good and kind. He had a hearty breakfast. He went late to the office— and he was hurrying. He didn't need to hurry. I would have taken care of him. But he was that conscientious."

Walt led her to the tall-backed chair in the foyer and she sank down into a pathetic crumpled heap.

Now the neighbors were thronging in. The body of the gentle typesetter lay serenely in the parlor and the silent procession moved past the sobbing mistress of Twin Oaks. Jeff stood at the head of the stairs looking wearily down. Walt leaped up and put his arms around him. "Oh, Jeff—Jeff!" Walt would not tell him what he had feared.

Jeff shook his head and wanly surveyed the sombre shrouded scene. "And him always worrying about a coronary, telling everybody else to nap during the day. Poor Mrs. Claiborne!"

Many people came. Quiet men, too, have friends. And Anne came towards midnight, and sat with the mourners. She came back early the next morning and prepared breakfast for the boarders, while Mrs. Claiborne protested, "You must let me work. I must keep busy. I mustn't think too much."

Sergeant Breen didn't say anything. He stood watching with his hands deep in his pockets. Slowly he ambled towards Mrs. Claiborne and thrust something into her hand. "You'll be needing expenses."

"No, no, Sergeant Breen. I have enough. I'll manage."

"Please, Mrs. Claiborne, don't make a fuss. I'd only drink it up the way I feel. Please take it."

Walt felt a great guilt in his soul. "My virtue is

only of words and dreams. *He* though of it. *He* and not I."

Anne was leaving now. She was holding Mrs. Claiborne tenderly in her arms. "I'll be here again tomorrow. Please let me come."

"You've been wonderful to me. God bless you, Anne. You've been a great help—and I can't thank you enough."

Walt walked her home. "You're good, Anne—solidly—truly good. I don't deserve you—pouring out words while you give your heart."

"Not jealous any more?"

"No, loving you is enough — even if I were not loved by you."

IX

They saw each other almost daily after that. Jeff fidgeted uncomfortably in her presence. He avoided her whenever she visited the Crescent office and Walt observed this and was troubled.

Anne understood. "Come to my home, Walt. Mother wants you to make our home your home. Use my room freely. You can write there to your heart's content. No one will disturb you—not even I."

And Walt came evening after evening. Often, when the nights were hot, Mrs. Sedley would bring them tea and silently depart.

Anne's quiet presence gave wings to Walt's pen.

"Just *be* here, Anne. Just *be* here and I'm content!"

Once she fell asleep in the large four-poster bed. He looked down at her, and, as though sensing his presence, she awoke and stretched out her arms to him.

They lay in each others embrace, speaking in hushed voices. Suddenly, Walt burst out,

"Anne! Anne! Is my song worthwhile—or am I

deceiving myself?"

"It's strong, Walt. It's different —"

"Because I break the rusty shackles that hold old words together. New phrases—living phrases!"

"But what are you trying to say?"

Walt's jaw sagged. All of a sudden he chuckled. "Is it that bad? And I thought I was putting it simply."

He tilted her chin to his lips and looked down at her serious intent eyes. "Let's get married, Anne."

Anne's eyes clouded. She looked startled, almost afraid. Walt bent gently to kiss her. "All I said was, 'Let's get married, Anne.'"

"It's not that simple."

He kissed her softly, barely touching her lips. "As simple as that!" he smiled. "Two people loving each other and wanting it to be permanent. So why not marriage?"

"But you said you didn't believe in rituals!"

"Try to understand, Anne. There's nothing any priest or minister can add to our love. But I want the feeling of knowing that people look upon you as I look upon you—dear to me, very dear to me. Openly dear to me."

"Isn't that yielding to convention? Understand me, Walt, I'm only quoting you."

"Yes, I suppose it is. But the prophecy is always in advance of the deed, and I cannot walk naked through the streets because some day people will understand there is no shame to the body beautiful. They wear clothes and so must I."

"And they wear prejudice, hate and meanness, and so must you!"

"That's a cruel thing to say!"

"But it's true, Walt. You know it's true. You see them in their chains—the Negro convicts; you see black folk caned and flogged and sold on the block, and you write about the flowers in the old French Quarter and the ships in the harbor."

Walt felt irritated. Jeff had said the same thing.

"Anne, it's not cowardice. You've got to believe that. Each must save himself. The South must heal itself of its own illness. It will be slower but surer. In the North I can cry out against exposure to slavery, but here where it is part of the pigment of your society I might as well try to flay your Southerners alive in order to cover you with another skin."

"If a thing is evil it's evil everywhere!"

"No, Anne. I don't recognize evil. There is no evil. There is only the man child trying to grow up. He's got to grow naturally. I won't stretch him on a Procrustaean bed! Not even with my songs."

"Then, Walt, you're wasting your time here."

"Wasting time? Is the time I spend with you wasted? Is the time I spend drinking in sound and color and pouring out my love of life wasted? For Heaven's sake, Anne—what devil drives men to a feeling of guilt for a moment enjoyed?"

Anne's calm eyes made him ashamed of his outburst. He continued, this time in subdued earnest tones. "Meeting you, being with you, loving you—don't talk of wasted time."

Anne shook her head. "It isn't that easy. Things don't get better by themselves. There are duties—responsibilities. Someone always depends on you—family, people in trouble. You just can't take an axe and chop off their hands. They have their hold on you whether you want it or not. What about your own kin folk? Don't they need you?"

"I suppose so, Anne. I guess you're right. I've been selfish. There's nothing really worth while I can do here. You must come North with me. Jeff isn't happy here and I'm just drifting. Why don't you say something, Anne? Will you come?"

Anne drew away. "I—I don't know. Your people —what are they like?"

"They're simple farm folk. I was born in New York, about thirty miles from New York City. The Indians called it Paumanok and the white men called it Long Island. I call it home. It holds precious memories of a childhood close to nature."

"But your people — your family — what are they like?"

"You've met my brother, Jeff."

"Yes. He's a little afraid of me. He dislikes me. Is he jealous of me for loving you?"

"Of course not! He's afraid I'll stay here and that you're the anchor." He bent his head and kissed her, a long reassuring kiss. "But I'm going back, Anne, and you're coming with me."

"Go on—tell me about your people, Walt."

"My father—his name is Walter too—couldn't fill our stomachs with what the land produced. He's a good carpenter so we moved to Brooklyn about thirty miles away. Yes, for our stomach's sake, a good enough reason, we moved from rural Paumanok to the populous pavements—and then I found I loved crowds, people, more than anything else. Mother's Dutch. She can't read or write, but she's a happy, brave woman. Father is quiet and brooding, but strong and hard as an oak knot. Mother is all love—all love and faith. My older brother's name is Jesse. I have two younger sisters, Mary and Hannah, and four younger brothers. There are things better left unsaid, but Anne, you've a right to know. There's a cloud—a few of them in the family sky. My youngest brother, Edward, has a child's mind. My sister Hannah is neurotic. Andrew has no sense of moral balance, and Jesse is worse. Trees do not always grow straight. Shall I go on?"

"Why do you say such cruel things about your own people?"

"Because you asked me—and I can't lie. I'm not cruel; I'm telling you the truth. You're going to meet them, you know."

"I can't, Walt. I can't!" Anne burst suddenly into tears and Walt looked at her in amazement.

"Now, you've *got* to tell me! There's no reason for these tears. Why do you hide yourself from me? What mystery is there about you? I've exposed myself to you completely — and you keep hiding yourself. Why? Why?"

"Hush, Walt, please! Mother will hear." She placed a finger on his lips and, after a moment, pressed him close to her. "Believe in me, Walt, a little while longer—until I am sure that you mean what you sing."

They were silent for a long time.

"Walt, there's something that shapes our lives and our longings—usually it's a person who leaves his print on you when you're very young. I know in my case, it was my Aunt Leah. She died when I was only ten— yet in the little while I knew her she left her indelible mark on my soul."

"She must have.been a strong and vital personality."

"Strong? Yes—in a quiet sort of way. Her husband was an invalid. I never saw or met him; but mother said he had fallen from the rigging of a sailing ship and was paralyzed. Aunt Leah worked as a seamstress. She worked night and day without complaint. Her face and hands were so thin. Once I found her crying alone. You know how the tears of an adult frighten a child. I ran to her crying, 'Aunt Leah! Aunt Leah! Please, please don't cry.'

She smiled and then put her arms around me 'Don't worry about me Anne, I'm very happy.'

I asked 'Then why do you cry, Aunt Leah?'

'Sometimes a person gets tired.'

'But you said you were happy.'

'I am, dear child, I am. When you do what must be done you can't help being happy. If you seek happiness you never find it.' "

Anne paused, looked up at Walt. "You believe that, too, don't you?"

"I have never consciously sought happiness for myself. I want to do—I must do what I'm supposed to do—," he stopped abruptly and laughed—"I really don't know what I want."

"Oh, yes you do. You're a preacher! You want to preach to the whole world in words of singing fire. —Tell me who influenced your life."

"There were many—"

"No, there was really only one. Think, Walt—your earliest memory."

Walt arose from the bed and stood near the open window.

"I suppose, in a way, you're right, Anne. My earliest memory is Elias Hicks. He was my grandfather's closest friend. Elias Hicks was a liberal Quaker minister, but to my childhood eyes he was a Hebrew prophet stepping from the pages of the mystic past. They threw him out—the others. They were intolerant and dogmatic and they could not bear his worship of the God within. My parents always went to hear him preach. He always talked of the God in man's own nature. He was no stranger to grief, for his four sons had died and he was like a great lonely tree against the sky. His wife and daughters loved him devotedly. He gave up hunting—calling it a cruel sport and in the revolution he, in common with the Society of Friends or Quakers, took no part.

When I saw Elias Hicks he was in the eighty-first year of his age. I can remember my father coming home at sunset, throwing down his bundle of kindling wood on the kitchen floor. 'Come, mother, Elias preaches tonight.'

Mother got the neighboring woman to stay with the little ones and I was taken along.

I can see everything clearly—the handsome ballroom of the Morrison Hotel, the sparkling pendants of the glass chandeliers—the settees and chairs filled with young and old. — There were men in uniform—and richly dressed women, and on a platform at the head of the room a dozen or more Friends, elderly, grim and with broad-brimmed hats on their heads. There were three or four women, too, seated at one side of the platform with Quaker costumes and bonnets.

Elias arose and stood for a long moment without uttering a word. Tall, straight, clean-shaved face, expansive forehead—long white hair. His face was illumined and glowing. Then he spoke slowly and with melodious resonance.

'What is the chief end of man? I was told in my youth it was to glorify God and seek and enjoy Him forever.'

Then he went on to say many things I could not understand and some that I shall never forget.

'The true Christian religion consists neither in rites nor Bibles, nor sermons nor Sundays—but in noiseless secret ecstacy and unremitted aspirations, in purity, in a good practical life, in charity to the poor and toleration to all.'

He spoke again and again of the 'inner light' and ended his preachment with the words 'There is but one Lord, one faith, and but one baptism, one God and Father, that is above all, through all and in all.' "

Anne looked at Walt as though seeing him for the first time. "Now I understand you better. His soul left its imprint on you. It's always that way. A young child with thoughts as soft as a downy pillow and then one comes and leaves an imprint. Souls are stamped one from the other and not born inside of us.

Walt, do you still insist on knowing all about me?" Anne's voice was low and hesitant.

"I'll take and cherish you as you are."

"No matter what I am?"

"I know what you are."

"Who am I?"

"You are the female form. A divine nimbus exhales from it from head to foot —"

"Stop it, Walt. Can't you be real? Must you always and forever quote poetry for everything you do?"

"Yes, because everything I do is poetry."

"From your memorandum book?"

"From my heart."

Anne's face softened. "How did we ever come to meet? Do you believe there's a pattern? Go on, Walt. Go on with your song. I'll listen—I can't help listening."

"I'm not making this up now, Anne. I've poured it out of myself before—many times before. I've written it down."

Walt sat down on the edge of the bed and read softly,

"*I sing of a woman's body*
It attracts me with fierce undeniable attraction,
I am drawn by its breath as if I were no more than
    a helpless vapor, all falls aside but myself and it,
Books, art, religion, time, the visible and solid earth,
    and what was expected of heaven or feared of
    hell, are now consumed,
Mad filaments, ungovernable shoots play out of it,
    the response likewise ungovernable,
Hair, bosom, hips, bend of legs, negligent falling
    hands all diffused, mine too diffused,
Ebb stung by the flow and flow stung by the ebb,

love flesh swelling and deliciously aching,—"

Anne opened her eyes and looked up at him. "Among animals is the voice of the male always more melodious than that of the female?"

"Why do you ask?"

"Then that is one of the secrets—the spell of sound."

"What are you saying, Anne?"

She closed her eyes and her lips formed a languid opening rosebud. "Kiss me, Walt," she whispered.

He felt the tip of her tongue play against his lips and he drew her closer to him.

She stirred at last in his embrace.

"What are you going to do when you go back to Brooklyn?"

"When *we* go back," he corrected. "Newspaper work, I suppose. Maybe your brother can help me get placed."

He felt her grow tense in his arms.

X

The following day at the Crescent Office Walt was again insistent. "Anne, I'm not curious, but I am concerned about you. I've told you the truth about my people. Now tell me all you want to tell me about yours."

Anne spoke evenly, as though reading a chronicle of simple facts. "My mother you've met. My father is a prosperous business man. My brother I've told you about. You'll meet him when you return—I know you will. They're all in splendid physical and mental health and so am I."

"Why do you keep speaking of *my* return, Anne? You're going North with me. We're going to be married."

She rose to her feet. His hand still held her wrist.

51

"There's something I must solve first—something that frightens me. It's not fair when you're near me. Go back, Walt. Let a year go by and then come to me again. And if you still want me —"

"Then I won't leave. I'll stay." He arose quickly. "Let's not play coy games, Anne. We belong to each other. We've known each other as intimately as my heart knows the blood-stream it pumps. I'll see McClure and tell him I've changed my mind. I'm staying."

"No, Walt. Jeff will grow to hate me. He's only fifteen. He's ill with dysentery. He's homesick. Take him home. Give yourself a chance to think, Walt. You're not thinking now. You're just feeling."

"Anne—Anne—is everyone logical but me? Do all love stories have to be frustrations and tragedies? To-morrow—tomorrow—tomorrow. Go away—come back —try this—try that. Why complicate our lives? Why put miles between us? Why torture ourselves when it's as primitively simple as Adam and Eve in a bower?"

"I can't talk to you, Walt, because you're too much involved in you."

"Talk, Anne, but say something that I can understand."

"Walt, you met me only a few short weeks ago. It was easy for me to fall in love with you. A woman responds to kindness, attentiveness —"

"Then it could have been anyone else?"

"I didn't say that."

"But that's what you meant."

"Still it *wasn't* anyone else; it was you."

"And tomorrow it will be someone else—that's why you want me to go away."

Anne's lip trembled. A curl danced foolishly over an eye brimming with tears.

"There couldn't be anyone else now any more. It's

different with women than with men. We don't change our loyalties so easily."

"But you said —"

"You don't understand, Walt. I suppose I could have been drawn to any one of many men if he had come like a romantic Lochinvar—as you did—but now you're part of me—like my arm—and I don't ask myself, 'Could it have been any other arm?' What could have been doesn't matter now. You are my own."

"Then why do you ask me to go?"

Anne pressed the back of his hand to her lips. "Walt, dearest, I'm sure of myself and what you mean to me, and now *you've* got to be sure. There's a restless love of life in you—and maybe it's not me you love but— the thought of it—the romance of it—the strangeness of the meeting. You've got to be sure. You've got to be sure."

"You're trembling. What frightens you?"

Anne shook her head. "It's not for myself —"

Pete thrust his seamed face at them through the suddenly opened door. "That same nigger, Miss Sedley. Shall I tell him to git?"

"No, Pete. I asked him to carry some packages for me. Tell him to wait."

Walt took hold of her arms above the elbows and looked down at her anxious face. "Anne, tell me what's troubling you. I want to help you."

Anne disengaged herself gently. "It's nothing that anybody can help, Walt. I'll be here again tomorrow. Could we attend the theatre in the evening? Will you be free, Walt? Dolores Fuertes is dancing. She is so strange, sad and graceful."

Walt watched her go. He stood looking after her as though piercing the opaque walls with his gaze.

"I know every pulse beat—every heart throb of her, her golden thighed warmth. Then why does she seem so strange—as though her life had nothing to do with mine?"

XI

Sergeant Breen met him at the door of Twin Oaks. Walt knew there was something fearfully wrong. Was he reliving the Chase tragedy? He could hear Mrs. Claiborne sobbing and a chill of fear paralyzed his tongue.

"Who—what? What is it this time? Is it Jeff —" he finally choked out the name.

"It's Paul Griffon. He's killed one of his students."

Walt leaped up the stairs. He heard Jeff's voice. "No, Mr. Griffon, you're crazy with grief. I won't give it to you. You can't make me!"

He pushed his way into the large room past a heavily bearded man who was intently writing notes in a thick copy book. Hewitt was there, and so was Caprin, staring down at a figure covered with a sheet, and crimson furrows on the rug. Two small slippered feet were all that were uncovered.

Walt stared at them and then his glance groped about the room, swept over the heavy ornate drapes, perceived a broken foil lying near the body, and then came to rest on Jeff—Jeff holding, with both hands, a pistol which Griffon was demanding. Griffon, his eyes wild, was reaching for the pistol in Jeff's grasp, while Hewitt attempted to restrain him.

As Walt began to understand what had occurred, Griffon sank back into a chair and covered his face with his hands, moaning, "His mother—I can't face her. Keep her away from me. For the blessed sake of Christ, keep her away from me!"

The odor of whiskey was heavy on his breath.

He lifted his tortured eyes to Walt. "It could have happened to anyone. The button broke off at the tip.

I didn't see it and lunged. He can't be dead. Why don't you listen to his heart? You're crazy, all of you. You God-damned doctor! Why are you forever taking notes? Why don't you get down there and help him? He can't be dead. His mother didn't want him to fence—I persuaded her. His mother—don't bring her here, for Christ's sake. I can't face her."

Jeff moved over to Walt. "Here's his pistol, Walt. I took it away from him."

Walt placed his hand on Griffon's shoulder. He heard Sergeant Breen murmur, "The boy's mother— Madame Matusin is here."

Griffon stiffened and rose slowly to his feet.

* * * *

Cemeteries can comfort with their peace—after a while—after the wound has begun to heal, but not while the grave is still open.

"Henri! Henri! Oh my God!"

"Madame, comfort yourself."

The rain—the heavens weeping—Death's bleak and desolate land—the dreariness—the mud underfoot. When the grass covers the grave it won't be so cruel.

"Anne—Anne! You came! You're always there when I need you."

Jeff is looking after Griffon. Griffon didn't attend the funeral. Where is all his boasting now? Griffon's harsh sobbing voice—"I can't face her again. For God's sake let me be."

Henri Matusin. It would have to be an only son! What to say—what to say—to the haggard drawn mother face underneath the black veil?

"He'll always be with you. It's we who are the dream. *They* are real—eternal. Your son lives, Mrs. Matusin."

"No. No. I won't feel the touch of his hand, hear his voice. I can't—I can't!"

Anne — Anne — If this is all — then all the more reason —

* * * *

Emanuel Caprin read the note with almost a leer of triumph.

"Griffon is gone, Walt. Jeff took him to the boat. He's leaving for France. Has a sister there. Life's funny, isn't it? There's no brag left in him."

Jeff nodded, "He's a broken man, Walt. He'll never fence again."

Hewitt shrugged his shoulders. "It's only temporary. He'll be a penitent for a day or two and then Griffon will be Griffon."

"I'll visit Madame Matusin tomorrow." Caprin removed his wet cape and shook it out. "She may have a miniature of the boy. She should have a portrait. It helps."

"Helps whom?" asked Hewitt cruelly.

"Mr. Hewitt, I don't have to take anything from *you*. Griffon had his rapier —"

"And I have my razor," laughed Hewitt.

"Get yourself another barber, Mr. Caprin," smiled Jeff—and then added quickly, "Mr. Hewitt didn't mean anything, I'm sure."

"Stay out of this, boy. Take a lesson from your brother. He minds his own business."

* * * *

"Dolores! Dolores!" The dancer bowed and waved a graceful hand.

Walt turned to Anne. "Aren't you pleased? The crowd is wild about her."

"What do their bravos mean? They applaud the Rowls on their tight rope—the bloody bullfight and a slave lashed after curfew. What do their bravos mean?"

"You liked her dance, didn't you, Anne?"

"It was graceful motion—and a child's eye is attracted by motion."

"You haven't answered me." They were walking past The Arcade and the stench of the traders' pens struck them full in the face.

"Walt, you, too, applaud everything. That's why I'm afraid. Where do you draw the line?"

"Around you, my dearest. You're all women in all ages and when I draw the line around you, then all is mine—intimately and completely mine."

"What a spot you've chosen for romance, my dear! They sold more than fifty human beings in these pens today—all of them guaranteed free from blemishes and maladies, but who was there to examine the purchasers?"

"What would you have me be, Anne?"

"Not all things to all men!"

"Anne, Anne, is it a fault to see God in everything? Why must you taunt me with fruit from the Tree of Knowledge? Why must I distinguish between beauty and beauty? It's the serpent's doing. Let me be Adam *before* he touched the tree—the Adam who lived by instinct and feeling. I love you. Analyze, tear it apart if you can. I love you. I love the touch of you—your voice—your nearness—every part of you—except your doubts."

"Walt, I'm afraid."

"Afraid of what?"

"Your love—a fierce passion. It isn't enough. What if my breasts should wither and my belly swell? If it were with child you'd glorify it and it would still be the echo of your passion—but if it were a tumor —"

"Stop, Anne! For God's sake stop!"

This time as he kissed her he sensed that it was lips he kissed. And beneath the skin of round enticing breasts are veins and glands and ducts, and women have their periods with bloody rags and their aches and groans—and teeth decay. But you're no child, Walt. You knew all that before. The rotting molding stump is beautiful to you. But *she* does not know and she lives with all that in her mind—and the future slays the present. Can you take fear and doubt to bed forever? Anne, you're a stranger to me. Our passion could have welded us—but your cold unripened thoughts come and stand between. And if I feel that strangeness now— how will it be afterwards on those mornings when we arise and look at each other across the table?

XII

Paddy Meager was the meekest of men. He was the printer of "changeable news," as he called it, while always with him he carried "the eternal word of God— the Bible."

He looked upon Walt as a volcano of flaming fires but wondered often if they were not infernal fires.

Now he observed with startled gaze that the fires had suddenly died.

"What's the matter? Aren't you well, Walt?" Paddy stopped the motion of the press and approached Walt with deep concern.

"No, I'm not at all well." His brain was pressing against his skull as though to shatter the walls of a prison. Was he lacking? Did he lack the balance of thought and opinion that was the ballast of most men? Come now, Walt—you suspected you were a demigod —a bit superior—a bit stronger than your brothers. Is it possible that on the contrary something was left out? What about Eddie? Can it be a family taint? Is yours a madness?

Through a haze he saw Paddy handing him a glass of water. He pressed it to his forehead and then suddenly emptied it over his head. Paddy was startled.

Now he was begging Walt to sit down.

"Don't grieve, Walt. Resign yourself—have faith. I never told you this —"

Walt kept thinking, "His words are going in one ear and out the other. Why doesn't he stop talking?" Yet he heard something of what the old printer was pouring out —

"My wife was very young. She left me after our first year. I looked for her everywhere. I found her in a brothel here in New Orleans. I forgave her—as Jesus would have forgiven her—I took her back and we were happy. She's in a sanitarium—but she'll be well soon —a year or two—she'll be well. We're very happy and it's faith — faith —"

"Walt, what's wrong?" Jeff ran toward him.

"Nothing, Jeff. A bit of dizziness. Here, lock the type; it's ready for you."

Homesickness! What other malady so cancerous? Eddie, with his vacant start. Is this what Jeff is suffering—a torture multiplied by miles between? Two small slippered feet from underneath a blanket. What if something had happened back home—Mary—Hannah. George hadn't mentioned mother in his last letter.

Walt walked more rapidly. If Anne loved him she would come with him — break all ties — resolve all doubts — "Thy people shall be my people —" "Do you find my daughter pleasing?" Griffon—so self assured—Griffon afraid. You're afraid, afraid of Anne, Walt. You don't want marriage—you're afraid of it. She might grow wearisome. Day after day the same face—the same voice. Go. Go—put miles between.

Maybe a change from Twin Oaks. A small room at the Fremont. There—that's better, Jeff, isn't it? No one at your elbow. And there across the street the teeming, swarming St. Charles Hotel with people from all parts of the world.

Jeff, your face is still hollow—and my heartache the same. What to do? What to do? Make a decision—*any* decision!

Now it becomes clearer. Jeff is homesick. Your creative work is at a standstill. There might be illness at home. You can always come back—You can write her. You can write each other. Yes, you'll go home. Jeff will be glad.

Back at the Crescent Office McClure made Walt's decision unavoidable. "You're a good writer, Mr. Whitman, but you don't belong here in New Orleans. It's not anything big you do that's wrong. It's a lot of little things. First of all there's the niggers. We take care of our niggers, sir. We give them shelter, food and even love; you talk to them on equal terms as though they understand what you are saying. You give them a suit too big for them to wear, Mr. Whitman. An' they puff up like big bellied frogs tryin' to fit into it, an' then they become a menace, sir—a damned menace!"

"Has my work been satisfactory?" Walt really didn't care. He felt a sense of relief.

"More than satisfactory, sir. And I'll pay passage for your return to the North. Damn it, man, I hate to see you go. Might as well know it isn't my choosing. Mosley of the Picayune is pining for a fight. I've been avoiding him. Not cowardice, you understand, but prudence. My wife is an invalid. A duel —"

"A duel?" Walt's question exploded. "What for? Why?"

"He's equally good with sword and with pistol. He keeps in practice—and I'm too damned fat. I make too big a target for both."

In spite of McClure's attempt at humor the man was greatly agitated. "You've been talking to his niggers and walking with them. Mosley makes you the issue—wants you out—says you don't belong here."

"But I haven't touched the Negro question."

"No, not in print. But you can't help being a Yankee. Your actions, I mean."

McClure was not enjoying the conversation. Walt watched him puff and perspire.

"All right, Mr. McClure. Frankly I'd meant all along to tell you that I intended to return. But I guess you don't want me back at all or ever. This just brings it to a head."

"No hard feelings, Mr. Whitman?"

Walt shook his head. His sense of relief mounted. McClure was a fine fellow—a fine fellow.

XIII

The steamboats lay two and three deep along the wharves, ocean liners and paddle wheelers—funnels and masts. The levee swarmed with varied creatures and reeked pleasantly with many odors. It was as though the warm sun coaxed and caressed everything to squirm and move.

Anne Sedley was at the dock, calm and reserved—just as when he had picked up her book. Walt dropped the bag he was carrying and ran towards her, while Jeff picked up his brother's burden and jogged slowly after him.

"No, Walt, please don't. Wait 'till you come back! —Jeff—" she turned to his young brother with a sudden gesture—"Walt loves you very much and I want to get to know you. Please don't resent me."

"I don't and I never did, Miss Sedley. It's just that I haven't been well out here. And I thought you'd make him stay."

"Why do you dislike New Orleans?"

"It's a different world here and my stomach can't stand it. The things they do to black people. They're kind and cruel at the same time. They're household pets or wild animals and there's no in between."

Her hand tightened around her handkerchief. "Tell me, Jeff, is it different up North? Is it really different up there? If I thought —"

"All aboard that's goin' aboard!"

Walt bent over her. There it was again—the physical alive warmth of her—the placid reassuring harbor —the oneness that was theirs—that no one else could share. "What do you mean, Anne? You mean there's a chance you'll come with me now? Come. Come, then! We'll send word to your mother."

"No, not now. Good-bye, Walt. Hurry! Hurry! Write me those wild crazy beautiful songs of yours."

"I'll be back, Anne. I'll be back for you. Keep well. Keep well, dear!"

Why was he leaving? Why? Jeff could go home alone.

The boat creaked and drew away from the dock. Walt's eyes remained fixed on Anne. Jeff was talking to him, but Walt paid him not the slightest heed. There were three feet of water between the boat and the dock. He could jump across that easily. Now there were four feet. He could jump that—rush toward Anne and take her in his arms. Now there were seven feet—twelve feet. What was Anne to him now? What had he said to her in farewell? Were they words she would remember—phrases she would caress?

As the Pride of the West found the channel and began its northward journey on the broad muddy breast of the Mississippi, Walt turned slowly to Jeff. "I could have said something original—something she would cherish. Anne expected me to, I'm sure. There are moments that need a word to preserve and enshrine them."

He drew his brother close to him. "I'm disappointed

in myself, Jeff. I left that wretched goodbye hanging in air. Poor Earl Chase could have done better. There was no poetry in that farewell, Jeff—only confusion and heartache."

Part Two

HOME IN THE NORTH

JEFF GREW STRONGER AND HAPPIER on the way North. Walt had overcome his torture of the spirit—grappled with himself and placed a determined foot on the neck of his doubts. Anne was none the worse for their encounter. Why should he flagellate himself with Puritanical remorse? They had met; they had loved. They might meet and love again.

The world is good—and all in it has a purpose. Meet life with exulting—the black, the white and the gray. Will to be joyous! Will to be joyous! "Hence vain melancholy of blackest midnight born!" No. No. Not Milton nor Shakespeare, nor anyone. My own I sing! My own!

Mere passion is it? Then passion let it be. I sound my barbaric yawp over the roofs of the world. Come now, my ship, full-bellied in the wind. On with the voyage!

*　*　*　*

Jeff brightened under the flame and fire of the rekindled Walt. By the time they had reached Chicago he was eager and curious to see all the sights and no longer in a frenzied hurry to get home.

They took a boat to Milwaukee, visited Mackinaw and Detroit, travelled leisurely to Cleveland and thence to Niagara.

At Niagara Jeff handed Walt a small package roughly rolled in wrapping paper. "Happy birthday, Walt!"

Walt turned away from the thunder of the waters that seemed suddenly silenced. He kissed his brother and then opened the package. It was a leather belt with a heavy metal buckle.

"I'll gird my loins in strength, Jeff—and incidentally hold my pants up. Thanks a lot, Jeff."

"You like it?"

"You bet. I like it a lot. I needed a new one."

He smiled as he drew out the frayed and worn belt he had worn up to that moment and replaced it with his brother's gift.

"I'm twenty-nine, Jeff—gray at twenty-nine. Wonder what I'll look like when I'm a hundred."

"Do you expect to live that long, Walt?"

"Why not? My body is strong. I live in no black fear-crammed world that worry creates and destroys. I live in the world as it is and revel in it. My blood flows strong. There's no poison in my blood—no cloud —no cloud."

His face set and became suddenly grave. "No cloud," he repeated and thought of Eddie's dwarfed mind, then trampled the dark mood and flung it aside. "I wonder, Jeff, how the folks are getting on. We'd better move a little faster from here on."

* * * *

When Walt entered the house his brother Edward looked up from the floor where he was seated playing with splinters of wood. He seemed to be staring through Walt and far beyond. Edward was thirteen and his vaguely groping mind had stopped growing at six.

Now Edward's voice was casual, as though Walt had not been away. "Walt, there's a hickory tree near the river. It's a big hickory tree. Father's a carpenter. You big hickory tree, I'll chop you down. Then Father will make a house — a house —"

He stared and stopped babbling and then lowered

his eyes to the chips of wood which strewed the floor.
Jeff remained standing in the doorway. "Hello, Eddie,"
was all he said. Walt walked over and put his hand on
Edward's head. Then he knelt and kissed him on the
forehead. Edward eyed him blankly.

"There's a hickory tree near the river —" he mumbled on and on as he moved chips of firewood aimlessly
on the floor.

"We're home, Jeff," Walt walked to the back door.
He heard the sound of an axe and peered through the
cracked pane. It was his mother who was picking up
the wood she had just finished splitting. He opened
the door wide as she came in.

"Hello, Louisa!"

She looked at him timidly as though she were going
to cry. "Walt, you're home, you're home."

Jeff took the firewood from her and deposited it
near the stove. His mother did not move. She looked
up at Walt, her hands at her sides, tears streaking her
cheeks. Her fingers fumbled awkwardly along the edge
of her apron. Walt placed his arms around her and
held her close to him for a long time.

Jeff stood watching Eddie move the splinters about
on the rug. He did not attempt to kiss his mother but
merely murmured, "Hello, Ma!"

"You're skinny, Jeff. You must be hungry, both of
you. Sit down. There's some cold meat."

She hurried to the pantry and brought out plates.

"We'll wait, Ma. We'll wait for Pa."

They had not long to wait. The elder Whitman and
Walt's brother George came in together. The father,
his hands streaked and grimy, his face stern and severe,
looked at his sons briefly, then walked to the wash pail
with no change of expression. "Jeff looks peaked,
Louisa."

George wiped his palm against his pants and held

out his hand to Walt. He ignored Jeff completely.

"Jeff looks sick," said the father tonelessly, splashing water on his face.

"Yes, Pa. He had dysentery but he's all right now. He'll gain his weight back."

Walt's mother had a radiant glow in her tired face. She was all eagerness and welcome. "Hannah's coming over tonight. She's been nervous as a cat ever since you left. Comes here no less'n three times a week. Dinner'll be ready when the soup's hot enough."

The mother stirred the soup vigorously and looked gladly at her two prodigal sons, although it was Walt on whom her glance rested with the greatest pride.

"What are you going to do now, Walt?" George, his hair dripping, reached over for the towel his father had dropped over the back of a chair.

"Guess I'll be back with some paper."

"Maybe the Eagle will take you back."

"Only if I take back what I said, and I won't. It's a dough-face newspaper. It won't change and I'm not taking back a word of it. You can't blow hot and cold on slavery. Dough-faces, that's what they all are, from the owner down."

Walt turned almost shyly towards his mother. "Can I set up my cot in Eddie's room, Ma?"

His mother looked at him, smiling happily. "Don't go worryin' none about bed and vittles. Whatever we eat you'll eat, and the same roof'll be over our heads."

The father led the way to the table. "Mother's right. You can give me a hand with the shingling I'm doin' for Matt Sykes, but don't you think I'm turnin' my own outdoors."

There was a long unbroken silence as they all sat around the table. Even Eddie bowed his head.

"Father, we thank Thee for our daily bread. Amen, and praise the Lord!"

II

The nights were terrifying in their loneliness. Walt clutched the pillow to his cheek and tried to imagine it was Anne he was kissing and caressing. Jealousy was tearing him apart.

"Write me, Anne! Why don't you answer? Write me every detail—what you do—whom you meet—what you feel for me."

Walt wrote to Anne constantly. His letters carried no news. Often they were literal copies of verses he had written and rewritten furiously in his crude notebooks.

The very first week home he wrote her:

"One hour to madness and joy!
O furious! O confine me not!
What is this that frees me so in storms?
What do my shouts and lightnings and raging
    winds mean?
O to be yielded to you whoever you are, and
    you to be yielded to me in defiance of the
    world!
O to return to Paradise! O bashful and fem-
    inine!
O to draw you to me, to plant on you for the
    first time the lips of a determined man."

At first his nights were ecstatic agony. He would smell the fragrance of her body; he would feel the roundness of her thighs and the softness of the tip of her tongue between his lips in the half dreams that raged in his brain. Then as he worked long hours beside his father, his sleep was sounder and his indecision less painful. How long to wait? Three months? A year? He would send for her—but first some regular income—a snug sum saved and put away—security—

the security that sets the mind at rest—money safely put away, rooted like a citadel or fortress.

Her letters were modest—patient—and his fears grew calm.

Walt was home. He swam and floated about the streets and opened wide his gills to the clatter and turbulence of New York.

A gold rush to California. The newspapers carried raucous columns and screaming advertisements.

Walt soberly eyed the frenzied Herald which was usually conservative and sedate. An advertisement in mighty letters proclaimed—

"Californians!

Ho! Hist!

Attention!

Our rubber boats and tents are unsurpassed.

You cannot face the gold rivers without a rubber suit."

And on that very page—"Startling Discoveries! The El Dorado of the old Spaniards is discovered at last. We have now the highest official authority for believing in the discovery of vast gold mines in California, and that the discovery is the greatest and most startling, not to say miraculous, that the history of the last five centuries can produce."

*   *   *   *

"Walt, I've been thinking on it." George, usually silent and reserved, moved closer to Walt as they strode down the road toward the river. "If you'd go with me — there's nothing to tie you down."

"There's a lot to tie me down."

"What?"

"Laziness—I guess!"

"You're not lazy, Walt. Lazy people don't sit all night studying and reading."

"Nobody's lazy when it's something he wants to do."

"Then you don't want to go West."

"No. I've just come home."

"It's no good being poor, Walt. It's like walking on this thin ice—afraid to let your weight down."

Walt took hold of his brother's arm. "It wouldn't be any better out there. They've gone wild—and only the tough and the brutal can take what's happening. There's crime and greed and hate. It's not for a quiet person like you, George. People get rich in New York too, if that's what you want."

"That's what everybody wants."

"Maybe some don't want it as hard as others."

"What do you want, Walt?"

"I'm too busy enjoying what I've got to want for much—but there are feelings I'd like to write down so they won't be lost. Great feelings—important feelings that I want others to have—and understand."

"But you're different from others, Walt—you know you're different. Most people aren't interested in your feelings about things, and the things you like most other people don't care for at all. With money it's different. Everybody understands that and always did, I guess. The best poem I ever read didn't sound half as good to me as "Payable to Bearer—One Dollar." It's no good being poor. Sometimes I hate to see morning come."

A feeling of guilt gnawed at Walt's insides. He burst out, "What's wrong with me, George? Why don't I have the consideration of a louse that grubs for its own food? I don't earn my keep and yet I walk around like a king—and tell you what to do or what not to do."

George grinned a slow abashed grin and a look of gruff tenderness warmed his dull eyes. "You can't help being what you are, Walt. Ma and Pa are sort of proud of you. They like having you around. I've heard Pa tell Mr. Sykes as how your talk is better than firewood to keep the house warm on a chill night. You sure can wallop the backside of words and make them do tricks for you."

III

Walt worked that afternoon, and in the evening sought the streets, the crowds—movement—the city. As he walked, his eyes came suddenly upon a lurid poster posted awry the cracked pane of a saloon window.

WORKING MEN!
Shall
AMERICANS
or
ENGLISH
rule in this city?

The crew of the British steamer have threatened all Americans who shall dare to express their opinion this night at the English *Aristocratic* Opera House! We advocate no violence, but a free expression of opinion to all public men.

WORKINGMEN!   *FREEMEN!*
Stand by your
Lawful Rights
AMERICAN COMMITTEE

"There's going to be trouble—plenty of trouble."

Whitman turned and looked curiously at the withered leathery hunched-up newsboy who peered up at him from below the tired brim of an ancient cap.

"Trouble?"

"Yes, it's all come 'count of that Macready actor—Charles Macready. He's been shootin' off his gab as how Americans aren't worth the price of a sick hog. Our money's good enough for him, though. He'll be getting his tonight and good."

Now Walt felt a tautness all around him. Men and women were hurrying with a brisker pace than usual— with grimmer faces than usual. He fell in with the general surge and heard muttered threats on all sides of him.

"His last appearance," he says. "It'll be his last appearance, right enough!" The burly, florid faced barber, standing in the doorway, drew his hand across his throat.

Now Walt remembered. There had been a temperamental flare-up involving the British actor Macready and the American player Forrest. In Macready's estimation American actors were generally "brutes not intelligences." As for Forrest himself, he was "a blackguard, a thick-headed, thick-legged brute, an ignorant, uneducated man burning with envy and rancor at my success."

Forrest, on his part, had used the term "liar" rather generously in his many bitter critiques of Macready. Several years before, Forrest had gone to the theatre in Edinburgh for no other purpose than to hiss Macready in his favorite role of Hamlet.

Yes, Walt remembered. But surely a spat between actors had not grown into a national feud! He quickened his pace.

The shouting of the mob at Astor Place sounded from that distance like the wailing and hooting of devils. The militia was there—uniforms, rifles and pistols.

"Where are the police? What need is there for the militia?" Walt was indignant and spoke aloud at no one in particular—and no one heard him. Rocks were already being hurled at the windows and over the sound of crashing glass arose shouts of "Tear it down!

Smash that palace of the aristocrats! Drive those kid glove bastards to cover! No English pucker-lip is going to insult us!"

The roar of the crowd was rent with the frightened screams of women.

"Walt, I followed you. There's going to be trouble. I was worried about you."

"Mary!" Walt drew his sister towards him.

"It seems crazy, doesn't it, threatening bloodshed over an actor's quarrel."

"And I thought all the hot blood was down South. Don't worry, Mary, it will pass."

"I'm frightened, Walt."

"Mary — Mary Elizabeth!" Walt put his arm around her to shield her as the menacing crowd pressed solidly against her. "Let's get out of here. This is no place for you."

They thrust, pushed and dug their way towards the fringe of the grim-faced mob where they breathed a bit more easily. A tall, gangling sailor volunteered, "I saw the police march in. There's worse trouble— much worse trouble inside."

"Let's go home, Walt!"

Mary Elizabeth was as wide-eyed as a child and as frightened.

Walt groaned, "They shouldn't have called the militia. That's a senseless thing to do! Americans don't like that way of doing things. Let them shout it out. You don't need a militia for a theatre crowd. Look at those young soldiers. They don't know in their own minds what they're supposed to do—and when humans don't know what they're supposed to do they do foolish, wild or crazy things."

"What's happening, Walt? You're so tall. What's happening?" Mary Elizabeth was half sobbing as she clutched at him.

"More folly! They've started stoning the militia—as though it were some sort of a joke."

There was a ragged rattle of rifle fire. "Blanks! Blanks!" roared the crowd. "Yah! Yah! They're firing blanks!"

And then a second volley—and then a third.

The shouting died away as though a storm wind had suddenly passed. There was a great silence—like a gasp of incredulity. Here and there a moan, a scream. Here and there a cry of terror—for there were struggling bodies and dark blood on the sidewalks.

Walt ran from Mary Elizabeth in his haste to reach the wounded. A father threw his arms over Walt's shoulders and hung like a dead weight as he sobbed, "My boy! Wyllis! Wyllis!" His son lay on his face in the gutter, the thick red pool around his head like a grim halo in the murky stream that lay stagnant along the curb.

There was a boy, his eyes bulging with terror or pain, trying to push his entrails back into the hole in his stomach. The boy couldn't have been over fifteen. Walt eased him to the sidewalk. People clutching heads, arms and legs moved wildly around him.

An echoing voice in his hollow skull was shouting, "There was no reason for it—no reason for it. Theatre actors—pride, envy, personal quarrels—guns, the dead —the dead. Mobs and masses of people have no soul. To keep your soul you have to be alone."

The boy—what to do with the boy! You can't let a boy bleed to death. But how do you stop the flow of blood? How do you ease the pain?

"I'll take over from here." The calm face staring at him was reassuring and confident. A male nurse from the city Health Department. He'd know what to do.

Walt got to his feet. "I can't do any good. I've got

only words—words." He felt ashamed of his own emptiness of skill and felt an awe and reverence for the
doctors who could stitch, bandage and heal—and the
male nurses who could look at blood calmly and say
"I'll take over from here."

"Come home, Walt. Come home!"

"Yes, Mary Elizabeth."

IV

Walt lashed himself in the days that followed—
condemned himself over and over again to hear his
own despairing sentence. "You're useless! You can't
create with your hands—nor with your brain either.
You caress life and death—gild them with words—and
call them beautiful. A gaping wound and you can do
nothing but moan. Stir your lazy hulk and work.
Build something—anything. Nail a shingle where there
wasn't one before. Saw a plank. Smash a rock with a
sledge and level the gravel to make a road. Do something!"

He determined to aid his father daily. Why not a
carpenter's trade? There were always night hours for
reading and study, if study he must. "Sweet is the rest
of the laborer"—the food tastes better and the lungs
breathe easier and the bath is more refreshing. Limbs
were made to function or they rot—so work, Walt
Whitman! Stir your sluggard, lazy hide. Work!

* * * *

It was in the late summer that he wrote to her these
words,

"I've found myself, Anne! I do believe I've found
myself at last."

That was the lusty routine and pattern for weeks
until Jeff came by and set his foot on the ladder of

their neighbor's house, whose roof Walt and his father were shingling.

"Walt, Judge Johnson wants to see you!" Jeff showed by his demeanor that he considered the news urgent and important.

Walt leisurely dismounted from the ladder and tossed the shingling hammer aside. "What did he say, Jeff?"

"Just said, 'Tell Walt I want to see him.' Guess that's clear enough."

"Tell Ma I won't be home for dinner, Jeff." Walt strode away leaving his father looking after him curiously.

At the Democratic Headquarters there were only two men at work—one the Negro janitor who was gathering up and cleaning the cuspidors, and the other Judge Samuel E. Johnson, bent intently over fresh copies of the Eagle strewn on the table. The Judge was short and stocky with a round flushed face from which a thin cigar projected like a stem from a bright red apple.

"Hello, Walt! Have a seat." He waved his hand in the general direction of three or four chairs near the table, while his eyes were still focused on the page he was reading.

Suddenly he brushed the papers aside with an angry snort. "The lordly Eagle with fear in its belly! Walt, we real Democrats haven't got a paper. We haven't got a voice. That's what I want to talk to you about." Then abruptly, "Why did you come back from New Orleans? Couldn't you make a go of it?"

"Jeff wasn't well—and I was in a rut."

"Did you kick up a row on the slave question?"

"No. Didn't touch it."

"Why not? Scared?"

"That doesn't even make me angry, Judge."

"I didn't intend to offend you, but what the hell —"

77

"There's not much difference in the way they treat Negroes anywhere."

"The devil you say! Do *we* treat them like slaves?"

Walt sprawled easily in his chair and looked at Ray Connors, the Negro janitor, shining up a cuspidor. "There's the answer."

"I don't quite get you, Walt."

"The South has one pattern of living and the North has another. The Negro isn't free in either. It doesn't answer the question to change the kind of shackles you put on a man. What's your idea of a Negro, Judge— someone to shine your shoes and clean cuspidors? Let him run against you for Judge and with all your free soil principles you'll resent his breaking out of the pattern your mind has set for him."

"Hold on there, Walt. He's got a long way to go before he's ready for my kind of a job."

"Wouldn't be so long, if we wanted it that way. One generation — or two — that's all — if we really wanted it that way."

"But whatever he's got stacked against him up North he's bought and sold like a horse in the South. Surely you're not comparing —"

"Judge, in the South a man takes care of his horse and his slave. He feeds them and even loves them. That's their pattern. The Negro slave is safe unless he tries to break out of that pattern. The North and the South, each with its ideological patterns and both of them bad. Both have to grow up—both the North and the South."

"Maybe you're the wrong man for what I've got in mind." Judge Johnson was dubious. "That trip to New Orleans didn't do you any good."

"Judge, I haven't changed my principles. I'll fight with everything I've got and everything I am to keep free soil free; but the South will have to settle its own problems."

"I wish I could be more sure of where you stand, Walt. A man's got to stand for something. Anyway, here's the proposition. The Eagle is wishy-washy—afraid to antagonize, afraid to lose votes for the regular Democratic candidate—afraid to lose the southern votes. The real northern Democrats, like myself, want to shout 'Free Soil' when the Eagle won't even whisper. A man or a party has to stand for something—damn it!

Let's go after Governor Cass. He's the king pin. We'll boost Van Buren for President! That's enough of an objective. The 'fill-in' is up to you."

"Anything personal against Cass?"

"Hell, no! I'm not asking you to do any grudge work for me. I just can't stomach a man who's everything to all men—full of piss and high purposes and sees no further than the ballot box. Cass is an obliging ass. Stick that in one of your poems—it rhymes."

"I don't share your opinion of Lewis Cass. He has served his country ably and honestly. All you'll succeed in doing is split the Democratic party wide open and let a Whig walk in."

"If the Democratic party isn't democratic then it deserves to be split. We've got to take a firm stand on slavery once and for all. You can't cure a cancer by saying it doesn't exist."

"*I* can't go all out on abolition, either. I suppose that puts me in the same class with Cass."

"Now *you're* rhyming," chuckled the Judge; then turning suddenly serious—"No, *you're* sincere, so there's some hope for you. When you finally organize your ideas you'll stand for something squarely. Right now you love everybody—but you'll realize that circumstances—history—events will force you to choose—and then you'll choose. Cass won't. He'll pick ballots like a buzzard picks the bones of a corpse without asking whose corpse it is. And there'll be plenty of corpses—plenty of them."

"Meaning what?"

"I mean the North and the South are heading for a break, and no honest man's going to be sitting on the fence. He'll have to be on one side or the other. Oh, I know—you'd like to say, 'Kiss and be friends. Peace on you and peace on you —' but life doesn't work that way."

"I'm not sure that you're picking the right man —"

"Neither am I—but I *believe* I am. Damn it—don't be coy. Anyway it's not a marriage. Quit any-time you want to. And—oh, yes—in case you need a location, there's a basement office for rent at 110 Orange Street. The Star has its office there and Alden Spooner's your friend. He can fix it up for you, space and all that. And here's another thing—draw on this account for the funds you need. Let me confirm your signature. I'll drop in at the bank to see that every-thing is in order. Draw what you need to live on. Are we agreed?"

Walt shook hands with the Judge and a warm ex-cited glow filled his body. He was a bit dazed at the suddenness of the offer, but pleased—very pleased. Here was a job and a challenge. Here he could be his own boss. Here he could be free. Now he could send for Anne. Now — now! No. Better wait a while. What would you do, Walt? Set up a home? You'd be anchored solid before you knew whether this is really your job. You couldn't come and go. You'd be rooted solid.

But you can't keep Anne waiting. What is she—wife or widow? She has a right to know! Her days are filled with anxiety. Her thoughts are of you—of you. Not yet. See how this works out—if it's perma-

nent. Permanent? Be honest, Walt—you are a vaga-
bond! You wouldn't *want* anything permanent except
your love of life. Permanent, permanent? Anne—Anne
—you're so far away. Anne Sedley's brother. You
ought to look him up. Brooklyn—she said he worked
in Brooklyn. She should have mentioned him in her
letters. Then you would have remembered. Write her,
Walt. Tell her what's happening. Then see what she
says. See what she says.

V

Walt stood in the street, frankly admiring the heavy
blocked poster he had designed.

"Free Soilers! Liberty Men! Free Men!
Here's your paper! Don't grovel with Cass
or blunder with Taylor, but come right up
and subscribe to the Daily Freeman!"

He lounged against the flaky and rusted lamp post
chatting with Alden Spooner as five or six newsboys
noisily shouted the merits of his paper. The September
day had a chilly tang and Spooner drew his coat collar
close. Walt thought, "New Orleans was warm — sun
drenched and warm." Anne hadn't answered his letter.

"Do you know a man by the name of John Sedley?"
Walt asked suddenly.

"Yes. He used to work for me. A fine copy boy.
Sorry he had to go. He left for New Orleans yesterday."

"Yesterday?" Walt was bitter with himself. Why
had he been silent? Why hadn't he asked before? He
could write Anne again. He drew the first copy of the
Freeman from his pocket lovingly, tenderly, and began
to walk home.

His mother met him at the door. She was fixing
up a mustard plaster for Mary Elizabeth who lay on
the couch with a patched quilt over her body.

"Don't you go worryin' none about Mary. This plaster'll burn it right out. What's that you're holdin', Walt? Your new paper!" In her excitement she forgot about the mustard plaster and let it fall on the table. She reached eagerly for the paper that Walt held out to her.

"Let me see it too, Mother." Mary's voice wheezed with hoarseness and her large eyes were alight.

His mother held it clumsily with her coarse fingers.

"Your own paper, Walt. Your own paper! Pa'll be glad that you're working."

"I'll read it to you, Ma." Mary Elizabeth stretched out her hands.

"Go on, read it yourself, Ma. Don't let Mary use her voice. It isn't good for her."

"There's too many big words in it, Walt. Jeff'll read it to me when he comes home. But it's your paper, your own paper." She pressed it to her lips before she gave it to Mary.

Mary Elizabeth frowned as she read. "But nobody's going to vote for Van Buren. You'll lose, Walt. You'll lose."

"It's better to lose with the right—"

"And which is right?"

"Van Buren is for Free Soil and General Cass begs the question."

"Hush, Mary Elizabeth. Walt knows what he's doing."

Walt seated himself at the table and watched with a faint smile the eager excitement of mother and daughter. Then he looked out through the window and arose slowly to his feet. He stood rigid as stone. The walls of his skull seemed to be crushing his brain. His body set and became immobile. Flames were shooting up against the sky. He could hear the clamorous shouting of people, the galloping of horses—the mad confusion of sound gone mad.

"What's wrong, Walt?" It was Mary's voice floating like tiny distant echoes against his ear. As for his mother, she held the newspaper fiercely against her breast and came anxiously to Walt's side.

George was running easily down the street towards them. Jeff was puffing at his side, yet he was the first to speak.

"They've got it under control now. We're safe here."

"Did the fire get to Orange Street?" Walt asked the grimly important question, although his heart told him what the answer would be.

George and Jeff both understood. They could not soften the blow. They nodded. Walt remained standing, trying to let his thoughts flow in an orderly manner. Would Johnson raise money to start somewhere else? Was this the end of the Freeman? Had it been doomed to die at birth?

There was a firm steadying grip on his arm. "Don't worry none, Walt. It ain't hard to start over—if you're not scared."

Walt looked down at his mother, the tension in his face suddenly relaxing. "I'm not scared, Ma."

* * * *

Walt arose late and as he entered the kitchen he saw his mother on her knees scrubbing the floor and Mary Elizabeth with a white wool wrapping around her throat doing the breakfast dishes. He was pouring himself a cup of coffee when his sister Hannah came in. Hannah was bony, tall and angular and at constant odds with the world and all it contained. She began at once on the business that had brought her.

"Ma, why didn't David Taylor give the paint job to Charles? Pa could've said something. He doesn't give a damn about me. Nobody in this family gives a damn about me."

She watched Walt calmly sipping the coffee and looking at her over the edge of the cup. "Well, now that you're burnt out what are you going to do—hang around Ma's neck like a leech and let her support and feed you?"

Walt did not answer. He didn't have to. Louisa looked up from her scrubbing and brushed the hair from her eyes. "Hannah, you leave Walt alone. He's thinking and planning. He's got a lot of learning or Judge Johnson wouldn't have asked him to run his own newspaper."

"You see," shrilled Hannah, "you don't care about me or Charles. Walt's your favorite. He can lie around like a pile of manure and nobody touches him—while Pa doesn't even put in a good word for Charles."

"Charles was drunk on the last job and messed it up," Louisa reminded her gently.

"And Walt is the perfect saint!" Hannah laughed mockingly. "Doesn't drink and doesn't bundle! Doesn't do anything, the lazy hulk!"

Walt spoke gently. "Hannah, why do you hate me?"

"I don't hate you!"

"But this happens every time you come."

"Then I won't come here."

"That isn't what I mean, Hannah." He stretched out his arm as she turned to go, and holding her skinny shoulder gently, drew her subbornly resisting to him. Suddenly she began to sob. Her slight form convulsed and shook in Walt's arms.

"I don't hate you, Walt. I love you. I don't know why I say mean things. It's myself I hate. Charles keeps drinking and there's times when he doesn't come home nights. And I'm there alone waiting—and I wish I were dead."

"Did he read my book?"

"No, he threw the first copy into the stove."

"Wait, I'll get you another one."

"He won't read it."

"He doesn't drink on Sunday. Give it to him on Sunday, Hannah. Once he gets started he'll find it interesting—and maybe it'll do some good."

"Nothin'll ever do him any good. He's mean and hateful when he's sober, just like when he's drunk."

Walt reached under Mary's cot and pulled out a flat box where he kept books and papers. He pulled out a paper-covered volume with frayed edges and thumbed the pages tenderly. On the cover in heavy black letters was the title:

Franklin Evans, or The Inebriate
A Tale of the Times by the popular
American Author, WALT WHLTMAN

He looked at the date. "1842. Seven years ago, Hannah, and I haven't gotten anywhere. Maybe Charles will profit by it. I didn't."

Hannah took the book reluctantly. "I'm telling you, Walt, it won't do no good and he'll throw this one in the stove too."

"Maybe that's where it belongs," laughed Walt. "My book on temperance in the fire and now my newspaper. God surely doesn't like my work so far."

"Don't be blasphemous, Walt." Louisa was pushing the box of books back under the cot.

"I'm not blasphemous and never could be. You see, Ma, God's a personal friend of mine."

He walked out into the street and watched the returning firemen galloping their horses back to the station. He wondered dully what their hurry was now that the fire was over and several blocks of the business section lay in ashes.

Someone called loudly to him from a carriage. Walt looked up. It was Judge Johnson. "I was coming over to see you, Walt. Hop in and we'll talk while I drive."

"Haven't been over to the shop, Judge, but I suppose we're burned out proper."

"Right down to the ground. Hi! We won't be able to get through here. Here boy," he called to a ragged smudge-faced urchin, "hold my horses and you get a dime."

They shouldered their way grimly and impatiently through the crowd and surveyed the shambles left by the fire. Here and there a broken wall projected itself up from the heap of ruins as though vaunting itself over the ashes around it.

"Let's go around to Myrtle Street. Better rent a shop before the others get going. They're still stunned. We've got to act fast."

"What do you mean, Judge?"

"You're slow, Walt. They haven't burnt the Freeman. What's a building but a body. The soul goes marching on! Rent another shop, Walt, and get to work! 'Victory with Van Buren!' That's the goal! Now get to work. And, by the way, don't try to get rich off subscriptions. Cut your price to a penny. Two cents is too damned much for us poor common people."

VI

"Blinding your eyes with that fancy work," the elder Whitman looked up from the Bible. "What's the good of it, Louisa? Sewing and darning are proper tasks for a home loving woman, but making flowers and petals out of thread —"

"It pretties up the house. There's no call to be angry." Louisa continued to bend over the pattern. "Go on with the reading, Father."

Her husband returned his sombre gaze to the huge tome and read slowly,

" 'And the Lord said unto Samuel, Hearken unto the voice of the people in all that they say unto thee; for they have not rejected thee but they have rejected Me, that I should not reign over them.' "

" 'And then Samuel anointed Saul.' " Mary Elizabeth raised her voice triumphantly as though exulting at demonstrating her familiarity with the text.

"Hush, child. Let your father read. You are ahead of the story."

Walt, leaning back in his chair close to the fireplace, exchanged smiles with George who sat opposite his father and commented, "And Kish had a son whose name was Saul, a choice young man and a goodly; and there was not among the children of Israel a goodlier person than he; from his shoulders and upward he was higher than any of the people." Then he added, "Prophets should be tall of height. Tall men are gentle and understanding."

"Don't know that size has much to do with it. I've seen big fools in my time." George arose from his chair and placed a stubby log on the smouldering embers. "Can't you stir yourself once in a while, Walt? You know you could have tossed that log in there just as well as I."

Louisa lowered the pattern to her lap. "Why must prophets be tall, Walt?"

"I've watched the little men, Mother. Usually their voices are loud. They have to assert themselves. They feel inferior and out of their resentment they rave and threaten. Their message is more often prompted by hurt pride than truth. I'm afraid of little men. We need tall prophets, tall presidents—tall leaders of the people."

"Saul didn't turn out so well," piped up Mary Elizabeth. "Little David did much better."

"There's no proof in the Bible that David was

little," said the elder Whitman closing the Sacred Volume. "All the Good Book says is that Saul was head and shoulders taller than the rest of the people."

* * * *

"Unprincipled traitor! Sticks a knife in the back of his own party!" Cass's furious press agent aimed a vicious blow at Walt's head. Jeff caught the enraged man by the elbow and held on.

The wrathful one finally wriggled free. "Let me go, damn you! You're his brother, aren't you? Well, tell him to stay away from me."

Jeff followed his brother to the street bench and the sullen crowd of precinct workers gathered about them. Posters showing the final election returns lay like shattered white fossils in the mud, churned up by the feet of the crowd.

Cass had lost the presidency by a narrow margin. Had there been no split in the Democratic party Cass would undoubtedly have won and Zachary Taylor, the Whig candidate—the slave owner—would have been defeated.

No wonder Cass' followers were bitter.

"What should I have done? What should I have done?"

Walt felt the chill of guilt. As between Taylor and Cass, Cass would have made by far the better President. His long and heroic record on many a battlefield against the Indians and his firm stand against the British, his valuable service as governor of the Michigan Territory were too fresh in the mind of Walt to be ignored. Zachary Taylor? Taylor was well meaning, but wholly unprepared for statesmanship. His military career had been marred by blunders—but his victories over the Mexicans at Palo Alto and Buena Vista had captured the imagination of America.

"Perhaps I blundered!" Walt groaned inwardly. "If

only Cass had not stressed his approval of the Fugitive Slave Laws I would never have permitted Johnson to persuade me. And now we have a slave owner for President! What should I have done? What should I have done?"

As for Judge Johnson, there was no question about his sincerity. "I'd rather lose with Van Buren than win with a compromiser." He patted Walt on the shoulder repeatedly and presented him with a flourish to the full-bosomed lady who teasingly occupied his comfortable desk chair.

"You poets should know each other" he chortled. "Adah, this is Walt Whitman. You know all about him."

"Not intimately," twinkled the poetess as she stared boldly and brazenly at Walt.

The judge roared. "That could be remedied, eh Walt?"

"Oh, stop, Lou, you're embarrassing the man." Then gravely to Walt, "I'm Adah Menken—if the name means anything to you."

Walt hesitated.

She twisted her lips wryly and nodded. "No, I can see it doesn't. Perhaps we have mutual friends—Henry Clapp?"

Walt nodded. "I used to know him when he was an abolitionist."

She clicked her tongue in mock sadness—"That was before Paris, and the flesh pots." She tossed her head, "Well, supposing you two go ahead and talk—and then later we'll have a chance to get acquainted. Don't mind me."

The Judge gave her a paternal pat on the knee and turned his attention to Walt.

"Walt, we've upped our subscriptions beyond the Eagle. That's fine! Let's make it a daily. It'll mean a lot more work for you —" he hesitated. "But you've got a life-time job if you want it."

"A life-time job!" Walt looked at his friend soberly. "What's your idea of a Democrat, Judge?"

Johnson's bulbous nose shone like a beacon.

"Why, generally speaking, he's a man who's loyal to the Jeffersonian principles of state sovereignty, but" the Judge waved a monstrous finger, "if you mean the slavery issue—then no state can make another state party to its crime by insisting that free states return fugitive slaves."

"And what's your idea of a National Republican or a Whig?"

"A man who believes in national supremacy as against States' Rights. Damn it—to Hell man! Why are you quizzing me?"

"Then the Republican party is the logical one to fight slavery—and if parties meant anything that's the way it would be."

"But there is a difference. We Democrats don't believe in national supremacy as against states' rights. We believe in the sovereignty of the state, — yes sir — the sovereignty of the state — and that includes the right of a northern state to refuse to be a party to a crime."

"That's clever debate, but it doesn't mean a thing. The Southern Democrats insist on state sovereignty to maintain and extend slavery, and the Northern Democrats insist on state sovereignty to refuse to be a party to slavery. You told me a man has to stand for something. Well, by the Living God, a *party* has to stand for something too!"

"Any regrets, Walt?"

"No, it's just that I want to know where I stand."

"What real difference does it make to you? You're a journalist. You can write the things you believe. I'm not dictating to you what or how to write. I don't see where the question of party politics affects you at all."

"Well, Judge, then take a calm objective, look at what I see,—the Eagle and the Freeman, bitter rivals, both speaking for the same Democratic Party. The Eagle seeing free-soil gradually enslaved and saying 'Let's not make that an issue—as long as we can keep our Democratic party in office,' and the Freeman saying 'Come all who love liberty! No compromise with evil! Slavery is evil!'"

"Well?" asked the Judge somewhat perplexed. "Then you agree! Surely our stand is the right one— the honest one. We can win the old Hunkers over. Time and circumstances will help us."

Walt shoved a sheaf of papers across the desk. "Take a look at our list of subscribers. Do you see any Whig names? And yet we're pretty much in line with what the Whigs want. The only ones that read the Freeman are the Democrats. We're labelled a party paper and our message doesn't reach the people as people; it doesn't reach Americans as Americans!"

"Well, we can't make the Freeman non-partisan."

"Why not?"

"Damn it, man, while we won't sell our souls for votes we're entitled to the fruits of our labors. Who the hell paid for this paper? If we educate the people we're entitled to their support."

"It doesn't reach the people."

"It does, Walt, it does."

"No, it's too much like a game of Rugby. Two teams kicking the same ball around. Your parties have gotten to be as confused as creeds—religions. People are born into one or the other. People belong to one or the other blindly without asking themselves why they belong."

"They know damn well why they belong!"

"Your active party workers do. Five dollars for passing out circulars. A job in the city or county. A relative who's running for office, — those are the bones and sinews of your party organization. If the Democratic Party can be for slavery and against slavery at one and the same time —"

"Well, what do you want to do?"

"Supposing I ignore parties and write for whatever paper speaks the truth — even if it is a Whig sheet."

"People won't understand, Walt. They'll call you a Benedict Arnold. They'll say you ran out on your party, that you have no political principles. Don't be a damned fool."

Adah raised her eyes from the book she was reading. "Gentlemen, more light and less heat." Walt ignored the interruption.

"So continuing loyalty to an idea eventually means disloyalty to a group."

"How do you figure that?"

"Because parties and groups are bodies that eventually change or degenerate — and ideas are eternal. There's Hunkerism among the Whigs and the Democrats both. The party names and the parties themselves don't mean a thing except as a device for political elections and personal ambitions. I don't want to be a Whig or a Democrat."

"What do you want, Walt? Do you really know what the hell you want? We've got a two party system and it's a good system."

"I want to be just a plain American. Why should the British system chain America? No Whig and Tory factions belong here. Liberalism and Conservatism like the Gingham Dog and the Calico Cat, both apparently at each others throats but both piously singing 'God Save the King.' Do I have to belong to a party?"

"Walt, you've got to be loyal to some group."

"I'm loyal to an idea."

"You just said you're an American."

"America is an *idea*—it's an idea of democracy—bigger than any party—bigger than any group. It's the biggest idea in the world, if only we'd realize it."

"Hurrah, hurrah for you, Patrick Henry! Any more beautiful words? Bah! Talk! Talk! Your thinking is muddled. You're perched on a pink cloud that's standing still when a carriage with wheels is what you need."

"No, Judge—I suspect I'm thinking straight, thinking the way I feel and not against my feelings."

"What does it all add up to, Walt?"

"Get yourself another editor, Judge. No hard feelings against you," he hastily added. "I'll stick around until you're set."

"Hell's burning, sizzling coals! you poets are all alike—building dream worlds in a vacuum and not lifting a brick to help keep a real one going. It's easier that way. It's escape. You want to eat the vegetables but won't help spread the fertilizer. I don't know why I like you. You irritate me no end—and yet I like you. I know you're wrong and yet I keep wishing you were right."

"Judge, you will get someone else? You won't just let things drift, depending on my staying —?"

"If that's the way you want it, Walt." Then abruptly, "What's eating you? There's something bothering you—something or someone. Can't you stay put? I'll get someone else—sure—but how is it going to look to the people you know? 'Lazy Walt Whitman can't hold a job.' First the Long Island Democrat, then the Daily Eagle; then New Orleans and the Crescent. Now you're fed up with the Freeman—and I suppose you'll be flying South for the winter like the birds."

"South?" New Orleans—maybe that was it—part

of his heart hunger. Anne's last letter—nothing about his coming, only "Your poems, Walt, I keep them in my Bible, — I'm beginning to understand them, — they belong there. Keep writing them, dearest. Yes, my brother came back to New Orleans. He's ill. When he gets well he'll return to Brooklyn. You'll see him then, for I've told him about you—almost everything about you except what belongs to you and to me and to no one else."

No word about the nature of her brother's illness. Was it the dread cholera that had broken out in New Orleans and was spreading over the nation? He thrust that thought forcibly aside. He didn't like thoughts of illness. Anne — Anne —. He could almost smell the fresh, clean muslin of her dress and the strange heavy odor of her hair. Slowly his desires, longings and gropings set themselves in determined ranks and marched forward. "Yes, Judge, I'm going South for the winter —but I'll not leave you stranded until you get someone else."

"Oh, hell, what's the use? Walt, I can't figure you out. You're either a lazy loafer who couldn't hold a job or a wild-eyed prophet out of the Bible — who *wouldn't* hold a job if the king went down on his knees, lest he surrender his freedom. Well, anyway it'll make news."

The Judge edged his tone with just a flavor of sarcasm. "Have you thought of a farewell message— something dramatic and stirring? After all, your exit ought not to go unheralded."

Walt grinned, "You could reprint my 'Dough-Face Song'." He pointed to the crudely set verses pasted on the wall:

DOUGH-FACE SONG
—Like dough; soft; yielding to pressure; pale.—
WEBSTER'S DICTIONARY.

We are all docile dough-faces,
  They knead us with the fist,
They, the dashing southern lords,
  We labor as they list;
For them we speak-or hold our tongues,
  For them we turn and twist.

We join them in their howl against
  Free soil and "abolition,"
That firebrand-that assassin knife-
  Which risk our land's condition,
And leave no peace of life to any
  Dough-faced politician.

To put down "agitation," now,
  We think the most judicious;
To damn all "northern fanatics,"
  Those "traitors" black and vicious;
The "reg'lar party usages"
  For us, and no "new issues."

Things have come to a pretty pass,
  When a trifle small as this,
Moving and bartering nigger slaves,
  Can open an abyss,
With jaws a-gape for "the two great parties";
  A pretty thought, I wis!

Principle-freedom!-fiddlesticks!
  We know not where they're found.
Rights of the masses-progress!-bah!
  Words that tickle and sound;
But claiming to rule o'er "practical men"
  Is very different ground.

Beyond all such we know a term

Charming to ears and eyes,
With it we'll stab young Freedom,
   And do it in disguise;
Speak soft, ye wily dough-faces-
   That term is "compromise."

And what if children, growing up,
   In future seasons read
The thing we do? and heart and tongue
   Accurse us for the deed?
The future cannot touch us;
   The present gain we heed.

Then, all together, dough-faces!
   Let's stop the exciting clatter,
And pacify slave-breeding wrath
   By yielding all the matter;
For otherwise, as sure as guns,
   The Union it will shatter.

Besides, to tell the honest truth
   (For us an innovation,)
Keeping in with the slave power
   Is our personal salvation;
We've very little to expect
   From t' other part of the nation.

Besides it's plain at Washington
   Who likeliest wins the race,
What earthly chance has "free soil"
   For any good fat place?
While many a daw has feather'd his nest,
   By his creamy and meek dough-face.

Take heart, then, sweet companions,
   Be steady, Scripture Dick!

Webster, Cooper, Walker,
 To your allegiance stick!
With Brooks, and Briggs and Phoenix,
 Stand up through thin and thick!

We do not ask a bold brave front;
 We never try that game;
'Twould bring the storm upon our heads,
 A huge mad storm of shame;
Evade it, brothers-"compromise"
 Will answer just the same. PAUMANOK.

The Judge glanced at the familiar lines and nodded. "Good enough as a statement of your principles—but what about a brief note of farewell?"

Walt slouched down at the desk. "In a week or two, or even now, if you wish, you may print this." Walt bent his head and scribbled.

Judge Johnson proclaimed the hasty scrawl aloud solemnly:

"After this present date I withdraw entirely from the Brooklyn Daily Freeman. To those who have been my friends I take occasion to proffer the warmest thanks of a grateful heart. My enemies—and old Hunkers generally—I disdain and defy the same as ever."

WALT WHITMAN

"And now, gentlemen, if you are completely done with business—perhaps we could eat?" Adah Menken turned wide eyes from one to the other and the Judge chuckled as though every little gesture of hers delighted him.

"You've been patient, Adah. You're entitled to the best. Come along, Walt."

VII

They walked arm in arm towards Broadway. The air was crisp and cold and Adah inserted her hand in the pocket of Walt's coat. He felt her fingers closing around his fist and tingled at the intimacy. It was close to the dinner hour and the avenue was crowded.

"Here, let's go in here." Johnson pointed to an old English oyster shop with dim candles burning.

"Atmosphere! Mood!" — Adah laughed, "Somewhere 'neath your fat belly is a poetic spark. Let's go to Pfaffs."

"No! Confound it! It's too far to walk, too crowded to ride and I'm starved!"

"You're the judge!" Adah shrugged her shoulders and started to lead the way in.

"Adah!" All three turned at the hoarse call. A tall dark-haired man stood swaying near the door. His collar was soiled and frayed and his long fingers grimy. "Hello, Steve!" Adah's face was grim. "What do you want now?"

The man called Steve drew himself up with hauteur. "Sorry, gentlemen. I thought I knew the lady. My mistake." He started to walk away holding himself stiffly rigid.

"Stop it, Steve!" Adah was at his side.

"I'm not troubling you, madame. Go about your business."

The Judge looked at Walt with puzzled eyes and a helpless lifting of his shoulders.

Then he looked intently at the stranger.

"I know that man. His name's Foster—Stephen Foster—a song writer. Hey, there, Mr. Foster, how'd you like to join us? We were about to have dinner."

Foster stared coldly at Adah as he answered drily, "So I deduced from your obvious destination."

"Please join us." Adah was contrite. "After all I am Judge Johnson's guest and I couldn't —"

Foster did not answer. He turned and walked with them into the oyster shop. As they stepped near an empty table Foster looked Walt up and down with purposeful rudeness.

"Limelight—everyone hungers for the limelight," he murmured.

"You're insulting"—Adah began.

"Sorry if my frankness gives offense. My name's Foster. Are you gentlemen going to wash up—or shall we order first?"

"This is the poet Walt Whitman." Adah's voice was calm.

"Never heard of him. I know the Judge though—even voted for you Judge—when the drinks were on the house. Order for me, Adah, will you—any brandy 'll do."

Adah seemed ready to burst into tears as she watched him stagger off to the Men's Room.

"He's from Cincinnati. Writes music. Quarreled with his father I guess, and the gutter's his home. Met him a few times at Pfaffs. I heard him play and said it was nice—now he bobs up like a ghost wherever I am."

The Judge reached bruskly for the menu. "I've heard him play. Sounds pretty good to me. Leave him alone, Adah. He'll be good company. I don't begrudge the man a meal, or a couple of drinks either. What'll you have to drink, Walt?"

"Beer."

"Didn't they give you the wine habit in New Orleans? All right waiter, one brandy, one beer and two Burgundys."

When Foster returned, his hair was neatly combed and his hands scrubbed. The splash of cold water had sobered him a bit.

"I was rude to you, Mr. Whitman. I apologize."

"Forget it."

"All right, then, it's forgotten. What kind of poems do you write, Mr. Whitman—naked abstractions that make our madness worse confounded—or people and palpable things?"

"People and things."

"Good. I'm going to like you after all."

Foster shifted his glance. "As for Adah, she's no poet; she's just a happy whore!"

Walt felt suddenly sick. The Judge half rose from his seat. "Now see here —"

"Oh sit down, Judge. Act your age. Adah knows what she is and what Margaret Fuller is—and the other Ada—Ada Claire—all happy whores."

"Don't mind him, gentlemen," Adah's face was white stone, "his mouth is a cess pool."

"Or an oracle." He shrugged his shoulders. "We won't talk about you. You're all of a type—hungering to be noticed if not for your brains then for your bosoms. But both must be exposed—exposed, did I say?—flaunted is the word." He stared mockingly at Adah. "To use your own exquisite words, you are the 'daughter of the stars, the white bosom with crimson roses.' You and they are the heroine of every love story, calling every tickling of your womb — 'the great romance' and changing your 'great eternal loves' as you change frocks."

The slap of Adah's hand sounded like the cracking of a twig. Foster did not even look startled. He grinned. "How unpopular is truth!"

Adah, in white wrath, picked up Walt's half-filled glass of beer and emptied it into Foster's face. The waiters approached on the run, while the Judge attempted to calm the poetess.

"You're as bad as he," she screamed and struck the Judge in the chest with her clenched fist. "You should have killed him for that. My host, my gallant host!" she jeered. "Thanks for a beautiful evening," and she ran out with the contrite imploring Judge after her.

Two waiters hovered around the table uncertain as to what the advancing proprietor expected of them. Walt had remained seated throughout, seeing and listening as though he were a million miles away. Now he waved the waiters away as Foster wiped the beer from his face with the napkin.

Foster suddenly grinned up at him. "Looks as though you're stuck with the check. I haven't a penny."

Walt was grateful for the six and a half dollars in his pocket—and more than a little hopeful the Judge would return with or without Adah.

"Do we eat?" Foster, still smiling, looked at him inquiringly over the menu.

And suddenly Walt felt like laughing. Was there no limit to this man's gall?

"We do," he smiled back, putting his hand in his pocket for the reassuring feel of the currency.

"Don't feel badly about Adah. You can't insult her type. If she had to starve for her songs and freeze for them—and die of loneliness for them—but it's the fashion to be the devouring queen bees of their salon —damn them all—Lola Montez, Ada Claire, Margaret Fuller, drawing out your strength and manhood in their selfish flight, — fondly bearing their bastards—as testimony to their alluring charm, and brilliant intellect. Bah! Perfumed rubbish!"

"And the men are guiltless?"

Walt tried to change the subject or at least cause it to swerve from its smoking rut, but Foster silenced him with a downward sweep of his hand. The sleeve of his coat touched and smeared the butter. With frowning concentration Foster applied the napkin.

"I'm going to leave New York," he said suddenly.

"Your going to return home?"

Foster looked coldly at Walt as though offended by a vulgar taunt.

"Home? A tomb of hateful memories. Mr. Whitman, I'm a bookkeeper. At least so my father says. I add sums and then subtract them like sand running in an hour glass. Tip it first on one end and then on the other—but I'm really not a bookkeeper, you know. —I'm a ghost; my father begot a ghost.—Oh, Christ, let's get out of here."

Walt paid the check and Foster led the way to the street.

The chill in the air made him tremble. "I'll tell you where I'm going. I'm going to New Orleans— where it's warm—where thin blood doesn't freeze. Thank you, Mr. Whitman. You make excellent acoustics for an embittered spirit."

"But why be embittered? You have youth—and life has much—very much to offer you."

Foster shook his head and looked at Walt pityingly. "Is that the poetry you write? Try this theme on your lute instead. They pour me out like wine upon the floor and stamp upon me with their muddy feet."

"Who does this to you?—You, yourself!"

Foster's face blazed as he clutched Walt's shoulders. "No! No! You're wrong. Has the still-born child slain itself? Man! Man! Do you know what it is to hear the maddening music of the stars—then put your lips to a reed—and out comes a piteous peep? I'd sing the stars out of their orbits if my talents were equal to my reach. I think the first thing I ever saw was my father's sneer. Then I died—and all that's left is a wraith—a specter that moves in the world unnoticed, unseen. He tips his hat. He greets. He calls 'Good Morning!', and nobody sees him or hears him. He sings and there's no music. He plays and there's no sound. Good night, Mr. Whitman. Thank you for the dinner and your attentive ear. You're a good fellow."

Walt felt concern for this torn and wracked companion. "Where will you sleep?"

"Don't worry about me. I'll be leaving for the South—for New Orleans."

"I've been there. Just came back. If you get in touch with me, I'll give you the names of some people —"

"Kind of you. Good night, Mr. Whitman."

Walt watched him go bending to the wind, pushed this way and that as he dug into it.

VIII

For days Walt did not write and he seemed to himself like a tightly sealed kettle seething and ready to burst.

"They're afraid — all of them! They're afraid! Afraid to grab the totality of life and mold it into what they will it. God created man in His Creative Image and man can create the world in his own image—and if my image is joy and the will to joy—I'll slap the reluctant clay around until it howls. But when do I begin? When do I begin? The years are hurrying and, if I wait, my song may die ere it is uttered—and the black slate sky will be unkindled by my singing—the quivering fears untouched—and the stricken fields—and humdrum hymns untouched—and the hacked, disfigured dead unblessed and tiny words of tiny men will nibble at the heart—and blind, doubting leaders —for want of a stronger step, will leave their petty snail tracks in the sands of time—while I remain a might-have-sung-the-song that could o'er leap horizons, shake every pillar of creation and reach the farthermost heavens."

And still he watched the days glide by —

"When do I begin?"

Then quite suddenly, unwounded by Foster's bitter epithet, a name called to him—to him alone—of that he was sure.

Walt, this is for you—and the moment now. She means you. No other will do. In some mysterious way she knows that you are waiting to reveal yourself.

It was the stimulating call to arms of one who signed herself "Margaret Fuller." Wherever Transcendentalism was discussed, the names of Emerson and Margaret Fuller cropped up. Walt had read her burning lines—and they had always seemed a trumpet call to him, for him—for him alone, but now there could be no doubt.

"No imitation of Europe is this land and life, therefore, this New World demands a new literature—its own!"

He must go to Boston. There he would see and hear this prophetess—and he would show her the outpourings of his soul—the new unfettered verse—his—his own.

But he wasn't ready—yet.

Part of him was far off. He needed Anne. During the long nights when his enkindled brain revelled in a mighty phrase, her face intruded calmly at the head of his bed. She watched him with maternal concern and the phrases dissolved into candle smoke. Then he would stare hard at the darkness as though to give substance to the dreams. Let the mystics speak of spiritual union. Let the Transcendentalists speak and write of mystic airy communion with the hidden truth —but he, Walt Whitman, needed Anne—the touch of her lips like the red haw in the autumn and the teasing fragrance of musk and roses that clung to her and all things near her.

Anne! Anne! Why had he left her? What must she think or feel of a love that can content itself with absence. His desperate hunger mounted with the dream food he devoured—and the more he tried to visualize her form—the more his anguish and remorse. Anne! Anne! I'm sorry! What? Again? Again pleading with her to forgive as that day on the docks.

Brave warrior—proud freedom-loving bard, serving on his knees —. Master your yearning, Walt, or it will master you. "No! No! New Orleans first—and then Boston. I need Anne! He must spin the flaming threads of his soul into the visible cloth of songs—more songs —of every mood—of every violent revolt against stolid austere tombs. Flame! Fire! Storm! Anne! Then he would announce himself. Then he would proclaim himself!

* * * *

Louisa wrapped the cold beef sandwiches carefully in thick brown paper, added a few hard-boiled eggs to the contents of the box and looked up at Walt. "Change your mind, son, an' stay home. You can have Eddie's room all by yourself and Eddie can sleep with Jeff and Andrew."

"Ma, I'll be back soon; a few months—at the most a year."

His father, who was reading the Freeman, spoke up sullenly. "Once you get a good job you can't seem to hold it."

Mary Elizabeth was closer to the truth. "Is it the girl who sends you those tiny letters?"

"A girl, eh? How are you going to support her, or do you expect to bring her here for me to feed?"

"Hush, Pa!" Louisa interrupted hurriedly. "A wife

will be a steadying to Walt—a good thing for him. It'll hold him down."

Walt half smiled. "I'm against slavery, Ma, where there's still free soil; but where there's slavery already," and he looked first at his mother's rough hands and then calmly at his father, "that's your problem."

His father's eyes were hard. "It wouldn't have to be, if you got yourself a job and kept it an' brought your earnings in. She wouldn't have to work so hard."

The bite of that arrow hurt. He pitied his father and mother and hated himself.

"Don't you be worrying, Walt," his mother persisted, embracing him hurriedly, awkwardly. "And come back home. Whatever we eat you'll eat, and the same roof'll be over our heads."

Part Three

SOUTHWARD AGAIN

It was a wretched trip from the beginning. "A trip into Hell!" Walt heard the captain's bitter soliloquy and had nothing to answer. The tension on the ship had been mounting hourly. The members of the crew were surly and insulting to the passengers.

As Walt leaned on the thick rail of the "Mississippi" and listened to the threshing of the great wheels he watched the faces of the people around him. They were drawn, frightened faces. Terror and the expectancy of greater terror to come was engraved on them. He had seen that fear grow more intense as he moved west and south. The dread plague of cholera was heavy in the land. Cincinnati had been hard hit. Some of the women, huddled in the stern, were puffing thin cigars or holding them unlighted in their mouths. Tobacco was supposed to be a preventative and so were garlic and vinegar.

He stopped off the boat at St. Louis, although the captain cautioned against it. He was appalled at what he saw—carts with the dead rolling by. "Bring out your dead! Bring out your dead!" the drivers intoned wearily.

The warehouse man waved him back. "Get back to the boat, Mister. There's no good of your stepping into this graveyard. The dead have been rolling past here from morning till night."

"Is it the same all over the city?"

"Just about. The poor sections mostly, though the rich ain't spared. Where you bound for?"

"New Orleans."

"It's worse in New Orleans."

Now Walt's anxiety was eating into his usually cheerful life-caressing soul. A great aching hunger taunted the anxiety into a frenzy. He wrote down scattered thoughts—burning phrases—in the little notebooks he made himself, pages crudely stitched or fastened with a pin.

He had written Anne from St. Louis: "Anxious about your welfare, dearest. The 'Mississippi' arrives October 3rd. The hour is uncertain. I dream that you'll be there. I love you! I love you! Walt."

How slowly the packet crawled down the river! If he could leap from the rail to the levee he could outdistance it on foot. Flow like a torrent, O mighty river. Leap forward with a sudden leap and hurl me quickly to her arms. He paced back and forth through the deserted lounge, his feet sinking into the heavy carpet. Even the card tables were abandoned. The passengers crowded the rails or locked themselves in their cabins.

"Memphis! Passengers make ready!"

As the great wheels slackened their motion the captain called out to the crowd on the wharf:

"Sorry! Cannot stop for cargo. Wait for the next packet!"

The laborers on the wharf continued piling bales and boxes as though they had not heard the captain's announcement.

As the ropes were drawn tight and fastened, the captain leaped to the wharf.

"Sorry, men, I can't take your cargo. I'm unloading my passengers in a hurry at each stop. The passengers are plenty frightened and each delay makes it worse."

A tall raw-boned planter shouldered his way through the dock-hands.

"Captain, we'll help your crew load—but we're not letting our stuff rot." Then turning to the packet he shouted with a heavy authoritative voice, "Don't let any passengers come ashore until this cargo's on board."

At this, an uproar arose both on the wharf and the packet. Women's voices shrilled hysterical pleas. Men's voices raged with blasphemies and threats.

The captain clambered back on board and winked at his crew, "All right, boys, load the cargo. Get the passengers off—and then we'll do business."

The crew grinned and set to work with surprising will. Soon all the bales were on board.

"Get to your cabins, ladies," suggested the Captain to two young school teachers and a gentle nun who stood nearby. "There's liable to be a difference of opinion and a lot of loose talk scarcely fit for a lady."

Walt heard the captain say softly to the pilot, "A two or three day lay over'll cool them off," and fitted the pieces together.

"Captain—" Walt began quietly.

"I'm busy, Mister. Stand aside!"

"What do you propose to do?"

"I'll write you a letter."

Walt had difficulty keeping his voice calm. "Is there going to be a delay?"

"Well, now, that all depends—"

Walt turned and saw the first mate take hold of a length of steel pipe. His glance darted to others of the crew who had finished loading. One caressed the stocky handle of a sheath knife.

Walt turned quickly to the nun. "Please, Sister, take these young ladies to their cabins; there's going to be trouble."

The three huddled together but made no motion to retreat.

"You can go ashore now." The Captain addressed himself to the small group of passengers that had been patiently waiting to disembark while the loading was in progress. It took but a few moments for them to scramble to the wharf. Then, as though some signal had been given, the crew of the "Mississippi," almost to a man, walked down the gang plank.

Walt asked himself, "In this quarrel, where do I belong?" and all the while he knew that he was watching detachedly from a great distance.

On the wharf the planters and their helpers leaped into action. They seized billets of wood and blocked the advance of the crew. The tall young planter's voice was soothing but sinister.

"Where the hell do you think you're going?"

"This is a free country, Jim Barrows. We're going ashore."

"What's the game?"

"We're charging double for taking your stuff down to New Orleans. The cholera plague —"

"Get back on board, you cutthroat bastards. Hey there, Captain, are you going to stand for this mutiny?"

The Captain made a weak gesture of protest. "I am out-numbered, gentlemen, as you can plainly see, and besides, my crew's demand seems reasonable enough. They're risking their lives in these trying days."

Barrows motioned the passengers who were lingering at the scene to move out of the way.

"We've made a contract with you on rates and you're going to live up to it."

The mate put out a heavy hand and thrust at Barrows to push him aside. The billet of wood in Barrow's hand landed with a dull thud. The mate dropped inert in a heap and lay still. The planters, grim-faced and jostling each other, carried the fight to the crew and forced them back up the gang plank.

"Hold your men off, Barrows!" yelled the Captain. "Let's talk business!"

Barrows bounded up the plank and caught the Captain by the loose collar of his coat. "You're damned right I'll talk business. Pull in your ropes and get moving or by cripes I'll break your thieving neck."

The nun spoke up. "This is disgraceful conduct on the part of Christian gentlemen. I am on an errand of mercy to the dying—and not even the tragedy of the fearful plague can calm your anger."

Barrows ignored her and twisted the collar a bit tighter. "Do you get going, Captain?"

The Captain's purpling face nodded and wheezed and Barrows released his hold. He dug a handful of bills out of a pocket and held them out to the nun.

"Use this as you think best, Sister. I don't mind *giving* it, but I hate like hell to be *robbed* of it."

II

Once out in the deep of the river the surliness of the crew wore off and the passengers, too, seemed in a happier mood.

Now the card tables drew the river gamblers and the shrill clatter of chips mingled with the steady hum of voices.

Walt sought the solitude of his cabin and without removing his clothes flung himself on the bed. Anne— and again, Anne. Anne—always Anne.

Now his thoughts wove enticing patterns. The caress, the kiss, the utter abandonment of their love-making. Surely she had been faithful to him in the months he had been away. Her letters yes—but her hunger, the delightful hungers that he had awakened in her, the hungers that he on his part had sublimated into his flaming song. Strange doubts—there might be someone else. A tall, strong, worldly, polished stranger. He, too, might have seen her in the street and begun a conversation. Then they might have walked together —an evening—perhaps a kiss—and then an intimacy that mocked him with its secret.

She would deny it — and he — Walt clenched his fists and whispered aloud as he rolled against the wall. "No! She hungers for me—only for me!" Her breasts —the roundness of them. The lips of her womb, like rose petals to his touch. What was it that drew him to her? Only that—the body—and was that all? Then why had he soared to heights of holiness at their first meeting and why did all the hallowed, airy daintiness congeal itself to thigh and touch and body against body —and was that all—and is that all?

Beatrice, does Dante know why he seeks you—and does he think he climbs? Oh, thin-voiced hunger! Oh, string finely vibrating — it sings like holiness — and stronger grows — and is it all flesh passion — worm against worm there in the darkness — beast against beast? And Man? — Thought ceases — hungers press against each other—pouring out their longings—their deep sunk longings with sudden mighty surgings —; now rest, tired bodies, now rest.

Oh, but that isn't all—Anne. That can't be all— not just a silken veil that nature casts over all living things for her own expanding—moving—growing purpose. For your calm *soul*, Anne. I know your *soul!*

And then the sleepless nights before the morning of the landing when for no reason at all he wished to die. And then the morning and Anne standing on the dock, much thinner but more wistful and tender, softly waiting for him—as though garbed in all the sadness of the lonely days.

He drew her to him very gently. "I came for you, Anne. I came for you."

She was silent but pressed against him with her eyes closed and her face upturned, gravely, for his kiss.

"Let's walk, Walt. It's not far—unless your bag is too heavy. Mother has a room for you."

He started to protest. "No, Anne, it's not possible. It can't be. We've got to be alone. Your mother would not understand."

"What wouldn't she understand?"

"That I consider you my wife."

"No, Walt, she wouldn't understand that."

"Why don't you tell me what's inside of you? What are you keeping from me? Maybe your brother can explain all the things you keep so secret. He's still here, isn't he?"

"I don't know where he is."

"Doesn't he live with you?"

"No, Walt. He's not been inside our house for eight years. I've met him only twice in all my life."

"I must meet him." Walt's voice was insistent.

"You will some day, and then you'll never come to me again. Oh Walt, why must you ask questions? Believe me they can only bring us sorrow."

"How? Why?"

This time she did not answer. They walked on in silence. The brownstone house looked bright and cheerful in the sunlight, yet Walt could not shake off the blackness of his mood. Even before they had climbed the stairs the door was slowly opened. Mrs. Sedley stood there, calm, gracious and hospitable.

"Welcome back, Mr. Whitman. A bath is ready for you, for you must be very tired from your journey."

"Thank you, Mrs. Sedley. I trust that you are well."

"This is our room, Walt." Anne led him to her spacious bedroom with the light frilly curtains and the old English furniture.

"Our room?" The blood swelled in his temples. He looked through the open door where Mrs. Sedley was placing tea and cookies on the table. "Our room?" he repeated wonderingly.

"Walt, close the door and take me in your arms. Don't be afraid. We won't be disturbed."

Mrs. Sedley did not even turn her head as Walt stepped slowly to the door to close it. The doubts, the fears, all questions and all things roared in his brain like the deafening waters of a mighty torrent and took on sunlight and flame as his hands fumbled with her bodice and she, yielding, inviting the strength of him, breathed softly against his cheek, "Walt, Walt, I've waited so long—it was so hard waiting."

III

The days that followed were like sleepy half dreams. They would walk together past the Old French Market where Mandy the Mulatto towered above the hucksters like a heaving volcanic mountain. The lava that she poured was thick syrupy coffee served in a mighty cup. Her large copper kettle flashed dazzling light—but a radiance no brighter than that of her eyes and her teeth.

"Hi-yi-yi!" her belly-shaking laughter poured out in such pure cascades of merriment that everyone and anyone had to smile.

Sometimes Walt and Anne would enter the old Catholic cathedral and, seated near the door, would listen to the vibrant sea of organ music that washed against them and covered them.

Then, if the day were not Sunday, Walt would walk Anne to Antoinette's Millinery, where she was employed as a sales clerk.

He would watch her glide among the latest French creations, bringing them with studied reverence to the

haughty clientele. And when she placed a hat upon a
head before the ornate mirror, it was with that devotion
with which pious workmen place a dome upon a
cathedral.

Once he went alone to Twin Oaks. Priscilla Claiborne came to the door. How much older she looked.
Little wisps of gray in her hair, a sagging of skin at her
throat, and lines—sharp lines near the eyes.

"Mr. Whitman! I'm so glad. Where are you staying?"

"I have friends —"

"How fortunate, Mr. Whitman. I had hoped you
were coming to occupy your old room. How is Jeff?"

"He's fine. All he needed was home."

Her face clouded. "Come in, Walt. It's early. I
don't have to prepare dinner for an hour and I want
to talk to you. You're easy to talk to and you do keep
a confidence."

Walt entered the familiar doorway and accompanied Mrs. Claiborne into the parlor. She sat close
to him and spoke in a hushed voice, looking about her
to assure herself that no one was listening.

"You understand—you wouldn't say anything."

"No, of course not."

She looked down at her nervous twiddling fingers
and spoke rapidly. "It's hard being alone. When Fred
died and we had been married only six years—I swore
I'd never think of anyone else. We were very happy.
He loved books—spent every penny on books—gentle
he was—quiet and gentle. The priest said he was like
a saint—and, indeed, he was. And when he went, all
of a sudden, in his sleep—my heart died with him.
But it's hard being alone. And when Mr. Chase paid
me the honor of asking me to be his companion, all the
loneliness flowed away like a long bad dream. Then
he died, just when I was beginning to feel happiness
again!

I thought maybe you mingling with people, knowing a lot of fine gentlemen, might know of some good person—a widower, perhaps. You won't mention this to anyone, will you?"

Walt's heart ached with pity.

"No, you may trust me absolutely. I understand your loneliness—and I want to help. Is Mr. Hewitt still here?"

"Yes, but Mr. Hewitt is not a marrying man. He spoke to me and so did the artist. But their talk isn't decent. They don't care about a holy life. They're sinful and selfish. All but Sergeant Breen. He's a good man but he drinks. He has a good heart and he sits watching me like a sad-eyed dog. He doesn't talk. He's a lonely man. I thought if you knew some well meaning man of near my age. There's only a small mortgage on Twin Oaks. I'll have it paid off in four or five years. This would be a nice home for a man that's intending to get married."

Walt arose slowly and she, fluttering fearfully, held on to his elbow.

"I'll try, Mrs. Claiborne. I'll keep it in mind. But don't lose faith. You never can tell what lies around the corner. Things happen—suddenly."

"Yes—they do—sudden and terrible. I don't know —I don't know. But you won't tell anyone."

Walt moved slowly to the door. Sergeant Breen was puffing up the stairs. He placed one hand against the column and rested. Then he saw Walt.

"Well, look who's here. How are you, Mr. Whitman—and how's your brother?"

"Both well, thank you. And you, Sergeant?"

"Can't complain. Can't complain. How are things up North—business, I mean—chances for a job in the building trade?"

"There's a lot of building going on. Always room for a skilled man."

"Glad to hear it. I've bought passage to Chicago. I'm leaving tomorrow."

Walt heard a tremulous moan. He saw Mrs. Claiborne cling pathetically to the sideboard. "Sergeant, you didn't tell me. This comes as a surprise. — Of course, I wish you luck—of course —"

Walt's heart contracted at the feeble quavering of her voice. "I must leave now, Mrs. Claiborne. But I'll be dropping in again."

"Please do." And as Walt walked heavily down the wide stairs he heard Mrs. Claiborne speaking rapidly.

"I didn't know you were planning—it comes as a surprise."

IV

Even the Creole woman, who poured their coffee, called Anne "Mrs. Whitman."

Walt's money was running out. Often they went together to the theatre—the St. Pierre—the St. Phillipe and most of all—the St. Charles. Life was good and Walt clung firmly to each moment and was supremely grateful for it. "We're together, Anne. That's all that matters. We can hear each other's voice, feel each other's presence. It's good this way."

There was, at times, a faint accusing voice. "What about the trumpet call, Walt? What about the thundering song of America—and man—and the glory of life?"

And then a defending whisper—"Perhaps you overestimate your strength—or the strength of any single person to shake the soul of man into life. Such monumental conceit, Walt! God's Will sweeps on to His own Purpose. What makes you think you have an appointed task? Be one with the masses—a blade among the grasses. Live small instead of great. Tend your tiny vineyard. Rejoice in the wife of your bosom, and leave the world to the inevitable Great Laws. Be content, Walt. Be content!"

"Anne, Anne, my darling." He woke at midnight and she stirred in his embrace. He clung to her, tightly pressing his lips against the lobe of her ear. "Does it please you to know that there has never been another —never?"

"I don't understand, Walt." Her senses were still dazed by sleep.

Walt persisted, "I mean that I have never intimately known any woman but you."

"I thought all men —"

"No, not all. Many, but not all!"

"But I thought their physical need was greater — I've always been told —" She was wide awake now, and her long lashes brushed his cheek.

"Man has done an excellent job of enslaving woman. Even their minds are meek and docile and bear the imprint of Man's arrogant doctrine. 'Man must sow wild oats, but woman must be a virgin.' 'Man is by nature polygamous, but woman is monogamous.' And you Anne—when you first felt the roundness of your own breasts and the stirrings of the great hunger within you, did not your thighs long to embrace and your lips hunger for the kiss? Is it not one hunger, just as intense, for both?"

"Walt, Walt, yes Walt. Hold me close. Hurt me. Hurt me. I did feel all that you say—and, until now, I thought it was sinful—and I was afraid."

"Oh, flesh of my flesh, bone of my bone—Anne, Anne—the hungers are the same—I knew it long ago. I know it now—and you and I have this to share which no other has shared with me. Oh, closest friendship— oh, dearest love—and all my yearnings find their rest in you."

Walt felt her tears against his cheek. "You're crying, my darling!" Then as he groped for the why of her tears—"I haven't asked you, Anne, to reveal yourself to me as I reveal myself to you."

Anne pressed her lips tightly to his—and her fingers stroked his hair.

* * * *

They were together constantly. Once as they loitered near the French Market, McClure chanced to meet them. He tipped his hat and regarded Anne intently while he spoke to Walt.

"Back here to stay, Mr. Whitman? Things have changed. The Crescent has a place for you. Glad to see you looking so well, sir. May I speak to you alone for a moment?"

Something in Anne's eyes made Walt hesitate. "I'll drop in at the office tomorrow, Mr. McClure. We can speak then."

"Make it between ten and twelve in the morning, Mr. Whitman. Good afternoon." He tipped his hat and turned briskly away.

After dinner Anne helped her mother with the dishes while Walt seated himself at the table in his room, lit the candles and turned the pages of the many notebooks he had filled with his outpourings. Suddenly Anne was in the room, frightened—tense with anxiety. "Walt, have you any money?"

"Yes, dearest. How much do you want?" He took out a large purse and began to open it.

"About twenty dollars."

"There's twenty-five dollars and change here. Take it, Anne. I have more in my pocket." He started to arise.

"No, Walt. Stay here. I beg you to stay here. I'll be back and explain everything—everything."

She was trembling with fright, and Walt, to reassure her, sank back in his chair. Then he heard a voice, in the room below—a boy's voice—not as deep as a man's but determined and hard. He resisted the impulse to clear up the mystery surrounding Anne once and for all. She had said she would explain. All right, he would be patient for a little while longer—a moment longer.

Then he heard her scream. It was a weird startling sound. He ran quickly down to find Mrs. Sedley holding Anne in her arms. Outside a wild riot of running feet was beating out savage sounds. He burst out of the door to find himself roughly challenged by a man holding a rifle. A lantern was raised to his face.

"Let him alone, Hank; he used to be with the Crescent. I know the man."

"What do you mean, 'let him alone'—the meddling Yankee son of a bitch."

Walt looked at the faces gathering around him. Young and old—all of them hard, angry, grimly set in cruel lines.

"There he goes!" shouted one of the men and pointed to the dimly lighted street. Walt caught a glimpse of a hurrying shadow leaping between the piles of lumber stacked near the drain. And the next moment, men and boys with clubs, pistols and rifles were swarming towards the spot where the fugitive had disappeared.

"We'll teach him! Put his hand on a white woman!"

V

Walt found himself running with them, shouting with them, though he was not conscious of what he was shouting. He hated the pursuers—not the pursued

—and, besides, he had never clearly seen the pursued. He picked up a rusty iron stake that he had almost tripped over and ran on in the darkness among men who swore bitter oaths as they jostled each other.

Now he was growing weary, but he knew that he must run on. Why was he grasping the iron stake so tightly? There was a rage in his heart against all the things he could not understand and, therefore, suspected. And he was afraid—terribly afraid. Of what? Of what? The iron weapon was a club which would smash the secret open and free him from the agonies of his doubt.

Now they were in a swampy field and the going became difficult and labored. There were three quick shots and the men roared questions at the one who had fired. "Did you get him? What did you shoot at, Clem?"

"I saw something move near the rail fence!"

The man they called Clem was advancing slowly to the spot, his rifle held at his hip. The grass was tall and the mounds of the swamp were soggy and slippery. In the pitch darkness the men tried to avoid the hollows and cursed bitterly as their feet sank into the slime.

"Beat the grass around you with your clubs. He may be playing 'possum."

They circled around and followed that direction with a certain caution, for the man that they were pursuing might be armed.

Walt, his boots heavy with water and mud, watched them move about him as he leaned against the fence to catch his breath. Now their voices were dying away; their figures were being lost in the darkness.

Slowly Walt grew calm. He looked at the iron stake in his hand and then dropped it into the tall wild grass. Let them chase whomever they wished. Anne would tell him everything. He saw the street lamps blinking far off and began to walk in their direction, but before he had taken three steps he found himself staring at something curled up in the grass—a living, squirming something. Walt drew back, his fingers groping in the thick wet growth for the iron stake he had dropped. He stared curiously at the mud-grimed boy who slowly straightened himself by holding onto the rails of the fence.

The boy saw him then and raised one naked arm as though to ward off a blow. "Don't, sir, I'm done. Don't hit me."

Walt drew closer. He saw it was a boy of about Jeff's age, pants clinging to his legs with swamp water and mud, shirt torn—and black stains oozing from between the buttons. Black stains—black? Blood!

He heard the yelping of dogs and then the boy whispered, "Shoot quick, Mister. The dogs'll tear me up. I'm scared of the dogs, but I'm not scared of dying quick."

The howling of the dogs drew closer. Walt stumbled forward. "Here, let me help you. You've got to get away."

"Can't make it, boss. Can't make it at all. He put two holes in me an' I'm just emptyin' out —"

Walt pulled out his kerchief and tore off the boy's shirt. One bullet hole was just above the nipple of his right breast. It was futile to stop the bleeding; the kerchief was soaked with blood and the flow went on remorselessly.

The boy pleaded, "Better go away. Quick. They'll be coming back. You must be a stranger, or else you're blind. I'm colored—high yellow they call it around these parts. Did you think I was white, Mister? Did you think I was white?"

The boy sank to his knees, his eyes bulging with terror as he heard the gallop of horses and the howling of the dogs growing closer. Walt spoke close to his ear.

"I'm from the North. I want to help you."

"Oh," gasped the boy, "I'm from the North too—Brooklyn. Better go away. They'll kill you if you try to help me."

The boy began to dig into the mud with both hands, frantically pressing his body into the soaking globs of muck as though to hide. The next moment, with a sudden sharp effort, he straightened up and thrust Walt away. As though the pits of hell had suddenly opened, the screeching, yelping dogs were leaping at him, the riders were beating at him with whipstocks, while their horses, stumbling in the bog, reared away as though wrathfully unwilling to carry their riders forward. Again and again the rifles cracked.

"How long does it take a boy to die?" Walt whispered to himself as he felt the mob thrust him roughly aside.

They were dragging the body away now and Walt remained standing while the rumble of the mob died awkwardly into a murmuring exhausted silence and the dark figures dispersed. He stood looking down at the grave that the boy had tried to dig in his terror. The Earth that had mothered him would not take him back to hide him. Now it was clear! All the secret and the mystery! Anne—Anne's mother—and this one—yes, it was all clear now. Anne's brother—a quadroon, and she too—of course!

* * * *

He found them rocking back and forth in their grief; Mrs. Sedley's face ashen pale and Anne weeping with strange singing moans as though rocking grief to sleep. He sat down at a chair near the door, and watched them.

"They lynched him, those murdering white bastards. They lynched John. They lynched my John," Mrs. Sedley whimpered.

Walt spoke softly. "You don't have to tell me any-thing now, Anne. I understand everything."

Mrs. Sedley spoke more calmly. "You mustn't be angry with us, Mr. Whitman. At first I thought you knew; then Anne told me you were from the North. She's a good girl, Mr. Whitman. There's been nobody but you. You know that, don't you?" She lowered her eyes.

"There's nothing for a quadroon girl to do but keep company with a white man—unless she marries a Negro. But that's hard after you've seen the bright-ness of the white man's world." Then abruptly, "Did they set the dogs on him?"

Walt nodded. What was the use of lying about it? "But the dogs didn't tear him. They were bloodhounds."

Mrs. Sedley rocked back and forth. "He shouldn't have come back from the North. They turned his head up North—the abolitionists did, with all their writings. And he came back home with those books. He said all men are equal. He was only sixteen—last May. The white devil bastards lynched a young boy—a good boy. John—my poor John—John, John!"

Walt, aching with pity, looked steadily at Anne. She raised her tortured eyes at last. "Don't hate me, Walt—Mr. Whitman, I mean. You don't owe me any-thing—not even hate."

She arose to her feet and walked slowly to the bed-room. Walt followed her. Mechanically she began to pack his bag, folding his clothes carefully. "Are you driving me away, Anne?"

"Yes, I'm sending you back to your own people."

"All people are my own people."

"It sounds nice—just like my brother John—just like the Bible."

"I mean it, Anne."

"So does the Bible, I guess, for all the good it does.

I've never been North, Walt, but is it so different there? Could you bring me into your father's house? Would they be glad if I bore your children? If you stayed here we could go on living like we do, but you couldn't introduce me to people like Mr. McClure. Remember how he looked at me and said he had something private to tell you. I'm sure I didn't look white to him. And then you'd be angry, first with yourself and then with me, and then you'd hate me."

"Anne, I love you. It makes no difference. I've got to live what I believe."

"You're a great poet, Mr. Whitman, and you mean what you sing, but songs are ahead of people 'by ten thousand years—maybe a million."

"I'm going to stay."

"No, you don't belong here—and besides it's going to be hard, the burial and all. You mustn't stay for that. People will talk—a quarrel. They'll call you nigger-lover. It's not safe. They'll make a lot of trouble for you."

Walt thought of Jim Barrows maintaining his rights with a billet of wood, captain or no captain, and felt ashamed. "What am I—just a spectator of other men's struggles? Why won't I fight for what I believe to be right? Speech isn't enough. Songs of courage are not enough. Deeds! Deeds are needed!"

Aloud, he said, "It can work. It must. Major Winchester is still the first gentleman of Memphis, and yet everyone knows that his wife —"

"No. No. His case is different. Walt, why won't you understand? Marcus Winchester was a citizen of Memphis, loved and respected. What do you know of the tortures he had to endure and is still enduring? He's a social outcast among the people he's known all his life."

"They've elected him to the legislature. They've accepted him."

"You're wrong, Walt. They've given him political office, but they've ruined him. They don't accept his wife; they ignore her and so he tries to forget the pain in drink. That's no answer. And worse than that— their son, — handsome, cultured — no white woman will accept him, and so he deliberately flaunts the Negro women in their faces. No, Walt, that isn't the answer."

"Anne—in God's name what is the answer?"

"I don't know, Walt. I don't know."

"Anne, I've been a silent watcher in every struggle —I won't give you up. If there's no trail we'll make one. I'll sing my challenge till the world will have to listen—Man—the Brotherhood of Man."

"And to the world it won't be a song at all. It'll be just this—'A white man married to a nigger!' "

Her eyes were dull and lifeless. Her face was gray and pallid. Walt looked down at her, waiting for her to say "Stay, don't go!" but oddly enough Anne seemed a stranger to him now—separated by an infinity of strangeness and awful space. What had happened to his hunger for her—his feeling of being at one with her? "A white man married to a nigger"—All men and women are equal. All men and women are equal. Color is pigment. She is no darker than a sunburned white girl. Her body—her mind—her feelings—the same, no different. "A white man married to a nigger!" All—all are the children of God. Why does she seem a stranger now?

He bent and kissed her curiously and the kiss was cold—as though all warmth had fled from her blood. "A white man married to a nigger —"

"Anne!" he repeated over and over, trying to re-capture his own longing for her, feeling a desperate shame and guilt at not being able to.

"Anne! Anne! I have plans for us, Anne! For you

and me! That's why I came back to you! I had to see you. I'm going to Boston. I'm going to gather and publish my songs. The poets have been following old trails. My trails are new. Their poems are of the old world as though America were a slavish suburb of their feudal estates. We have declared political independence but our literary lives feed on the crumbs dropped from their tables. I sing America proud and independent! Anne —"

It seemed as though she did not hear him. She fastened the buckle of the strap with hurrying fingers and left the grip lying at his feet. Then she sat near her mother and stared straight ahead.

"You'll write to me, Anne?"

"Yes, I'll write to you if you wish."

"Anne, I'll write you often—more poems than ever."

Her voice was toneless, dead. "Will they still be love poems?"

"They'll be nothing but love poems, Anne."

He felt oppressed—by the room—by them. Was it pity or love that still beat its feeble wings like a tired bat in his heart? "Mrs. Sedley, I'm going now. I share your grief more than you can understand, and yet I feel I'm in the way."

"It's no fault of yours, Mr. Whitman, and I don't suppose it's any fault of God's. I really don't know whose fault it is."

She arose and opened the door for him. He went out quickly and did not look back. There were men gathered in the street near the gas lamp. They looked at him with cold hostility as he passed them. Walt felt afraid—clammy. He was not afraid of them but of something inside of them that he did not want to recognize—something inside of *himself* that he did not want to recognize. Drive it out—the rotten moldy indifference to cruelty. Lash conscience into life. A dark-skinned boy dying against a fence.

> *"The hunted slave who flags in the race at last,*
> *And leans up by the fence,*
> *Blowing and covered with sweat,*
> *And the twinges that sting like needles his breast*
>   *and neck*
> *The murderous buck-shot and the bullets,*
> *All this I not only feel and see but am . . .*
> *Damnation and despair are close upon me*
> *I clutch the rail of the fence*
> *My gore presently trickles thinned with the plenti-*
>   *ful*
> *Sweat-salt ooze of my skin as I fall on the reddened*
>   *grass and stones*
> *And the hunters haul up close with their unwilling*
>   *horses,*
> *Till taunt and oath swim away from my dim and*
>   *dizzy ears."*

VI

The ponderous threshing of the wheels beat against his brain. The drone of voices from the barroom lifted and fell—a wearying torrent of sound. Hunger—physical hunger—aching feverish hunger.

Walt sat on the edge of his bed turning the same sweet mad vision over and over in his mind. Distance blew upon the ashes of his longings and there was fire.

"What did your mother mean?" he heard himself asking again and again—and then that nearness, that blood-throbbing, all-knowing tenderness in Anne's eyes as she leaned towards him—the smoothness and roundness of her skin, feeding the famished tips of his fingers with the joy of touch.

He reached in his pocket for the wrinkled notebook.
To set it down—to channel all that flaming outpouring
into fixed patterns that he might preserve the moment
and its meaning—to make it live eternally so that he
need not dread its fading.

The stub of pencil in his great hand dug deeply into
the paper as though to engrave rather than write each
word: —

> *"One hour of joy is mine*
> *I'll not this joy confine*
> *The wild red flame of wine—"*

He clenched his fingers around the page and tore
it from the book. His temples were knots of rage. "Be
damned, you driveling insipid rhymes! I'll not be
chained to you. I'll say what I *want* to say!"

He beat with his fist against the wash stand near
his bed, shouting, "I'll tear myself open and write what
I want to write—write what I want to write—"

This time there was a rebellious exultation roaring
in his veins. He did not hesitate to pick a word or
rhyme pattern but wrote fiercely, gloating over the
swiftness with which the sweet anguish poured itself out.

> *"O the puzzle, the thrice-tied knot, the deep and*
> *dark pool, all untied and illumined.*
> *O to speed where there is space enough and air*
> *enough at last!*
> *To be absolved from previous ties and conventions,*
> *I from mine and you from yours!*
> *O something unproved! something in a trance*
> *To escape utterly from other anchors and holds*
> *To drive free! To love free! To dash reckless and*
> *dangerous*
> *To court destruction with taunts, with invitations!*
> *To ascend, to leap to the heavens of the love indi-*
> *cated to me!"*

He read and reread the lines. "That's it! That's the

way! A new free trail—a mighty trail. The strong will blaze it—break it through, smash it forward. The weak will click their tongues in disapproval and then one by one shamefacedly and tardily set their feet to it."

A cold stinging delicious chill made his hair roots tickle—he felt a sense of thundering power that would grind stars and planets into pigments for his brush.

"Give me a canvas big enough," he raged in dizzying ecstasy, "and I will paint myself!" He was breathing heavily now, muttering ecstatically aloud. He had discovered himself — freed himself. No chains — no shackles. This was the moment he had been waiting for. "Nothing will stop me now! Nothing!"

He saw himself like a colossus striding assuredly from continent to continent and swarms of human beings looking up in wonder. "Who is this giant?" they were whispering from pale and frightened faces, and he was answering them, "I am Walt Whitman, one of you—no different. You can be as big as I. Grow— grow quickly—don't stay small—grow quickly so that we can walk together, laugh together, shout together!"

The day had darkened rapidly. Walt lurched against the wash stand and lit the lamp. He adjusted the smoking wick. Then he wrote in a frenzy as though afraid that this intoxicating sense of power would ebb and leave him helpless.

"*Out of the Rolling Ocean, the crowd, came a drop*
    gently to me,
Whispering I love you, before long I die.
I have travelled a long way merely to look on you
    to touch you,
For I could not die till once I looked on you
For I feared I might afterward lose you.
Now we have met, we have looked, we are safe,
Return in peace to the ocean my love,
I too am part of that ocean my love, we are not so
    much separated

*Behold the great rondure, the cohesion of all, how
    perfect!*
*But as for me, for you, the irresistible sea is to sep-
    arate us,*
*As for an hour carrying us diverse, yet cannot carry
    us diverse forever;*
*Be not impatient—a little space—know you I salute
    the air, the ocean and the land*
Every day at sundown for your dear sake my love."

*   *   *   *

In the fevered days that followed he seldom left his
cabin. "Hurry, hurry; there is so little time. Chatterton
wrote at sixteen and died at eighteen. Shelly had
written magnificently at twenty. Keats had penned
immortal sonnets at twenty-one. Yes, they died young.
They were old men at twenty. It took you a little more
time to find yourself, Walt; but you're greater than all
of them, vaster, far greater, taller, broader, spreading
yourself among the planets. You can see way over the
tops of them. Walt, you'll shake the world with your
shout. Your laugh will ring above the porcelain tea cup
prissy chatter. Proper lords and ladies will bite their
lips in annoyance. Scented Euphuists will find their
dainty lace work torn to shreds. You've shocked them
out of their smugness, Walt. You'll show them the well-
filled hair-fuzzed belly and the common-to-all navel
under the prince's purple, the serviceable breasts red-
nippled under the queen's robes and the crinkly hair
under her armpits and over her womb. No sham, Walt,
no hypocrisies—the Negro your brother, a little bit sunburned, — but your brother.

Wait! Wait, Walt! What about Anne? Prove what
you say! Back! Back to her! No barriers now. It's in
your song. It's in your heart. It's in your soul. Back!

But the great striding, threshing wheels are pressing

the Pride of the West northward and you're going North, Walt. You're going to keep going North, now that your rage is spent, and you're leaving Anne. You know you are, for songs and truth are ahead of people by a thousand—or maybe a million years."

Part Four

LEAVES OF GRASS

Hannah was off on a spitting, snarling tear again. "You lazy hulk! Eatin' the flesh of Ma and Pa. Every piece of bread is their sweat and their blood. Can't hold a job. Too good for a job."

"Hush. Walt's just come home. Give him a chance to get set." Louisa did not take her eyes off the quilting as she sewed rapidly, rocking her thin body back and forth with almost every move of the needle.

"You might at least help Pa with the buildin'. Thirty-one years old an' still hangin' around their neck."

Still Walt did not answer. His silence whipped up her fiery tirade. "Lazy, that's what you are, an' wastin' your time writing dirty poems!"

Now Walt was on his feet, his arms lifted in rage. Suddenly he let his arms fall limply to his sides. "What's dirty, Hannah—the manure on our farm? Its life-giving strength is in the grain and the vegetables you eat. What's dirty, Hannah—your womb that opens its lips to give a beautiful child to life, or the lips of your mouth that call things dirty?"

"Look at him, Ma! Listen to him! That's what he talks about. He's as crazy as Eddie—crazier!"

Walt did not answer. He walked out of the house and turned down Myrtle Street, plunged in dark abysmal thoughts. What had he accomplished with his life? What could he hope for? Why did he have a conviction of a great destiny—a mighty thundering in his heart when in fact all that he sensed within himself were vividly colorful adjectives, raging crashing verbs, a maddening sense of a giant's strength and no single task to spend it on. And was he really strong? Horace

Greeley's pen was mighty. Daniel Webster's voice was a ringing trumpet. What was *he* that he felt such greatness?

No sooner had a desolate sense of melancholy pervaded him than just as quickly he tore it to shreds. He put his foot on the base of a nearby lamp post, drew out a memorandum book and wrote: —

"I will not be a philosopher and found any school ... But I will take each man and woman of you to the window and my left arm shall hook you around the waist, and my right shall point you to the endless and beginningless road. Not I—not God—can travel this road for you."

Poor Hannah. She was not to blame. No one was to blame for what he was and said. She and her slouching watery-eyed husband. Poor Charles, his poverty—his drunkenness. Hannah—Charles—they needed love, affection. He must not be angry with them. If only Hannah were there when he got home. He would put his arms around her and press his lips on the narrow wrinkles that bitterness had autographed. He could almost kiss the sharp thin lines away if only he would be patient. Regret! Remorse!

He hurried back, but Hannah had already left. There were, however, other visitors. His older brother Jesse had come over to see him and Andrew was with him. It had been a long time since Jesse had spoken to him. Jesse had his own friends, men who had their regular tables in tavern corners night after night, with cards, drinks and women. Andrew had been much in Jesse's reckless company, but now there was something of fear and guilt in both their faces.

"Got to talk to you, Walt." Jesse's voice was brittle and insistent. Louisa, who was filling the warming pan with coals, looked sideways at her sons. "Better talk to him, Walt. Jesse is as fidgety as a cat." Then she hurried up the steps to warm Eddie's sheets.

"Can't talk to you here! Let's walk!" Andrew and Walt followed Jesse into the street. They crossed over to a bench before Ernst Schmidt's red brick grocery store and sat down together.

Andrew was the first to speak. "Jesse's sick," he announced solemnly, "damn sick!"

Walt looked at Jesse curiously. Jesse sat grim and silent!

"What's wrong with you, Jesse? You seem to be all right."

"I'm going to kill myself!"

Walt stopped thinking with the impact of the threat. He looked at Jesse intently and suddenly realized that he had never really seen him. Jesse had a bulging Adam's apple. His ears were set away from his head. There were pathetic white streaks in his tangled matted hair. There were a few black hairs projecting from inside his nostrils.

No, he had never seen Jesse before. Jesse had always been there—like the chair—the rug—the table—like his mother—like his sisters. And he had never really seen them. They just passed back and forth across his vision.

Death! That word makes one look intently. What have I lost? Great God, what am I about to lose? Let my eyes explore you minutely, my brother, for you have been a stranger to me.

Your neglect, Walt—*your* neglect, Walt. You're bound up in yourself and you don't really see anyone else. Jesse's teeth. One is half broken. And there's a sore on his lip. Haven't you ever noticed? He says he's going to kill himself. Never talked that way before. Why? Why?

"That's the way he's been talking ever since he found out," Andrew commented tonelessly.

"Found out what? Jesse, can't you talk for yourself?"

"I've got the shameful disease. I've had it for more 'n a year. That's what the doctor says."

Walt felt a weird sense of unreality in the scene. This situation did not belong here. Poverty — yes. Misery—yes, but three brothers sitting there like Job's comforters discussing something that just didn't seem to fit.

"Are you sure? Is the doctor sure?"

Andrew answered, "That's what Jesse keeps sayin'. I was at the doctor's with him but the damned old medicine man wouldn't say a word to me."

"Does your wife know?"

"No. The doctor says I may have passed it on to her. I'm afraid to tell her anything. She's an empty-headed old bag but it would be a hell of a trick to play on her just the same."

"Jesse, I ought to have broken your head when you kissed Gwen. Why the hell can't you keep your hands off my wife?" Andrew did not look at Jesse as he spoke. He spat the words out sullenly with bowed head at the ground.

Walt felt his head whirling about in a turgid sea of sweat. He wanted to run away from his brothers— from the ugliness beating against his ears. What could he do? There was no way of solving ugly things like that. Some diseases had the fangs and venom of hell in them.

What about your perfect world, Walt? Maybe it would be better for all concerned if Jesse hanged or drowned himself. No, Walt, where are your concepts now? There is no evil. Nature seeks its eternal harmony —and there are moments of transition that seem like discords. There are strains and reactions to the breaking of nature's laws—there are . . .

His voice sounded odd to his own ears as he asked,

"Can't it be cured? What did the doctor say?"

"It's too late. I should have come to him sooner, that's what he keeps saying over and over again. Walt, do people go crazy from what I've got? That's what the boys have been saying, and I'm believing them." Then quite suddenly Jesse began to sob, his whole body shaking and the tears crawling in ugly botched streaks down his chin.

Walt put his arms around Jesse's shoulders and kissed him on the cheek. "Don't Jesse. We can heal this thing. I'm sure of it. We'll see the doctor together. Go home. Get a good night's sleep. I'll knock at your door at nine tomorrow morning. Don't worry, in the meantime.

And you, Andrew, don't go telling Mother or Hannah or anyone about this. There's no use making everyone worry."

He watched Jesse and Andrew walk off together and his heart seemed dragging him down to the pavement. He wanted to sink down inert and prone as though by his lying down, the winds of the evil that he denied would fail to see him, sweep over him and let him be.

II

"Life's dreadful and ugly!" Mary had found out the secret of Jesse's vacant stares.

"No, I'll never believe that." Walt was firm, insistent.

"You're blinding yourself because you don't want to see things as they are."

"I see them very clearly, Mary. And nothing is ugly. Everything is strange, wonderful, mysterious— everything but fear."

"And the Cholera?"

"Yes, and the Cholera — the red blotches, the warmth, the fever, the chills, all patterns—patterns. Everything but fear."

"And hunger—and poverty—and death?"

"And hunger ends with feeding; and poverty weaves dreams; and death no one alive has ever experienced. No, Mary, you mustn't tear life apart that way. All of it is life—all of it—the rich mold, the precious rot that nourishes the seed and the growth—it's all velvet— and you can't play a song with one string on your fiddle."

"You just talk words. Are those the things you write?"

"Yes, Mary."

"People won't believe you."

"I don't want them just to believe me. I want them to hear my song and feel it in their blood until they sing with me."

"You're just trying to wish things away. You can't do it. Nobody can."

At night Walt wrote ecstatically, tasting a fierce sweetness as he rooted out a dead word to plant a living one. In the day he worked at his father's side, rejoicing in the fibre-tearing teeth of the saw and the driving power of the hammer. And this went on for weeks and months, until Mr. Lees, who edited the Brooklyn Daily Advertiser, stopped to admire the bearded carpenter, his eyes twinkling with amusement.

"You're not fooling me, Walt. A Messiah bogey is what you've got. Christ was a carpenter and so you must be one."

Walt, on the top of the ladder, leaned against the eaves and smiled down at the jovial editor. "Thanks, Pilate, for the verbal crown of thorns! Or is it a job you're hinting at?"

"If you can dismount from Pegasus and write straight copy, it's a job; if you can't, keep on shingling."

Walt came leisurely down the ladder. "I'll take the job for part time anyway, just for the finger exercises and the pay—but don't use my name on the copy."

"Why not?"

"I'll be selling you words at so much a paragraph. I'm saving my name for something better."

Lees grunted. "Look here, Walt, do you want a job or don't you?"

* * * *

Night after night, Walt took from the wooden box underneath his bed the essays that he treasured more than the books piled one on top the other—his essays and poems.

Margaret Fuller had called to him again. Whom could she mean but him? "He will come! It is inevitable! He will come impassioned as our vast prairies rooted in strength—free, fresh, savage, luxuriant!"

But, in the meantime, let the pen travel the old old familiar trails. And so Walt wrote for the Advertiser as he had written for the Crescent—vignettes, descriptions, innocuous accounts of persons and things, until Daniel Webster, on the seventh of March, 1850, spoke these words:

"I repeat, therefore, Sir, that here is a well founded ground of complaint against the North, which ought to be removed, which it is now in the power of the different departments of this government to remove; which calls for the enactment of proper laws authorizing the judicature of this government, in the several States, to do all that is necessary for the recapture of fugitive slaves and for their restoration to those who claim them."

"It will make God most wrathful," murmured

Louisa as Jeff read the paragraph to her. "It's against Holy Writ."

Jeff was furious beyond speech. His lips were tight and his eyes hard and cold.

Walt entered a few moments later and Jeff handed him the paper without speaking a word. At first swift glance he nodded in approval. Yes, Webster was right. The abolitionists, with their extreme acts, were doing no good. There must be no talk of secession. There were several statesmen of the South who had spoken against slavery. A little more time—and they themselves—but wait—this was incredible! Was the North being asked to share the crime—to restore a fugitive slave to his chains? Was this a sincere appeal for peace from a great American or an obsequious bid for the presidency of the United States?

Walt, restrain your indignation. Think now! Remember! *You* felt that way once. *You* thought once that was what states sovereignty demanded of you—and you wrote it—yes, you did! Maybe it's not Webster you despise at this moment, but your own past self. Maybe a man always despises his own unworthiness in another. But Daniel Webster, the statesman — mature of judgment, — that could not be *his* conviction. There had been talk of Webster's income—dealings with clients—and money gifts—but always the stirring eloquence and stalwart demeanor of the man had swept rumors away like driftwood before the rush of the rapids.

Daniel Webster, a dough-face? Walt let the paper fall to the floor. "Hand me the Bible, Jeff."

"I know what you're looking for, Walt—Deuteronomy, Chapter 23, Verses 16 and 17. I looked it up a few minutes ago."

Jeff set the heavy Book on the table and opened it where he had set the marker. Walt read aloud: "Thou shalt not deliver unto his master the servant which is escaped from his master unto thee; He shall dwell with thee even in thy midst in that place which he shall choose in one of thy gates, where it pleases him best; thou shalt not oppress him."

"What's the answer, Walt?"

"I don't know, Jeff."

"I hate compromise."

"When it brings peace?"

"For God's sake, Walt! Slavery is wrong! Wrong! Wrong! Compromise here is approval. I'd rather leave America forever than be a party to this."

"Jeff, where would you go where there wouldn't be some form of slavery? Is fifty cents for a twelve hour day freedom?"

"Yes. At least a man's not bought and sold like a horse or mule. No, Walt, I'll not be a party to this. It's a mortal sin. God, what a wicked world! When the Negro finally breaks his chains and crawls to us for help we kick him in the face—and then they have the gall to say 'There's nothing in the Scriptures against it!' "

Why had Webster kept that verse in Deuteronomy out of his speech when he had asserted that there was nothing in the Old or New Testament that attacked the institution of slavery? Had this brilliant orator, who knew the Bible almost by heart, overlooked the verse—or had he conveniently ignored it?

Thousands upon thousands of copies of Webster's speech flooded the land, and that flood was turbid and murky when the clear light finally shone upon it. In the minds of at least the northern readers, fear—flattery —self-interest vied with each other to shout for love and peace.

This then was expediency.

The lawgivers from the North were thrusting back

the spectre of secession and war by eloquent flattery of
the representatives of the South as though they could
heal a cancer by spreading butter upon it. Judge Johnson had been right. History creates issues that must
be faced! The issue no longer was "Shall the South
keep house in its own way and the North keep house
in its own way?" The issue was clear. "Shall the North,
by returning fugitive slaves, become partners in the
institution of slavery?"

"Face the issue! Why don't they face the issue
honestly?" Suddenly Walt felt a sense of guilt and
shame. Who was he to urge others to face issues?
Anne! Anne!

Jeff's accusing silence taunted him. Walt felt he
must defend his previous stand. "Look here, Jeff, don't
look as though you've won your point—because you
haven't. Yes, slavery is wrong—terribly wrong. So you
cure it like any other illness. You prevent its spread
and then treat it carefully to heal it, slowly and thoroughly. You don't kill the patient in order to cure the
disease. You've got to treat the South with understanding—but this —"

"You like this better, Walt?"

"No, of course not! It's dishonest. Webster should
have told them firmly that we can't compromise on
principles—that we can't be their partners in slavery."

"That would have meant secession."

"And if it had?"

"Would you fight to prevent it?"

"Fight?"

"Yes, with a gun—with a bayonet?"

Walt hesitated. "I don't know. That might be
slavery too—holding the states in the Union against
their will."

Jeff looked at his brother with condemning eyes.
"Damn it, Walt. Just what *do* you believe?"

*   *   *   *

Congress quickly adopted the Fugitive Slave Law making it a crime to harbor a fugitive slave. There it was—the deed! Not suggestion—not theory—but the deed!

Walt felt a sense of greater guilt than ever before —an oppressive shame that he could not shake off. Nor was he alone in this. The angry whirlwind of God seemed to be stirring the land. Emerson, usually calm and deliberate, wrote: "This filthy enactment was made in the nineteenth century by people who could read and write. I will not obey it by God."

Whittier mourned Daniel Webster as:

> *"So fallen! so lost!*
> *The light withdrawn*
> *Which once he wore!*
> *The glory from his gray hairs gone*
> *For evermore!"*

A portrait of Webster was beginning to take shape in the minds of the masses. "Webster is cunning. Webster is ambitious. Webster has dreamed of himself as the preserver of the Union and the logical candidate for the presidency."

Now the North shuddered and recoiled from him. "Fugitive Slave Law! Fugitive Slave Law!"

"There it is, Walt. Compromise! Compromise!" Jeff taunted. "Why don't you go back to New Orleans? Then you won't have to worry about returning a runaway slave to his owner."

Walt did not answer. He felt hollow and empty inside as though all certainty and faith had melted away. "By what light shall a man travel? Why isn't the right more clearly defined? Why can't the signposts be clearer?"

What about it, Walt? Are you really trying to see? Are you really trying to hear? The same World Soul that speaks from within Emerson speaks from within you. Listen to its message—the message of the God Within.

III

Hannah came in breathlessly. She threw off her shawl and clutched Walt's shirt with her long thin fingers.

"I shouldn't have gone, Walt. But it's done and can't be recalled, I guess."

"Gone where, Hannah? Calm yourself. You're trembling and quivering all over."

"There's a lady that tells fortunes and talks with the spirits."

"Hannah, you shouldn't have gone."

"I know. I know it now. But when days tear you apart and you see darkness ahead—you can't help wondering about tomorrow. Everybody talked about the knockings and the marvels—and so I went to the house where they were staying. They are a strange family, Walt, but they can talk with the dead. They know things they couldn't know unless it was revealed to them."

Walt's blood ran cold. "What did they tell you, Hannah?"

"We held hands. The room was dark. They called upon the spirits to answer. They knew a lot of things about us. They said we had a younger brother who was sick—and then they mentioned Jeff."

"Go on, Hannah. What did they say about Jeff?"

"They said they saw him lying white and still—bleeding." Hannah tore herself loose from Walt's grasp. "But maybe they don't know; maybe they're lying. A lot of things they said aren't true. They said we had a brother who was a writer and that he was married and that his wife was pregnant — so they can't be right!"

Walt stood stock still staring at his sister. — Anne! Anne! With an agonizing effort he disciplined his speech, "Hannah, who are these people? What do they want? How much did you pay them?"

"I paid only three dollars. There were many people there. It was at the home of Reverend Griswald. They have seances there almost every night."

"I am astonished that a minister permits such things."

"There were a lot of people there—reporters from the newspapers, yes—and more than one minister."

"And did no one speak out against such dark actions?"

"No one."

"Three dollars! Hannah, you can't afford to throw money away."

"I thought it would bring me peace."

*   *   *   *

The next evening Walt lost no time in calling upon Reverend Griswald. He found him in his study speaking with his colleague, Dr. Hawks.

"Good evening, Mr. Whitman. I presume you have already met Dr. Hawks, or at least listened to him preach."

"No, I'm sorry."

"Indeed you should be." The tall clergyman smiled and motioned Walt to a chair.

Walt hesitated as both dignified men waited in silence for him to speak.

"My sister was here yesterday evening —" he began abruptly.

Reverend Griswald knitted his forehead. "She did not introduce herself to me. There were many observers here. In fact, our home was crowded with them."

"She said there was an admission fee of three dollars."

Reverend Griswald frowned. "Your sister is in error. No admission fee is charged for entrance to my home. There were free will offerings. Some gave and some did not."

Walt strove to conciliate the minister. "I may have misunderstood her. No doubt I did, but Reverend Griswald, did I misunderstand her report of what followed?"

"What did she report?"

"That there were attempts to communicate with the dead."

"And did she say whether or not such communication actually took place?"

"She did. She said they prophesied the injury or death of one of my brothers."

Dr. Hawks interrupted angrily—"Your sister has told you an untruth. I remember the woman now. Thin, gaunt and obviously under great emotional stress. She was told that she had a brother who was a writer and that his wife was about to bear a child—and that is all that she was told."

Walt sat silent, his thoughts beating against one another with angry wings.

Anne—Anne—can this be true? I can write—I can find out, But Hannah—what about Jeff? What about the grim prophecy? There is something wrong and evil in all this? What plot? What scheme?

Reverend Griswald was speaking calmly. "It seems clear there has been some exaggeration or distortion in the report your sister gave you."

Walt rose to his feet. "But how can you permit such things in your own home and with your approval?"

The white-haired minister shook his head. "I am no witch hunter, Mr. Whitman. An honest appearing woman, Mrs. John Fox and her young daughters, Margaret and Kate, lay claim to communicating with spirits of the departed. I give them a fair opportunity to demonstrate their supposed power. As distinguished a man as William Cullen Bryant is coming to this evening's seance. You, too, are welcome if you care to stay."

Walt was silent.

"Afraid?" Dr. Hawks smiled pleasantly so that his word was not offensive.

"No—not afraid, but resolute in my refusal."

"Why?"

"Were I of your calling—a minister of God, I would answer from the Holy Writ, from the Book of Leviticus —'Regard not them that have familiar spirits, neither seek after wizards to be defiled by them.' "

Dr. Hawks nodded "And you might quote an even greater stricture from Leviticus—'And the soul that turneth after such as have familiar spirits, and after wizards to go a whoring after them, I will even set my face against that soul and will cut them off from among his people.' "

"Well then—how do you approve?"

Dr. Hawks leaned forward in his chair and spoke gently. "It is clear that the Scriptures intend to exclude from Grace all those who are *possessed by the Devil*— not those who communicate with the blessed spirits of our departed dear ones."

Walt arose from his chair. "This is why I shun your sermons and your preachings and listen to the God Within. How subtly Writ can be twisted to suit desire. Something within me cries 'That which cannot bear the sun's bright noonday light is ugly in the sight of God!' Dark rooms and knockings! Reverend sirs, I want no part of it."

"Just a moment, Mr. Whitman." Reverend Griswald walked quickly to the doorway leading to the parlor. He called gently, "Mrs. Fox, may we ask you to join us for just a moment?"

The woman who entered was fresh, clean and joyfully vital. Her face beamed and her smooth rounded figure cast a healthy glow about her. "Good evening, gentlemen. My daughters will be down directly."

"This is the poet and journalist Walt Whitman, Mrs. Fox. He has shown an interest in your gift."

She extended her hand, and after a slight pause Walt took it firmly in his own.

"Mrs. Fox, permit me to say at the outset that my interest is far from approval."

"That is as you will. I do not ask for anyone's approval. People have ears to hear sounds. If my daughters and I have a spiritual ear to hear sounds most people cannot, that does not require anyone's approval."

She paused and looked at Walt with friendly eyes. "Stay this evening and see and hear for yourself."

He asked "Can you hold a seance at noon, in the sunlight and in the open?"

Dr. Hawks murmured, "Do you think that darkness is evil?"

"No, darkness is only the absence of the sun—but it conceals too much."

"These are my daughters, Mr. Whitman."

Walt saw before him two pretty girls—buxom and blushing. "Margaret is fourteen and Kate is eleven. Do they look forbidding to you?"

"No, Mrs. Fox. They look very lovely—and so, for that matter, do you." Walt wanted to leave but Mrs. Fox restrained him with a gesture.

"Tell Mr. Whitman, darling, — tell Mr. Whitman how it first happened."

Margaret seated herself on the piano bench while Kate leaned against her.

"I don't know if mother told you about our house in Hydesville. Sister and I often heard tappings and finally I answered by tapping. Then I said 'I will tap out a question like the rhythm beat of words. Are you a spirit world? If you are a spirit, tap twice!' And then it came clear and distinct—two taps. From then on the tappings increased and I knew that many, many spirits were crowding together to get their messages through to the living—and I was so glad that I could understand and give those messages to the living." Margaret's cheeks glowed. She sank down upon her knees, "I thank Thee, Divine Father, that Thou hast made me a medium between the spirit world and the world of the living."

Reverend Griswald was deeply moved. "Amen, Oh Lord, Amen!" he murmured.

Margaret arose to her feet and approached Walt, smiling. "Will you stay, Mr. Whitman?"

Walt let his hand rest lightly on her hair. "No, my dear child. I, too, hear a voice. And the voice says to me 'Come out into the sunlight, Walt. Do not explore the graves or seek the dead. Let them rest with Me in peace—and as for the living, let them listen to no voice but the Voice of the Living God who speaks to all His children from within. He needs no mediums and no oracles. His voice is not in the thunder and the lightning—nor in the tapping and the knocking, but in the human heart. No marvels—but the marvel of His Great Eternal Laws. No miracles but those all men may do and witness. No caste—no class—no favored ones. All—all are His children.' "

"You're something of a preacher yourself, Walt?" growled Reverend Griswald, somewhat annoyed.

"Don't browbeat the child." Dr. Hawks was indignant.

It was at that moment William Cullen Bryant entered the room. He recognized Walt and extended his hand. "Do you still believe that this is the best of all possible worlds?" he rumbled in his rich deep voice.

Walt nodded. "I do" Then he looked slowly around the room at the two clergymen, at the frowning Mrs. Fox, and then at the venerable poet, "And are you, Mr. Bryant, still afraid of death?"

* * * *

Hannah was still waiting when Walt returned.

"Why did you lie to me, Hannah?" Walt's voice was gently reproachful.

"I didn't lie."

"They didn't tell you about Jeff."

"They began it—about you—and then as I left them I saw a sign 'Fortune Teller.' I wanted to know more —" She began to cry.

"No. It's no good, Hannah. These fortune tellers —if they tell you bad luck's coming, you'll pine yourself into the grave long before the sorrow comes. It's far easier to bear a trouble when it comes than to anticipate it and count the hours till it arrives. It's God's own blessing that we cannot know the date of our illness or our death. Maybe the Fortune Tellers do know something—and if they do—let them keep tomorrow till tomorrow comes. Forget what she said about Jeff."

"And shall I forget what she said about you?"

* * * *

Try as he would, he could not throw off the question "Is Anne with child? Is she bearing me a child?" He quieted himself, "She would have written? She would have written! Nonsense! A Fortune Teller's word! God of Life, why are people so frightened— why do they walk with heads turned backward or with eyes fear-bulging beyond the day — and beyond the night —? Why do they huddle in dim closets with the dead? O God of Life, Who desirest Life. Teach us Life! They don't want to learn! Cults with lulling names—Mystic Truth—Pure Light—Transcendental-ism—Escape! Escape! Escape from Granite Justice and Iron Duty. Escape into words and dreams—and to misty Olympian peaks that need but a lazy wish and no climbing. Oh God, why do they run away from your great, shining, radiant gift of Life? Why do they run away?"

IV

"Walt, what was the name of that lady author?" George looked up at Walt from the newspaper he was reading.

"Which author, George?"

"You know the one I mean—the editor of the Dial. Was it Margaret Fuller?"

"Yes. What about her?"

"The 'Elizabeth's' gone down near Long Island. There's no detail in the papers, just that it's gone down and that she's supposed to be on the passenger list."

Margaret Fuller! Her clarion call for the New American Poet had blown on his lazy fires. He had dreamed of seeing her—meeting her—and she would have known him as the one she sought. Too late! Too late!

The next morning brought the tragic tidings. So close to home! Her husband, Baron Ossoli and her infant son—they too had died, and the waves that had carried her almost home—almost home—washed their lifeless bodies tenderly to the shore.

Walt writhed in bitter remorse. "It's too late now! I should have gone to Boston. I would have shown her my songs—and then she would have known—and declared it. Now *I* must reveal *myself* — and that will be difficult—impudent and difficult."

He continued to work at his father's side, finding greater and greater contentment in the physical labor and strenuous exertion that kept him bodily alert and well.

Anne—Anne! If I could go again to New Orleans. If I had the money to make the trip—if there weren't so many forces, troubles, barriers keeping us apart— Anne, why didn't you come back with me—to guide the soul of me—the groping, uncertain soul of me; why weren't you more resolute?

Tomorrow?—Perhaps!—You can never tell. — A story—an article—an unexpected revenue and New Orleans is altogether possible. Another day—another week. She is not destitute. Anne is not destitute.

Times are troublesome. Why should he bear all the burdens of the world? Let statesmen worry about the state. Each to his own.

His father had learned of Jesse's tragic ailment and grieved inwardly. He was darkly morose and silent. "Man's life is vain and full of trouble"became his litany.

And Walt struggled against a terrifying melancholy.

* * *

The affairs of the nation moved like pale marching shadows around Walt's heart. He was conscious of them, but they seemed distant and far off. Webster had lost the nomination but the Whig Convention, which had spurned him and nominated General Winfield Scott, had adopted a plank approving and acquiescing in the Fugitive Slave Law. What had been gained? What a muddle of thinking! Where in the election was there to be a real issue of principle? Franklin Pierce, the Democratic nominee, was a plain unvarnished party man. Offices and patronage were his chief concern. Judge Johnson came to ask Walt once again to wield his pen politically, this time in behalf of Pierce.

Walt shook his head wearily. "I'll ask you the same question I asked you then. What's the difference between the parties?"

Johnson ignored the question and announced, "I'm still a party man. Pierce is a loyal Democrat. He'll take care of his party. When there was an issue I was willing to fight for my principles. Now that there is no issue —"

"What do you mean 'there is no issue?'"

"Walt, why don't you keep abreast of the times? Why don't you find out what the people are thinking? The tendency now is 'There doesn't have to be a general conflict between the North and South.' The tendency is compromise. Hell, man, it's the best opinion of the land; compromise rather than chaos."

"You too, Brutus?"

"In an age when there are no Caesars, don't expect a Brutus. We have no men of great stature. We're playing chess on a big chess board with little chess men —so let's forget making the world over and let's talk practical politics."

Walt sensed the frustration in the other's soul. "I liked you better, Judge, when you first began the Freeman. It was more than a name then."

"Forget it. Are you with me for Pierce or aren't you?"

"What does he stand for?"

"Damned if I know."

"Then, if there's no issue, it becomes a question of personalities. Man to man, if it weren't a question of party, whom would you choose?"

Johnson rubbed his chin thoughtfully, then fumbled in his pocket for a cigar. "Scott's a great man—a fine looking man—six feet five, and all courage—but there are certain personal flaws which if brought to the attention of the people —"

"Is that what you want me for? To help libel a true patriot?"

Johnson paid no heed to the remark other than to say, "When a man runs for public office his life is public property and Pierce happens to be fortunate in having a blameless record."

Walt laughed. "No achievements, therefore no errors, but he does have party loyalty."

Johnson blurted out, "Stop grinding your gums on dream food! Why the hell can't you be practical? Use the machinery you find and build whatever you've a mind to build. You can't build anything with words. Nobody hands you perfect tools. You take what you get —sharpen them yourself and do the best you can with what you've got. You can't accomplish anything standing outside of both parties the way you're doing. Get inside one of them and work from within. You can have your old job back at the Freeman with a bit more pay."

Walt shook his head. Johnson turned to go. "There's a better job in it for you—a government job. Pierce is sure to win and he takes care of his friends. No? All right, suit yourself. Why should I waste any time with you, anyway?"

Walt shook his head, but inwardly he wept. It would be nice to have an income that would lighten his mother's burden—relieve her of her daily drudgery, and his father was getting along in years —.

"Lazy Walt." No, it's not indolence. Let me feel that a thing has meaning and I'll make of my long nights days of Herculean labor—but it must have meaning to mankind everywhere. It must have the power of resurrection—the power to make dead souls arise, walk and be glad!

"Give me O God to sing that thought
Give me, give him or her this quenchless faith
In Thy ensemble. Whatever else withheld
Withhold not from us
Belief in plan of Thee enclosed in Time and Space
Health, peace, salvation universal."

V

Jenny Lind was appearing at the Castle Garden. Johnson handed Walt a ticket. "Don't say I never did anything for you, Walt. You can sell this little billet for fifty dollars; it's up front with the elite."

Walt thanked him and quickly made his way to the box office of the theatre. The waiting line curled almost around the block. Louisa would like this too— the magic voice—the magic name.

For two hours he waited until, hot and perspiring, he faced the tiny window and the sullen clerk.

"Could I trade this ticket for two further back?"

"No! Sorry! We're not in the barter business. There's a long line behind you. Will you please step aside?"

Walt moved away and stood watching the line. He felt hurt at the discourtesy and convinced that a ticket worth fifty dollars was a luxury he could not alone afford.

The fourth man in line called to him. "When's your ticket for?"

"Monday night."

"What row?"

"Ninth row center."

"All right, stay where you are. We'll do business."

Walt waited. The man's turn was reached.

"I'm Bigelow of the Evening Post. Give me two for Monday night."

"Sorry sir. Only the music critics receive passes."

"Who the hell is asking for a pass? Sell me two tickets."

"The nearest I have is eleventh row first balcony."

"I'll take them."

"You're Walt Whitman, aren't you?" He held the tickets out to him. "How's about it? Is it a deal?"

Walt nodded smiling, and the exchange was then and there made.

Bigelow took him by the arm. "Buy you a drink. Gosh it's hot!"

As they sipped chilled wine Bigelow rambled. "Saw you at the Reverend Griswald's the other night—guess it was a month ago. Did you see the show?" Then, without waiting for an answer, "Hell, man, there's so damned much knocking and tapping around the country you can't hear yourself think. A hundred sinkers a night! Walt, we're in the wrong business. But then, again, the honest knocker is worthy of his hire. Good show though, damn good show. Holy Moses—a hundred dollars a night."

Walt smiled. "Jenny Lind is getting far more. I've heard that Barnum is paying her a hundred thousand dollars for her American tour."

"You've heard right enough. But that's different. She has a legitimate talent."

The man sitting next to them laughed and turned a leering face to them as he banged his whisky glass on the bar.

"Legitimate talent, hell! It's all publicity! She's got a Jew backing her—or she'd be back with the rest of the dumb Swedes—singing for pennies."

Walt felt sick at the man's hate.

"Is P. T. Barnum a Jew?" he asked.

"Maybe he is, for all I know. But that guy Goldschmidt that sleeps with her—he's the shrewd one.

Why the hell don't smart Jews and dumb Swedes stay where they belong?"

There was a disturbance near the door and a slender young man came towards them, grim and white-faced.

"My name iss Goldschmidt," he said slowly and with difficulty. "You speak my name und name uff my fiancee."

"Glad to meet you, Mr. Goldschmidt," boomed Bigelow without turning, and with a sudden wild motion he swung his fist hard at the foul-mouthed one. The blow caught the slanderer on the ear. The metal chair tipped and its occupant crashed violently to the floor.

"Gentlemen, gentlemen," pleaded the bartender.

"You're not meaning him, I hope," laughed Bigelow. Then facing the white-faced youth, "Glad to meet you, Mr. Goldschmidt. Heard you at Leipzig last year. Can I buy you a drink?"

"You hit me when I wasn't looking." The drunk was crawling to his feet.

Bigelow got off his stool. "You scummy son-of-a-bitch. Open your mouth again and so help me I'll kick your teeth in."

Goldschmidt looked at Bigelow for a long moment. "There is much about this great democratic country that I do not understand. If you will forgif me —" he bowed and left.

Bigelow turned to Walt, shrugging his shoulders. "Can't say as I blame him much. That was Otto Goldschmidt the famous composer—pupil of Felix Mendelssohn. He's been engaged to Jenny Lind for the last six months. Funny how hate can twist things cockeyed. She's given away fifty thousand dollars to charity—right here in America—but go reason with a slimy gutter rat. Come on, Walt—another one—gotta wash the taste out of my mouth."

* * * *

Louisa sat stiffly silent as they cheered and applauded. The vast audience was wild with delight.

"Bravo! Bis! Another one, nightingale, — give us another!" Walt too was on his feet clapping his hands until his shoulder blades ached. Jenny Lind bowed again and again. She seemed so tiny on the huge stage. Now the stamping began—a rhythmic beating of feet that made the walls tremble. "Encore! Encore!" She raised her hand and motioned the pianist to her side. Both bowed their appreciation. She raised her hand for silence. "Thank you—thank you, dear friends—for your welcome to strangers. You have made my future husband, Mr. Goldschmidt, and myself very, very happy. Your country is so young and people say it has no tradition like the countries of the old world—but your country has a great and noble tradition—as old as the Bible and as new as tomorrow's dawn—and that tradition is the perfect equality and brotherhood of man. Oh—new and beautiful country, — the world — the old tired world needs you — God bless you, America!"

The vast audience was momentarily hushed. Then the applause began again as the crowds thrust their weight towards the exits.

"She should stick to her singing," mordantly opined the elderly lady seated near Louisa. "Cobbler, stick to your last."

Louisa slowly arose to her feet.. "She has a good and understanding heart."

"No instrument music is like the human voice; it flows directly from the heart," thought Walt as he tried to shield his mother from the mass of movement around him.

He breathed softly to his soul "O God, can *I* thus stir the sleeping with *my* songs?"

VI

The next night Walt went alone to the art exhibit at the Brooklyn Art Union. The exhuberant young artist Walter Libby stood laughing mockingly in front of a painting.

"Fol-de-rol and a Hi-nonny-ho!" His sharp voice quickly gathered curious observers to the spot. "Sorry to disturb your art studies, good citizens, but what is this mummy doing outside of its pyramid?"

One dignified matron bent forward to better observe the signature on the painting. Then she quickly drew herself up to the fullness of her short plump stature—"Young man, this painting is a Corot."

"It's a forgery then—an unblushing fraud! Corot couldn't have committed this foul crime!"

Walt approached and eyed the painting with great interest. It was a formal landscape done with classical skill—and that was all. He was about to venture an opinion endorsing the young artist's views when he heard a strangely familiar voice hush the group with a note of authority.

"It is undoubtedly a genuine Corot."

Walt recognized Stephen Foster in the same instant that Foster discerned him, but before either could approach the other, Libby thrust himself squarely in front of the composer.

"What makes you, sir, an authority on the authenticity of a painting?"

Foster placed a calming hand on the artist's shoulders.

"Easy there. Don't make this a personal quarrel."

"It *is* personal. When your whole life is your art it can't help but be personal."

Foster's face turned pallid. "I see what you mean —and I agree with you. As a fellow artist I agree with you."

Libby was slightly mollified.

"Oh, then you paint? May I know your name?"

"Stephen Foster. No, I don't paint. I compose Ethiopian melodies—you may have heard 'My Old Kentucky Home' and several others in a similar vein."

Libby extended his hand warmly with all traces of truculence completely erased from his features.

"Glad to meet you, sir. Yes sir—very glad to meet you! I like your work. There's something truly human in your songs."

Foster turned and presented Walt with a brief "The poet, Walt Whitman." Libby gave a quick, almost imperceptible, nod in Walt's direction and turned back to Foster.

"What makes you so sure this is a genuine Corot?"

Foster pointed to the painting as a teacher might do in instructing a class. "Corot was a draper by profession—a milliner and costumer of some sort. You can readily see that such training would incline him to formal or classical creation. At first this is the type of thing he did in France and in Italy. I've seen many of them; but as soon as he came under the influence of Rousseau and Millet—he began to look at nature —"

"Mr. Foster, you are a scholar and a gentleman." Libby embraced the composer warmly while the crowd surrounding the painting laughed. "I thought Corot was *born* a Barbizon. I admit my ignorance. Yes, sir, you are a scholar and a gentleman."

Foster made a wry grimace. "Mr. Whitman can testify that I am neither. However, now that the art issue is settled, I find myself extremely thirsty."

"Agreed. Hey Bill!" Libby called to a friend on the other side of the room, "I'm buying!" Then in a quick aside, "That's William Mount. He'll be over in a minute. That Negro study is his."

The three regarded the subdued colors of the Negro

scene in admiring silence. Finally, Libby chirped blithely to Foster, "Mount paints like you sing—a tragic lonely quality. Here he comes now."

Walt lifted his eyes from the painting and faced the three young men. He was glowing with an eagerness to praise their zest, their eagerness, their work.

"This is America—this is our own! I shall write in the journal of your work and call it good. It should appear in the Evening Post within the next week."

"A friendly or even unfriendly press, Mr. Whitman, and we eat. Ignore us and we die." This last sally was Mount warming to the occasion, — and the wine was good.

Walt's praise of the young artists appeared in the Evening Post as promised.

"A sunny blessing, then, say I, on the young artist race!"

He was overwhelmed with demonstrations of their appreciation. The entire circle of young artists beseeched him to address them.

"What do I know of this form of art?" he asked Foster. "It would be impudence on my part to offer them counsel."

Foster shook his head. "All forms of creative art have origin and purpose in common. You have very much to tell them. Your simple unschooled honesty will be refreshing. There is so much confused chatter about tendencies, schools, impressions, expressions, cubes and Heaven alone knows what that a simple clear lucid opinion is sorely needed."

"Foster, why don't *you* give the lecture?"

"They didn't ask me."

"And if they had?"

"I would repeat Ruskin to them — 'They should go to nature in all singleness of heart, and walk with her laboriously and trustingly, having no other thought but how best to penetrate her meaning; rejecting nothing, selecting nothing, and scorning nothing.' That's creed enough for an artist, isn't it?"

"Almost—but not enough for me."

"What else, Walt—what else is needed?"

"To put one's naked self into the painting—so that the artist and the painting are one—more even—so that the painting contains all there is of the artist—until the painting is himself!"

"You can't mean that, for then the artist would be always and forever painting himself instead of what appears to his eye."

"Foster! Foster! I am not interested in what appears to the artist's eye. I want to know how it appears to his soul. The thing itself and the mood which it induces—the flowing tide of emotion aroused by the object or the scene, eternalized upon a canvas—that is what a painting must be if it is to be art."

"Words—more words!"

"No! No! It is the same with literature and the same with music. If the sensitive creator of it seeks to convey the mood and the emotion that he feels he may make the sky more blue and the wing of the gull more white and thus give the lie to the eye in order to convey the truth of the heart."

"A lie? Can a lie be art?"

"But it won't be a lie; it will be the true and direct communication of the artist's sensitive soul to the soul of him that beholds it, putting as it were a microscope to his inward eye."

"Not bad!—Not bad!" murmured Foster. "You'll lecture to them?"

"I will."

"It won't be Ruskin."

"No. It will be Walt Whitman."

* * * *

Walt's first lecture on art was a tumultuous wall-shuddering success. The small hotel room that had been wheedled from the manager as his contribution to culture was foggy and murky with smoke, but the good-natured crowd applauded and cheered every sentence, and Walt beamed his gratitude to every corner.

Foster was not there. He had left for New Orleans to seek inspiration for his "Ethiopian ballads," as he called them, but Walter Libby and William Mount clung to Walt with fervor and vied with each other in serving him and ministering to his every need.

"Your throat must be dry. Here's water and lemon."

"We'll walk you home, Mr. Whitman. We insist."

Oddly enough the loquacious youths were silent as they left the lecture hall—and Walt could not help asking "Why this sudden gloom?"

Mount replied slowly. "It's not easy, Mr. Whitman. Parents object. The environment thrusts at you with a thousand jibes, 'Make an honest living'—'Get yourself a job'—'Idler'—'Wastrel'—'Did you sell a painting?' —'Does anyone want it?' "

Walt nodded, "I know. I know. The same slurs are the poet's lot. Shall we compare bruises?"

Mount laughed, then reverted to his graver mood.

"Frankly, Mr. Whitman, shall we go on painting?"

Walt stopped abruptly and faced them in the darkly shadowed street. The city was asleep and the moon seemed like a pale frightened traveller avoiding the thickets of the clouds as it sought the clearings of the sky.

"Did I hear you correctly, Mr. Mount?"

"You did."

"And you, Mr. Libby?"

"I don't know. Lately I've asked myself whether I have anything to give a canvas beyond the paint?

I've sold one painting in the last eight months and that to an opulent friend whose quality of mercy is evidently greater than his appreciation of art."

"You speak a strange language for an artist. If you have to ask the question 'Shall I create?' then for Heaven's sake as well as your own—don't!"

Walt went on more calmly. "In the writing of books, in the field of drama, in the composing of music and in the painting of scenes, there will always be the fiercest rivalry and competition. Almost every human being believes himself to be gifted in at least one artistic talent. I do not like to believe in any 'God-given' aristocracy—even an aristocracy of genius! It offends my idea of democracy. So, gentlemen, in our competitive fields, only a few will be heard, or seen or understood; the results, whether recognition or oblivion,—if that's what you're seeking—rest with Providence—the effort lies with you."

"You've left us where you found us. You've told us nothing." Libby's voice was bitter.

"Then I haven't made myself clear. The glowworm does not ask 'Shall I glow?' The spider does not ask 'Shall I spin?' And the artist—creates because he must."

"Thanks for your trying to help."

Walt grasped both men by their arms—"I wasn't talking to you. I was talking to myself!"

VII

Jeff entered quietly and started for his room. His head drooped wearily.

"Jeff, where have you been?" Walt was anxious.

"Meetings, Walt. Abolitionist meetings. Talk of rifles and gunpowder."

"That isn't the answer."

Jeff shook his head as though rebuking a child. "Sometimes I feel like *your* older brother. When the rights of Man are ground under-foot, God hates a coward."

"No, Jeff, no. War doesn't solve anything. It kills people and keeps hate alive."

"That's a question for your conscience to decide. I've made *my* decision."

"You're young and hot-headed."

"There's one thing worse than being young—and that's being too old to care or do."

"It's treason, Jeff."

"So was the Revolution!"

"Jeff, don't do anything you'll regret."

"Then I might never do anything at all, Walt. Don't lecture to me. Just leave me alone. Besides, you've never been sure of where *you* stand, so why confuse *me?*" Jeff slammed the door behind him.

* * * *

The family moved to Cumberland Street—that is to say, the father, mother, George, Jeff, and, of course, Eddie. Walt did most of the loading and unloading of the furniture himself. His father would have nothing to do with the moving and watched with resentful sullen eyes. " 'Man is a tree of the field' the Bible says, and he should be deep rooted like a tree. This movin' around is against the Law of God."

Scarcely had the furniture been arranged and the first supper prepared when the elder Walt collapsed with a groan, his head striking the edge of the door. Walt's arms were around him, — the first time he had ever embraced his stern father. Jeff and George helped carry him to his bed. Louisa unlaced his shoes, directing her sons with an anxious flurry of words. "Jeff, get Dr. Holt. Run quickly." Jeff was already dashing out of the door.

The elder Walt lay bleak and dark against the pillow. Louisa, wringing her hands, stood bending over him. Walt tried to calm her. "He'll be all right, Ma. The doctor'll be here soon."

His father, opening his eyes very wide, muttered, "Bring Eddie—bring me Eddie."

George came back into the bedroom leading his brother by the hand. The poor boy looked at his father uncomprehending. A tear began its slow journey from the corner of the elder Walt's eye. "Eddie, I wish I could do somethin' for you. I wish —"

The boy's lips moved soundlessly. "You can make me a house, Pa. Chop down the hickory tree and make me a house. You've got a big hammer, and a big saw, and you can make me a house."

The father's hand reached out to caress his son, and the boy, frightened at the gesture, drew back. The gnarled hand fell limply and Walt thought his father was resting with half-opened eyes.

Finally—finally Dr. Holt drove up. He busied himself at once with the stricken man. The family followed his every movement—waiting—questioning.

The doctor spoke softly. "It's paralysis—a stroke. You should be prepared. I don't think he has much chance."

Walt watched the doctor leave, dreading the thought of entering the bedroom again.

* * * *

This is all, Walt. There isn't anything else. Your father is dying. The light's gone out. The little bit of earthly motion is over and all the litanies, the prayers, the processions, the dreams of future life are hollow sounds — empty tumult of sobs and laughter in a vacuum.

"Walt, what are you staring at?" Louisa's tired drained voice drew him to her side.

Poor mother, not much joy in her life. So many babies died at birth. Was it five or six? And of her prolific tortured yield, Jesse doomed, Hannah warped, Andrew sneering at truth and goodness—like Jesse's shabby echo—and Eddie—well Eddie, with his stunted mind, was happier than all.

Why was he, Walt, trying to fill the Universe with song when there was no music there? Just cold balls of mud rolling endlessly through meaningless space. What was there to sing about?

"Just to live is torture!" whispered Walt to the emptiness that was his soul. "I can stand physical pain even if they tear my flesh, but this black emptiness—There's *got* to be a reason, a pattern! There *is*—there *is* a pattern. The thoughts I think—*I* didn't create them. Why am I pitying the clay? Father no longer suffers. *I* suffer watching him. He is at peace or at rest. Why should I torture myself with thoughts of death? Father will never experience death. No one ever did. The dying feel no pain—even though death be only oblivion. Only the living grieve—and the living have power not to grieve. The living have power to exult—the living have power to laugh, to sing. The living have power to laugh all death away.

"*The beautiful touch of Death, soothing and be-*
numbing a few moments, for reasons,
Myself discharging my excrementitious body to be
burned, or rendered to powder, or buried,
My real body doubtless left to me for other spheres,
My voided body nothing more to me, returning to
the purifications, further offices, eternal uses of
the earth."

That's it. All is beautiful—except our fear of things. All is life unending. All is real and eternal—the sweat, the teeming dung and the stars—all beautiful. Cease, O spiteful differences among men. There is so little time. Why use the bayonet? Your fellow man will die. A few more years will slay him.

Anne, I need your comfort—the calmness in your eyes. Your serious face floats over my pillow. You are wiser than I. My knowledge is words—words like chess-pieces. I move them around in tune to my own writhings—but you know. Men guess and women know. Eternal feminine—so wise, so sure, — offering men your breast, your thigh as to a suckling child with a strong condescending maternal tenderness. You, — *you* know—and your knowing gives me strength. Anne —I haven't written you for so long. I promised you love poems—only love poems.

"Dearest Anne,

*Once I passed through a populous city imprinting
    my brain for future use with its shows, archi-
    tecture, customs, traditions,*
*Yet now of all that city I remember only a woman
    I casually met there who detained me for love
    of me,*
*Day by day and night by night we were together—
    all else has long been forgotten by me.*
*I remember I say only that woman who passionately
    clung to me.*
Again we wonder, we love, we separate again,
Again she holds me by the hand. I must not go,
*I see her close beside me with silent lips sad and
    tremulous."*

VIII

His father's approaching death made Walt hurry. It was as though the days were pressing on each other's heels and shouting with confused voices: "You've only a little while, Walt. Put your songs on paper or they will die with you, forever lost, forever lost."

And so Walt thrust his pen at the empty sheets and scratched them into life, letting his clamoring blood write rather than his fingers.

"I have said that the soul is not more than the body,
And I have said that the body is not more than the
soul.
And nothing, not God, is greater to one than one's
self is.
And whoever walks a furlong without sympathy
walks to his own funeral drest in his shroud,
And I or you pocketless of a dime may purchase
the pick of the earth.
And to glance with an eye or see a bean in its pod
confounds the learning of all times,
And there is no trade or employment but the young
man following it may become a hero,
And there is no object so soft but it makes a hub
for the wheel's universe,
And I say to any man or woman, Let your soul stand
cool and composed before a million universes—"

Death, life, birth—everything—everything must sing. Blow away the ghosts and the spider's webs. "I'm not afraid of death," he told his soul and he walked slowly and curiously among the gravestones.

Then he stood silent and waited and felt the sweet peace rather than the Fear he had feared—and saw the grass pointing upward joyously like tiny prophet fingers, and he wrote:

"I believe a leaf of grass is no less than the journey-
work of the stars,
And the pismire is equally perfect, and a grain of
sand, and the egg of the wren,
And the tree-toad is a chef-d'oevre for the highest,
And the running blackberry would adorn the par-
lors of heaven,

*And the narrowest hinge in my hand puts to scorn
  all machinery,
And the cow crunching with depress'd head sur-
  passes any statue,
And a mouse is miracle enough to stagger sextillions
  of infidels."*

The aching tempest in his brain and heart was suddenly stilled. He had gathered them together, all the memorandum books, fragments and scraps of paper where he had carved out jagged phrases, sharp-edged singing blades.

"Leaves of grass! This is my field of growing things. My book is done! Mother," he called, "Mother, my book is done."

He gathered them all together and held them tightly—ecstatically. His mother looked at him tenderly. "Walt, I don't understand what you write. Do you think people will like it?"

"*I* like it and I'm people, but *they* still don't know what they are and I do—so I must show them what they are—what they really are."

"You're getting to speak like you write, Walt," wailed Louisa, "and now I can't understand you at all."

* * * *

"Anne! Anne! I've found the answer. Jeff said I wasn't sure of where I stood. My soul knew all along but it had to teach my mind. There is no devil but Fear. There is no evil but Fear. There is no disease but Fear. Fear is the womb which spews forth suspicion, hate and war. Fear renders men and nations insecure. Fear is the mother of crime and violence. Fear is the spur of cruelty. Fear is the root of envy. I have found the lamp. Anne! Anne! I have found the lamp. There are two lamps—one is Knowledge, but its light travels slowly like a weary stream soiled with the lies hurled into it by despots that fear. My lamp

is Joy—the Will to Joy—the Will to Exult. Fear cannot live in such a flame. Anne, my darling! Come to
me! My book is done! My soul sang it and now my
laggard mind understands its greatness. The Newest
Testament of All—the Book of Joy exulting!"

*   *   *   *

Anne did not come. Instead she wrote:
"Poor Walt, how sad and dark must be your soul,
if you must sing so loudly to disperse the shadows!"

*   *   *   *

Anne, why won't you understand! My soul is no
different from the souls of all the children of Adam.
What drives my Fear away will drive all Fear away—
the Will to Joy! The Will to Joy! Oh God, let me
heal—heal—heal! Let me heal the sick sun—the dying
stars and the withering race of man! The Will to Joy!

IX

The publishers had been earnest—attentive, detached and very polite when he interviewed them, but
all of them had been brusque and impatient when it
came to reading his work. One of them had skimmed
over a song or two displaying an up-raised eyebrow
flicker of interest.

"You can't expect us to use these words—'aching
love flesh'—'belly pressed to belly.' What are you trying to do, shock people into talking about your book?"

Walt eyed the man coldly. "You're not interested?"

"Yes—if you expurgate some of these words."

Walt gathered his papers together and towered like
a giant over the man. "You want me to emasculate
my book. Would you have agreed to being born without a penis?"

"You are insulting, Mr. Whitman."

"But not blasphemous enough to deny God His Handiwork."

Walt's pride could not stand such rebuffs. "I'll be my own mid-wife," he resolved grimly. "I'll print it myself."

He strode quickly and wrathfully to the Rome Brothers Print Shop at Fulton and Cranberry Streets.

"Mornin', Walt!" Andrew Rome was working the huge shears and chewing a colossal wad of tobacco. His silver gray hair gave him a gentle benign appearance.

"Where's Jim?"

"He'll be in soon. We're getting an order for five thousand posters from the Freeman—and an order of ten thousand posters from the dough-faces. Looks like the dough-faces have more cash."

"They always have had."

"What's on your mind, Walt?"

"I've got a book I want to set up myself. May I use your type and press? I'll not interfere with your jobs—and I'll buy the paper myself."

"It's all right with me, Walt, but better talk to Jim. He doesn't like anyone else using the press."

Walt cleared a space near the window and began to arrange the pages. This song would be the first:

"I celebrate myself, and sing myself,
And what I assume you shall assume,
For every atom belonging to me as good belongs
to you."

It would appear—this book—this golden trumpet Book—in beautiful binding! An announcement or two in the press—then the lifted eyebrows—the interest-kindled eye, the rising chorus of voices—the queries, "Who is this great prophet who strides among us like a giant? He is one of the people. See the laborer's clothes he wears. He is a powerful voice in the land—

much more, the writer of a new Bible—the mighty herald of a joyous dawn. He is the lusty awakening spirit of America itself. Why didn't we know until now that such a man was among us? Can you not see the truth of what he says—the brave, clear, flowing, singing, uncompromising truth? Exchange your black cassocks for an open shirt, your prayers for honest ringing laughter and throw away dead words and outworn phrases."

Mother, you said they wouldn't understand—but they do, they do! See? They buy my book by hundreds, and there's a new bonnet for you—and toys for Eddie, and a dress for Hannah—and the best doctors for Jesse—and a nice home for Mary—and new suits for George and Jeff. You see, I wasn't lazy. God had given me a volcano of a heart and I couldn't cover its flame with ashes. Now you see it burst forth. It gives fire and light. The whole world sees—understands, loves me for what I show to them.

The creak of the heavy door made Walt at once conscious of his exact temporal whereabouts. Jim Rome entered the shop and began immediately to don his leather apron. His brother went directly to the point. "Jim, Walt's got somethin' to ask you. Wants to use our presses."

Walt felt this blunt presentation was lacking in adequate appeal, so he stated his request simply and with just a note of urgency. "I'm doing a book, Jim. I've written it. It's all here. It's the best I can do. It's got to have a nice looking body—a cover that will make people know it's important. I'll pay for all the material I use. All I want to use is your type and press. You can charge me anything you like."

Jim walked over to the high desk where the pages were spread. His cauliflower ears stood out like knobs from the sides of his head. He looked at the first page curiously. "It doesn't rhyme!" he finally announced with grave solemnity, "but it sounds pretty good." He glanced at page after page, then turned back to the title. " 'Leaves of Grass'," he read. Then abruptly, "Say, Walt, I've got some case-type with flowers and ferns tooled in. Make a nice heading. You going to have a paper cover?"

"No—cloth."

"It'll cost you almost a hundred dollars for five hundred covers."

"I've got it."

"How many copies you going to run off?"

"About a thousand."

"Well go ahead, Walt. It's agreeable with me."

*   *   *   *

Day after day and far into the night Walt worked, and no God-intoxicated priest ever offered a sacrifice with more fervent devotion. Each letter was holy to him. He hesitated about changing a word or a phrase in the slightest, for this was to be the new singing Bible —the Bible of America, and from that vast pulpit it would go forth to the world!

His name—should his name appear?

No, not on the cover. Did Moses place his name on the cover of his Book? No, the name of the author would not appear on the cover, — but in the body of the verse, there "Walt Whitman" would appear—in name occasionally, but in spirit everywhere—all of it, all of it he, — all of it Walt Whitman.

His picture—that must be there. People must sense that this was the voice of a laborer, a common man, and yet unique in his vision. His name would tell them little—but his picture —.

A plate would have to be made. He carried a photograph of himself to an engraver named Hollyer who offered to do the plate and case-type both for six dollars. Hollyer's judgment of the picture itself was candid. "It's not a portrait, but it will do. Could be more dignified, you know—more in keeping with the literary profession."

Back to the print shop. The ripened fruit was about to be gathered—*his* Book! He watched the hollow-chested woman sew the binding, — *his* Book! He smelled the glue pots, felt and fingered the green cloth for the cover and answered as best as he could the many questions of the rugged brothers Rome.

* * * *

Jim Rome looked over Walt's shoulder and commented casually, "It's gonna be a nice lookin' job, but who's gonna buy it?"

Walt was about to answer when a sudden loud crash sent a chill of fear and anguish through him. The copper oil can perched on the shelf had been jostled by Jim's elbow. It now lay on his precious pages, pouring itself out blackly in awful stains.

He wanted to leap forward but his limbs became rigid and would not respond. Andrew was the first to move. He picked up the half empty oil can and threw it fiercely aside. Then he clutched the upper layers of the pile of sheets and handed them to Walt. "There's about two hundred pages spoiled, Walt."

"Two hundred pages!" That meant two hundred books less. Walt felt an urge to shout and rage against Jim, even to strike him with his fist, but only for a moment. It had been an accident. The brothers had been kind—even generous. His voice was toneless. "That's all right. Eight hundred copies will be enough."

"There's not enough cloth for half of the covers, Walt. Let's bind some in paper to sell at a cheaper price. You can always bind them in cloth, you know."

"Yes, I suppose you're right."

Three books were bound that afternoon, — sea-green cloth with the title in gilt. And Walt, hugging the first copy close to his side, felt as though he were soaring aloft on eagles' wings and that all of the world could see his flight.

As he walked block after block he would open the book from time to time, examine it page by page, close it, caress the covers with his finger tips, quicken his pace and hurry on. "My Book! My Soul! My Book! My Song! Myself!" He almost wept in his joy. Large and thin—only ninety-five pages, and one-third of the book consisted of his lengthy prose preface or intro-duction.

As he entered his home his mother was closing the bedroom door. She put her fingers to her lips. "Pa may get some sleep. He's been moanin' all night."

"Ma, let me go in for just a minute. The book is done. I've got to show it to him."

He moved past his mother and slowly opened the bedroom door. His father's eyes were resting calmly on him. "Pa, this is what I've been working on. It's done now. I wanted you to see it."

There was no flicker of understanding in his father's eyes. Walt kept on talking. "Pa, I haven't been lazy. I couldn't help myself. I tried to keep jobs, but all the time there was something inside here calling to me." He drew closer to the bed. "This is it. The book. It's good, Pa. It's good."

Louisa gently pulled his sleeve. "Hush, Walt. I don't think Pa hears you. Maybe if we're quiet he'll sleep."

They walked back to the kitchen. Louisa reached for the book. "It's beautiful, Walt." She held it fondly. "But where's your name on it?"

"It's inside, Ma."

"I'll ask Mary Elizabeth to read it to me."

"I'll read you some of it, Ma, right now."

He turned the pages, seeking desperately something whose words she would understand.

"Read me something religious, Walt."

Walt turned the pages more slowly. "Here's something, Ma. It's all religious, but here's something." He began to read:

"Why should I wish to see God better than this day?

I see something of God each hour of the twenty-four, and each moment then,

In the faces of men and women I see God, and in my own face in the glass,

I find letters from God dropt in the street, and every one is sign'd by God's name,

And I leave them where they are, for I know that wheresoe'er I go,

Others will punctually come for ever and ever."

And as to you Death —

No, he would not read those sharp phrases. He turned back to the previous verse:

And I say to mankind, "Be not curious about God —" And he halted. He could not read her the rest. She would not understand.

His mother looked at him proudly, her hands resting in her lap. "If you've got God and religion in your book it's a good book, Walt. But it doesn't sound much like the Bible. There's not much peace and comfort in it."

"But there is, Ma—the peace and comfort of love and joy and friendship among men. That's what all of it's about."

Louisa nodded. "That be good Quaker teaching, my son, but 'tis not good to be joyous overmuch, for are we altogether sure of our salvation?"

X

Walt had his Book! Now how to get it into the hands of readers. He left his first copy at home in his mother's care and then he went to the print shop early and waited for six more copies of his book to be bound.

Tenderly he put the six copies into a carpet bag and began to make the rounds. His first call was at The Corner Book Shoppe where he was courteously greeted by the scholarly Dr. Limpet, who owned and managed the austere and well stocked book mart.

"A beautifully bound book, Walt. Now let's see the contents."

Walt waited patiently while Dr. Limpet perused several pages. Finally he suggested, "If you could take twenty or thirty to sell at a dollar a piece —"

"No, Walt. You haven't even got a publisher's name or imprint on it. It doesn't look right for an author to peddle his own wares. Have there been any reviews of your book? What do the critic say about it?"

"Dr. Limpet, why don't you put a few copies where the customers can see them?"

That was as far as Walt got. Dr. Limpet's eyes seemed glued to the page he was reading. He looked up shocked and flushed. "Do you expect me to ruin my business utterly? Such vulgarity! What would happen if a lady were to read lines like these?"

"She *might* become a woman!" Walt reached over and took the copy from Dr. Limpet, replaced it in his carpet bag and set out for the next shop, leaving Dr. Limpet staring after him over the top of his spectacles, following Walt's indignant progress, with half-open mouth.

"Let me take it home overnight," suggested one friendly book seller. Walt thought that was a splendid idea, for after all what could a reader gather of him by fluttering a few pages. He distributed his six copies at various and sundry book stalls and then came home to find his brother George bent over the volume.

"There's a lot of powerful words here, Walt, and you sure do throw them around. The parts about slavery make good reading. That's what you should still be fighting, Walt, — slavery."

Walt said simply, "I am," and let it go at that.

The next morning he made the rounds once more —Drummond's Book Shop, where the lady in charge handed him back his book as though removing a dead reptile. She glared at him in frigid offended silence and refused to discuss it.

Blake's, where Mr. Blake told him kindly and sermonically, "There are *some* things which are personal and private, Mr. Whitman, and scarcely suitable for public proclamation."

Reef's, where the erudite young man told him haughtily, "None of this can properly be termed poetry. It is a coarse mixture of the Bhagavad-Gita and the New York Herald. Read your Whittier and Longfellow again."

From Reef's he walked to Swayne's Book Shop. Edward Swayne polished his glasses with nervous concentrated attention as Walt talked.

"Enthusiasm is quite usual in parents and authors, Mr. Whitman. Suppose you consign fifty copies to us and we'll display them. We'll even try to push them for you."

Walt, overjoyed, hesitated. "Would you mind holding off for three days? I'd be most happy if the book would appear on display July 4th."

"The connection is obvious, Mr. Whitman. A sort of poetic Declaration of Independence. All right— July 4th it is. Why not try Fowler and Wells—or have you been there? Fowler is a bit eccentric, but he's a good bookman. Talk to him."

Walt felt a warm glow now. He had been expecting more obstacles—more discouragements—and had extended his jaw pugnaciously. Now the tautness in him relaxed and he walked with a more confident stride.

Mr. Fowler was busy showing a customer his treasured limited editions. "Six-fifty for that one," Fowler murmured casually as the customer asked the price.

Walt drew closer. It was an Addison first edition. Still six and a half dollars was quite a price. He drew a quick breath as the customer nodded, "Very well, Mr. Fowler. You'll have my check for Six Hundred Fifty in the morning."

"Six Hundred and Fifty Dollars?" Walt almost shouted the words. The buyer, an opulently dressed mild-mannered broker, gave Walt an amused glance. "Yes, you heard correctly. Now that I have consummated my purchase I must confess that I consider it a rare bargain at the price. Good day, Mr. Fowler, and good day to you, sir, whoever you may be."

When the customer had left Walt addressed himself to Mr. Fowler. "My name is Walt Whitman."

"Oh yes. I've read your Free Soil articles. Very well done, Mr. Whitman. A bit emotional and undisciplined, but on the whole eloquent—quite eloquent."

"Oh?" He raised his eyebrows as he examined "Leaves of Grass." "Your work?" Then surveying him intently, "You have an interesting head, Mr. Whitman. Bumps—contours—I presume you've studied phrenology." He fluttered a few pages. "Interesting. Style unrestrained, free. Leave a few copies with me and I'll see what I can do. By the way, I should like to examine your skull—your head, I mean—a most interesting head."

Walt smiled at Fowler's praise of his cranial fea-

tures. "Why should my head be interesting? Its shape,
I am sure, was determined by my position in my
mother's womb or by the pressure exerted on it during
parturition—or even perhaps by the amount of time
I was permitted to lie in one position as an infant."

Fowler made a deprecating gesture. "Not entirely
—not entirely, Mr. Whitman. There are regions of
power in the brain, and these pressing from within
determine the shape of the head."

"My book will be a clearer indication of any poor
powers I may possess."

"Or lack," was Fowler's dry comment.

"I'd like them to sell for one dollar—paper copies
seventy-five cents."

Fowler's sole comment was, "The usual forty per
cent to us, Mr. Whitman. Send us a hundred copies."

"Will you display them?"

"Yes, we can give you a fourth of the window."

"Could the display of my book begin July 4th?"

"Superstitious or patriotic, Mr. Whitman?"

"There's no superstition in me."

"Then it's patriotism, of course. A laudable sentiment."

"Much more than sentiment, Mr. Fowler. It's my
very life."

"I see—an American poet."

"*The* American poet."

Mr. Fowler raised his eyebrows and smiled. "What
monumental egotism! — No, no offense!"

"On the contrary, I admit it and wear it like a
shining garment."

"What?—your egotism?" Now Fowler was rather
taken aback. "I'm quite busy, Mr. Whitman. Send me
the copies, and I might suggest that you leave several
review copies for the press. Would you pay for a com-
mercial advertisement?"

Walt nodded. "Most willingly!"

"Then advance us ten dollars."

"But you'll have my books —"

"Mr. Whitman, an edition that does not sell brings only the price of fuel on a warm summer evening."

"But this book is different —"

"I've already drawn the parallel of authors and parents."

Walt opened his purse. Some few small coins and six silver dollars huddled abjectly and pathetically in the worn leather as though seeking each other's companionship in their loneliness. "This is on account. I'll bring the rest this afternoon with the books."

He hurried home and began to wrap and bundle the books tenderly—lovingly—carefully. "Ma, I need four dollars."

Louisa went at once to the small pewter tea pot over the fireplace. There was not much left after the doctor had been paid. Well, George was working at the waterworks and Jeff was presently employed full time, so conditions were not too desperate.

"Take five dollars, Walt. You'll pay me back."

Walt stacked the books and bound them firmly. Now there were three bundles of his beloved "Leaves of Grass." One bundle was destined for Swayne's and the other two for Fowler and Wells. Walt placed the two bundles in the wheel barrow and grasped the handles with a will. He began the long trek over the sidewalks with wild drum beats in his heart. He was a pioneer blazing a singing trail through a wilderness of tangled thicket. He was treading a new pathway for others to follow. His strong arms held the wheelbarrow steady. People paused to stare, shook their heads and went about their business. Let them stare! This, his load of books, was a battering ram to break down walls of indolence, stupidity, mummified cliches, inane platitudes—moldy expressions of still moldier minds. This was more than a new book. This was a new age, — a new and shining age! The age of which all mankind had dreamed.

Forward, then! Can't you see, you people who hurry about your dwarfish tasks and trivial doings, that I, Walt Whitman, am blazing a trail over the cobblestones, carrying a cargo more precious than all the caravels of the East Indian trade? I carry the Bible of America — the new singing Bible of Humanity, written with black fire on white flame. If only you had the vision—if only you would look into these bundles! But you will—you will—and then you will say, "Who was this man who moved among us like a prophet? Why did we not know him at once, his garments of a laborer, his trade of carpenter, his love of men —?"

People *were* watching. They were smiling too—some of them laughing openly at the sight of a bearded, starry-eyed man wheeling a barrow of books straight ahead without swerving to the right or to the left, his beard bent backward in the wind. He carried the books to the rear of the first bookshop on his list.

"Give me a receipt, please."

"Sale or consignment?"

"Consignment."

"Very well."

And so it went. And now the wheelbarrow was empty and again people stared at the sight of a gray bearded giant wheeling an empty barrow across the cobblestones. He did not realize his lips were moving with the words of his songs until a grocery boy remarked loudly to no one in particular, "Crazy people talk to themselves."

XI

Early in the morning of July 4th—almost at dawn —Walt haunted the windows of Swayne's and Fowler and Wells. The display at Swayne's was modest—a single copy of "Leaves of Grass" among scores of books of other American poets.

But Fowler had kept faith as to the promised "one-fourth of the window." The display was neat and geometrically sound. Three piles of books pyramided, two books open to the photograph of the author and one book at the apex invitingly drawing attention to the poem "I Celebrate Myself." The show card in circumspect and modest lettering gave the title and price of the book.

Walt lounged delightedly against a street lamp watching the customers enter and leave the book shop, wondering if they recognized him from the print in his book. Should he enter? No, that would be too immodest. Then again it might annoy Mr. Fowler.

Oh, if he could fling a stone in Swayne's window, the crowd would be sure to gather. "Who did it?" they would shout. "Why do you not display my book properly?" he would retort.

Be patient, Walt. Your book is out. It's only a matter of time—a customer glances idly at it—then bends his glance intensely—he tells another—and he another —

"Come in, Mr. Whitman!"

Lorenzo Fowler stood in the doorway of the shop smiling affably. As Walt entered the book store he perceived that his book was being held open in the large hairy hand of a stalwart interested reader.

The man looked up and examined Walt from head to foot with scrupulous attention to every detail.

"Is this your genius, Lorenzo?"

Lorenzo Fowler nodded soberly and then addressed himself to Walt. "This is my brother Orson. You remember I asked you on a previous occasion if you were interested in phrenology. Well, my brother would like to pursue the subject further—if you are interested."

Orson Fowler gave Walt no opportunity to answer. "You have doubtless heard of Dr. J. C. Spurzheim and his scholarly work 'Phrenology'."

"I received the volume some time ago."

"Then I presume you read it—or did you follow the example of some scoundrels who write reviews from rumor?"

"I read it carefully."

"I have opened a Phrenological Cabinet on Nassau Street. I would like to give you a reading without charge."

Lorenzo suggested mildly, "Perhaps you would be interested in the results of my cursory examination, Orson."

"Here!" He placed his thumb against Walt's temple and began to move his fingers slowly through the graying hair. 'There is sublimity and amativeness shown—and a poetic or visionary genius clearly indicated."

Orson Fowler frowned his disapproval. "A truly scientific examination requires more accurate measurements. I still suggest a visit to my study, — or" and he scrutinized Walt intently, "are you one of those naive souls who consider Phrenology on a par with the nonsense of Palmistry."

"I have formed no opinion about Palmistry."

"You may dismiss any consideration of that spurious art—for it can tell naught of the future and little of the past—unless the hands go unwashed, but the chart of the brain of man—that is quite different!"

Walt smiled at the Fowler brothers. "I do not doubt

that it is a science—but I wonder at the flattering qualities you discover me to possess."

"Not all of them are flattering:" Lorenzo indicated with his index finger a declivity behind the ear. "You have a failing."

"And that is —?"

"Indolence, sir."

"But you maintain that I have the gift of Poetry."

"I said the *genius* of Poetry."

XII

Walt had received twenty-five dollars for each of his last three lectures. The first he had called "Art and Artists." The second he had titled "Tom Paine—American," and the third he had named "Religion and Democracy." But, now that the New Dawn Women's Club had scheduled him jointly with Mrs. Amelia J. Bloomer, Walt felt distinctly ill at ease.

"I should never have accepted," he told Mary Elizabeth. "I don't know anything about this Bloomer woman and I'm not anxious to engage in a debate with her."

Mary Elizabeth was delighted. "I'll go, Walt. I must hear you."

"No, Mary, I beg of you."

"You're frightened—Walt, you're frightened. But you needn't be. What is there to it? Mrs. Bloomer will speak on the enslavement of Woman by Man, and you will speak on the enslavement of Man by Woman—and you'll divide honors. For every man that tyrannizes over a woman, there are at least two women who lead their husbands by the nose."

Walt laughed at Mary's outburst of chatter. He shook his head soberly. "No, Mary. The women that will attend this meeting will not be in the mood for banter. I had better prepare carefully—and I'd be wise to start preparing now."

Walt had anticipated meeting, in the person of Mrs. Amelia J. Bloomer, a hawk-faced bespectacled shrewish champion of Women's Rights. When he arrived at the lecture hall a few moments early he found a pleasing eloquent young lady whose only distinction in appearance was a pair of wide pantaloons, neatly tailored, in place of a skirt. He eyed them curiously on being introduced to her. She laughed—a liquid gurgling laugh. "Nothing sinister about these, Mr. Whitman. If a woman is to work side by side with men, she should wear garments that permit her freedom of movement. Agreed?"

Walt nodded. "How do you meet the Scriptural injunction about woman not wearing the garments of a man and vice versa?"

Mrs. Bloomer knitted her brow as she answered quickly, "That was one of the first objections to this garb. Leave it to clergymen to oppose reform. Be frank, Mr. Whitman, would a man be seen in these?" She stretched her pantaloons to their full width. "I think the Scriptures refer to perversions of sex and do not prohibit comfortable clothing."

The women who had collected in small groups throughout the hall were abruptly called to order by the chairman of the evening. At the sound of the gavel, they promptly took their seats and gave their complete attention to the chairman's opening remarks.

The chairman was Sara Payson Willis, an extremely popular author who wrote under the name of Fanny Fern. She was an attractive, plump, fair-haired woman who, all the while she was speaking, kept constantly glancing at Walt for approval.

"This meeting is only one of hundreds that are being held throughout the land. The emancipation of

Woman must come as surely as America will witness the emancipation of the Negro. The lot of Woman enslaved is, in a certain sense, far worse than the lot of Man enslaved. Men have often rebelled with arms against their tyrants, while we, of necessity, must attempt to win our freedom by an appeal to their slumbering sense of justice. It is my privilege to present one of the most able leaders of our Freedom Movement —Amelia Bloomer."

There was a slight uncertain burst of handclapping, —for many of the women present were attending such a meeting for the first time. It was quite different when Amelia Bloomer had concluded her remarks, for then the applause was almost an ovation. She spoke simply of the restraints placed upon woman from ancient days until the present. "The husband could flog his wife by law—and in some lands he had the power of life and death over her. There are peoples today where the woman replaces the ox and plows the field while her husband sits idly by and watches. In our own day and in the modern scene our efforts for freedom are met with ridicule by those whom God created male—or else we are given honeyed phrases to calm our indignation. 'You are the queens of our homes. We hold you upon a pedestal. You are nobler and finer than we.'" Her eyes flashed fire, "Our answer is we do not seek to be your goddesses any more than we will tolerate serfdom at your hands. We demand the equality of standing at your sides in whatever tasks you do—and we will not be denied!"

Although Walt had prepared his lecture word for word, he determined to pursue the theme of Amelia Bloomer's message. He traced the whole story of Woman through the ages—marriage by capture— marriage by purchase—polygamy and concubinage and concluded,

"We see, then, that Woman has constantly aroused in Man a certain ambivalent emotion. On the one hand Mother love and the appeal of her beauty inspired him to an ecstasy of reverence and worship— and on the other hand, desire sated, — he despised her frailer physical power, denied her mental stimulation and kept her from his counsels and his side. The result was that the slave hugged her chains and even now there are women who enjoy their thralldom. They cling to strong Man wistfully—make an ornament of their frailty — diet to the point of famine — faint to arouse pity and assume that a weak woman is the truest representative of her sex, while Man, true to the old savage pattern, calls her his 'star in the sky' before his sex dream disperses and his 'chain' and 'shackle' afterwards. You are quite right. You ask neither their sting nor their honey. You ask for the dignity and freedom which is your right. Go forth, then, each to your desired task—some into medicine, some into law, some into the fields of commerce—if that is your desire, but remember too, once having obtained your freedom, that the sturdy, intelligent, devoted wife and mother has a career as gloriously satisfying as any other."

There was applause—but also the staccato conversation of hostile criticism.

Mrs. Bloomer shook hands with Walt and launched at once into her comments on his speech.

"You seem to imply, Mr. Whitman, that Woman is, in her very nature, weaker than Man —; Man has kept her physically weak by his enslavement."

Walt looked at the rapidly growing circle crowding around them and answered slowly, "I don't see how this has any bearing on her right to freedom, but Woman is obviously less aggressive and at a certain disadvantage in a purely physical sense."

"We deny that!" chorused the group about him. "There are stories of Amazons —"

"Yes," interrupted Walt "stories of Amazons who amputated their right breasts in order to better draw the arrows on their bows. Even in legend your physical limitations are shown."

"Oh—rot!" Fanny Fern's voice drowned out the rest. "Your Slavic peasant woman—your Indian squaw refutes your argument."

Walt looked her straight in the face "Nevertheless it is the man that rapes the woman and not the woman that rapes the man—and in even the more peaceable union it is the man who is the aggressor in the physical act."

Now there was silence—tense and blushing—but silence, and Walt continued quietly.

"You will have to admit that in the ancient wars, even in the days of the cave man, woman was inconvenienced at times by her periods and her pregnancy. It is not expected of a woman seven months pregnant to battle the tiger or lead an attack. Nevertheless Woman has labored in the field and farm with endurance equal and often superior to that of Man. There is no war between the sexes. Man's ignorance has enslaved you and your indolence and inertia have kept you slaves. Man would much rather have a full companion in his great loneliness than a spiritless serf in his dwelling."

Fanny Fern thrust an envelope into his hand. Walt knew it was the fee for the lecture and thanked her as he crushed it hastily into his pocket.

* * * *

Walt brought her a copy of his book. At first she seemed a little annoyed that the cover of his book was so like the cover of her own successful volume entitled "Fern Leaves."

"Imitation is a sincere form of flattery," she remarked coldly.

"I urge you to believe that a printer's material at hand determined the form of the cover."

"And the title? Was that also coincidence?"

"No. I chose the title because my faith is horizontal rather than vertical. A field of grass is more my faith than a tall deep rooted cedar."

"You mean that all of us—the gifted and the lethargic—are alike blades of grass in the meadow of the world. It's a thought. I can't say that I agree with it —but it's a thought—and you're forgiven." She smiled for the first time during the interview.

"I don't know when I'll be able to give your book my complete attention. I'm doing my autobiography in the form of a novel—and thus I'm much absorbed with me — but —"

"It isn't a large book. The pages are few—" Walt wanted desperately a favorable comment from so renowned an author.

"I understand. I'll read it at once—and perhaps speak of it in my column."

Walt arose to go feeling a great gladness in his heart. She stayed him with a gesture.

"You were blunt and outspoken in your lecture last Tuesday—or rather in your remarks after the lecture, yet you didn't say whether or not you approve of free love."

Walt hesitated, torn between a knowledge that she expected him to approve—and the conviction of his own heart.

"No love is free except self love. All others require an investment."

"No epigrams—please."

"Do I approve of promiscuity? Is that what you are asking?"

"I didn't ask you that. Surely it's possible to love more than one person in one's lifetime. If it's all right for the man isn't it equally all right for the woman?"

"I was afraid that there would be many in the new movement that would seek to imitate man's vices instead of his duties —"

"You're begging the question."

"No—on the contrary. If you ask should the women have the freedom to live as they choose, and with whom they choose, whenever they choose, I would answer that there should be no difference in the freedom of man and the freedom of woman, but when you ask if I *approve* of free love —"

"I see I have a Puritan to deal with. I'm afraid I'll find your poems dull,—but,—" Suddenly she extended her hand, "Come to my home this evening. We're having some interesting guests—artists, composers—an intimate group."

Walt, offended, sought escape "I have some writing —"

She shrugged "Some other time then."

Walt left in silence, asking himself bitterly "What do they want?" And by "they" he meant women generally.

* * * *

July fifth—no notice in the Criterion or the Tribune. No review in the Ledger. Nothing by Fanny Fern.

July sixth—still no review. Better drop in at Swayne's. See if any copies have been sold. No copies sold! No notices! No reviews! You've *got* to notice my book!

By heavens—I'll write a review of it myself! Who'll publish it? I'll write it now. I'll tell Fowler it's the review of a literary friend who wishes to remain anonymous.

And Walt wrote, angered by the apathy against which he could not struggle—convinced that the indifference of the reviewers was a conscious common hostile front against him, an attack by silence. He wrote furiously—gritting his teeth.

"An American bard at last! One of the rough, large, proud, affectionate, eating, drinking and breeding, his costume manly and free, his face sunburnt and bearded —"

Walt then described his style and content with equally shrill trumpet blasts. Then he took the review to Fowler.

"A friend of literature and of myself has written an appraisal —"

Fowler read the review, then looked up with an amused twinkle. "A literary friend indeed!"

Walt saw at once that Fowler knew, nor was he abashed. "Very well, Mr. Fowler, I wrote it myself, and I'll keep writing and shouting through the thick smoke in their eyes and the thick wax in their ears. I know it's a good song I sing—yes, more than good—great—the only American voice in a chorus of ancient continental shades, ghosts, echoes and shadows."

"We haven't sold one copy, Mr. Whitman, but your book is nevertheless being discussed by book critics. We passed out five review copies. It is the usual custom. Soon, no doubt, we will hear what they say. In the meantime—no, don't tear it up—we'll print this 'literary friend's' opinion in the Democratic Review. A cousin of our Mr. Wells writes a literary column there. Have no fear! Your anonymity will be respected."

July seventh!—and now the reviews and notices were appearing. The one in the Boston Intelligence was cruel:

"Bombast, egotism, vulgarity and nonsense. The beastliness of the author is set forth in his own description of himself and we can conceive no better reward than the lash for such a violation of decency."

Walt smiled. A reaction anyway.

Here were assorted clippings that Fowler had sent by messenger: —

"A poet whose indecencies stink in the nostrils."

The Christian Examiner wrote—"Impious libidousness."

And this clipping brutal—"Walt Whitman is as unacquainted with art as a hog is with mathematics."

Walt revelled in the attacks. "Let them talk about my book but not ignore it."

I'll walk—towards Swayne's. What's that in the gutter? A white shaking indignation possessed him. *His* book—the pages are stained with sewage and ordure. Let it lie there. You have other copies—other copies. No—pick it up. It is holy. Wipe it off with your kerchief. Can it be that no one understands?

July eighth. Go home and rest, Walt. Maybe tomorrow the reviews will be better. Half sleeping—half working. Morning is a long way off.

"Any mail, Mother? I don't know what happened to me. It must be almost noon."

"The mail is on the window sill."

Yes—the Democratic Review—his own write-up. Yes, there it is—prominent at the top of the column: "Every phrase announces new laws ... You are come in good time, Walt Whitman!"

A moment's glad flame—and then—no joy in that review —

Empty, hollow—a fool's evaluation of his own stupid vaunting self!

Walt, your father is groaning in the next room. The sound tears at your heart. There's nothing you can do, so shut the door and you won't have to listen. Mother is staring at you. What about your Will to Joy now? Is there beauty in groans, Walt? Is there beauty in pain? I don't know—don't know. I don't know anything any more. But somehow it's needed—the pain is needed. A beautiful child is born in pain—and mothers forget the pain and bear again.

Mother—patient, plodding Louisa—She's staring at you across the table—trying to say something to forget the groans—to close her ears to the groans. The groans don't mean anything, Walt. Your father's unconscious; *he* can't feel his pain, but *you* can, Walt— *you* can feel it. No, it's your idea of what he feels that tortures you—you imagine he feels pain—but he doesn't feel pain—doesn't feel pain—doesn't feel pain—therefore, *you* shouldn't feel pain.

"What do they write about your book, son?"

A sound of a heavy body falling—Walt runs to the bedroom, his father's bedroom. All twisted and knotted up in the bedclothes his father is lying off the bed. There is a heavy odor of urine. His father, paralyzed, has emptied his bladder in the moment of his convulsion.

Walt lifts his father's shoulders back on the bed. Inert. Still. Calm. Eyes half open.

"Pa! Pa!"

No pulse beat.

Final—end—that's all—that's all—that's all.

"Pa, you should have waited! You should have waited!"

* * * *

What was it Epictetus had said about death?

"Do not say 'He has been taken from us'—but rather 'He is restored.' See how the black earth opens its arms to receive its own, — and the grass whispers,

'Welcome, brother—Welcome.' " Now the earth holds him completely. Now you can rest.

Walt heard his mother, his brothers and sisters weep—and he grieved for their grief—not for his own.

* * * *

Mr. Swayne puckered his lips, knitted his brows and tried most painfully to be kind. "It's no use, Mr. Whitman. The readers won't have it. Better take back the copies. We have no room to stock them."

Sick at heart, Walt pleaded. "Keep them for a little while longer. The reviews may help the sale."

"Oh, very well—but really it's not much use."

I mustn't think of failure. I mustn't take any books back. Better stay away from the booksellers for a week or two; keep writing; keep pouring it out, Walt—like a mighty roaring stream with waters frothing, seething, boiling—hurling rocks—exploding through cliffs—

> *"O you hastening light! O the sun of the world*
> *will ascend, dazzling, and take his height—and*
> *you too will ascend;*
> *O so amazing and so broad! Up there resplendent,*
> *darting and burning;*
> *O prophetic! O vision staggered with weight of*
> *light; with pouring glories!"*

What am I doing now? Just raving—shouting—screaming. I'll try again—

> *"O sun of real peace! O hastening light!*
> *O free and ecstatic! O what I here, preparing,*
> *warble for!*
> *O the sun of the world will ascend, dazzling, and*
> *take his height—and you too, O my ideal will*
> *surely ascend!"*

No! No! No! Don't take it away from me, God—Thy Holy spirit—the visions that I see, and leave me only sound and fury. I'll try again.

> *"O take my hand Walt Whitman!*

Such gliding wonders! such sights and sounds!
Such join'd unended links, each hook'd to the next,
Each answering all, each sharing the earth with all.
What widens within you Walt Whitman,
What waves and soils exuding?
What climes? what persons and cities are here?
Who are the infants, some playing, some slumber-
*   ing?*
Who are the girls? who are the married women?
Who are the groups of old men going slowly with
*   their arms about each other's necks?*
What rivers are these? what forests and fruits are
*   these?*
What are the mountains call'd that rise so high in
*   the mists?*
What myriads of dwellings are they fill'd with
*   dwellers?"*

Part Five

EVE OF CONFLICT

"Walt, George thinks you can get a job at the Water Works. He'll talk to you if you want him to. You can still lecture, you know. Jeff's been raised a dollar and a half a week."

"All right, Ma. I'll talk to him." Anything—as long as no one disturbed the sick, gray desolation of his thoughts. Come now, Walt, *will* yourself to rejoice! Be true to your song!

"I've been to Pa's grave." Louisa sat stiff and straight, her gnarled hands folded.

Walt murmured softly. "Pa should have waited. I wanted to show him. Pa should have waited."

Eddie's voice came monotonously from the next room. "You great big tree. My father's a carpenter. He'll chop you up and he'll make a chair—a table— a house —"

A strangling cud-like melancholy pressed against Walt's throat and heart. "What have I achieved more than Eddie? He babbles and I babble, and to the world there is little difference. I'm thirty-six years old. Schubert had already completed his work at thirty-one, Chopin at thirty-nine. Why do I have this sense of destiny? No, it's not a mad delusion of grandeur, for if I'm grand then every man on earth is grand. I'd give my heart's blood to prove that every man's the same—leaves of grass making the green meadow of the world. Well, Walt, it's done—the book and you are one. You stand or fall together. Nothing else must distract you. The book is you. You are the book—One —One."

Mother's voice again. Why—why must she keep breaking in!

"You haven't eaten, Walt! And you don't talk like you used to. You don't use the strong words —"

"I'm writing it all down, Ma, and there isn't much time."

"Jeff said the job in the Water Works is still open."

"I'm not taking that job, Ma. I'm writing some more poems."

"But you said —"

"I don't know what I said."

"Did you try on Pa's coat, Walt? If it doesn't fit I'll give it to Jeff."

"My shoulders are too big for it. It doesn't fit. Better give it to Jeff."

"The mail's in, Walt. A post card from Jesse. He's lonely and he can't ever get well, he says. He says, 'Tell Walt to visit me; he'll know what to do.' And there's a letter for you."

Walt regarded the name on the envelope for a long moment before it had any significance for him. "Emerson. R. W. Emerson." Then a sharp stab of joyous eager realization—his nerves afire!—Concord—Concord, Massachusetts! Concord! That's Ralph Waldo Emerson! A letter from Emerson—from Emerson— Emerson! Louisa's question hung lightly in the air. "Emerson—isn't that the minister?"

Walt's fingers were clumsy as he carefully tore the edge of the envelope so as not to injure the contents.

Even before he read the words he sensed their warmth
—that these were good words—praising words:

Concord, Mass., 21st July, 1855

Dear Sir, — I am not blind to the worth of the wonderful gift of "Leaves of Grass." I find it the most
extraordinary piece of wit and wisdom that America
has yet contributed. I am very happy in reading it,
as great power makes us happy. It meets the demand
I am always making of what seems the sterile and
stingy Nature, as if too much handiwork, or too much
lymph in the temperament were making our Western
wits fat and mean. I give you joy of your free and
brave thought. I have great joy in it. I find incomparable things said incomparably well, as they must
be. I find the courage of treatment that so delights us
and which large perception only can inspire.

I greet you at the beginning of a great career,
which yet must have had a long foreground somewhere,
for such a start. I rubbed my eyes a little to see if this
sunbeam were no illusion; but the solid sense of the
book is a sober certainty. It has the best merits, namely,
of fortifying and encouraging.

I did not know, until I last night saw the book
advertised in a newspaper, that I could trust the name
as real and available for a post-office.

I wish to see my benefactor, and have felt much
like striking my tasks and visiting New York to pay
you my respects.   R. W. EMERSON

Walt gave a great shout—a shout of folded lungs
expanding—a triumphant shout at sneering doubts
and haughty jeers turning their backs and fleeing. He
stood like a colossus and roared a sound that had no
words. Then he threw his arms around his mother.

"Ma! Look! The book is good—great. Emerson!

Emerson praises it. There'll be many others now. Listen, Ma, listen to what the great scholar Emerson writes. He's a very great man, Mother—one of the greatest men alive!"

Walt declaimed the letter with booming voice and Louisa listened very much impressed and more than a bit awed.

"He wants to visit me, Ma."

"We could fix up Pa's room for Mr. Emerson. Invite him, Walt, invite him."

"I will. I will. But first let me show this letter where it will do some good."

Walt leaped into battle like a lion. He shook himself like a Samson aroused—and the ropes fell apart. Now let the Phillistines come! He had the shot and the shell now. Swayne's first. No, first a contact with a periodical. He needed a job—cash, and at once. If he could sell a few poems to the Home Journal— perhaps even contribute regularly. Willis was the man to see—Nathaniel Parker Willis—Fanny Fern's brother. He could use her name and Emerson's letter—

"Mr. Willis is in Boston. He will return next Friday. Would you care to see his assistant, Mr. James Parton?"

"I would."

"I'll announce you," then after a pause—"you may go in."

Behind the desk Parton, in his shirt sleeves, was pasting a layout. "Damn it, a man's got to do everything himself. Cut, paste —! I'll be mopping the floor next. Go ahead. Talk to me while I'm working." He glanced up quickly at Walt and then back at the layout. "Whitman — Whitman. Didn't you write some verses recently? Haven't had a chance to look them over—but my fiancee finds them interesting. What can I do for you, Mr. Whitman?"

Walt began resolutely. "I've just received a letter from Emerson—praising my verses. Perhaps a column or a regular contribution in your Journal—"

"Our customers haven't Emerson's taste—unfortunately. We're dealing with the masses and their literary pabulum must be judiciously synthesized. My fiancee's success is due to her instinctive knowledge of what people want—the smile—the tear—the moral and the happy or heart rending ending."

"Your fiancee?"

"Fanny Fern is her pen name. I'm engaged to marry Sara Willis. You've read her work I'm sure."

"I've met her."

"Yes—so she said. A Women's Rights meeting—wasn't it?"

Walt nodded and waited for Parton to continue. Parton looked extremely youthful — twenty-eight or twenty-nine at the most, and Fanny Fern was a matron of forty.

"Tell you what I'll do. Submit a few of your verses and if we can use them from time to time we'll pay you five cents a word."

Walt had a vision of drops of blood being weighed in a balance—to be bought at so much per drop.

"If we can't use them, we'll tell you so."

Walt's need was immediate. "How soon will I hear from you?"

"Damn it man—how can I tell? If it's an advance you want—ask the girl for fifty or seventy-five." "Alice!" he called abruptly, through the half-closed door. "Make out a receipt for Mr. Whitman in the sum of seventy-five dollars. The name is Walt Whitman." He stretched out his hand. "You'll be hearing from me."

The seventy-five dollars would not be touched. Let the debts pile up. This was for New Orleans. A little while and he would come to her. Anne—by this time wounds have healed. Now you see how simple it all is. This concerns you and me and no one else. We are already one; there is nothing to decide; nothing to discuss.

* * * *

Carry me, O heart. Push open that door. Firm, proud footsteps. You're asking no favors now. Calm now. Matter of fact. That's it.

"Good morning, Mr. Swayne. Yes, I know you're busy. My friend, Ralph Waldo Emerson, may visit me shortly. Yes, I said 'my friend.' I thought you would care to meet him. A great scholar—quite right —indeed he is. Yes, I received a letter from him only this morning. Oh yes, he wrote me. Let me see now —where did I put it? Oh, here it is. Yes, of course. There's nothing too personal. By all means go ahead. Read it."

Mr. Swayne's eyebrows raised themselves ever so gradually until they almost met his scalpline. "Very, very fine comment, Mr. Whitman. This letter—may I show it to some friends? There have been several inquiries about your book. Perhaps you had better let us have some copies."

"I'll leave the letter with you when I bring the books tomorrow."

Without looking backward Walt knew that the book clerks were gathered around Swayne. He could hear the hushed whispers and Swayne's now altered verdict.

"Remarkable style. I quite agree with Emerson. That is why I accepted the book at once for display."

Walt did not gloat. He turned at the door, nodded and left at once for the establishment of Fowler and Wells, where the letter created something of a sensation.

"This could mean a lot, Mr. Whitman." Fowler tapped his glasses against the letter. "It's most important. This could mean world fame for your book. Ah, that's the answer—a second edition with this comment on the cover. Here is something else that will please you, considering that this lady gets one hundred dollars a column for her writing."

Fowler handed Walt a galley proof. "Fanny Fern sent this to me. She wants me to show it to you before it appears in the Ledger."

Walt read, and once again the fullness of joy exploded in his heart and crashed against the walls of his body like waves of mighty music. "Thou hast turned my mourning into dancing," one frolicking segment of his brain kept singing as he read. Praise! Praise! Approval! He had always craved approval—longed for it as a child longs for it. Even when his stern father had smiled once as he swung an axe with tiny hands and split the wood—there was a glowing heart-warming blessing in that smile. Naked and empty would be his heaven with no loving God there to approve, "Well done! Well done!" And man's approval too!

What had cheered him in the lonely hours? The thought of future recognition. How dependent he was on his fellows. He wanted people—all people to like him—to like him. Come, friends, pierce the walls of my loneliness. Say to me, "We understand and love you, Walt." Now everything is radiant. Everything is good.

A column in the Ledger—and about you! And here's a sketch by Fanny Fern—brief but good.

What does she say? What does Fanny Fern say about my songs? "Well baptized; fresh, hardy, and grown for the masses—'Leaves of Grass' thou art unspeakably delicious —"

There was a shadow in the room. Walt sensed an interloper.

"The lady seems interested." Wells, who had approached to listen, thrust his bald pate forward and leered into Walt's face. "She is overwhelmed—swept away by your exuberant masculinity."

"An understatement, Mr. Wells," Walt replied calmly, and then his mind and heart flashed back to Anne Sedley. He had written her constantly but had heard from her rarely. He had sent her fragments of verse, strong verse, verses like these. He must get those verses back! Some of them could be included in the second edition.

How could he tactfully request the return of those verses. He must explain his need. The Book is everything! Anne should be pleased. Now—now there was nothing that could stop the surging of his mighty torrent. He would pour himself out to a world alertly attentive at last! But first he must get those verses from Anne. They must not sing to her alone; they belonged to the world.

Dear Anne: The painful years have ripened and brought forth fruits of joy. Read the enclosed comments and share with me their flavor. If these lines seem to you self-centered, reflect that the memory of a lover's caress is far from the thoughts of a woman in labor. So must my thoughts center on the child I bear from my soul's womb. Under separate cover I am sending you "Leaves of Grass." Some of your sunlight helped them grow.

I have no copies of many of the verses I sent you.

They are desperately needed for my next edition. Could you gather them and send them to me?

Is your mother well? Please write me at length.

Best love,
WALT.

Early in September Walt received in a neatly wrapped package all of the letters and all of the verse he had sent her. There was a note—a puzzling, torturing note that accompanied them.

Dearest Walt: You are wrong. A woman in labor *does* think of her lover, sometimes to curse him when the pain is great and sometimes to take strength from his presence.

You were not here, so you could not know—and it is best that way. The letters and the verses are yours to do with as you will, but listen to me, Walt—songs like yours are a thousand years ahead of people—or maybe a million years.

You have two children, Walt—your book and your son, and both are twins—conceived alike in love and truth. Your book when born was disdained, but, when a little grown, finds favor.

Your son, now small, is smiled at—fondled—but then a few more years and he will feel the bonds, the downward look, and all your singing cannot change it till twice ten thousand years or more have passed.

You tremble. You did not know. You would rush to my side. And would my kiss or your son's wistful prattling sweep away what's real? Don't come, Walt. Don't even write!

Mother is well. ANNE.

Hannah! The Fortune Teller—so there was something behind the jabber-jabber! Tea leaves—darkness —black magic—

Walt, try to face it! You have a son. Anne has borne
you a son! There must be a right and a wrong for
every problem. You have a son. Anne has borne you
a son. Out of her honest love she has borne you a son.
No other man ever caressed her. No other man ever
knew her. "Do not fear me for my skin is darkened
by the sun—yet I am lovely." The southern sun tints
the skin and ripens it but men don't understand. You'll
teach them, Walt. How? By bringing Anne to you.
And if you did? Would Emerson or Mrs. Emerson
greet Anne with natural hospitality—or Fowler—or
Louisa or George—or Jeff? Oh sweet mouthings of
"God's children all"—oh honeyed hymns of "brotherhood of man"—the discreet belchings of man's Sunday
breakfast troubled by a conscience.

My son. Is his skin dark as ebon or is it like Anne's
—almost white?

I'll answer her tomorrow. Things will change. Circumstances may alter.

But Walt did not answer her—not "tomorrow" nor
the morrow after that. He would go to New Orleans
when the new edition was complete. He would see
his son. He would see his son—his son—his son. But
first finish the book. It must be mighty—perfect—
complete!

II

He worked furiously, begrudging himself moments
of rest and sleep.

"You've set that poem fifty times," commented
Andrew Rome drily.

"And it isn't right yet." Walt looked at the galley
proof with an impatient expression. He repeated over
and over again—

"Demon or bird!

Is it indeed toward your mate you sing?
Or is it really to me?"

"Bird or demon!" sounded a deep rumbling voice close at hand. Walt was startled and, for a moment, resentful of the interruption. He turned slowly around. The man who faced him held out his hand stiffly. He looked like a New England farmer, hardy, stern and weather toughened. His beard, unlike Walt's, was but a thin fringe that framed strong features.

"I've come a long way to meet you, Mr. Whitman. My name is Henry Thoreau."

There was a tense peculiar pause as they explored each other. Thoreau — Emerson's friend — Thoreau. Walt slowly grasped the outstretched hand. "I'm honored, Mr. Thoreau, deeply honored."

"Won't you be as candid and honest as are your songs and admit that, at the moment, I disturb you?"

"I'm proud and happy that you came. Mr. Thoreau, you're coming to my home for tea and cakes. This shall be a holiday."

"May I glance at those proofs?"

"By all means."

Walt felt intoxicated, elated. Henry Walden Thoreau, the famed hermit of Walden Pond—the man who lived within himself—had come on a pilgrimage to *him!*

"Emerson planned to accompany me but a siege of illness altered his plans. I do not easily alter mine." He lifted his intent eyes from the proofs. "Come, let us walk. Tell me of your songs."

Walt opened the door for Thoreau. They both walked rapidly with long strides, talking all the while. It was Thoreau who spoke for the most part.

"It is unusual for me to pay visits. The best part of a man is in his thoughts—his book. As for the rest —his limbs, parts, organs and habits, they differ but slightly from the beasts of the field—and, may I add, to his disadvantage."

"Then why, may I ask, did you honor me with this visit? You have my book."

Thoreau smiled. "Egotism—the delusion of grandeur. I said to myself, 'Who is this Walt Whitman that sings as eloquently of the virtues of men as I speak of their follies. Let me see if his body, carriage, demeanor, garments and life comport with his song as mine do with my speech.' You don't mind my studying you and making a few observations?"

Walt did not answer.

"Don't be offended, Mr. Whitman. We are very much alike except that you see men as they should be and I, alas, I see them as they are."

"Now as to your songs—you have consciousness or awareness of your powers," and Thoreau began to quote from the verse he had glanced at.

Demon or bird! (said the boy's soul),

Is it indeed toward your mate you sing? or is it really to me?

For I, that was a child, my tongue's use sleeping, now I have heard you,

Now in a moment I know what I am for, I awake,

And already a thousand singers, a thousand songs, clearer, louder and more sorrowful than yours,

A thousand warbling echoes have started to life within me, never to die.

"You know your power of expression and proclaim it with blaring trumpets. It might, however, seem a bit immodest to project yourself rather than your thoughts."

Walt answered quickly. "I do not believe in false modesty. The ego is as much a part of every living thing as its cells are. I won't put pantaloons on it, as though in people's eyes it were a thing of shame I covered."

"As long as you are on that subject, Mr. Whitman, may I observe that your poetry displays a very noticeable lack of trousers. Is that candor really necessary?"

"That to me is the holiest of holies, Mr. Thoreau."

"Lack of trousers?"

Both men laughed. Walt continued earnestly. "Once man has learned complete honesty with himself he will understand his brother. A woman has legs, Mr. Thoreau, not limbs. She has breasts and a womb, just as a man has a penis and testicles and not 'organs of sex.' You wince, Mr. Thoreau, but what is there to blush about? Did God create only what is above the navel and the devil finish the rest?"

"But this is bound to shock—and the real beauty of your verse will suffer."

"That is the real beauty of my verse—its truth."

"The ministers of the gospel and the priests of the church will anathematize you."

"Can they blaspheme truth? Then let them begin with the 'Song of Songs.' Let them proscribe the Bible."

Thoreau laughed. "There is a spiritual significance to the 'Song of Songs' in their eyes—the Church as the bride of Christ."

"And I ask, what do they mean by spiritual? The body is as spiritual as the soul. The hungry stomach aches for real bread. The hungry lover longs for his love's real caress. The tired body needs a real bed, not words."

"Your conversation takes poetic patterns."

"I can't help it. The truth is so simple and men befoul it with dainty lying words because they will not face it. But this is my home, Mr. Thoreau, and you are most welcome."

Louisa was making cupcakes and the warm sweet

aroma filled the room like incense. Thoreau seemed truly glad he had come.

"You may believe me, Mrs. Whitman, that this is the longest pilgrimage I have yet made. The woods near Concord are my world, and I know every tree, every boulder, every hawk's or squirrel's nest for twenty miles around."

"Don't you get lonesome?"

"For what? For people who are more or less my own image? Here I've travelled all these miles and found that your son and I are very much alike."

"But don't you find people more interesting than animals?" Mary Elizabeth fingered her apron shyly as she almost whispered the question.

"No!" Thoreau's eyes lost their smile and chilled.

"You sound as though you've been hurt, Mr. Thoreau." Louisa's voice was soothing. "Mary Elizabeth was just making conversation."

"I apologize, my dear, if I frightened you. I'm so much with animals that I growl and bark. Am I forgiven? Please join us here at the table."

Mary Elizabeth eagerly pulled up a chair and sat with an air of veneration that warmed Thoreau's heart and thawed his conversation.

"You asked if I was hurt, Mrs. Whitman. No one can hurt me. I've learned from the boulders how to be hard and from the oak trees how to sink my roots deep into the earth rather than in the shallow surface of men's affections."

"That proves you've been hurt at one time or another."

Thoreau smiled at Louisa. "That's what my sister Sophia keeps telling me, but no one has hurt me since childhood—and children are very sensitive."

Walt leaned forward, pouring the tea into Thoreau's emptied cup. "Tell us of your childhood."

"I remember best the poverty—I felt poor where now, possessing even less of material goods, I feel immensely rich. My sled had no iron runners like those of the neighborhood boys. And they laughed at my sled and said 'It isn't worth a cent.' Such trivial things one remembers."

And then Thoreau spoke of the beauty of the forest —of the habits of the wild things—of Walden Pond— of surveying—gardening—carpentry—of the wealth he owned as the gift of Nature—and suddenly he was gone, after thanking them for their welcome.

Mary Elizabeth said, "I think he's still hurt about that sled." Then she added "There's a letter for you."

Walt saw the name Home Journal on the envelope and experienced a sinking of the heart as he remembered that he had submitted no verses to Parton. He read the formal note with fury at his own forgetfulness. Dear Mr. Whitman:

Having failed to receive your literary contributions within a reasonable time, we must ask you to return the loan or advance in the sum of seventy-five dollars granted you some time ago.

Trusting that this will have your prompt attention, we are

> Very truly yours,
> HOME JOURNAL,
> ALICE CARTER,
> *Secretary.*

Walt hastily gathered four poems that he had not included in "Leaves of Grass" and mailed them to the Home Journal—"Attention Mr. James Parton."

He received them back three days later exactly as he had sent them with no note nor comment.

However, Walt felt no dismay. His star was ascending.

Thoreau's visit was but the herald of the parade
of the famed and the celebrated who in the weeks that
followed came to pay their respects. John Burroughs,
the young naturalist, eager, enthusiastic, paid frequent
visits to his home. Then came Moncure Daniel Conway, to whom Emerson had said of Whitman, "Americans abroad may now come home, for unto us a man
is born." Conway called his coming "a pilgrimage."

Then came William Cullen Bryant, whom he had
met once long before, and A. Bronson Alcott, who was
Emerson's dear friend.

"We have truly arrived, Ma. Your eyes have seen
it." Walt's arms went softly around his mother. He
watched Bryant and Alcott depart together. "Don't
you see, Ma, it took them a little while, but now they
understand!"

Yet the next morning, when Walt spoke to Fowler,
his high spirits were abruptly cooled.

"How are they going, Mr. Fowler?"

"Two copies sold—and yet everyone is discussing
the book here in New York. Walt, there's your pattern
of man's opinions. One bellowing ram and a million
lamby 'amens'! They haven't even seen the book and
yet they debate it."

Walt's face was grim. "It will help, I suppose, if
we print Emerson's letter."

"I thought so too at first, but, on reflection, that
letter was personal to you."

"Nothing is personal to me. My book and I are
one."

"Come now, Walt. You may offend a great and
good man."

"I'll risk it. You've assured me that you'll publish
the second edition. Very well. Right on the cover we'll
use the sentence from his letter—'I greet you at the
beginning of a great career. R. W. Emerson.' "

Fowler shook his head. Walt plunged on. "I'm going to answer him publicly. In this second edition we'll print an appendix, and there, with the favorable press notices, we'll print Emerson's entire letter and my reply. Here, let me show you what my answer will be."

He took a piece of wrapping paper and began to write rapidly:

"Thank you, dear Master, for your praise. My first edition of a thousand copies readily sold. I much enjoy making poems. Other work I have set for myself to do, to meet people and the States face to face, to confront them with an American-made tongue; but the work of my life is making poems. I keep on till I make a hundred, and then several hundred—perhaps a thousand. The way is clear to me. A few years, and the average annual call for my poem is ten or twenty thousand copies—more, quite likely. Why should I hurry or compromise? In poems or in speeches I say the word or two that has got to be said, adhere to the body, step with the countless common footsteps, and remind every man or woman of something.

Master, I am a man who has perfect faith. Master, we have not come through centuries, caste, heroisms, fables, to halt in this land today."

Fowler looked from the letter to the enkindled face of the writer. "For one whom I believed to be a truthful man this is an egregious falsehood—'one thousand copies sold.'"

"It will be so. You will see."

Fowler smiled. "As a prophecy I can perhaps accept it—especially since you have Emerson's endorsement."

Fowler read on. "Not one solitary dram of modesty," he wondered audibly.

Walt's reply was deliberate. "Modesty is as much

a lie as pride. There's no room for it in me; my song takes up all the space."

Walt haunted Fowler in the days that followed.

"How many books? How many sold?"

Walt was convinced that the world must be shocked out of its lethargy and brought violently face to face with this book. He would not be dissuaded.

Fowler shook his head and clicked his tongue as he watched Walt's frantic attempts to publicize his songs. "It's indecent, Mr. Whitman."

"The contents?"

"No, the method! You're forcing the book on the public!"

"It's a sick public and it needs my medicine!"

The second edition was ready by June, and Fowler and Wells waited with trepidation for the reviews. They came smoldering in angry attacks, coarse abuse, threats of prosecution!

Walt was outwardly calm—inwardly exultant. Fowler was frankly worried. "Don't press for more publicity. We've kept our promise. Now let's wait and see what happens. Surely the book can walk on its own legs from this point on."

"Whether it can or not we've got to break through their stupid sanctimonious Jericho walls. Let trumpets blow! We'll make a breach. I'll write some more reviews anonymously. Let's din it in their ears. Let them damn it but read it. Let them stone Moses but be redeemed from slavery!"

"Is there no limit to your vanity? Now you are Moses!"

"It was a figure of speech, I assure you."

"My literary Spartacus. Why not take a trip to New Orleans if you're determined on an emancipator's role and a martyr's death."

"It's the whites I'm trying to free, Mr. Fowler.

They're chained much more than the Negroes—and what's more tragic, they love their chains."

"Those are powerful ideas, Mr. Whitman, but your book isn't selling and your ideas are strangling on my shelves."

Walt did not answer. He picked up the carpet bag that held a few copies of his beloved book and began the long walk home.

III

The newsboys were shouting their wares of the moment's novelty with more gusto than ordinarily. "Fremont for President! Republicans name Fremont!"

Walt was in a rebellious mood. "My book is greater news!" It was a release from his own bitterness that he sought, and then as he grew calmer, "Fremont's a man, at least, but whom do the Democrats name—moth-eaten anaemic politicians like Buchanan and Fillmore. Is America grown so stupid and apathetic that it no longer cares who represents its forward course?"

Walt felt a spiritual kinship to Fremont. The intrepid trail blazer who had won California for the United States had captured the imagination of the nation. But as Whitman mused upon Fremont's chances for victory he remembered what had happened to General Scott. He had learned that political skill and careful organization far out-weigh the appeal of personality. But what a personality John Charles Fremont was!

"He is the very spirit of my song! He stands squarely for freedom!" Here was a man who could conceivably lead the mighty cause—anti-slavery—to victory, for Fremont was a magic name across the nation.

His pioneering expeditions westward through unexplored wastelands, his explorations and mappings in the face of incredible hardships, his crossing over the Sierras by paths unknown even to the Indians—all these things and more had woven an epic that stirred hearts through the length and breadth of the land.

"Walt, there's your man and your message!"

Neither Fremont's court martial nor his resignation from the Army had weakened his hold on the hearts of the people. Almost every newspaper in the land had championed his cause. And then when gold had been discovered on his desolate stretch of land, no hero in all the stories of romance and chivalry appeared so resplendant in the press of the land. John Charles Fremont, pioneer, explorer, soldier, millionaire senator from California had first been offered the nomination of the Democratic party.

"I shall not sanction the introduction of slavery into the territories," was his reply, "nor shall I endorse the Fugitive Slave Law."

Walt sought out Judge Johnson and found him in the office of the Freeman with two of his precinct lieutenants. The bottle on the desk was almost empty and the Judge kept banging the littered desk with his hand and saying nothing. He looked at Walt as though not recognizing him, then he waved a heavy hand in the direction of his helpers.

"That's what I told them, Walt. The Freeman stands for Free Soil, but you can't switch parties. We're a democratic paper."

"Why wasn't Fremont *your* candidate, then?"

"He's a Catholic. A Catholic can't win. You gotta be practical. Want your old job back, Walt? You can have it. I've got a lot of stuff here—a lot of stuff on Fremont. He's an embezzler, that's what he is! What's the Republican party? A young pup that hasn't even been housebroken yet. No organization! Haven't got a chance!"

"Most of the Free Soilers are going over to the Republican party. Why don't you?"

One of the precinct captains ground his cigar against the sole of his shoe disgustedly. "That's what we've been telling him, but talk to him and talk to the wall."

The Judge rose unsteadily to his feet. "I've been a Democrat all my life. A man's got to be loyal to something. Clear out, all of you. What the hell are you wasting my time for? Talk! Talk! Talk! Jabber! Jabber! Jabber! Why aren't you out working your precincts? Footwork—knocking on doors—that's the way to win an election. Frenchy Fremont—hero in spangles—who the hell does he think he is?"

Walt left at once. He heard the annoyed bellowing of the Judge even after he reached the street. He filled his lungs with clean cool air and walked rapidly homeward.

He must strike a blow for Fremont—especially if the attack was to be one of slander. Fremont had made his position on slavery clear. The issue was there!

No wonder that Emerson and Whittier had thrown their eloquence eagerly into his cause. The newly organized Republican party had nominated him with the slogan of "Free Speech, Free Press, Free Soil, Free Men, Fremont and Victory" and the whole nation shook with wave upon wave of wild unbounded enthusiasm and clamor for "the colonel," as he was affectionately called.

Walt, too, found himself thinking in ringing, declamatory phrases—seething with them. He quickened his step. Louisa greeted him at the door.

"Son, Mr. Thoreau was here again. He said Mr. Emerson is coming to see you in a few days."

"Emerson—coming here." A sudden pulse singing, dizzying swoop to the skies. Walt stooped and kissed his mother. "Thank you, Ma. I've got a lot of writing to do—a lot of writing that I'll want to show Mr. Emerson when he comes."

But first on the Fremont issue. For a brief moment he would put his Messiah's trumpet, "Leaves of Grass," aside and lay about him with a flaming sword where men would *have* to listen, for this blow was to be struck in the arena of their immediate hates and prejudices.

"Have done with lies. Why speak of political parties ? There are no differences between parties. Each is a selfish gang of office seekers. No, there are no differences between parties, so elect a *man*—a *man* regardless of party."

He wrote, "Dough-faces, hypocrites, ward heelers —a plague upon them all! I wasn't born a Democrat— I was born an American—and as an American I shall speak!"

No, this would not do. Too much fire and no wood. Prometheus without light. Set forth your ideas logically and coherently; put them down in even prose.

And so Walt wrote, pausing to gasp for breath, so swiftly did the thoughts and the ink flow. First a general survey of corrupt politics and then to the particular:

"Whence the delegates of the politicians? Whence the Buchanan and Fillmore Conventions? Not from sturdy American freemen; not from industrious homes; not from thrifty farms; not from the ranks of fresh-bodied young men; not from among teachers, poets, savants, learned persons, beloved persons, temperate persons; not from among ship-builders, engineers, agriculturists, scythe-swingers, corn-hoers; not from the race of mechanics; not from that great strong stock of

Southerns that supplied the land in old times; not from
the real West, the log-hut, the clearing, the woods,
the prairie, the hill-side; not from the sensible, generous, rude California miners; not from the best speci-
mens of Massachusetts, Maine, New Jersey, Pennsylvania, Ohio, Illinois, Wisconsin, Indiana, nor from the
untainted unpolitical citizens of these cities."

Walt paused to read what he had written.

"Generalities! Emotion! So what? I'm not a dried
up lawyer; I'm a poet and I'll write as I feel!"

He plunged his pen into the ink.

"Stript of padding and paint, who are Buchanan
and Fillmore? What has this age to do with them?
Two galvanized old men, close on the summons to depart this life, their early contemporaries long since
gone, only they two left, relics and proofs of the little
political bargains, chances, combinations, resentments
of a past age, having nothing in common with this age,
standing for the first crop of political graves and gravestones planted in These States, but in no sort standing
for the lusty young growth of the modern times of
The States. It is clear from all these two men say and
do, that their hearts have not been touched in the
least by the flowing fire of the humanitarianism of the
new world, its best glory yet, and a moral control
stronger than all its governments."

Again Walt hesitated,

"What am I saying? What facts am I giving?
Never mind, I'll pour myself out."

He plunged on.

"It is clear that neither of these nominees of the
politicians has thus far reached an inkling of the real
scope and character of the contest of the day, prob-
ably now only well begun, to stretch through years,
with varied temporary successes and reverses. Still the
two old men live in respectable little spots, with re-

spectable little wants. Still their eyes stop at the edges of the tables of committees and cabinets, beholding not the great round world beyond. What has this age to do with them?"

Walt sought the telling phrase — the powerful image.

"A pretty time for two dead corpses to go walking up and down the earth, to guide by feebleness and ashes a proud, young, friendly, fresh, heroic nation of thirty millions of live and electric men!"

Let it be a pamphlet—let it be an article in the press—let it be anything—but let it be read! He had scrawled at the top of the first page "The Eighteenth Presidency." That would be title enough.

The knock at the door aroused Walt from his furious writing. Walt looked inquiringly at the somber mustached face of the process server.

"Are you Walt Whitman?"

Walt nodded.

"I'm sorry, sir, but I must leave this with you." He handed Walt a legal summons, turned on his heel and left.

All of a sudden, Walt felt cold and oppressed! A law suit! A trial! He stared at the title of the case. "James Parton vs. Walter Whitman." He unfolded the summons and read the ad damnum,—"In the sum of one hundred dollars." He supposed that included court costs and interest.

"Monday morning at 9:30 A.M." Yes he would be there. He did not need an attorney. He would plead his own case. Why be alarmed? This was no criminal charge. He was being sued for money. He had a valid defense. There was no fine or prison involved. Why be disturbed? Yet the day and the hour named in the summons hung over his head like the sword of Damocles.

Forget it! Sufficient to the day is the evil thereof. So Walt worked on his political article—striking out a phrase here and there and inserting a more valid one.

It was late afternoon when Walt was done with it. He rolled it up and carried it eagerly to Pfaff's where he knew there would be plenty of listeners. Right now he needed approval—approval that he could see and hear.

IV

Charles Pfaff, almost spherically round and jovial, was polishing the mirror in back of the bar. His beer cellar on Broadway near Bleecker was the Mermaid Tavern of the Johnsons, Beaumonts and Fletchers of New York. Under the very sidewalk of Broadway it nestled impudently, blissfully, cozy, snug and alive with jest and song.

It was still early for customers but there were ten or twelve frequenters near the bar, and Clapp—bland, dapper, the always clever and sometimes insolent Henry Clapp—was already at his table in the corner reserved for the celebrities. There was a dark-haired strikingly beautiful woman with him. Clapp had been working on his column for the Saturday Press as Walt approached and gave him a brief glance as he continued with his notes.

"Walt, you're early. Talk to Miss Claire for a while, will you? I've got to finish this column." Without looking up he introduced them. "Ada, this is Walt Whitman."

The woman nodded. Walt looked down at the soft petting dark eyes and fresh-cheeked beauty of Clapp's companion. "You are very beautiful," he said evenly.

"An auspicious beginning," remarked Clapp, drily, without looking in their direction.

The woman laughed as a child laughs, and her

mild knowing eyes narrowed and sparkled. "And you're a handsome man. Now what will you make of that, Mr. Clapp?"

"The beginning of a beautiful amour."

"Come now, Henry, you're embarrassing Mr. Whitman."

Clapp pushed back his chair and laughed. "Dear girl, you couldn't embarrass Walt Whitman if you burnt every fig leaf on the planet. He just doesn't embarrass."

"How delightfully interesting—and almost a challenge."

"To burn your fig leaves?" Walt, who had been listening patiently, sank down on a chair that seemed almost too frail to support his weight. He looked at Ada Claire with so artless an expression that she colored.

"Your glance is too candid, Mr. Whitman. You seem to be looking right through my garments."

Walt looked straight into her eyes. "I am, but what should embarrass you in that? You were discussing fig leaves. My next thought followed logically."

"Really, Mr. Whitman—"

"Yes?"

"There are some things that are private, you know." Coyness did not become her, yet she affected the reaction. Whitman remembered Blake the Bookseller saying something very similar to this with regard to his frankness in "Leaves of Grass."

"Why so?"

"Because everyone understands they're not to be discussed."

"Why not?" Then he noticed the crucifix about her neck and asked, "Do you believe that God is all Good?"

"Yes —"

"And there is no evil in Him?"

"No."

"Then all that He created must be good. Why should man arbitrarily decide that the navel is less perfect than the dimple? A navel, after all, is that point at which life was fed you as through the stem of an apple. Is the stem of an apple to be covered up?"

"Shall we change the subject?"

"As you wish."

She pointed to the rolled sheaf of papers. "Is that one of your songs?"

"No, it's a view on politics—or rather—yes, it *is* one of my songs."

"May I?"

Walt nodded.

She read blithely aloud, skipping from page to page as a stone skips over the water. Clapp had interrupted his writing to listen. "Fremont can't win," he announced decisively in the midst of Ada's declamation.

"What makes you so certain?" Walt was the questioner.

"I've smelled the venom in the witch's brew they're preparing, and what a slimy pudding it is!"

"What specifically?"

"That he's a swindler, an embezzler of public funds, that he's Catholic, anti-Catholic, a drunkard and a bastard. A smear campaign. What effect can your fine general phrases have against an attack like that? Besides, it takes money to run a campaign, — money and organization. The Republicans are a new party. The Democrats are rooted in every village and township. They're already clamoring that if Fremont wins it means secession and disunion. Those are powerful weapons, my Olympian bard, — and your thunderbolts are squibs."

"What's wrong with this article, Henry? I think it

reads very well." Ada was obviously sincere and Walt was grateful.

Clapp shook his head. "I can't put my finger on it, but it lacks something; it lacks a detailed, methodical, logical array of facts. Walt, you're too much the impatient prophet and too little the careful architect."

"What are you trying to achieve with this, Mr. Whitman?" Ada's eyes were serious now.

"This is only part of it. I'd like to sweep away all the sick thoughts, all the corroded and festering dogmas, all the attic trash of creeds, rituals, superstitions, fears, prejudices, hates that infect and envenom America —"

"Whoa, there—all that with one article?" Clapp laughed. "The new Messiah—preaching what?"

"That's just it. Preaching the Messianic Age when there will be no Messiahs, or when each man will be his own Messiah, preaching the religion of America— the seeking of Truth. The world is swarming with saviours, each trying to shove his unique brand of salvation down the throats of babies before they can yell their folded lungs into normal functioning."

"And you're another!"

"No, I'm a poet—a doctor for sick souls."

"And you offer them what?"

"Clean, eager minds — free healthy bodies — a boundless sky for growth."

"That's all?"

"Yes, that's all, but it's a bigger all than anyone has ever offered them before."

"What about God?"

"He's self-evident."

"In what?"

"In all things and in all processes."

"I want to know more about Him, O prophet!"

"Ask Thoreau and Emerson."

"They haven't an answer—at least no answer for me."

"Then whom will you ask? Has the priest beheld His face? Has the puritan minister smelled the sulphur of the Hell's fire he preaches? To paraphrase Archimedes—if I had a broom big enough I'd sweep all the images, idols, hackneyed prayers, Sunday morning manners off the earth and leave the universe clean and sweet again."

"You'd be sweeping earth's saving graces away."

"There's too much pageantry and cant—too little soul."

"Ceremonials instruct."

"They become idols in themselves."

"That's your Quaker training."

"I'm not a Quaker—although their views are in my blood."

"What are you?"

"I'm a plain freedom-loving man—that's all the definition I want."

Ada Claire smiled a strange intimate mischievous smile that warmed Walt's blood. "And it's all the definition *I* want." She glanced at a small mirror in her hand. "Henry, I'll leave you with your friend. Bring him tomorrow evening if he cares to come. You *will* care to come, won't you Mr. Whitman?"

Clapp, his moon face ruddy, arose courteously as Ada prepared to leave. He helped her on with a neatly tailored coat and watched her step quickly and assuredly past the curious and admiring men at the bar to the stairway beyond. Walt remained seated, pleased yet sweetly troubled by the Mona Lisa smile and the ambiguous invitation. His eyes followed her until he heard Clapp chuckle. Then he asked, "Just who is Miss Claire?"

Clapp puckered his lips tightly as though reluctant

to speak. Then in the matter-of-fact tone of one who relates statistics, "She writes rather well—a pagan, lusty and sensual, but pretty, as you see, and as determined as a cobra. She's the mother of a four year old son."

"Did you say *Miss* Claire?"

"Yes, quite distinctly."

"I see —"

"No, you don't Walt. You neigh like a lusty stallion in the mating season, yet you're as shy and naive as a debutante. Your pen soars on mighty wings but you can't keep up with it—or are afraid to—Galahad in Sir Lancelot's armor—too pure for Guinevere."

Walt winced. Was this the echo of Anne Sedley? Was he being charged with inconsistency as between word and deed?

Clapp quoted loudly, " 'I turn the bridegroom out of her bed and stay with the bride myself. I tighten her all night to my thighs and lips.' "

Walt frowned. "Not in the way you mean, Henry. I meant that I am he—I see myself in all men."

"How fortunate! Your verses should have a commentary. In that case you'll not be envious of Ada's present lover—Pierre Poncelle." Clapp laughed. "You'll see yourself embracing her—and that will be sufficient for your pleasure. Sing on, O poet, of vicarious joys. Nor dip your tootsie in the cold, cold sea."

"Maybe you don't understand the purpose of my verse, Henry?"

"Oh, has your verse a purpose? I had thought of it as an explosive hysteria brought about by a plethora of verbosity—a game in which you coin new phrases because you're fed up on platitudes—a gymnastic exercise with words as acrobats; but I hadn't considered the possibility of a purpose in your madness."

"Clapp, have you any other reaction to the world than mockery?"

"Yes—disgust. And you —?"

"Wonder."

Clapp looked at him with interest, sucking in his lips so that his round face became broader than long.

"Walt, you actually believe the junk you write! You're an infant—a bearded infant. Get that look of awe out of your eyes. It's a stinking scummy world. Grow up, my friend."

"Until I reach your height, Henry?"

Clapp paled. "You can be nasty too." Then abruptly, "You said you had a purpose."

Walt did not answer but stared at Clapp oddly. He was thinking, "Are men really alike? Is there really anything in common between Clapp and me?"

"I should like to see Miss Claire again." Walt spoke as though he were expressing a casual wish in the privacy of his own room.

Clapp winked. "All right, Walt. Tomorrow evening at nine. Pick me up at my office and we'll take a coach from there."

V

Ada Claire's ivory pink-tinted apartment was spacious and luxurious. Its alert mistress was a most eager and gracious hostess and twittered about charmingly from guest to guest. Walt found himself conversing with an earnest youth whose restless eyes roved constantly to glance about him as he spoke. Thomas Bailey Aldrich was his name, and he hovered broodingly over a glass of sauterne as though he hated it and only politeness compelled him to sip. The conversation skipped lightly from politics to art and from art to poetry.

"Doctrinal authority is as fatal to literature as it is to religion. It stifles growth. Therefore, there is rebellion —" Thus the young Aldrich.

Walt seized on the pause. "Precisely. You have seen this rebellion in my 'Leaves of Grass.' I have not imitated the ancients or the classics. I have dedicated myself to the new—the free—our country—America."

"Do not claim complete novelty, Mr. Whitman. I find something of William Blake in your content, and a great deal of the late Elizabethan and Jacobean in your form."

"My verse may suggest these thoughts to you, but if you read me carefully you'll find my metre is my own. Men who are renowned scholars have admitted this to me."

Aldrich shrugged his shoulders as though signifying the futility of further comment. Walt could not restrain himself.

"Perhaps you would be interested in Mr. Emerson's appraisal of my book." He reached into his pocket to bring forth the letter but Aldrich stayed his hand.

"Don't trouble yourself, sir. I've already read the letter in the Tribune. It was most unwise to publish it. You'll pardon my saying so, but Emerson was quite displeased when he heard of it."

"But why? It was his honest opinion."

"Really, now, Mr. Whitman, don't pull my leg. One does not commercialize on one's friendships. Mr. Emerson felt that his letter was personal to you."

Walt's heart sank. He suddenly realized that in his frenzied eagerness to push the New Bible before the gaze of the unheeding world he had offended a man who had stretched forth his hand in a gesture of honest appreciation.

Aldrich surveyed his empty glass as if deliberating whether or not it was his duty to have it replenished.

At that moment Ada Claire approached them. "Would you be willing to read to us from your poetry?"

Whitman arose eagerly. "Yes, I'd be most happy to."

Aldrich smiled faintly. "Mr. Whitman, you might at least pretend a modesty that you lack."

"Then, young man, instruct me in pretense. In spite of my years I do not know the art."

Walt was angry. He did not realize he had raised his voice so that the others in the room had turned in his direction. A young broker from Wall Street—Willie Winter—careened sullenly toward them holding his glass on a level with his eye as he surveyed them belligerently. The dreamy young lady who sat near Aldrich attempted levity. "Shall it be nasty noisy pistols at dawn or will you be content with hurling pens and ink pots at each other?"

"Come, now, I'm sorry if I've offended." Aldrich extended his hand.

Willie Winter, who had drunk a sizeable bit more than was good for him, and now stood, legs wide apart, facing them, pushed Aldrich's hand aside. "Don't beg his pardon, Tom. He offends everyone with his bawdy rhymes—bad verse at that—blusters as though he were God Almighty and poses as a bearded prophet out of the Old Testament."

Clapp walked over to Winter at that point and pushed him, protesting, firmly onto the sofa. "No, Walt, don't read to us. We're swine. We're so in love with clever words and cunning epigrams that your bald-headed truth would only make us snicker. Go home, Walt. You're not good company for clever people."

Walt did not answer. He walked to the bedroom where his large hat was lying, picked it up quickly and without a word of farewell went to the door. Ada, troubled and deeply concerned, was there before him.

"I don't understand them, Walt. Do they envy your honesty? Do they squirm at their own lack of simple truth? Please come here tomorrow evening. I want to talk to you alone."

He nodded. His eyes were intently upon her and yet it was not of her that he was thinking. He was thinking. "Young men — youth — arrogant, assured, cocky — know-it-all youth but alert, alive youth — if youth could not understand his message, what good — what good —?"

Walt faced the chill wind with a plodding steady pace. Could it be that his whole thesis was wrong? Were the Clapps and the Claires, the Aldriches and the Winters humanity? And were the prophets of old insane, unique and abnormal? Were their flaming words, tiny counter currents against the flood, or lofty, aspiring white-caps on the waves of a general flow for good that all men shared? Were the prophets the exceptions to the downward flow of Man? No, for once the prophet was dead and his strong personality was no longer a challenge to the envy of his contemporaries, then *all* revered, *all* admired—and even worshipped.

His mother, who had been bending over the stove prodding smoking coals, greeted him excitedly. "He was here, Walt — a fine Quaker kind of man — Mr. Emerson."

Emerson! Emerson himself! *He* had been there.

"Where did he go? When did he leave?" Walt could not restrain his chagrin. "Why did this evening have to be so maimed and disfigured when it could have been so beautifully spent with a great soul?" kept running achingly through his heart.

Louisa saw his agony. "Don't take on so. He'll be back, Walt. I told him you were spending the evening out but that you might be back before eleven. He said he was going back to Concord at sunrise and that he wanted to see you tonight before he left. So I put the kettle on, made hot biscuits like those Mr. Thoreau liked so well and opened up some marmalade."

"That was nice. That was fine."

Walt embraced and kissed his mother, then hurried to his room. He must show Emerson some of his other work—his newer work—Enfans d'Adam, for example.

It was only ten-thirty. Another half hour. Walt's spirit was tumultuous with anticipation. Then Emerson had not been entirely offended by his letter. Emerson had come to see him. In a little while they would be sitting side by side, he and Emerson—Walt Whitman and Emerson, Walt Whitman—and Emerson.

Promptly at eleven there was a sharp tap on the door. Louisa, who had donned her prettiest white apron and Dutch hat, arose eagerly from her chair. She opened the door. Clapp stood in the doorway quite drunk.

"Sorry, Walt. Came to apologize." He lurched in striking his top hat against the half opened door. It toppled off and rolled crazily in a circle.

Walt took him by the arm, while his mother picked up the hat. "Come in, Henry. Sit down. Sober up. Mr. Emerson is on his way here. Mother, give Mr. Clapp some black coffee, please."

Clapp bowed formally to Louisa, then without removing his cape sank down on a chair near the table.

"Words, smart talk, clever digs—and you like a bull in a china shop! Sorry, Walt. Sorry for all of us. I apologize."

Walt did not hear the second knock, did not notice his mother open the door for Emerson. He was coaxing Clapp to sip the black coffee. He looked up to see Mr. Emerson watching the scene with a quiet amused smile. He arose at once. They shook hands and then Walt introduced Clapp. Clapp straightened up with great but unsteady dignity. Emerson recognized the name.

"The Saturday Press has annoyed our Boston friends—ruffled their austerity and disturbed their traditional poise. But truly, Mr. Clapp, I'm afraid it's all in vain. Pointed epigrams and barbed jibes will not do it. Walt Whitman with his blunt honesty might."

"In that case the Saturday Press had better go out of business." Clapp tried to be ironic.

"It no doubt will," said Emerson drily. "And now, Mr. Whitman, may I congratulate you in person on the trail you blaze—but as you blaze your trail don't strike too deep or you may kill the tree."

"I merely expose what is beneath the bark."

"There's not much doubt of that," smiled Emerson.

Louisa took Mr. Emerson's cloak and from that point on the conversation was a dialogue with Clapp occasionally throwing in a word, sometimes pertinent, more often not.

"Perhaps you are right, Mr. Whitman, in your frankness on sex, but don't over emphasize. The human body has many organs besides the organs of reproduction. It has also a brain which could be of considerable importance."

Walt persisted. "Yet every part of the body moves in response to the law of sex. Each movement of the male, each movement of the female, even their thoughts are masculine and feminine—his to attack and hers to surrender. The dance, the conversation, the courtship, the home, the dreams—the desires."

"You over-simplify, Mr. Whitman. What about the masculine in woman and the feminine in man? The cleavage is not as distinct as you would make it. Oddly enough, you who boast of masculinity—there is so much of the feminine even in you. I can't quite define it, but it's there."

Walt nodded. He had been brooding about this. "Yes, I've thought of this often and yet my heart cries out that man and woman must supplement one another and not compete with one another in the same tasks."

"The thirty-first chapter of Proverbs, Mr. Whitman?"

Walt nodded.

Clapp laughed mockingly. "Chain her to the spinning wheel, boys — keep her safe from the naughty world.

Let her weave; let her spin
But only keep her safe from sin.

There, that's poetry for you. Charming picture."

"What's wrong with it?" asked Emerson mildly.

"What's wrong with it?" Clapp taunted. "What about the new emancipated woman like Ada Claire?"

Walt faced him squarely. "Mr. Emerson hasn't met her. As for me, I don't know anything about her, Henry. But what's your point? Does freedom for women mean that she shall swagger about male brothels imitating the base in man—using his oaths, be partner in his drunkenness? Does it mean vice on equal terms, or does it mean a voice on equal terms, a hand on equal terms, a vote on equal terms, a mind on equal terms?"

"You grandly give her a share in all virtues and none in the faults."

"Because her desire to be free is proper and noble, while her right to harlotry was always there. She need not fight for that. Man is only too anxious to grant her that."

Clapp chuckled. "Preach that from the pulpit, ye hypocrites. Woman's ancient right to harlotry! Hurrah! Hurrah! You have that right, but please don't! And you, Walt, are you any different? You've glorified what you now condemn." Clapp fumbled in his pocket. "Here's a copy of what you wrote only a week ago. Read it, Mr. Emerson. That's the thirty-first chapter of Proverbs rewritten by the modern prophet, Mr. Walt Whitman."

Emerson surveyed him coldly and made no move to accept the crumpled page Clapp thrust at him. Clapp arose and leaned for support on the table. He read loudly, as he swayed to keep his balance:

TO A COMMON PROSTITUTE

*Be composed — be at ease with me — I am Walt
  Whitman, liberal and lusty as Nature,*
Not till the sun excludes you do I exclude you,
*Not till the waters refuse to glisten for you and the
  leaves to rustle for you, do my words refuse to
  glisten and rustle for you.*
*My girl I appoint with you an appointment, and I
  charge you that you make preparation to be
  worthy to meet me,*
*And I charge you that you be patient and perfect
  till I come.*
*Till then I salute you with a significant look that
  you do not forget me.*

Emerson looked up at Walt inquiringly as though asking, "How about this?"

Walt spoke slowly. "I don't condemn and I don't approve. I just understand."

Emerson hesitated and then nodded. "I think I understand. You meant it in the sense that no publican or sinner ought to be ostracized. Is that it?"

Walt hesitated. "No. Anything I say will not be as clear or direct as I've already said it in my verse."

Emerson could not repress a faint smile. "You mean that I'm too obtuse to comprehend your real meaning?"

"No, I mean that a song is more than a lesson or logic. I do not discipline my songs as I do my actions —for there is a need once and for all for a poet to reveal all of himself so that others may not nurse secret thoughts in hidden dens and by the darkness make them evil. There is no evil but fear and darkness. Bring your most private thoughts into the sun and they become realities to be coped with, not evils to be condemned. That's the purpose of my verse—to make people understand their real selves and not cringe with shame at the whisper of desire, but walk erect proclaiming themselves fearlessly."

Emerson shook his head. "No, Mr. Whitman, the danger is that you feel too intensely. Understanding has to do with logic, which has definite rules. Emotion too must be channelled and harnessed. May I see your Children of Adam? I shall have to leave soon and am most anxious to glance at some of your new works."

Walt, as eager for approval as a child, spread the papers before him. Emerson read the lines beginning: " 'To the garden the world anew ascending.' " He nodded approvingly. " 'No harps nor halos in some remote geographic spot beyond the stars—but an *earth* that's heaven.' I like that in your songs—this earth a Garden of Paradise if we but will it. What I have whispered you have sung."

Then he read aloud, " 'From pent-up Aching Rivers' " and repeated the words softly. He looked up. "You have a genius for coining an original phrase— strangely but aptly formed." He read on. Suddenly, he ceased nodding. His face became severe. "No, Mr. Whitman, you can't do this. You'll overreach yourself and destroy your work. There's a limit to what people will accept in frankness."

Clapp swayed over Emerson's shoulder and chuckled. "Lordy me! 'Singing the phallus—singing the bedfellow's song'. Walt, why don't you write about the privy in the same poetic way? It's so big a part of life it's a shame that it must go unsung. I do most of my serious reading there."

There was a long silence. Emerson regarded Whitman calmly. "Your friend put it rather crudely, but indeed, why not, if you're consistent?"

"I am consistent. I admit there is beauty in all these things, though people deny them. All natural processes are divine and good, and full of wonderful mystery—but somehow we don't sing of ashes and of dung—and nature seems to whisper to us 'bury both beneath the earth, not because of shame but to enrich it with eternal chemicals.' So, if nature says 'Conceal' I will conceal—but unashamed, as one buries a treasure."

Clapp laughed out loud. "So it's become a treasure now. All hail to the New Poetry!" He gestured wildly with his arms and recited with drunken levity, "A man's ambition must be mighty small to write his name on a toilet wall."

At this Emerson flushed, then whitened with anger. "I must leave now or I will be late. But truly, Mr. Whitman, if ever you come North I shall be pleased and honored with your visit."

Louisa, who had gone to her own room during the discussion, reappeared. "You didn't touch my marmalade and jam, Mr. Emerson."

"Oh yes, and very good. Yes, very good indeed!" He bowed as he took her hand and Louisa looked up at him as one looks at beauty.

"Can I drop you off anywhere, Mr. Clapp? I'm

taking the coach to the station. It's at the next corner."

"Thank you, Mr. Emerson—and if I've offended you in any way —"

Emerson ignored the apology.

A slight cold rain began to fall. Louisa trembled with the chill.

"Better take your mother inside, Mr. Whitman. I can see the carriage from here. Goodby and thank you again for your hospitality."

The coachman had been waiting patiently. Now he came down and assisted Clapp to the carriage. Clapp looked at Emerson with a dazed yet eager expression.

"Mr. Emerson," he finally exploded. "I've wanted all my life to meet you—and now when I do I'm in no condition —" His voice trailed off as he leaned against the side of the coach and vomitted.

Emerson watched him pityingly, thinking all the while, "Are we all trying to escape from ourselves—to Heaven or to Nirvana—are we all forever struggling to escape?"

VI

Walt could not sleep that night. Doubts and regrets assailed him, leered at him, frowned at him. If only Clapp had not come. If only he and Emerson had been able to speak their hearts. If only—if only—if only —!

Then a thought struck him that gave his panicked emotions direction. Why shouldn't he publish the third edition of "Leaves of Grass" in the very stronghold of Puritanism—in Boston itself?

The next morning he hurried to Fowler. Fowler did not hesitate. He pounced lithely on the idea while it still trembled on Walt's lips. "Of course! Why not?

That precious Emerson letter has Thayer and Eldridge interested. They'll publish for you. I'm sure of it. I'll write to them at once."

That evening when Walt lifted the ornate knocker on the door of Ada Claire's apartment he carried with him his Children of Adam. A woman would admire where a man might envy. Authors are as jealous of each other as are mothers of precocious children.

Ada Claire would understand the whole stream of his thinking and feeling far better than Henry Clapp, for Clapp would stand on his own literary values—and resent the novel ones of another.

Ada—Ada Claire! Walt mused as he waited for her to answer the door. There was a warm, secure inviting intimacy in her every gesture as though all her airy dancing conversation were a thin flowing gossamer veil over her assured glowing body. Now Walt sought her as he would seek a cheerful fireplace in a strange cabin.

What secret do women know? What secret do they pretend to know? Anne, Anne—why should the same hunger—the same yearning draw me to each feminine form? Is it no different with me than with the burrowing worm, the bat, the rooster, the owl, the insect? Mate—mate—mate—a shimmering silken net in Nature's hand. Cast the net over male and female. Chirp insect, hoot owl, crow rooster, sing poet—all the same —until fulfillment—then shrink back wearied until nature casts her net again? And this is all there is to romance—and all the love stories of the ages—and all the fallings in love? Assuredly, if roosters could write they would create their own barnyard Romeo and Juliet—Heloise and Abelard—and all the other roosters and the hens would nod and cluck, "What a great love story! They fell in love. It was a love match.

They knew when they saw each other —" etcetera, etcetera and etcetera.

Anne—Ada—aching love flesh the same—yearning the same—but yet *not* the same, for Anne remained, firmly there, anchored to his brain—his life—sharing the substance of his thought, his work, his hopes for man. She was mate and more—she was friend, companion, wife. Wife? Why should love stories end at Marriage? They should begin then. What went before was only glow—silk threads—silk nets—Nature's silk net. O, to understand this thing for what it is—and not define it by the name of Love. One *climbs* in love; one does not *fall* in love. Anne, you know that! One does not slip and trip and *fall* in love. The tears, the heartaches, the laughters and the daily chores, the aches, the pains—even the days and years of togetherness are rungs by which we climb in love.

And love is loyalty—open—honest! A plague on all misnomers! Give ear, O aged Casanovas, you Tristans and Isoldes, Lancelot and Guinevere, Helen and Paris, sly twittering dowagers! Know the thing you gloat on for what it is—and do not sanctify sneaking treacherous adulteries and every urge in heat with name of "love."

Walt lifted the shining knocker once more. He heard a distant clear-voiced perfunctory "Come in!" and walked into the large scented parlor, still wearing his wide-brimmed hat. She had approached him unobserved while he stared curiously at the baroque decorations of the large room, and now she reached up and swept his hat from his head with a flourish and a merry cascade of laughter.

Walt blinked. Her gown was of dazzling splendor and her fingers were radiant with jewels. This was so different from what he had expected. This was so different from the clinging, languorous, sensuous-lipped

Ada Claire he had already catalogued in his mind. This Ada was assured, strong, sparkling, regal. This was beginning to look oddly like a scene from Mark Anthony—a Queen, no less! He had the peculiar feeling that Clapp had a hand in this, that he stood somewhere like Polonius listening or watching. Some mocking jest, no doubt.

He looked so awkward and uncertain standing there that Ada questioned him. "Is there anything wrong, Walt, or are you chilled through by the wind? Sit down and I'll bring you a glass of sherry or muscatel."

"No, no wine, please. Maybe later." He sat down stiffly on the edge of the sofa and waited for her to speak.

"Are you still angry over last night? Henry's a boor when he's drunk. And as for Winter, I told him he was no longer welcome here."

"You shouldn't have."

"Criticism of a man's work is one thing. Personal abuse is quite another."

There was a sudden shrill yelping that startled Walt. Ada hurried to the door of her bedroom, picked up an alert white terrier and snuggled it against the blushing whiteness of her breast. For a long while she seemed oblivious to everything but the dog.

"Why did you ask me to come this evening?" Walt asked the question with blunt directness.

"I wanted to explain—to apologize." She tossed her hands with an impatient shrug of her shoulder. "Must you have a reason? I wanted to hear more of your work." She patted the dog, with tender fingers, as she spoke and lowered him to her lap. "Fanny Fern has praised your volume in most glowing terms."

Now Walt was pleased—anxious to speak of nothing but his songs. "I've brought a rather lengthy bit with me—Children of Adam. It will appear in the third edition."

Ada put the dog down and took the pages in her hand. Walt watched her, aglow at her concentrated interest. She sat very close to him as she read; then abruptly in the midst of a line she turned to him. "I rather liked your prose poem in behalf of Fremont. Don't take Clapp too seriously. He's in love with his own verbosity which he mistakes for wit."

Walt smiled. "He didn't offend me"; then gravely, "I'm inclined to think he's right in his prediction that Fremont will lose, and it panics me to know that, in this great democratic nation, slander and intrigue, carefully organized around political clubs motivated by no other purpose than jobs and patronage, can crush a man of principle. A Buchanan for a Fremont! A Buchanan, jelly-like, flowing around and under obstacles, inserting himself slyly here and slyly there, moving his principles about like pawns on a chessboard to suit each occasion!"

"Now don't *you* become the cynic and the pessimist."

"I'm not. I never could be. Every pulse beat in my veins beats out the faith that nothing can prevent the democratic process from flooding the land—that America is truly the will of the people—that the very rush and flood of its moving waters cleanse and purify; but I also see the evil that greedy men plot, plan and execute, while the good pour out their convictions in shouting and in song—and the steam escapes and does no work."

"You mean optimists are inefficient and let their dreams and wishes suffice?"

"Exactly that."

"Then the optimist must harness his dreams and force them to work."

"Yes."

"And so an optimistic dreamer like Fremont must learn from Buchanan's methods."

"To compromise his ideals, no! To organize, yes! —To organize, delegate, build cells, groups that will do the work in every corner of the land and not trust to a giant wave of sudden idolization."

"His wife is a practical woman. Jessie Benton knows what she's about. She'll guide him, never fear. She's very clever, writes his material, I understand. Walt, how well do you understand women? I've never asked you—but are you married?"

"Yes—lacking ritual or ceremony I would say that I was."

"What do you mean lacking ritual? Then it's no marriage at all. Surely you don't call my relationship to Pierre marriage?"

"No, I don't think so. Although I suppose it could be."

"Heaven forbid!"

Walt smiled. "On the contrary—Heaven bids."

"Preacher? Puritan?"

"Oh, no. You asked me. I did not volunteer."

"And you —?"

"I loved, mated and begot a child. I wanted the mating to be permanent—marriage—the closest and most intimate friendship."

"No priest? No minister?"

"What could a priest have added—and yet I would have gladly done that as the world's conventional way of saying, 'Here before you all I take to me the dearest, closest friend!' "

"Then you're *not* married?"

"Please, Ada, don't cross-examine; try to understand."

"Which shall I understand—what you say now or your poems? Your songs of a blaring stallion—the male glorified, or your shy pious definitions—and virginal blushes now? You see, Walt, I'm much more honest than you. Wine tickles my palate and the touch of a man is pleasant to my body. I do not dull my palate with the same wines but seek variety. I do not sublimate my desire in song but in acts. Who is being honest—you or I?"

Walt reflected. "So they, these 'liberated women,' *do* understand what moves them! Ada did not let herself be fooled by undefined desires! Within her she knew her yearnings for what they were—as real as food hunger."

There was a heavy flesh scent in her perfume that now enticed and yet offended Walt. He felt uncomfortable. It still seemed to him that Clapp was hiding somewhere in that room—perhaps behind a drape—enjoying all this to the full.

"Honesty? Very well, Ada, let's try to answer it." Now *he* would be blunt. "Who paid for this apartment and your gowns?"

"Pierre partially, if that's what you mean." She did not seem at all embarrassed.

"Where is your son?"

"In an excellent boarding school under competent supervision." This quite proudly.

"Where is his father?"

"On the concert stage. He is a famous and talented pianist."

"Would the father have preferred a permanent union with you?"

"Perhaps." Her tone was chilly, her eyes hard.

"Then, Ada, you don't know what love is—not for your child nor for anyone. What you feel, the romantic urge, is beautiful, intoxicating, but less in intensity, far less, I am sure, than the hog feels for the sow, the rooster for the hen, the ape for his mate."

Ada was furious. "You could use more apt illustrations, you know—the flowers, the birds and the bees."

Walt snapped back, "Why should I? Let the romancers do that. I'm describing what you call 'love.' It remains nothing but a tickle of your love flesh, a sensation of the nerves, a biological misty ecstasy that even the angleworm enjoys. Even in the animals there must be something of the feeling of procreation, protection and even permanence—loyalties, we call them."

He stopped abruptly. "If I continue in this vein, I'll be most disagreeable. I'll leave now. You won't understand my song."

Ada's eager touch restrained him. She had been biting her lips with annoyance. "No, please don't leave. Why think of leaving? I do, Walt, I do understand. With you it's different. I'm puzzled. Your songs seem to glorify the physical and yet you speak of moral restraints. I haven't known your kind of man. Don't condemn me. Teach me."

"I don't condemn anyone—not even myself."

"Then let's enjoy each other's companionship. Stay with me tonight. Pierre is in Virginia. His life is like mine. Whom will we be harming? He'll not be back for several days. Walt, stay here. Stay here." Her hands were resting on his shoulders. Walt did not say a word and his long calm silence enraged her. Her full lips twisted. "You're a cheat and your songs lie! You arouse, tease and excite with words, and then you mock."

"I don't mean them that way."

"Then why don't you write what you *do* mean?"

"Don't be angry, Ada. Just forget that you read what I wrote."

"You glorified a prostitute—and revile *me!*"

"I did not glorify her. I accepted what she honestly stands for—an outlet for a physical need. She sells her commodity honestly. You cover it with lace and ribbons and call it by names I don't understand."

She half screamed and started to slap him and then quite abruptly she clenched her hands and sat down. This was too much like a play. Both of them felt that way. He walked slowly to the door, stopping to take his hat from the piano. She remained huddled on the sofa, fighting to control her hurt pride.

"Walt, I was only teasing you." There, she had finally swallowed the red urge to scratch, kick and slap him. She laughed. "It was all an act. The Temptress and St. Anthony. The woman scorned. Now please behave and read me your songs."

She arose and came toward him smiling, her huckles weaving enticingly, as though hers was the final victory. Walt opened the door and left. He heard her scream, "You damned Joseph!" as the door closed behind him and he rather pitied her.

* * * *

Fragment of thoughts—broken like glass. Pour them in a stream. Channel them. Think, Walt. Organize your thoughts!

The Song of Songs. "Do not fear me that I am black, for the sun has tinted me." Anne, what's wrong with my song? Leave it to Ada, scorned and furious. She'll tell Clapp. And then, they will laugh at the shy, frightened timid singer of lusty songs. But there *is* a difference! There is a difference between things that can face the sunlight and sneaking things that crawl down dark alleys. "Pierre is in Virginia. Nobody will be harmed." Time-honored chivalric moralities that make of adultery a boast but of keeping the lady's name a secret, a virtue.

O knights in shining armor! O Lancelot sneaking to the bed sheets of Queen Guinevere. Sing, bard— and tune your lyre—O sing these deeds of glory! A Paris for a Lancelot and a Helen for a Guinevere. And poor, poor Ada—with virtue withered like hay. If every bitch in heat could sing, her love songs would outdo the classics!

Bathe, Walt! Give yourself the feeling of being clean again. Bathe and think of Anne, the wisdom and understanding of her, the dark, dark cleanness of her. But you can't live alone—with her alone—set apart— the objects of vicious stories and grim hostility. Even though your love is real and good. You live in a world of people and people won't let you choose your values —people won't let you. They'll accept a dalliance with Ada but they won't tolerate marriage with Anne.

Anne, dear Anne, you were right. How right you were! My song is too far ahead of people. My song is far too swift and even *I* can't quite keep up with it or I'd have come to you. We would have each other— our own world loftier than theirs. But then the mob won't let us—I saw your brother die—what would they do to you, to our son—in the South, in the North —what would they do to you? Thoughts are black and thoughts are white, but skin, just skin, the color of leather—dark earth—light earth—earth—earth. Did God breathe unto the white man and sneer into the black—or what—or what? Anne, help me! Help me think! I'm just guessing—but *you* know!

VII

There was the matter of the summons he had received—the law suit.

Walt waited for more than an hour until his case was called. He searched the courtroom for James Parton but could see him nowhere. Then when at last the weary clerk called out nasally "Case of James Parton vs. Walter Whitman," a slender, bald, stooped, bespectacled attorney answered "Ready for the plaintiff."

The judge looked curiously at Walt who stood silently before the bench waiting for someone to say something.

"Are you the defendant?"

"I am, your honor."

"Have you counsel?"

"The matter is too small, your honor. May I plead my own defense?"

"You may." Then turning to the lawyer, "Mr. Jensen, you may proceed. Mr. Clerk, swear the witness."

The lawyer leaned forward in the attitude of one communicating a confidence to the court. "Your honor, I don't believe it will be necessary to bring in my client. As a matter of fact I was certain that the defendant would default."

The court replied drily "Obviously your expectations were vain. The defendant is here and ready for trial. Proceed, counsel."

Jensen drew a file from his portfolio. From the file he carefully extracted a document which Walt recognized as the receipt he had signed.

"The defendant has not been sworn, your honor, and I desire to call him as my witness."

"You will be bound by his testimony."

"That is satisfactory, your honor."

"Very well, then. Swear the witness, Mr. Clerk."

Walt interrupted at that point. "I have no objection, your honor, to taking an oath if that is necessary. I believe we can agree upon the facts leaving the decision to this court."

The judge smiled and murmured—"A little irregular—but let's see how far we get."

Jensen held out the receipt between his thumb and forefinger. "I believe the defendant will admit his signature."

"Well, *show* it to him!" roared the judge impatiently. "Don't wave it in front of his nose."

Walt nodded "That is my signature."

The judge reached down, took the receipt from Jensen's hand and read it aloud.

"Received from James Parton the sum of Seventy-five dollars as an advance." He glared at Jensen over the rim of his glasses, "An advance for what?"

"The defendant can explain."

The judge looked at Walt kindly. "Perhaps you can enlighten us."

Walt stated his case briefly. "I was asked to submit some of my verse for possible publication in the Home Journal and assumed that the Seventy-five dollars was an advance to be deducted later from any monies due me."

"A fair assumption," agreed the court.

"Your honor," broke in Jensen, "perhaps we had better continue this matter and I'll bring in my client."

"Are you willing that this matter be continued, Mr. Whitman?"

"I have no objection."

"Very well then. Two weeks from today."

As they left the courtroom, Fanny Fern came rapidly toward them from the stairs.

"Was the case disposed of?" she inquired coldly.

Jensen sought to explain, but she waved his explanation aside. She turned her eyes upon Walt as though he were a loathsome object cast out from her world. "To obtain a loan from my fiance on the strength of your acquaintanceship with me and then to refuse payment, is scarcely in keeping with the preachment of your verse."

Walt was aghast. "But it was not a loan; it was an advance."

Fanny Fern's face grew pallid with hurt and anger. "It's hard to know exactly what you do mean. Your conduct and your words are at eternal loggerheads. I presume your discussions with Ada Claire and your visits to her home were cold impersonal expositions of your honest and rigid moralities."

So that was it! He had declined her invitation and accepted Ada's. The rest was either slander or imagination. He faced her squarely, conscious of the fact that curious passers-by were inclining eyes and ears in his direction, but determined to answer her slur.

"I did not come to your fiance for a loan. I have never asked anyone outside of my immediate family for financial aid at any time. I came to submit literary material for the columns of the Home Journal. I did not suggest the advance; Mr. Parton did, and I assumed it was to bind our bargain and to be deducted later from any monies due me."

Fanny Fern favored him with frosty distant attention and, when he paused, snapped at him.

"Why don't you speak a little louder? Let the whole world hear of your injuries."

Walt felt hot anger surging at his throat. He saw, however, how futile it would be to continue —

"You may tell Mr. Parton that I won't appear to defend this suit two weeks from today—or any other time. I'll return the advance to him. Good day, Miss Fern."

Walt knew in his empty heart that New Orleans was farther away than ever before. But if his book sold—if "Leaves of Grass" sold —

VIII

John Brown—John Brown—John Brown of Kansas
charged with:

> Confederating to make rebellion and levy war
> against the State of Virginia.
> Conspiring to induce slaves to make rebellion
> and insurrection.
> Murder of Thomas Boerley, Fontaine Beckham,
> Luke Quin, white persons, and Shephard
> Heyward, Negro —

Walt, Walt—have you an opinion? Guilty or innocent?

"I don't know."

Think! Feel! This man urged slaves to arm themselves rather than wait for their tyrants' bounty.

"Bloody—bloody were his deeds."

Can freedom then be won by other means?

"I don't know."

Thoreau champions Brown's martyrdom.

"I have no quarrel with Thoreau."

Wake up Walt! You are the poet! Sound your
lyre! Cry out! Accuse! Defend! Take any stand, but
let your voice be heard!

> *"I would sing how an old man, tall, with white*
> *hair, mounted the scaffold in Virginia.*
> *(I was at hand, silent I stood with teeth shut close,*
> *I watched,*
> *I stood very near you old man when cool and in-*
> *different, but trembling with age and your un-*
> *healed wounds, you mounted the scaffold.)"*

Part Six

WAR YEARS

March, 1860! Angry words—bloody talk of war! Secession! "We have the right to secede. We will go our way and you will go yours." "No, there will be no secession—not without violence!" Harper's Ferry and John Brown's trial—and Walt planning his third edition of "Leaves of Grass."

Walt had come to sedate, blameless Boston. Charles W. Eldridge of Thayer and Eldridge met him at the station and accompanied him to the hotel. He beamed his good tidings.

"I have some encouraging news for you, Mr. Whitman. The Atlantic has accepted your 'Bardic Symbols' for publication in the April issue. That means you're being accepted. Ah, yes, you're very definitely being accepted."

Walt was pleased. "I'm anxious to see Thoreau and Emerson. How can I communicate with them?"

"No difficulty whatever."

"How's that?"

"Mr. Emerson spoke to me only yesterday afternoon. I told him you would no doubt be at our office at three. He said he would be sure to call. It is five after three now, and Mr. Emerson is always punctual."

Throb, oh heart! I shall walk in the company of the great. Walt, Walt, what is happening to you? Who are the great? Are they, too, not leaves of grass in the even meadow of mankind.

As they entered the display room of Thayer and Eldridge, Walt felt a glow of affection—almost of reverence for the sweet, white-haired scholar who came forward eagerly to clasp his hand. Emerson was obviously painfully troubled about something. A slight frown creased his forehead. His white hair was a silver aureole in the austere shadows of the bookshop as his eyes dwelt on Walt.

"Come, Mr. Whitman, I'm sure Mr. Eldridge will excuse us for an hour. Let us walk in the Common. There's a warmth and brightness in the air that is most invigorating."

Walt felt a sense of profound awe in the presence of the gently smiling sage. He tried to speak and could not, for he was afraid that anything he might utter would be less than Emerson expected of a poet he had praised so highly.

It was Emerson who began. "I hear that you have also written on political issues."

"As a journalist, yes, occasionally." Walt was still sensitive to Clapp's outspoken and depreciating criticism.

"Buchanan is a tired and pathetic figure." Emerson shook his head, "Mind you, I do not trust leaders who proclaim, 'I am the Way, — the heavens absolute! I am all Truth! Follow me!' But on the other hand, unfortunate is the nation whose leader tries to be all things to all men. Bewildered Buchanan! What a sorry mess his weakness has brought about!"

Walt was most eager to disown a share in the guilt. "As you know, Mr. Emerson, I was for Fremont!"

"Yes, yes, I remember."

Emerson paused beneath an elm tree and turned slowly to Walt. Walt's eyes were fastened on the tiny white stubble of Emerson's cheek. Even the hair roots were white. "Emerson and I" he was thinking. "Emerson and I." What was Emerson saying? "We've had four years of blundering with a cabinet who keeps public opinion away from the ears of the President. I do not believe Buchanan is guilty of treason against anyone but himself. He has sold his integrity for the handclasp, the pat on the back and the flattering smile. I'm afraid I am much the Jeremiah but I see a wave of blood sweeping over this land of ours."

Walt looked closely at the troubled face of the saintly scholar. "Can anything prevent it? Is there still time?"

Emerson did not answer directly. He mused for a while then asked quietly, "What do you think of Stephen Douglas as a candidate for the presidency?"

"That he is quite *willing* to be President."

Emerson laughed a short chuckle of a laugh that quickly subsided into a quizzical smile. "Much *too* willing! Self interest—how it twists one's viewpoint. He *must* be President, therefore, he marries twice from the South as an ambitious calculating king would make an alliance."

Walt felt that a gesture of defense was proper. Then, too, it gave him a sense of power to rebuke Emerson even mildly.

"It might have been love."

Emerson raised his white brows.

"It might have been—but the rest of his acts are in conformity with his wooing of the South by promises the North will not tolerate."

They walked on in silence for a while and then began to retrace their steps. Walt paused and faced Emerson. "I've withdrawn from party politics although

I used to be quite active in the Democratic party. I cannot understand the continuing strength of the Democratic party, — one party that covers two distinct viewpoints, slavery and anti-slavery, with a brotherly blanket of the crass things they have in common— political jobs, political honors, political profits, individual self-pampering, self-interest."

Emerson quickly agreed. "It will break apart. The southern democrats do not trust a northerner and the northern democrats cannot overcome self interest sufficiently to proclaim their true convictions. A house divided against itself —. The democrats will split and lose because they are untrue to themselves—as untrue as is their leader Buchanan. This man Lincoln —" Emerson paused.

"What of Lincoln?"

"I don't know. He appears to be sincerely bewildered and uncertain, but just as sincere in his search for an answer. For such there is hope; but for those who are confused because self interest seasons the chaos, there is no hope."

They walked to Beacon Street and, as they strolled together leisurely, Emerson spoke up gently but with painful candor. "Walt, if I may call you by your given name, I mentioned before that I was distressed. Let me be frank with you. I'm afraid your work is being rudely censored. Try to understand that my wife is one of the most hospitable of women and for that matter so is Sophie Thoreau, Henry's sister, who keeps house for him, but both these women have put thumbs down on you with a finality that dwarfs all masculine obstinacy. You would have been my house guest. I wanted that very much, but —" Emerson paused as they walked and said abruptly, "You should not include Children of Adam in your third edition."

"So that's it!" Walt smiled. "I'm afraid I can't escape the Children of Adam, nor do I want to, for I love them in spite of—or should I say, with their cussedness."

Emerson was nevertheless far too serious to dally with his objective. "What affect can a description like this possibly have on women, children, and the many, many immature adults — 'Limitless limpid jets of love?' "

"Would you expurgate certain passages from the Bible?"

"There *is* a difference."

"I fail to see it."

Emerson shook his head. "The Bible gives the *facts* of the story—the narrative of what happened. You stir up the emotions consciously by detailed description."

"And the Song of Songs?"

"You go much further than the Song of Songs. Insofar as you inventory the physical charms of a male or female form there is little difference, but when you dwell enthusiastically on each detail of the act of sex with vivid and original descriptive phrases the result is in some cases to offend, in others to attract, but in all cases to excite emotionally."

"And since when is the song of a poet only an appeal to logic?"

"Walt! Walt! You will not understand. Let me tell you in simple practical terms that a parent does not want the book around where his children can read it."

"Whose fault is it? The fault of parents who have cried 'Shame' where there is no shame, or mine, who sees beauty and truth as one?"

Emerson's voice was serenely patient. "We're not discussing guilt or blame. The general public will not accept it and the beauty of the rest of your work will be lost because of your obstinacy. Yield a bit—in order to conquer."

Walt lashed out, "What about your criticism of Buchanan? No, the Union, now and forever, one and forever, one and inseparable. Mr. Emerson, I will not amputate because a badly educated society prefers one-legged men. I'll write the truth as I see it."

Emerson bit his lip in vexation. "I had hoped to persuade you." Then with a quick look at Walt, "As fair a man as Whittier threw your book into the fire."

"Other books have been burned—and they gave the greater light for it. But tell me, Mr. Emerson, I must still insist—are your views on poetry different from your views on politics? Is compromise permitted and sanctioned in one and not in the other?"

Emerson smiled. "Let's have dinner together, Walt, at the American House—and I warn you I'll persevere. You've got to eliminate some of those verses."

They walked up and down Beacon Street. Emerson did indeed persist. "You have the right to glorify the body beautiful. I do not agree with Luther and Saint Bernard nor with any who hold the flesh to be a maggot sack rather than the divine work of God— but you go too far."

Walt suggested, "Let us dine together this evening and then we can pursue the subject."

Emerson was uncomfortable. "Walt, this dinner should be in my home. My wife —" he hesitated, then continued ruefully, "should never have glanced at your book. You've sung yourself out of many a dinner and supper."

"I sincerely regret that I can't be Tommy Tucker." Walt laughed, although he mused inwardly that his ostracism would prove expensive, what with coffee at five cents a cup and nineteen cents for beefsteak. It would have been far cheaper to have been Emerson's house guest.

"Change some of the words at least," pleaded Emerson, kindly. " 'Seminal wet' is not even poetry. 'Jelly of love' might be. Why should the greatness of your work be cast aside because of your stubbornness?"

"Compromise of principles is a suicidal game, dear master, and he who yields in the slightest will surrender in the greatest." And then Walt quoted firmly:

"I will effuse egotism and show it underlying all,
*   and I will be the bard of personality,*
And I will show of male and female that either is
*   but the equal of the other,*
And sexual organs and acts! do you concentrate in
*   me, for I am determin'd to tell you with cour-*
*   ageous clear voice to prove you illustrious,*
And I will show that there is no imperfection in
*   the present, and can be none in the future, . . .*
And I will show that nothing can happen more
*   beautiful than death . . .*
I will not make poems with reference to parts,
But I will make poems, songs, thoughts, with ref-
*   erence to ensemble, . . .*
And I will not make a poem nor the least part of
*   a poem but has reference to the soul . . .*
Behold, the body includes and is the meaning, the
*   main concern and includes and is the soul."*

Emerson paused in the leisurely pace of the walk and faced Walt. "What a pity that those who need your songs most will not read them—and those prurient ones whose passions they will excite will devour them. I should like you to meet my friends. Perhaps Sunday afternoon —"

"No. I've heard of your literary circle—"

"And?"

"I shy away from those who live mentally in splendid isolation."

"You're not being fair to judge them without meeting them."

At that moment Mr. Eldridge rode by in his carriage. He checked his horses with a firm compelling hand. "Good afternoon, Mr. Emerson. Would you honor me with your presence at my house Sunday afternoon? It will be a welcome to your companion. I have already invited Mr. Thoreau."

Emerson tipped his hat in acknowledgment. "I shall be most happy to accept." Then turning to Walt as Eldridge drove off, "How on earth did he manage to snare out hermit Thoreau? Did he use you for bait? Sunday afternoon then, I'll call for you. And now, let's have dinner."

II

The dining room of the American House was almost empty when they entered.

"Perhaps it's too early for you, Walt."

"No, I rarely eat by the clock—and besides, a table is to me an altar—a pulpit—acoustics —"

Emerson nodded understandingly and addressed the buxom and breathless young waitress who had hurried to their table from the far corner of the room.

"That's Mr. Melville over there," she whispered with wide eyes, "the man that lived with cannibals."

Emerson turned quickly in the direction from which the girl had hurried and Walt followed his glance with equal eagerness.

"No. She must be mistaken. What would Melville be doing in Boston?"

The man in the corner arose slowly and placed a coin upon the table. He walked leisurely to the coat

rack and, as he turned, the light of the lamps, added
to that of the sunset, illumined his handsome bearded
features.

"It *is* Melville! Wait, Walt!" Emerson arose and
walked quickly toward the other. There was a brief
conversation between them and as both men approached the table Walt could hear Emerson urging
"A cup of tea. Surely you have time for that."

Walt arose and faced the man who scarce a decade
before had loomed like a restless giant upon the literary
horizon.

What had happened to Melville?

Why had oblivion come upon him?

Such prose as Moby Dick contained was flaming
lava pouring from a mountain of fire—and now the
fires were dead and the mountain cold and barren.

Melville murmured, "I recognize Mr. Whitman
from the print in his 'Leaves of Grass.'"

They were seated.

Melville's bearded face was exceedingly pale. He
seemed nervous and agitated. "I am returning from
a lecture in Danvers. My stay in Boston will be brief."
He lapsed into a silence, his eyes studying the table-
cloth as though he were ill at ease and preferred to
be left alone.

Walt felt a great pity for the man. If only the lips
would open and the hidden anguish pour out—

"Your adventures must provide you with an in-
exhaustible store of material for lectures."

Melville raised his eyes and looked at Whitman
with a faint smile. "It provides me with an easily exhaustible supply of cash. I speak badly, that is to say,
I ramble into the abstract—and people are fond of
pictures—stories. I have, therefore, anchored myself
to two topics—one for those who insist upon an elevated subject. For them I discourage on Statuary in

Rome, and the indiscriminating others I tell of the South Seas."

Emerson strove to encourage him to further speech.

"You seem to be constantly seeking distant horizons. You have kindled the flame of adventure in the hearts of young and old."

Melville looked startled instead of pleased. He sat grimly upright. "Mine is no adventure towards the Unknown. Mine is an escape—an escape from the hell within me and around me—"

He turned to Walt. "I read your 'Leaves of Grass' —your constantly repeated shout that 'all that is, is best.' "

Walt felt the smart of the slap and only pitied the man.

"Sometimes a truth has to be shouted!"

"But yours is a lie!"

Emerson reached across the table and placed a quieting hand upon Walt's arm. It was an unnecessary gesture. Walt was not offended. He knew that the shadows that sometimes hovered around his own sun had engulfed and overwhelmed the other.

"And your lie," Melville continued coldly, "stirs the lie in my soul almost to revival while I shout it down with 'Peace, peace thou liar in me, telling me I am immortal. Shall I not be as these bones?' "

Walt said softly, "And the bones too are eternal!"

The gentle answer infuriated Melville. "An eternal madness—an eternal realm of the dead and the dying. We are full of ghosts, you and I. We are as graveyards full of the buried dead."

Emerson shook his head. "Whom are you fighting? What are you fighting?"

"A Father known to me chiefly by his rod."

"You admit the possibility of the Father?"

"I admit nothing, — only that dogmas planted in youth cannot be utterly uprooted."

He turned to Walt with the dark pupils of his intent eyes piercing like gem-tipped drills.

"I know you, mine ancient enemy. You represent all that I despise. For you the universe sings of ecstatic joy. You are the wordy apologist for God. You see only His love and not His cruelty—if He exists at all. And I see the Universe stripped of the verbal garments with which you'd clothe its ugly nakedness—its pitiless savagery—its dark pursuing Nemesis. I know emptiness and cruelty and night. I know the white-capped pastures of the sea—and I know that just below the waves monsters devour each other with savage tearing bloody jaws. I know the surface civility of man—and below the waves —"

Emerson's tight lips opened. "Is Night the only truth and Daylight false? I asked you before, whom you are fighting—and now I know without your telling me. You are still on the mad hunt for Moby Dick. Your own soul is the infinite sea where he tears your limbs and mocks your harpoons. And you feel yourself drowning—sinking—with no hope—no trust—no faith. Somewhere in your youth there came the Great Insecurity and terrified you and engulfed you — until you mistrusted everything and everyone—those nearest you—mother—kin—friends—life. That is your Moby Dick!"

Melville's voice was low. "You hint that melancholy has touched my mind—that I am insane—"

"I did not say that —"

"Say what you mean then!"

"I have already done so. I seek no quarrel with you."

Melville arose from his chair. "Please do not misunderstand. I know of your excellent repute. Your disciples, and they are many, regard you as a saint. You are a good and sheltered man. The four walls of your calm existence shut out the terrors that are. But let either of you see what I have seen—blood, famine, hate—the sullen mocking shroud of the sea that covers the dead and the dying—until nothing can escape—nothing — then perhaps — you'll seek annihilation as your fondest goal — complete annihilation, and you, Mr. Whitman—your song will die in your throat—" Melville hesitated, white and shaken by the strife within him. He continued more calmly.

"My quarrel with you is not personal—therefore, more real—but less vindictive." He pointed to Walt as he smiled at Emerson. "This man and I were born in the same year. He and I are Esau and Jacob struggling in the womb of literary America. I am afraid that my poor blind father will give *him* the blessing! Good evening, gentlemen!"

Emerson did not try to restrain him.

* * * *

For a long while after Melville had left, the gentle sage of Concord and Walt did not speak. Emerson was the first to break the silence.

"I wonder if his Schopenhauer-infected malady would have been healed had his stirring book received a warmer welcome."

As for Walt, he was busy fumbling among the worn news clippings in his wallet. Emerson, thinking that Walt was about to pay the check, hastened to say—"Remember, I am your host. Please Walt —"

Walt had found what he had been seeking. He unfolded the paragraph he had selected from among the contents of his wilted pouch. "Mr. Emerson, I have carried this paragraph with me for many years. The faith-empty man who just left us wrote these words in

. his book 'White Jacket.' I could have sworn then that .we thought and felt alike."

Emerson's voice was kindly as he reached for the almost illegible paragraph. He remarked to Walt. "Man is not consistent. Esau had his gentler moments; he, too, wanted his father's blessing. Approval—approval—approval—God's or man's—but without it the soul withers and dies."

Emerson studied the excerpt, holding it close to his eyes.

The shadows were darkening. The waitress brought a lamp to the table and Emerson held the limp worn paper to its glow. He read aloud—"Escaped from the house of bondage, Israel of old did not follow after the ways of the Egyptians. To her was given an express dispensation; to her were given new things under the sun. And we Americans are *the* peculiar, chosen people—the Israel of our time; we bear the ark of the liberties of the world. God has predestinated, mankind expects, great things from our race; and great things we feel in our souls.

We are the pioneers of the world; the advance guard sent on through the wilderness of untried things, to break a new path in the New World that is ours ... for we cannot do a good to America but we give alms to the world."

Emerson regarded the scrap of paper wonderingly. "It's hard to believe that the tragic man we saw wrote these lines—but then, the same *Saul* that pursued David to slay him—wept aloud and called him 'My son!' "

"Madness?"

"Perhaps. The unreal world born of terror where things imagined become true."

"But much of it *is* true!"

"What do you and I know of truth? Only that we still seek it."

"And Melville?"

"— has given up the search."

III

They had spent a pleasant hour in the spacious parlor of the Eldridge home. The sun streamed in on them through the window-framed picture of gentle hills and long rows of elm trees. Dusk came softly so that they were scarcely aware of it.

Now the maid lit the candles and retired, leaving the teacups upon the table and the men to themselves.

Emerson remarked pleasantly, "We had become quite content with contemplation and lack of motion until you came, Walt—like a deus ex machina blowing a trumpet call to action."

Thoreau, who stood leaning against the casement observing the last glow of day, inquired without turning, "Trumpets have called men to action worse than those of beasts. I dislike fanfaronade—and you, Waldo —what great actions do *you* contemplate now that our Gabriel is here?"

Emerson's eyes had a peculiar quality of radiance that kept others at a reverent distance. Only Thoreau seemed ever unconscious of it, and his direct and familiar form of address to Emerson shocked the others. Emerson smiled slightly.

"The elements conspired to bring to this new world pilgrims of every origin, and out of their differing views and common hunger for individual liberty a nation was born. You and I, Thoreau, have more or less become hermits, accepting this infant nation as but another child in the family of the nations of the earth. Mr. Whitman sounds a trumpet—a mighty ringing blast—

that tears away the cobwebs of habitual thought and proclaims 'Lo, this land is different;—this America is the greatest experiment in the brotherhood of man that all of history has witnessed. It is more than that; it is the hope of the world.' "

"And the trumpet call?" Thoreau now turned so that he faced the others.

Emerson continued gently, "Is a call to us to move consciously forward in the path that Providence has worked out—and not drift aimlessly with the flood, relying upon the original impulse of the fathers of our country to propel us forward."

Eldridge coughed delicately as though afraid to interrupt the dialogue, then ventured, "Yes, Mr. Emerson is quite right. I consider Mr. Whitman a truly American poet in that he recognizes the uniqueness of our country, its destiny as a teacher, as a guide —"

"Piffle!" Thoreau spat the word with such vehemence that Emerson frowned his annoyance. "America is a child like all children—living its fresh primitive youth till the marrow dries and the arteries harden and following the pattern of all nations to pride arrogance—blustering clamor for empire —"

"Why will you not concede that America is different from the others?" Walt spoke slowly as though groping for the apt expressive phrases of his verse. "In France, it is the French and the stranger, in Germany, the Germans and the stranger, in Italy, the Italians and the stranger. Here no man is a stranger, or all men are strangers. This land was conceived in the very idea of the freedom and equality of all."

Thoreau answered with a touch of bitterness. "Have patience, my friend, and you will see a homogeneous Yankee evolve out of your diverse peoples and that stereotyped Yankee will despise the stranger with all the arrogance of a citizen of any land of the old world.

We will adopt the stern exclusiveness of other nations
—to thrust away rather than to welcome."

"You have no faith in people."

"Precisely. And that is why the animals of the
forest are my chosen companions."

"And your presence here this afternoon—?"

"Only to make comparisons and conclude that my
woodland retreat is better by far than the loftiest of
mansions—even those dedicated to the mouth worship
of God."

Eldridge was shocked. It was apparent that he was
trying to harness words that he might send galloping
furiously at the stern and bitter Thoreau.

Emerson, completely unperturbed, for he had
listened to Thoreau's misanthropic diatribes for years,
commented evenly, "If a man is to be cynical of his
fellows, let him begin by being cynical of himself, for
he is of the same clay and substance. Cynicism is the
attitude of a mind and soul which assumes itself
superior—"

"My position exactly." For the first time that afternoon Thoreau smiled. The tenseness vanished and
everyone enjoyed a pleasant laugh.

Thoreau continued "But Whitman here sees every
ego as important as his own—conceives of every benighted anthropophagite as his equal. Don't you,
Whitman?"

"One can devour a fellow man with the teeth of
finance or the proclamation of caste. Even the preacher
may consume his hearers with the threat of Hell. I see
the retreating shadows of night in all men as I see the
first rays of dawn in all men."

Emerson looked up at Whitman with an intensity
that made the others silent.

"Mr. Whitman, you are a forceful preacher and a
remarkably pious one. Hereafter I shall consider your

verses as sermons and understand them better. But as for your Enfans d'Adam —" He arose slowly and shook his head, "I don't know but that my demand for a fig-leaf to cover your verse is a sign of my own fault or defect—and, therefore, the Voice in the Garden finds *me* ashamed and *you* unashamed."

* * * *

When Walt returned home from Boston·he found his mother weeping in her room. "They've taken Jesse away, Walt. They've taken Jesse away."

Jeff, who had been sitting with his head in his hands, greeted Walt darkly. "They had to, Walt. He picked up a bread knife. He's violent."

Louisa moaned, "I've been a God-fearing woman all my life. Why did God —"

Walt soothed her. "There are laws, Ma, great, powerful laws, like two and two are four. You can't break those laws."

"A God of vengeance!" murmured Jeff bitterly.

"No, Jeff. Gravity's not a bad law. It's a great law. It holds the house down; but don't lean too far out of the window. There are great laws—great eternal laws. I'll visit him, Ma. I'll go now."

* * * *

Jesse recognized Walt. He beat against the bars of the cell.

"Take me out, Walt. They're keeping me here. I ain't done nothin' wrong. I'll be good. Put me anywhere. I'll stay quiet."

He thrust his hands through the bars and touched Walt's cheek. He sobbed and cried, "How's Ma? How's Eddie?"

Walt kissed his brother's hand and strangely enough Jesse calmed himself a little. The cell smelled like a urinal and Walt saw his brother's clothes scattered about as though he had thrown them everywhere about in his anger or despair. The spittle and tobacco juice that ran down Jesse's chin, rough with hair stubble, made Walt's heart ache with pity and his usually strong spirit felt a sense of helplessness.

The warden surveyed him with cc'd hostility. "Time's up!"

"I'd like to bathe my brother, if I may."

Inmates moved like silent ghosts along the corridor, stopping to stare at Walt until the Warden ordered them away.

"He sure can stand a bath, but he's liable to hurt you if you go in. He's a dangerous syph case, you know."

"Yes, yes, I know. May I bathe him, please?"

"Sure, go ahead. You can get a pail of water in the kitchen—and some soap too." He turned abruptly and moved down the narrow corridor.

Walt hurried eagerly. He felt a strange bitter exultation when his brother docilely submitted to the soap and water. He scrubbed him thoroughly and then Jesse dried himself awkwardly with a towel, repeating over and over, "It feels good, Walt. It sure feels good."

Walt tidied up the cell and mopped the floor. The Warden came back shortly to watch him and to tell him where to pour the dirty water.

When Walt made ready to leave he kissed Jesse on the cheek and the Warden exclaimed, "Whadduya know? You must be a missionary—or a minister. Religious man, huh? Well, I've got a cousin who gives coffee and sandwiches to the bums on the Bowery—if they accept Christ."

"And if they don't accept him?"

The Warden's face flushed with rage. "Say, mister, are you trying—"

Walt took out three of the four dollars he had in his pocket. "Buy yourself some tobacco—" The Warden's face showed the proper reluctance. "—and will you sort of—be good to my brother?"

From the asylum Walt went to Jesse's home. He found Martha sitting in the darkened living room with three of her neighbors. Without comment he drew aside the curtains and let the light in. Then he seated himself on the threadbare sofa near his sister-in-law. Martha did not speak. The silence became gloomy and oppressive.

"I've been to see Jesse," Walt began. Then abruptly, "Where are the children?"

"They're visiting with Nancy. Nancy said she'd take them for a few days until Andrew comes back from the hospital."

Walt felt his insides collapsing. "Andrew in the hospital?"

"His lungs. I thought you knew."

"No, I didn't know."

"You—so interested in your book you don't see the world around you."

"May I see you alone for a minute?"

The three neighboring women looked as somber and malignant as the Three Fates at not being a party to the conversation. Walt drew Martha into the kitchen.

"Martha, I'll see that you get three dollars a week as long as Jesse is ill."

Martha's strained face softened. "That's help a lot, with the sewing and washing I'm doing. The neighbors have been nice. They look after the children when I'm working. Mrs. Gilbert brought over some bran muffins. Did Jesse ask about me?"

Walt wept inside. Great God! Jesse had perhaps infected her with the same disease that had reached his brain—and Martha was asking —

"Yes," he lied eagerly, "Jesse kept saying, 'Tell Martha not to worry. If I was mean to her and to the children it was my sickness. Tell Martha I love her very much.' "

Martha listened curiously. "It doesn't sound like Jesse. He must be very sick. Did he say he needed anything?"

"No."

"I'll bring him some tobacco on Sunday."

"Don't take the children to see him."

"No, Walt, I won't take the children."

Walt felt a numbness as though blows could no longer give him pain. "Come, Great Laws—strike, beat, kick. I feel no pain—just the sound of the blows!"

* * * *

Jesse's children were at Nancy's. He must see the children. The old ramshackle house where Andrew and Nancy lived spread its ugly decaying boards over an almost barren plot of ground. The pile of wood and the narrow and rotting outhouse shed were prominent in the bleak landscape. The door of the shed clung there desperately by one rusty hinge and Walt felt the abjectness of its plea.

Maybe inanimate objects feel all that man feels. Yes, he would write about bits of refuse—the cigar butt and the match swirling down the gutter to the sewer. Now they come lovingly together. Now the currents carry them apart. No, such things do not feel. Human beings feel. Human beings feel many things. Animals feel strength, fears, pain—but human beings feel so many things—mighty rivers of feeling sweeping upward to the stars, then down with dizzying speed, now up again.

Walt, why are you here? Andrew is sick. It's his lungs again. He's in the hospital. Anticipate what's

272

darkest. Expect the worst. Then whatever happens will be easier to bear.

There was no one in the house. The cat opened lazy eyes as it dozed near the stove. The pendulum moved sleepily back and forth.

Where were the children? It was late afternoon. School was over. "John!" he called. "Gail! Where are you?"

He waited for a long moment then walked out into the yard and sat down on the edge of the porch. No one came. Nothing stirred. He arose and walked to Myrtle Street and the more crowded sidewalks. Crowded sidewalks usually drew him like a magnet—sent dark thoughts scurrying away. People, all sorts of people— laughing, cursing, sullen, good-humored. What did it matter? People.

He returned home in a mood so despairing that he repeated over and over to himself, "It will pass. There were other dark moments and they passed. This darkness too will pass."

Early the next morning he set out once more for Nancy's place. He must see the children. He must see John and Gail. His heart was flooded with pity for Gail, only nine, thin and wistful. He should spend more time with her. What hospital? Andrew was sick and he had omitted to ask the name of the hospital. Jesse and Andrew—both ill, and he with his joy songs! Escape—wishful thinking. Emerson had said "pious" —called him "pious"—a piety of verse, alas, and not a piety of deed. Unworthy—unworthy—unworthy!

He thought for a fleeting moment that he saw Gail near the barber shop. No, what would she be doing in the doorway talking to the man who was leaving? Gail was only nine, sensitive, intelligent, swooping like a graceful bird from one mood to another, dainty and wistful. Yes, Gail was a sweetly tender child, and that girl in the doorway couldn't be Gail because Gail was shy, with just a hint of coyness, and would not talk to strangers.

Walt stopped abruptly, a frozen anger pressing against his heart. It *was* Gail, and the man had given her a coin. Gail was begging! Now she was accosting another man. That man brushed her rudely aside. The barber came out and shooed her away just as Walt hurried to her and took hold of her thin arm.

Gail looked up startled, then smiled. "Hello, Uncle Walt. I haven't seen you for a long time. Uncle Andrew's been sick. He's coming home from the hospital tomorrow. You heard about his sickness?" she nodded excitedly. "When he coughs into his handkerchief blood comes out—that's what makes him sick."

"Where's your Aunt Nancy?"

"She's sewing. You know the hat and overall factory on Jefferson Street—that's where she sews. We've been staying with Aunt Nancy. Are you coming to our house, Uncle Walt? Come to our house."

Walt bowed and put his arms around her. "What are you doing here, Gail?" How thin she was. There was scarcely any weight against him.

Gail repeated, "Come to our house, Uncle Walt, and tell me a story. John says you make all your stories up—but they're true, aren't they, Uncle Walt?"

They were walking now, her little hand swallowed up in his big steadying grasp. At the hat shop the foreman told Walt Nancy had just left, and Walt, his blood one great aching stream, hurried to confront her. He suddenly realized he was almost dragging Gail by the arm and slowed his pace.

Nancy was fumbling with her coin purse near a fruit store when Walt caught up with her. He gave Gail a quick gentle pat on the head "Run along home,

Gail. Run along ahead of us. I want to talk to Aunt Nancy."

Gail went slowly away, turning her head from time to time with a puzzled look directed at Walt.

"Nancy," he burst out, "Gail was begging."

He had expected a startled exclamation. Instead Nancy's reply was brief and sullen. "We've got to eat."

Walt took hold of her shoulders and faced her squarely. "But they're not your children. You have no right —"

"Are you taking care of them?"

"I'll try to help. Does Martha know? She wouldn't consent to this. Begging! Begging!"

Suddenly he realized people were staring and he dropped his hands.

"It's not dishonest to beg." Nancy's voice was hostile and stubborn.

"No, it's not dishonest—but Nancy, what's it doing to her? It's killing her spirit inside, making her whine where she should ask, kneel where she should stand —"

"Don't talk to me in fancy words, Walt. Our stomachs are empty and poetry doesn't fill them. I work hard, sewing hat bands and more hat bands until my fingers don't belong to my body any more. Then there's the medicine—and hospital for Andrew. His lungs are very bad—both of them. Then Jesse gets sick and Martha sends me the children. Whom should I ask for help—George or Jeff, when Jeff is saving every penny so he can get married. Or your drunken brother-in-law Charles, the old devil—or you, when you're so busy trying to save the world that you haven't got time for your own flesh and blood?"

Walt shrank—winced—questioned himself furiously and protested in his agony. "Everybody's my flesh and blood. Everybody!"

"Then don't jump on me for setting the children

to begging. They're asking help from their own flesh and blood. It's all in the family! Comin' in, Walt? Let's not quarrel. Come in an' have some supper with us. We won't wait for John. He's working Broadway."

Was she purposely trying to torture him more?

"Made a dollar and twelve cents yesterday and would have made more if the policeman hadn't frightened him." Then abruptly, "How's Ma?"

"She's well, Nancy. She doesn't know how sick Andrew is."

"Better not tell her anything, Walt." Nancy's eyes softened for the first time since Walt had spoken to her. "Don't mind me, Walt. I get nasty sometimes. I wish I could be like you, happy and liking people instead of hating them like I do. I tried to read your book but I can't make anything out of it. Are you selling a lot of copies?"

"No, Nancy, I'm not."

"Then why don't you get back on the newspaper? Coming in, Walt?"

"No, Nancy. Ma's expecting me. I'll come tomorrow and bring you some money. Don't let John and Gail beg. Please don't let John and Gail beg. It isn't good for them."

Nancy did not answer. She went into the house and closed the door behind her. Walt heard Gail singing inside the house and Nancy's voice shrill and hard telling her to stop—and Walt felt sorry for everyone that had ever lived.

IV

Only a little while ago John Brown had mounted the scaffold and the rope that strangled his voice now unloosed a million others. Some shouted "Devil!" Some shouted "Martyr!"—but everyone shouted.

Walt shook his head. "John Brown's bloody sword the answer? Not that way. The slow way is best. It takes a little while for things to grow."

All the noise, confusion, flaming speeches of the abolitionists swirled and heaved about him like the appearance of molten lava—but appearance only. Walt nodded approvingly when Lincoln was elected. "He's as real as earth—made of firmer stuff than Buchanan and truer stuff than Douglas." Then he asked himself, "Firmer stuff?" — to what end. War! Hasn't the South the right to its own way of life? Why hold it in the Union against its will? What is there in common between the plantations of the South and the factories of the North? Socially different—economically different—climatically different. Yes, but if they divided, any foreign power could destroy each separately. "A house divided against itself —" But did Lincoln see clearly through all the petty hates, the real basic differences? Who was advising him? And if you, Walt, were called upon for a great message what would you say?

"Man—Man—Man must be free."

A noble dictum—a grand generality—but tell the plantation owners to free their slaves and turn their crops into weeds, their homes into ruins. Tell them to turn their proud rule into the hands of the Negro majority and accept a meek minority status. Go on, Walt, be consistent. *You* be the banner—the symbol of the equality of man. Send for Anne Sedley and for your son—*your son—your son* —! Too soon! Too soon in the slow growth of man's soul.

Come now, Walt, sculpture your convictions clearly in your own mind.

"The South must solve its own problems. No rash threats *from* the North—but no spread of slavery *to* the North."

277

"But what of the Fugitive Slave Law making you a partner in evil?"

"It is an unwise corrupting law."

"If a thing is evil, stamp it out."

"No, it will outgrow its evil part and cast it off like dead leaves."

"Is that all, Walt Whitman? But what of your song—your song of the Freedom of Man? What can you achieve for others if you yourself don't know? You know the *direction* your path must take, but you don't know what to *do*."

"I'll admit it. I'll confess it. It's just as Anne says. I don't know what to do. I only know what must be. My song is ahead of people by a thousand years—but I believe my song—I believe in America—Oh God, — how I believe in America—teeming, swarming with brave yearnings, the America where that song of mine will first come true!"

V

It was futile to argue and shout back and forth—back and forth—in the Senate—in the halls of Congress. Men did not seek truth through debate. They mustered phrase and gesture to arm their stubborn prejudice. And yet the debates and orations continued furiously.

But now quite abruptly only the newsboys were shouting. A heavy silence froze all else—a silence more dangerous than clamor. Men read the headlines in deathly quiet, tightened their lips and walked on.

There was a morning when Walt read curiously, "Fort Sumter Fired Upon!" Almost resenting the annoying interruption to his work on "Leaves of Grass" he murmured, "Hot heads. Impulsive fire-eaters. An insane act. Such things don't happen! Men of America aren't going to kill each other. One country—one flag—one language."

But guns *were* fired. That was real. Guns were real. Now what path?

Louisa's eyes were grief-dulled. "George has gone and joined up."

Walt murmured, "He shouldn't have gone, Ma. The whole thing will be over in a few weeks."

"You'll not go, Walt?"

"No, Ma. I can't kill. If this continues I suppose someone's got to fight, but I can't kill."

"That is good Quaker teaching, my son, but George has joined up. Tell him he's wrong."

"But I don't know what's right any more." Walt covered his face with his hands. "The Union must be preserved or each half goes under. To preserve it we must kill—to preserve the whole family we must kill members of the family. I cannot stain my hands with blood so I applaud George, laud his courage and I stay home so that my hands are clean. Mother, I wish I knew what was right to do."

* * * *

The guns that he could not fire exploded in his brain—and the wounds that he could not inflict flowed from his pen. His verse was of the war; he could write of nothing else.

> *"Come up from the fields father, here's a letter from our Pete,*
> *And come to the front door mother, here's a letter from thy dear son.*
> *Lo, 'tis autumn,*
> *Lo, where the trees, deeper green, yellower and redder,*
> *Cool and sweeten Ohio's villages with leaves fluttering in the moderate wind.*

*Where apples ripe in the orchards hang and grapes
   on the trellis'd vines,
(Smell you the smell of the grapes on the vines?
Smell you the buckwheat where the bees were lately
   buzzing?)
Above all, lo, the sky so calm, so transparent after
   the rain, and with wondrous clouds,
Below too, all calm, all vital and beautiful, and the
   farm prospers well.
Down in the fields all prospers well,
But now from the fields come father, come at the
   daughter's call,
And come to the entry mother, to the front door
   come right away.
Fast as she can she hurries, something ominous, her
   steps trembling,
She does not tarry to smooth her hair nor adjust
   her cap.
Open the envelope quickly,
O, this is not our son's writing, yet his name is sign'd
O a strange hand writes for our dear son, O stricken
   mother's soul!
All swims before her eyes, flashes with black, she
   catches the main words only.
Sentences broken, 'gunshot wound in the breast,
   cavalry skirmish, taken to hospital,
At present low, but will soon be beter.'*"

* * * *

The defeat of the Union forces at Bull Run was a
stunning shock to both North and South. The North
writhed and questioned in a panic, "Will Washington
itself fall in the next assault?" As for the Confederate
forces, their triumph was incredible in their own eyes.
A fever of over-confidence swept through their armies.
"To the offensive *now;*—at once! To the offensive!"

In the meantime General George McClellan had

inspired the faith of his colleagues by his victory at Hart's Farm and by his efficient organization of the Army of the West.

Short in stature, young in years—only thirty-five— he was given immediate command of the Army of the Potomac. He built a disheartened multitude of raw recruits into a highly disciplined, magnificently organized war machine—poised to strike and then he sat back and waited.

"To the offensive now; to the offensive!" This was the anxious plea of the President.

Walt watched with gathering horror as the armies of the North and South called for more and more men and guns. The great nation, his beloved America, was cleaving asunder—and all he could do was watch.

McClellan answered Lincoln's urgings for immediate action with silence. In vain Lincoln pleaded for an attack upon the rapidly growing rebel army. Now the press and the public grew frantic in their clamor. "How long will we wait? While we delay the Confederates build powerful batteries along the Potomac and gather strength from hour to hour."

"Wait," was McClellan's cautious reply to the press. "The enemy is far more powerful than you think."

As Lincoln pressed for action, McClellan grew contemptuous and hypersensitive. "What makes you think you can judge the situation as well as I?"

Lincoln removed him from command and appointed General Pope in his stead.

Pope was beaten at the second battle of Bull Run and Lincoln, swallowing the indignities that McClellan had heaped upon him, summoned him to command the now demoralized army of the Potomac. The defense held firm. At Antietam Lee's invasion of the North was checked, but McClellan again became cautious and refused to pursue the attack. He surveyed the field of the dead and the wounded with a strange melancholy dread that chained him to the spot and fettered his limbs.

Lincoln at once relieved him of his command and elevated Burnside in his place. Then almost at the same moment he prepared an Emancipation Proclamation which defined the issue so sharply that neither foreign powers nor local politicians could straddle the fence.

France and England were thus prevented from recognizing the Confederacy, as they fully had intended to do, for on the issue of Union they could favor and even champion the South's right to secede, but on the issue of Slavery their public opinion must be regarded.

Now the North seethed with the zeal of a righteous cause on the one hand and swellings of the heart—forebodings—and remorse at the costly human sacrifice on the other.

McClellan, embittered by his removal from command, and never an opponent of slavery, denounced the Emancipation Proclamation:

"Is it idealism or guileful maneuverings? If it is sincere idealism why does Lincoln permit slavery in those portions of the South occupied by Union troops? No, friends, he is attempting to stir up the slaves of the South to rise up and do his fighting for him."

There gathered around McClellan partisans of the "peace at any price" persuasion, and as the dreary months brought slaughter without victory, Lincoln's unpopularity grew apace. No one spoke up in his defense. It was enough if men were silent.

Now few of the North spoke of victory. There were battles, casualty lists, appointments, demotions, and battles again. There were the wounded—the living—and the dead—and reports—reports—bulletins—and more battles.

* * * *

His mother stood thin and bowed in the doorway. "The neighbors told me there's been many men lost at Fredericksburg, Walt. Get the paper, Walt. Get the paper."

Walt hurried out and bought a New York Herald. The casualty lists were not there.

"Mother," he comforted her, "there are other camps and many battlefronts. You don't know where George is serving."

The next morning's Herald carried a long list of the dead and wounded. Walt, disregarding the snow and the cold, spread the paper against the wall of the saloon near the news stand and checked each name carefully. There was a numbing shock and then a sharp piercing pain across his heart as he read and re-read, "13th Division—51st New York Volunteers, George Whitman."

"George! George wounded!"

He must go to him. Perhaps the wound was slight. He was short of funds, but he must travel at once to Washington. Washington! That's what the Herald said —"Hundreds of wounded men have already been transported to hospitals in Washington."

His mother's anxious face was pressed against the frosted window. She had been waiting—waiting. Sharp snowflakes stung her face as she thrust the door open.

"Mother, I'm leaving for Washington today."

"George?" Louisa's lips framed the name in scarcely a whisper.

"George has been wounded. I'll find him and take care of him."

Jeff came in a moment later. He carried a rolled up Herald in his hand. His forehead was clouded. As he unloosened his woolen scarf he saw that Walt and his mother knew.

"You're going to him, Walt? Better take the ferry

to Jersey City and get a train there. You can get one this afternoon."

"I'll need some money."

"Here's ten dollars, Walt. They've cut me to fifty a month. I wish I could let you have more."

Walt shook his head. "I can't take it, Jeff. You'll have to look after Ma and Eddie. Then's there's your wife and the baby, and Martha and Nancy to help. I'll get to Washington all right. Don't worry about me."

"Take five anyway."

Walt took the five dollars, dressed warmly, kissed his mother and left the house, all in the space of a few moments.

Again his thoughts become incoherent. What had happened to George? Was it an amputation—or some other disfiguring wound? There should be ways of protecting arms, legs, eyes, — arms, legs, eyes.

Once men fought in armor. Not many were hurt that way. Limbs are too vulnerable, too vulnerable. A whole body is beautiful—a complete body—the Union must be preserved. Amputations are ugly—the Union —

Walt dozed darkly, leaning his head against the train window.

"Below the surface of the sea monsters devour each other —"

In his fantasy Walt saw Melville looking at him with white face and narrow eyes. "Now do you see?"

"I see and *yet* I believe. Let my heart burst like the fabled bird with the expanding flood of its own song, — but the song—the song must live!"

Strange dreams — distorted visions — amputations. The body must be complete. Paste on the leg. Sew on the arm. No, no, not that way; the stitches show, the glue shows. Sew the South to the North. Make the stitches strong. No, no, not that way—complete—complete—complete. America—complete—complete!

VI

"You can't get rooms in Washington, Mister. Haven't you got a friend or a relative in the city?"

The puffy-eyed clerk of the cheap lodging house was trying to be helpful. The manager who emerged suddenly from his office offered the time-worn venerable cliché, "Don't you know there's a war on, mister?"

Walt reached for one of his memorandum books. Somewhere on the inside of a cover he had noted the address of William Douglas O'Connor, a fighting abolitionist and a spirited writer. Ah, there it was—394 L Street.

"How do I get to L Street?" he asked the clerk.

"It's only a few blocks west from here. You can walk it. What number on L Street?"

But Walt was already striding out of the door. He had observed the way the numbers ran and was sure he could find the place.

It was dismal and cold and the hour was late when Walt tapped at the door of the O'Connor apartment. The door was opened almost at once by a genial black bearded florid-faced young man in stocking feet who had evidently been lying on a narrow sofa near the stove. The large white pillow still bore the imprint of his head.

Walt was recognized at once and cordially welcomed. "Hello, stranger. Come on in! Don't tell me you're doing a column on the horrors of war. What brings you to Washington?"

Walt walked in, pleased at the undisguised friendliness of O'Connor. O'Connor pushed a chair at him.

"Use that, Mister, and take the strain off your spine. What's your assignment?"

As Walt prepared to answer, a tall, tired looking young woman came into the living room, nodded pleasantly at Walt and began to pick up the scattered sheets of newspaper.

"You remember my wife Nellie, don't you Walt? She remembers you well and speaks of you often."

"Of course I remember you, Nellie."

Walt arose and took her extended hand. "Wasn't there a little boy?"

O'Connor frowned and lowered his head. Walt knew at once he had blundered. Nellie O'Connor lost all color. Her lip trembled and she looked past Walt with anguished tortured eyes.

"Our son died, Walt. He was playing with the rocking chair, pushing it back and forth and laughing. Then it tipped over and broke a souvenir cup. I scolded him—Bill scolded him, too."

"That had nothing to do with it, Nellie. It had nothing to do with his being sick. He caught cold— he had a fever. His lungs —"

"I know, Bill. I'm just telling Mr. Whitman how it happened. When he went to sleep he was kind of flushed. Before morning he was dead."

"Nellie, you promised —"

"But I keep thinking it really didn't happen. I used to get up three times a night to see if he was breathing. He seemed so tiny. Sometimes I'd wake him from his sleep just to be sure he was alive. All right, Bill, I won't talk about it—any more. I'll make you some tea, Mr. Whitman."

As she hurried from the room O'Connor arose and stood looking down at Walt. "I tell her not to talk about it, but I'm worse than she is. I can't get one thing out of my mind, Walt. I scolded my youngster for tipping over that chair and breaking that cheap little souvenir cup. He whimpered, and finally I kissed him goodnight. He smiled after that and went to sleep. That must have fixed it up with him, Walt. Children forget their hurt feelings quickly—don't they? You don't think it bothered him—the scolding, I mean. That couldn't have made his lungs—his condition worse, could it?"

Walt felt his heart rise and swell with grief. He wanted to weep. "Of course not, Bill! You're imagining things. Remorse—regret. Don't do that. All of us feel that way—guilty, when a dear one goes on."

O'Connor kept on tonelessly, "It's sinning against God to complain. We've still got our little girl. That's what pulled Nellie out of it—having to take care of our little girl. Philosophize all you want to, Walt, about how wonderful life is—but it hurts. It hurts horribly." O'Connor smiled a wry twisted smile. "But you just keep on—just the same, doing the same things. There it is—and what choice have you?" He tore himself out of his mood with a savage effort. "But you haven't answered me, Walt. What brought you here?"

Nellie paused as she served the tea—paused to hear. Walt thought, if I tell *my* troubles maybe it will take their mind off *theirs*.

He spoke rapidly. "My brother's wounded. His name was in the published list. I don't know if they've brought him to Washington, but I feel quite sure he's here."

Nellie's eyes poured out her concern and sympathy. She became alert, eager to suggest, anxious to help. "Why don't you hire a carriage and make the rounds of the military hospitals?"

"I left without funds—and haven't been able to find lodging."

Nellie made a quick gesture of resolve. "Bill, Mr.

Whitman can stay with us until he gets settled. He can use the sofa if it's long enough. He's taller than you."

O'Connor grinned and nodded. "That's the way it's going to be, Walt. You won't get lodging anywhere. Families of wounded men have been pouring in. Government officials—yes," he grinned, "even Republicans and Democrats are doubling up."

Walt did not protest. He stayed that night, gratified for the warm and genuine friendship offered him and anxious to set out early in search of his brother.

"No information!" "No record!" "Our clerks can't keep up with the reports." "Be patient. By the end of the week perhaps." Such were the responses to his anxious quest.

Walt returned to the O'Connor apartment late that afternoon. The door was locked. He sat down on the top stair to wait. Then he heard the whimpering of a child. It came from behind the locked door. Walt arose quickly and took hold of the knob.

"Peg! Open the door! It's Uncle Walt!"

How could Nellie leave a child of five alone, especially after the tragedy?

"Peg, don't be afraid. Open the door!"

The whimpering increased in volume. Now Walt could make out childish sobs. "Don't Ma! Don't Ma! Peggy's scared!" Then he heard Nellie's voice with a touch of madness in it—"Walk slowly, little darling, and I'll catch up with you. Wait for me, my son."

He flung his shoulder against the heavy door. "Nellie!" he shouted. "Nellie! For God's sake open the door!"

There was no answer. Walt, his heart chilled with an overwhelming terror, beat with his fists against the door and looked frantically about for some heavy implement with which he might shatter it.

He stepped back a few paces, resolved to break either his shoulder or the door in the next attempt. Suddenly the door opened. Nellie stood there, her face flushed and her throat raw and bruised. Tiny drops of blood flecked the skin. Her hair, straggly and disheveled, added frenzy to the madness of her eyes.

Walt's eyes saw all, the knotted rope thrown over the rusty water pipe that was exposed high over the sink—the overturned chair below it—the frightened, weeping child clinging to the mother's dress sobbing and gasping for breath, her little body trembling with every intake of air.

"Another minute and it would have been too late!" Nellie spoke the words calmly and then suddenly burst into tears. Walt took a firm hold of her shoulders and seated her on the sofa. She covered her face with her hands.

"I can't live, Walt. I can't go on living. His little body's in the earth and the rain falls on it. And he's all alone."

"Nellie, it's against God's law to throw away the gift of life." He drew the sobbing little Peg towards him, but she still clutched the skirt of her mother's dress with her tightly closed tiny fist.

"I know. I know; but I can't help it. Every minute of living is torture. I'm not finding fault with God; it's just that I don't want to live."

"You've had a great shock, Nellie. And the world seems to you like a bad dream. But catch hold of it! Take hold of Peg and Bill. They love you and you would take all the light out of their lives if you did this foolish thing."

"I've tried—Oh Holy Mother Mary, I've tried, but it gets worse—the thinking, the grieving! You've made a beautiful world, God—but take me out of it. I can't bear it."

Walt watched her sob, wondering what Bill would feel if he knew—if he knew—

"I'll have to tell Bill. You have to have someone with you all the time."

"No, Walt, don't tell him. He's had too much sorrow. I promise I'll not try anything like this again."

"How can I believe you?" He grasped her arm gently. "You're not to blame. Your grief is stronger than your will. You mean to keep your promise but you might not be able to fight off your despair."

"I know I'll be all right now. He can't be tied down with me day and night. We'll both go crazy. If I could only sleep—if I could only get a few hours of sleep so I wouldn't think."

"Please don't talk about it now. Try to calm yourself." Walt whispered the words, "You've given Peg a shock she may never forget."

"I know—I know. Come, Peg, let me wash your face. I'll comb your hair. See, there's nothing to be afraid of. Mother is smiling. Mother is happy again."

Nellie guided the bewildered child to the bedroom where the heavy pitcher of water stood in its ponderous bowl on top of the clothes chest. Walt watched her bathe the child's frightened and flushed face. Then he heard footsteps and stepped out into the hall. O'Connor waved a cheery greeting, "Any luck?"

Walt shook his head and laid a restraining hand on O'Connor's shoulder. He motioned him away from the door.

"Bill, Nellie's been more hurt than you think. She's melancholy. She'll have to be watched."

O'Connor's eyes glazed with unspeakable despair. "I felt it, Walt. I was afraid of it. Did she try to do away with herself? Is that what you mean?"

Walt nodded. "It will take time for the wound to heal."

O'Connor moved to the doorway. His face was weary and gray with dejection. Walt followed.

Nellie stood facing them. One hand held a large coarse comb. Walt saw that Peg's face was clean and her hair neatly combed. The bruises on Nellie's throat were livid purple swellings. She looked at Walt for a long moment. Her eyes were lifeless. "You told him, Walt. You told him."

O'Connor shook his head. "Stay with us, Walt. You'll be helping us." He walked slowly to Nellie and looked at the dark welts on the white skin. He suddenly held her close in his arms and broke into a labored sobbing. "My darling! My darling!"

Walt turned away. "It's better this way," he thought. "Bill can do his writing at home. He doesn't have to leave her—until she has learned to live with her grief."

Outside he walked the streets till midnight. So much sorrow—so much pain. Could there indeed be a malicious power, a vast malicious power that ruled the universe and watched the living things rend and tear each other—and, when a frightened human being ran to a cave in his terror, that sardonic infinity of malice would clutch it squirming in his hand and push it writhing and struggling back into the clearing—back into the battle, shouting "You can't escape!" Why he, Walt, had done that very thing to Nellie. All she had asked was oblivion. But he had pushed her back to the life *he* found palatable. *You* must live because *I* love life!

And then Walt went back to the O'Connor flat. Perhaps the door was locked. No. He opened it gently. There was a sheet and a blanket on the sofa—and a pillow. How quiet the rooms were. Blessed sleep that so resembles death—forgetfulness. No, there was the

sound of voices in the bedroom. No sleep for Nellie.
No escape for her. A cage! A trap!

Walt didn't mean to listen—and yet somehow the
words were audible.

"I'll try to make it up to you, Nellie darling. I
need you so." Nellie answered softly, and all that Walt
could hear was "Forgive! Forgive!" The voices rose
and fell—and then suddenly it was morning.

VII

Walt scanned every bulletin—every casualty list.
He wrote his mother of hopes that he was far from
feeling. Each clerk referred him to another. Each de-
partment made plausible excuses and explanations.
Walt insisted patiently, "You *must* have a record of
George Whitman. After all, it isn't a Smith or a Jones.
The name is Whitman."

For days on days he made the rounds—from hospital to hospital, from church to schoolhouse, then to
the government buildings, all of them filled with the
stench of blood and drugs, all of them swarming and
writhing with men in sweaty agony. Here a man
sobbed, a deep strange sound, and then a young boy
scarcely sixteen cursed profanely as the nurse tried to
turn him on the cot.

Walt helped one, then another, and found a slight
relief in his agony. In the evenings he wrote—wrote
fragments of the horrors he witnessed sitting near the
bedside of the afflicted. Aching, weeping words sought
for expression:

"I onward go, I stop,
With hinged knees and steady hand to dress wounds,
I am firm with each, the pangs are sharp yet un-
avoidable,

*One turns to me his appealing eyes—poor boy! I
never knew you,*
*Yet I think I could not refuse this moment to die
for you, if that would save you.*
*Oh, on I go, (open doors of time! open hospital
doors!)*
*The crush'd head I dress, (poor crazed hand tear
not the bandage away,)*
*The neck of the cavalry-man with the bullet through
and through I examine,*
*Hard the breathing rattles, quite glazed already the
eye, yet life struggles hard,*
*(Come sweet death! be persuaded O beautiful
death!*
In mercy come quickly)."

The nurses and doctors hurried about with sagging lips, glumly scowling their complete exhaustion as they found themselves swamped beneath so great a heap of suffering.

The lists were posted and Walt searched each page for his brother's name—searched in vain.

"I'm going to Fredericksburg," he told O'Connor suddenly.

"You'll need a pass. I'll try and get you one."

That very afternoon Walt had the precious pass —the pass and fourteen dollars that Bill thrust into his coat pocket. "You'll pay me back when you have it, Walt. Don't argue about it."

"Good people—good people," was the constant refrain in his heart. "Their own loss aching—they feel *my* anxiety."

Nellie was better now. She laughed at times. Bill had been patient, so patient with her.

"Thanks for your kindness, Bill."

Walt placed his arms around Bill and kissed him on the cheek. "Hey, don't do that," laughed Bill awkwardly. "What's the idea? You sure are the effectionate kind."

Walt felt embarrassed. Even Nellie was laughing. He had shown his affection frankly and these good people were amused. He would like to take the whole world in his arms. Why did they laugh?

He wandered for hours among the rows of tents at Fredericksburg. Behind one hospital tent was a heap of arms, legs and hands that had been amputated. He grew faint and sick and his breath caught inside his lungs so that he could not breathe freely.

He asked the question mechanically of everyone he met.

"Do you mean Captain George W. Whitman?" asked one of the chaplains he accosted. "You'll find him in the officers' quarters on the other side of the hedge."

He had found him! He had found his brother! A Captain? He felt a glow of pride in the midst of his anxiety. "Perhaps it is someone else with the same name," thought Walt to himself as he followed the path through the hedge. Then he heard his brother's voice and entered one of the larger tents. Three of the men lay in cots covered neatly with several blankets. Two others were attempting to nurse a flame in a small camp stove. One officer was seated at the table writing. One side of his face was bandaged but Walt knew him even before he faced him. He touched his shoulder gently.

"George, you're not badly wounded?"

His brother, startled, arose quickly, and Walt pressed him affectionately back into his chair.

"Just a hole through my cheek, but nothing dangerous. A bit of grape shot. How's mother?"

"She's going to be much better when you finish that letter and send it off to her."

"Poor Mother! There was a nasty infection. I couldn't write for a while. It's good to see you. Walt, these are my friends—Lieutenant Esposito and Captain Cohn. Captain Cohn's wound is almost the same as mine, except that the grape shot is still in his jaw." George continued rapidly, "Major Ellis has read your book and likes it. He even understands it—so he says." He motioned to a young man lying in the cot near the stove, his eyes fixed kindly upon them.

"Major, this is my brother, Walt. You read his book—now you can tell him yourself what you think. Go on, Major, tell him." Still the young man made no sign of recognition. George bent quickly and seized his wrist. The two officers near the stove slowly rose and moved towards him.

"Call a doctor, Gil. Call a doctor. Quick! I'm afraid he's gone. I can't find a pulse beat."

The harassed doctor who entered the tent soon after, merely nodded. "Well get him out of here right away. That'll give you men a little more room for a few days."

"He was very young to be a Major." Walt tried to break the gray, heavy silence.

"He was twenty. Started out as a medic and then asked to be transferred to the infantry. He was soft like. I never could figure him out, Walt. He kept saying he wanted to heal and not kill. Yet once he got into the infantry—"

Two soldiers came in with a stretcher and soon Ellis' cot was gapingly empty.

Walt broke the taut silence. "What did he see in my book? What did he like about it?"

"He said it was a broom that swept clean—an honest broom that left no dust anywhere. He wanted to meet you. He kept saying that you knew what you were about, where almost everyone else was muddled."

Walt felt like shouting in desperation, "I'm just as lost as the rest, just as bewildered." Instead he arose and nodded to the officers. "Maybe I can be of some help to the medical staff. Will you excuse me?"

"Stay here with us—lodge with us, sir," suggested Captain Wilber Cohn earnestly, slowly turning his bandaged face towards Walt. The others added their urgings. "Sure. We've talked ourselves out. You'll give us a fresh slant."

George added his plea. "Stay here, Walt. I'll be going back into the lines in a few days, so let's see a little of each other. You'll have a chance to tell me more about the folks."

Walt nodded. "Thanks, friends. I'm really grateful."

Walt felt an immediate urge to look into the very heart of all the agony he sensed around him. He took his leave and hurried down the path past the hedge to the long sheds which were being used as hospitals. Nobody paid any attention to him as he entered the first shed. They were performing operations in the ward. There was no special operating room. The air reeked with odors and shook with groans, curses and screams.

A group of sanitary commissioners made the rounds of the beds with mechanical regularity and severe important visages. The wounded men turned away as they passed.

"Piss on them!" gritted one bearded veteran lying on his face as he tried to push himself towards the head of his inclined bed. Walt placed his hands under the arm-pits of the embittered one and slowly eased his position.

"Those damned jackals parading around here taking notes while our guts are rotting. Why don't they stop to give a man a scrap of tobacco, a drink of water or a lift when he's all cracked up?"

He got confidential with Walt. "Sharpen your eyes on those chaplains—the big one and the little one. Me with three pieces of shrapnel in my ass and they telling me the meek will inherit the Kingdom of Heaven."

Walt stayed on. He needed little sleep. From bed to bed he moved, changing linens when linens could be obtained; helping men to the toilet when they could walk, carrying their bed pans when they could not; dressing festered wounds; holding a man down with his weight during an amputation—reading the Bible to those who asked for it. Often he sat on the floor with the wounded men for whom no beds could be found.

So used was he to the stench of antiseptics that the chill air away from the camp seemed like a vacuum that he could not inhale. Often he reproached himself, "I should be writing my songs. The 'Leaves of Grass' must be complete. It must be, for it will be eternal!"

But no time for that. The wounded men begged him to write letters to their dear ones, and so he wrote long, long letters until his fingers, cramped and numb, seemed glued to the pen.

At night he carried a lantern down the long corridors of agony. From hospital shed to hospital shed. "Can't you sleep, Fred? Let me read to you."

"Get me the doctor. He can give me something to stop the pain."

"He's in the next ward. He'll be here soon. Please let me read to you."

"Like hell he will. You lie in your whiskers, you bearded bastard. He never comes around. Go 'head, keep talking; read to me—read and be damned!"

VIII

The Spring grew warm and sultry. George was back in action somewhere near Chancellorsville. More wounded were being moved to Washington from Fredericksburg. Walt went along with a hundred and thirty badly wounded men. He fanned them as they were jolted down the rough roads in the wagon, wiped the sweat from their foreheads, carried their bed pans to and from the wagons when the caravan halted at intervals.

There was a Negro soldier badly slashed in the groin by a saber thrust lying alone in the last wagon where medical supplies were stacked. Walt would not have known he was there if he had not heard a sharp cry of pain as the horses gave a sudden tug at the wagon.

"Could you turn me, sir? The jolt threw me directly on my wound."

Walt climbed into the wagon and carefully stepped over the piles of supplies. The Negro smiled. "And my cry was heard. And the Lord sent—There, if you'll just lift the shoulder. Thank you." The Negro lapsed into silence as though Walt were no longer there.

Walt sat down on a half-filled burlap sack. "Would you like an orange?"

"Yes, thank you. Would you mind, sir, — I mean, may I ask your denomination, sir?"

Walt was puzzled for a moment. "I mean, are you Lutheran, Baptist, Catholic, Moravian, Quaker — or what?"

"Why do you ask?"

"I've been getting many a bargain, brother, salvation and bananas, salvation and milk, salvation—always salvation. White folks are more worried about saving my soul than healing my wound. What brand of salvation do you sell?"

"Why are you bitter?"

"Why not continue with condescension and reproof? You were going to say, 'Here we white men are giving our lives to save you from slavery—and you are not properly grateful.' "

"No, I wasn't going to say that. Our slave ships brought you here in the first place."

"What *were* you going to say?"

"When was your bandage changed last?"

"I'm sorry. No, better not touch it. It's been draining. There's a tube in the wound."

"May I ask again, why are you bitter?"

The Negro was silent. Walt felt an impulse to speak —to tell this man about Anne, about his child—to break the wall of mistrust. The wagon jolted on and Walt could not find the words. The man was educated, intelligent—a freed slave perhaps. Walt found himself dozing from exhaustion. The Negro lay there watching him, and he was too tired to speak.

In Washington Walt made the rounds of the hospitals, slept and ate with the medics who accepted him unquestionably as one of them.

The streets were choking and congested with humanity—all of it noisy, clamorous, critical, swarming near bulletin boards, famished for news from the battlefront.

Walt visited the prison hospitals. There were rebel prisoners there among the wounded—hostile, cold, defiant. They rarely spoke to Walt and when they did it was a brief aloof thanks for a kindness done.

* * * *

"General Meade replaces Hooker!"

The set-back at Chancellorsville was the final cause of Hooker's removal. General "Stonewall" Jackson had struck suddenly and had found General Joseph Hooker entirely unprepared. More than that he had encircled the right flank of the northern forces and caught General Howard napping so that the retreat became a stampede.

Things were not going well with the North, although the South had lost its greatest and most beloved hero. General Thomas Jonathan Jackson was dead. From the battle of Bull Run he had carried away a nickname that his forces had lovingly bestowed upon him — "Stonewall" Jackson. He had battled superior northern forces and defeated them. The South could ill afford to lose him—and the North correctly guessed that such a man would not easily be replaced. "Stonewall" Jackson was dead—shot by his own men as he reconnoitered with a small staff of officers, — shot by his own men. Yet even as he lay dying he had given the orders which first broke Hooker's center and then forced him to retreat.

Stinging charges—furious accusations were hurled at Lincoln. "Politicians pick your generals—and, while you play favorites, the North is being routed."

The Lieutenant who stood near Walt groaned his disgust. "Stupid, blundering fool! Can't he make up his mind? Why does he experiment with appointments? If only we had a leader!"

The crowd around the bulletin board turned their faces toward the Lieutenant, as though expecting more in the same vein.

A fat man with pompous side-whiskers proclaimed solemnly, "That's what comes of having a damned atheist for President!"

"He's not an atheist. It's malicious for you to say so," protested a young lady who stood near the Lieutenant. "President Lincoln prays to God and believes in God."

"Words, nothing more. Hypocrisy to get votes. What church does he belong to? Answer that, miss. That's the proof of a man's religion—church affiliation, church membership. Founded on a rock, miss, founded on a rock. I could understand him even if he were a Jew or a Catholic, but this way he's nothing—a bag of wind, miss—a bag of rhetorical wind."

Walt interrupted boldly, "And Thomas Jefferson? And Benjamin Franklin, and Thomas Paine—were they also bags of wind, my friend? And Thoreau and Emerson and Burroughs—are they also bags of wind? Might not that wind be the Spirit of God?"

"You malign the founders of our country and its poets, sir! They were and are church men—devout church men —"

"On the contrary, my brother," Walt interrupted mildly, "but they did proclaim the Unity of God and the brotherhood of man."

"That's no religion. That's taking refuge in empty words. That's backsliding — rebellion — untrammelled atheism —"

"Cool off, mister." The Lieutenant drew himself up stiffly and turned to Walt. "Are you by any chance a Jew?"

Several people in the crowd turned suddenly to listen. Even the young lady stiffened and stood coldly aloof. Walt debated in his mind whether or not to answer, but almost at once he heard a ringing shout:

"Yes, by the broth of Aunt Bridget's mulligan stew!" It was William O'Connor who interrupted noisily, yet good naturedly. "Sure an' our President's name is Abraham, the father of the Jewish people he was—and our friend here has a beard—and so have I —and so has Grant and Meade and a hundred generals, and so did our Lord Jesus and they are all Jews— —and so was Mother Mary—and so am I and my name's O'Connor."

Someone in the crowd laughed. The Lieutenant

flushed angrily. "None of that shanty Irish humor appeals to me."

O'Connor laughed. "It wouldn't. Humor is a sense of proportion, an' where there's no sense there's no proportion."

Then the Lieutenant lost his head completely. His handsome face flamed red. He pulled his pistol from its holster. The young woman screamed and recoiled. Walt thrust both his hands forward and struck down the arm of the enraged officer and the bullet discharged into the ground. The crowd milled around in a frenzy and would not be calmed.

An army officer pushed his way through the crowd. "Lieutenant!"

The young officer's hand moved sharply upward in salute, his face above his tight military collar still swollen with anger.

"You fired that shot?"

"Yes, sir."

"Is there anyone who wishes to make complaint?" No one spoke.

"Your name and company, sir."

"Lieutenant Gerald Smythe, sir. Co. F, Cavalry, 112th Volunteers."

"You will return to your quarters and consider yourself under arrest."

IX

O'Connor greeted Walt with the keenest delight, "Nellie's much better. Come with me and see for yourself." There was a glow of health in Bill O'Connor's bearded cheeks and Walt, as he listened, felt as though some benign power were removing part of his burden.

Why must I bear the weight of every grief I know?

But then I share the joys—so fair arrangement, I'll not rebel.

O'Connor was garrulous. "You moved quickly, Walt, when you struck his arm down—and I am grateful. After all it was my quarrel. You might have been injured."

"No, it was any decent man's quarrel."

They passed a general store and Walt spied a forlorn rag doll in the window. Before O'Connor could protest Walt had made the purchase.

"Children seem to prefer rag dolls—more room for the imagination, perhaps."

"Sympathy—maybe."

"I don't know, Bill. You may be right—and a child's reputed cruelty may arise out of ignorance of the harm he does."

"And an adult?"

"No, an adult justifies his cruelty under the cloak of an ideal."

"You're a strange man, Walt. You walk with us—and yet you're apart from us. Your emotions are those of a child or of a very wise old man. I can't for the life of me make up my mind which."

As they climbed the stairs Walt felt an oppressive tug at his heart. The closed door—Nellie—the closed door. What was concealed behind it? Closed doors—kick them open. Closed doors—break them open—and then Nellie herself stood in the doorway—and Walt felt a great relief.

"Welcome to you, Walt. I thought you had forgotten us completely." She saw the doll and shook her head. "You shouldn't have done that. Prices are so high with the war and all. Peg! Peg! It's Uncle Walt."

Peg came out of the bedroom cautiously. At first she wouldn't touch the doll. Then slowly as the attention was taken from her she approached it where it lay on the sofa.

"That's a safe gift, Walt." Nellie watched Peg tenderly as she spoke. "Rag dolls can be mended." Then she smiled up at Walt. "Don't fear for me any more. I walked in the dawn yesterday on my way from Mass, and I saw the drops of dew hanging under the rail fence and the sun was shining through them making them look like diamonds. 'How beautiful,' I whispered. 'They are like the tears of yesterday.' "

"Stay with us, Walt." Bill was insistent.

"No, your heart is bigger than your space."

"Well, this night anyway. You've got to read to us some of your verse. My writing's been pretty flat. Maybe I can borrow a spark from your fire."

Walt stayed and read his verse with the exulting joy of one who suddenly uncovers a treasure long lost and long despaired of.

Three days went by and then Walt resolved he must crowd his friends no longer. Off he went to serve as a volunteer nurse once more. There were, however, no extra cots for volunteers.

"You're not getting any rest sleeping on the floor in the hospitals. There's an attic room on 6th Street near Pennsylvania Avenue, Walt." O'Connor reached in his pocket for the address. "Nice old lady runs it. I told her you'd call. Tell her I sent you."

Walt lost no time in hurrying to the lodging house. 456 Sixth Street. That very morning he had received a check for fifty dollars from the Times, and had paid O'Connor the fourteen dollars he owed him, so he felt in a rather opulent mood. He reflected, "Strange— that a few dollars in the pocket brings one such a comforting feeling of security, no matter what his philosophy may be."

"Are you Mr. Whitman, the poet?" The kindly

old lady, whose gray blonde hair was tightly curled and whose thin shoulders were somewhat stooped, looked up at Walt with a deference almost reverent. The ornate locket she wore seemed too large for her small flat bosom. "Are you the man Mr. O'Connor sent?"

She continued as though an answer was entirely unnecessary. "Of course you are—just as Mr. O'Connor described you. I had many callers who wanted the room but I kept it for you."

"Thank you. Is it well-lighted?"

"Yes, you will find it entirely satisfactory for your writing."

"And the price?"

"Four dollars a week."

"May I see it? No, it won't be necessary. I'll gladly take it, Miss —"

"Mrs. Quentin Raymond."

Just then a spindly little dark-haired girl with an eager excited face came running towards them. "Grandma! Grandma! Come quick!" she called. "The President is riding by—President Lincoln!"

Walt hurried to the door. He felt suddenly overwhelmed. He was as eager as the child who had called out. His glance rested first on the young cavalry lieutenant who rode stiffly at the side of the President. There was something familiar about that scowl. Walt remembered and frowned. It was the young lieutenant who had been placed under arrest only a few days before.

"Are the good always so surrounded? Doesn't nearness to kindness receive a glow?" Then his eyes dwelt intently on the tall sombre figure of a man who rode a large gray horse at a slow pace. Behind both riders were a score of mounted troops, their sabers clicking sharply as they moved closer.

A crowd had gathered, but a crowd that was

strangely silent. Walt looked at Lincoln. The tall black top hat, the flapping dull bleak coat — all dark — all black — the severe, melancholy brooding face deeply lined.

"Looks like an undertaker," growled a tailor who had left his shop in haste. "And he is. He'll bury the whole country before he's done."

"Keep your damned mouth shut or I'll shut it for you." An army wagon-driver lifted a fist as big as a ham and the tailor subsided.

The President had heard the sound of the disturbance and turned his face slowly in that direction. He looked at Walt quietly, intently. Walt felt a strange desire to shout "Cheer up, Mr. President! You have friends—loyal friends. We're all behind you in this!" He opened his lips but no sound came. Suddenly Walt smiled and waved his large hat. The President inclined his head in a slight bow and rode on.

"What a fool I am!" Walt felt a writhing shame raging within him. "To grin like a clown; to wave my hat in a silly gesture, while *he* broods over the dead and wounded. I should have nodded to him solemnly, with dignity. What will he think of me? If the lieutenant recognized me he'll say sneering uncomplimentary things—vicious things in the President's ear. Why do I worry so about what people think of me? The President—the whole weight is on him—on him. Could he have avoided war? Should he have permitted secession—peaceful secession? Why hold the South by force? What's wrong with divorce? Yet—a house divided—! No, it was the only thing he could do. Union or destruction. Union or dismemberment by jealous nations. He couldn't turn back. Thoughts—echoes of thoughts —fragments of thoughts swirling up—sinking—then swirling up again. Who's right? Who's wrong?"

"Did you see him? Did you see the President?"

The little girl was dancing up and down, clapping her hands and looking up at Walt eagerly.

"Yes — I think I did."

X

"Prophets and leaders should be tall men." Walt had occasion to repeat his conviction often in the days, weeks and months that followed.

What strange arrogance and vainglory little men affect to cover their uncertainties, — little men like McClellan, — little men like Douglas. But then, had he not himself been accused of being an egomaniac? Come now, Walt, confess—don't you dress as you do, stride as you do and seek the populace rather than solitude because you crave attention, admiration and more? You want everyone to like you, to love you.

Yes—but let each man express himself freely and frankly as I do. I do not consider another's popularity as an encroachment upon the domain of my personality; nor do I create rationalizations to bolster up my prejudices—for I have no prejudices and no delusions of personal grandeur. A poet yes—but very like a flute through which the breath of God blows music if I keep the passages clean.

Not so McClellan. He is petulantly selling himself out to those embittered Democrats and even to thousands of Republicans who would declare the war a mistake—the sacrifices vain, and would sue for an Armistice on almost any terms, assenting even to secession.

On a platform repudiating the war McClellan had permitted himself to accept the Democratic nomination, and although in his letter of acceptance he had rejected that platform, the issue remained what the Democratic convention had first declared it—"Immediate armistice under McClellan or to continue the struggle to preserve the Union with Lincoln."

Walt watched from afar and contemplated a nation tearing itself to shreds with fears, doubts, uncertainties, remorse—and worst of all, loss of faith in itself.

He brooded much. America—new shining land, youthful giant among the nations, have you indeed lost faith in the brave path to the freedom of man? Then die—forever die all hope of man upon this planet— for where is there another uncharted continent on which to cast up another such highway?

"Leaves of Grass"—my Gabriel trumpet call! It's all there—my own unfaltering faith. And Lincoln, mocked, reviled with "stupid," "boor," "incompetent," "blunderer," "ugly," "weakling"—does Lincoln himself still have faith?

Would my voice—would my voice —? What could I counsel him?

Each man has his task. Write! Heal! Preach the Will to Joy. That is *your* task. Lincoln must face his own.

*   *   *   *

Walt sent the completed verses of "Drum Taps" home for safe-keeping. Mary Elizabeth read them aloud to Louisa and to Hannah.

"From the stump of the arm, the amputated hand,
I undo the clotted lint, remove the slough, wash off
 the matter and blood,
Back on his pillow the soldier bends with curv'd
 neck and side falling head,
His eyes are closed, his face is pale, he dares not
 look on the bloody stump,
And has not yet look'd on it.

I dress a wound in the side, deep, deep,
But a day or two more, for see the frame all wasted

and sinking,
And the yellow-blue countenance see.

I dress the perforated shoulder, the foot with the
bullet-wound,
Cleanse the one with a gnawing and putrid gang-
rene, so sickening, so offensive,
While the attendant stands behind aside me holding
the tray and pail.

I am faithful, I do not give out,
The fractur'd thigh, the knee, the wound in the
abdomen,
These and more I dress with impassive hand, (yet
deep in my breast a fire, a burning flame).

Thus in silence in dreams' projections,
Returning, resuming, I thread my way through the
hospitals,
The hurt and wounded I pacify with soothing hand,
I sit by the restless all the dark night, some are so
young,
Some suffer so much, I recall the experience sweet
and sad,
(Many a soldier's kiss dwells on these bearded lips)."

Mary Elizabeth remembered. She remembered the
boy on the sidewalk the day of the riot and Walt's
awkward helplessness. "Guess he must have learned
how."

* * * *

Louisa, Jeff and all of them sent contributions in
money and Walt knew the skipped meals and the
threadbare clothes that made these contributions possible. Emerson and Alcott and hosts of friends sent
gifts of currency and tobacco to Walt. "Tell us—please

tell us what more we can do," they wrote. There was a substantial check from Clapp and a brief note:

Walt,

I'll send more from time to time as my fiscal circumstances permit. Good work, boy.

Ada Claire passed away yesterday. Her agony was great. Hydrophobia caused by a bite of her dog. She spoke of you often. There's no logic about life—or death either. Damn it!

Fondly,

Henry Clapp."

Ada Claire dead! Like Cleopatra from the bite of an asp—or dog—what difference does it make? But to romance it does! Exits must be dramatic—theatrical! Last words like Goethe's "More Light!" or Hale's "I regret that I have but one life —" What if a great man or queenly lady in extremis should exclaim "Ouch, my poor stomach!" or die on a toilet stool? It would gravely offend the romancers!

She had called him "a damned Joseph." Joseph—. What happened to Potiphar's wife afterwards—afterwards when Joseph was in prison? Did she speak of him often—or think of him? Or did she cast her eyes on some other young lad who would delight her nerve ends? Poor Ada! Poor Ada! Poor anyone that loves life so lustily and dies so quizzically. Bite of a dog—bite of a dog!

XI

The Emory hospital had many wounded confederate officers in the convalescent ward. Often Walt came there as he made the rounds of the wretched, passing out fruits, candies and other little gifts to the wounded and the sick. They, the rebels, were proud, defiant and bitter. Walt knew better than to argue the question

of secession with them, but as he gently befriended
them they lost their reticence. A few even persisted in
a stubborn attempt to get an expression of opinion
from *him*.

Captain Odds Butler was only nineteen. He had
left a leg at Chancellorsville but none of his belligerent
spirit had abated. He pounded his fist on his artificial
limb. "There aren't two rights, sir. There's only one
truth—one right, and the South is right. We have the
right to secede, sir. That goes with freedom. If a woman wants a divorce does that give her husband the
right to butcher her?"

The handsome youthful confederate Major who sat
smoking in his wheel chair grunted. "Go get yourself
another figure of speech, Captain Butler. The South
don't want a Yankee husband. It's attempted rape,
sir—that's what it is. We've never been married to the
North and never will be. God wouldn't bless such a
union any more than He'd bless the marriage of a
nigger to a white."

Walt, seeking to avoid argument, lifted his empty
bag and prepared to leave. He was very tired. He had
visited the wounded that day in the overcrowded wards
of six hospitals—this was the seventh—and there was
an article to be completed for the Brooklyn Eagle.

Captain Butler spoke up petulantly. "You're chas-
ing our friend away, Sedley. Choose another subject."

Sedley! Sedley! Anne!

Walt turned slowly and faced the young Major.
"Is your name Sedley?"

"Yes. Ralph Sedley."

"Have you a brother Will?"

"Yes. Do you know him?" The young man's pale
face brightened. Walt searched each feature. There was
a very definite resemblance. He was not imagining it.
Almost Anne's eyes. Not quite the depth and beauty

of them. *Almost* Anne's lips—not quite the gentle fullness of them.

"Is your home New Orleans?"

"We must have met, then. You know my family?"
Major Sedley leaned forward eagerly.

Walt said slowly, "I think I've met your sister."
In that same instant he regretted his words, for if the
elder Ralph Sedley was in reality Anne's father by
his mulatto mistress, it would be secret—secret.

"But I have no sister." The young major leaned
back on his pillow.

Walt nodded slowly. "Then I must be mistaken."

* * * *

"Walt Whitman—I've been looking for you! You're
famous! You're an immortal legend in your own life-
time."

Walt recognized the voice and turned to grasp the
outstretched hand of his former publisher, Charles
Eldridge. Walt saw at a glance that Eldridge had fallen
on difficult days. His one-time publisher correctly in-
terpreted his glance.

"*Almost* broke, Walt—not quite." Eldridge's manner was agitated as it had once been reserved. "The
war wiped out our southern credits, and that was the
end of the Thayer and Eldridge honeymoon. What are
you doing here—besides being an angel of mercy?"

"A scribble here and a scribble there, Mr. Eldridge.
A sort of free lance war correspondent for the papers
that accept the sparse fruits of my pen."

"How are you fixed—shall I say numismatically?"

"Head well above water—for the present."

"And your writing —?"

"A few poems of what I've seen of war—'Drum
Taps' I call them."

"Pound away, Walt. Beat that drum of yours. Blow

the cheery trumpet! But tell me frankly, is it as good as 'Leaves of Grass?' "

"It's a part of it. It's all one book—one song, just as each of my limbs is a part of me."

Walt felt it was his turn to question. He had a desire to help this man without offending him. "What are you doing these days, Mr. Eldridge?"

"A scrivener of accounts, after a fashion. Major Hapgood is army paymaster. I'm one of his many clerks. And say, Walt, just in case you're interested, he needs a good penman to copy some reports. It pays well."

Walt smiled. "Mr. Eldridge, until the royalties of my book take care of me such tasks must not be too lightly regarded. You think your recommendation will help?"

"Almost a certainty. Let's go up now. Why wait?"

As they walked they asked each other the news. Eldridge was in excellent spirits.

"I get the Boston and New York papers here. My room's quite cold and if you spread the papers between the blankets it helps."

"Nothing new in New York?"

"Nothing except a chorus of ink-slinging editors telling our generals how to win the war—and a human interest story like the tragic death of Foster for the headline."

"Stephen Foster?"

"Yes, the composer. You knew him?"

"I met him once. He was young—very young. He was in difficult circumstances."

"I don't remember all the details, Walt. Some sort of accident. He lived in a cellar. Drink and all that. Fell and cut his throat on a broken pitcher. Left a wife and child."

"What other details would there be? What more is there to add?"

Eldridge dropped his careless manner. "You tell me, Walt. Why? Why does weakness so often walk hand in hand with genius? Foster, Poe and the rest of them—why is it harder for them?"

"I don't know, but perhaps—strong rapids break through the walls of their narrow carved canyon—the result of too frenzied a pressure. Moral hernias—ruptures—failings—or Moby Dick."

"What's that?" Eldridge's query was sharp and abruptly jerked Walt out of his darkening mood.

"Too great a loneliness; for the gossamer threads a poetic spirit flings about him rarely catch and hold to a material anchorage."

"But he was admired everywhere. His songs are loved."

"Then there was another emptiness."

"In other words?"

"Poets must eat."

*   *   *   *

The entrance before the tall building was besciged by a throng of crippled soldiers squirming and struggling to hobble up the stairs that led to the fourth and fifth floors. A few of the wounded men recognized Walt. They began to shout: "Hey, let this man through," and cleared a way by thrusting with their shoulders against the thickly jammed crowd.

Walt tried to dissuade them but Eldridge, grateful for their assistance, propelled him to the foot of the stairs where two sentries stood guard with muskets and bayonets. From there on the crowd thinned out and the two climbed the stairs in silence. They walked down a wide corridor.

Major Hapgood was bending down intently, inserting the key into the door of his office when Eldridge presented Walt. He straightened up and looked at Walt appraisingly. "Oh yes, I remember the name. Something about an indecent book, I believe."

Walt's nostrils dilated. "As indecent as the Bible."

"A modest comparison. However, we shant pursue the subject. You write legibly, I presume."

"I can testify to that, Major," interrupted Eldridge before Walt could answer.

"Give us three or four hours a day at a dollar an hour. How will that be? You can start right now if you wish."

Walt nodded.

"And I say there—Mr. Whitman—no offense intended. I don't get much chance to read so I trust Dame Rumor, a nasty hag with a spiteful tongue."

Walt used the additional funds he earned to buy oranges, tobacco and candy for "the boys." It was a sacred routine now. He heard them whisper as he entered the ward—"Walt—there's Walt Whitman. Could you write a card for me—just a line or two?"

From bed to bed—sometimes no more than a word —often a friendly caress, a rumpling of the hair. The doctors nodded their awareness of his presence brusquely. The sanitary commissioners with their endless taking of notes stared at him coldly. Chaplains passing out tracts and religious pamphlets hurried about. The nurses were friendly, for he made their tasks lighter.

XII

From one of the beds came a soft boyish call. "Come here, Santa Claus. What have you got for me?"

The boy couldn't have been over sixteen. Walt reached into his bag. "Name it, my boy—candy, tobacco or a stamped envelope for a letter home."

"Repent! Repent!" came a sudden shout. "Repent and seek ye the Kingdom of Heaven."

A young missionary with pleasant voice and earnest eyes thrust a pamphlet into the hands of the boy.

The boy smiled faintly, "I'm not ready for the Kingdom of Heaven yet—so if you don't mind I'll have some of this man's candy instead."

"Candy is temporal. Salvation is eternal. Be saved from the eternal fires of Hell, my boy. Find the peace that passeth understanding. These are the days of judgment, my good lad. Behold the Judgment of the Lord. God's wrath will consume the sinners—but your soul will be saved. Our Lord Jesus shed his blood—"

Now the boy's eyes were wide with anguish.

"I shed mine too—"

"But He shed His blood that you might be saved to Eternal Life!"

"I didn't ask Him to."

"But He did it out of His love for you. He was crucified. He bled from His hands and from His feet where the nails—"

The boy's face turned deathly white. He beat his fists against his forehead.

"Stop it, you fool!" The interne who had approached on the run gave the startled missionary a violent shove away from the bed and then whispered angrily, "This boy's had both his legs shot off."

Walt slowly calmed the young soldier, kissing him repeatedly on the forehead. The boy's thin fists unclenched. He sobbed, and placing his hands around Walt's neck drew him down to the pillow. He kissed him hungrily, as a girl might kiss her lover.

"Son—dear boy—" Walt soothed him. "Don't let anything frighten you. Don't go worrying about Hell's fire, my child. Trust God's love. I've got a niece named Gail. When she's good I love her and when she's bad

I love her too, and is God less than I am? Will *He* hate where *I* love? Will He punish His children with the fires of Hell?"

The handsome missionary flung himself back at the bed again. "You lying anti-Christ! You don't belong here. Where's your authority to be here? You're not a doctor or a nurse. You spawn of the devil!" Moisture drooled from the corner of his lip. "Now I see it clearly. You're after his immortal soul with your sweet speeches."

In a frenzy he turned to the boy. "Don't listen to his lies. The blood of the lamb washes clean. The blood of the lamb —"

A gray haired priest approached and put his hand on the man's shoulder. "Haven't we had enough talk about blood, friend? Let's talk about something more cheerful. Let's talk about the Sermon on the Mount instead. Religion is a gentle thing."

The interne was not as patient as Walt or the priest. He grasped the missionary firmly by the wrist. "If you don't get out of here quick now I'll dump you in the latrine—so help me!"

"I'll talk to the commissioner about this!" The missionary retreated, slowly, walking backwards. "You can't keep Christ out of hospitals. He belongs at the pillow of the sick—near the head of the dying. I'll talk to the commissioner, you anti-Christ!"

"For Christ's sake, shut up!" groaned the young interne disgustedly, then, seeing the shocked expression in the kindly face of the priest, he murmured "Sorry, Father!" Again he turned bitterly to Walt. "That's what we're up against—not enough medicine, a handful of nurses, no cots to speak of—but Hell's fire served steaming hot!"

He glanced briefly at the chart at the foot of the

bed. "Eat as much of the candy as you want, soldier. It isn't going to hurt you."

He went on to the next bed, calling to Walt over his shoulder, "Carry on, pop. These boys can stand a little soft stuff."

Walt took the boy's hand in both his own. "Where are you from, son?"

"New Jersey."

"Ever get over to New York?"

"Lots of times."

"When you're in New York be sure to drop in at my mother's. Here's her address. There'll be cakes and jellies." That was the formula Walt always used whenever a wounded boy said he hailed from Brooklyn or thereabouts.

"It'll be a little while —"

Walt knew what the boy meant. His legs—

"What's your address, lad? I'll bring the cakes to you."

The boy grinned at him. "I'll wait for them here."

The Will to Joy! The Will to Joy! Rise, rise from the muck. Split it with fire! Rend darkness to shreds! Melville, false prophet! I have seen all that you have seen—the blood, the anguish and the hate—and yet I hover above the teeming ferment of creation—partner with God—yes, partner with God, knowing in the ever-striving soul of me that all that is, is at it *must* be and is, therefore, — good!

* * * *

"And I say to mankind, Be not curious about God,
For I who am curious about each am not curious
about God
(No array of terms can say how much I am at peace
about God and about death)

I hear and behold God in every object, yet under-
stand God not in the least."

 * * * *

"Why should I wish to see God better than this day?
I see something of God each hour of the twenty-
four and each moment then,
In the faces of men and women I see God, and in
my own face in the glass,
I find letters from God dropt in the street and
everyone is signed by God's name,
And I leave them where they are, for I know that
wheresoe'er I go,
Others will punctually come for ever and ever."

XIII

Andrew was dying. Jeff had been as gentle as he could, but he had made that tragic fact very clear to Walt in his last letter. The letter had given other disturbing information. Louisa had denied herself food that she might feed the soldiers that came to her door bearing Walt's greeting. She was in very poor health.

Walt tortured himself with a feeling of guilt. "You were too generous with your invitations and young soldiers are lonely!"

Hour after hour Walt sat in the little reception room of the lodging house brooding. Should he return to Brooklyn—to his mother—to Andrew—and leave the wounded who so desperately needed his affection, or should he say, "My duty lies here."

His eyes came to rest on the alert and pretty child who had once so joyously announced that Lincoln was riding by. The dark-haired little girl, Harriet was her name, was playing with an assortment of dolls, caressing them and talking to them with mature maternal solicitude. Now she had them properly seated and propped up against the back of the sofa, — all of them but her rag doll, which kept wilting sadly and falling forward on her face.

"You stay there now. Sit up straight, Dorothy. What's wrong with you? Haven't you any pride?"

Why do thoughts keep repeating themselves?—Peg and the rag doll. The same thoughts then; the same thoughts now! Why does she love that rag doll best? The others are new and charmingly dressed. The others sit properly erect and don't fall foolishly on their faces. Are children fond of things that give them room for imagination or are they naturally sympathetic! Does God love his human rag dolls best?

Aloud he called, "Harriet, may I ask you a question?"

"What kind of a question, Uncle Walt?" She came over to him and rested one tiny hand on his knee.

Walt looked at her reverently as though he stood before an oracle. "I've been helping sick and wounded soldiers here—helping them get well, and now my brother in Brooklyn is very ill. My mother isn't well either. Shall I go to them or stay here?"

Harriet pursed her lips and frowned and Walt felt a great tenderness at the little pucker of concentration that appeared at the top of her nose. Finally she looked up at Walt and said simply, "You've only got *one* mother, you know."

"Out of the mouths of babes —"

Walt bent his head and kissed her hair. "You're a dear, precious child, Harriet, and a very wise one. Thank you."

Part Seven

WHAT SONG DO YOU HEAR?

Walt was home. Louisa, her face alight at the joy
of his return, hurried about preparing a simple cold
lunch, while Walt protested with earnestness that he
was not hungry.

"You're sure George is well?"

"Completely recovered."

"And you saw the President?" Louisa's voice had
much of worship in it.

"Not once, but many times, Ma," Walt went on
after a moment's silence, "He has a great burden to
bear—a task that God placed on his shoulders. There
seemed to be no other way. I don't know, Ma. I don't
know the right or wrong of it. Does God want men to
make war?"

"I don't know what God wants, Walt. His wisdom
is beyond my understanding, but I don't think He wants
slavery for any of His children. The President is a
good man. You can see that in his face. Of course, he
doesn't want war, but he can't help himself."

"He could stop it this minute with his word. Both
sides are tired of blood."

"And then what would happen? The slavery would
still be there, and the hate would grow again—and
there would be more wars."

Walt looked lovingly at Louisa. He had seldom
discussed problems other than domestic with his
mother. Now he was eager and curious to hear her
opinion.

"Would you say he was doing the right thing? Maybe time and patience could have solved it without war."

"What do you mean, Walt?"

"I mean this awful suffering—the dead and the wounded. The thousands and thousands of dead and wounded. The thousands and thousands of homes draped in black. Widows, orphans, ruined farms, ruined cities—hate, bitterness, disease—"

" 'Tweren't Lincoln's doing. The sickness was there. The boil had to bust—and he just pierced it."

"No, Ma, it isn't as easy as that. If you saw what I saw. If you saw the bloodshed—"

"There was a heap of blood when you were born, Walt."

Walt arose from the table and put his arms around his mother. From the next room came Eddie's droning voice, "My father's a carpenter. He'll chop you down, you big tree, and then he'll make a house—he'll make a house—he'll make a house—"

* * * *

They all came that evening—gathered to see Walt and hear the news from the front, — all except Andrew who was still in the hospital. Nancy was there, and Gail and John. Jeff's youngest daughter, whom he had named California, slept like a cherub in Louisa's room.

Nancy thrust five dollars into Walt's hand. "You'll give this to the wounded soldiers. Buy something they need."

Walt felt an impulse to weep. He remembered how Nancy had let John and Gail beg for coins.

"Walt, do you get a lot of money from people who want to help?"

"Yes, Nancy. It amounted to more than five thousand dollars and people are sending more."

Hannah raised her voice shrilly. "That's the way

322

this rotten world is. You got to have an arm or leg off before anyone offers to help."

Jeff, who was smoking his pipe in silence, asked suddenly, "Been writing any more poems, Walt?"

"Yes, Jeff. Poems of the war. Simple, direct. You'll like them."

"Can I understand them?"

"You'll understand these." Walt turned to Louisa. "Ma, you haven't thrown out any of my papers, have you? I wrote you not to sweep out a single scrap."

"Son, you'll find everything as you left it. Mary Elizabeth saw to that. The poems you sent are on the table in your room."

Walt went quickly to his room and came back eagerly with several sheets of paper. Hannah, looking skinnier than ever, exploded, "Must we listen to that mess of words again? Can't we just *talk?*"

Mary Elizabeth looked up from her knitting. "Unwind yourself, Hannah. Sit easy. We can learn things from Walt."

Walt ignored Hannah's interruption and went on unruffled. "I don't know if this should be a separate book or not. It's all I—so it should all be in 'Leaves of Grass.'"

"Yes, it's all you. Everything in this family is all you." Hannah arose from the edge of the sofa. "You laugh at us with your big words—think you're smart and we're just hogs. Here you sit, nice and easy, all of you, while Andy's coughing up his blood—dying."

"Don't say these things to Walt, Hannah. You know what he's done for the wounded men. You shouldn't keep carping at him." Louisa tried to calm her daughter, but Hannah would have none of it.

"Sure he takes care of the whole world, except his own family. Nancy starves. Gail and John go begging. Jeff works his fingers to the bone trying to help the family. And you and George go off to save the world. Charity begins at home."

"Be still, Hannah." Louisa's voice cut sharply and Hannah closed her lips. Louisa chose her words carefully. "People can't help being what they are, and Walt here can't help what's inside of him any more than a cow can help giving milk. *I'm* not complaining, Hannah, and you shouldn't, because Walt is an important man. What he writes makes people feel and think, and when people feel and think there's hope for 'em. Mr. Emerson came to see Walt, didn't he? And if Mr. Emerson listened to him you can listen to him, too. Sit down, Hannah, and behave yourself."

"No, Ma. I'm not staying. I'm going to Andrew. He's my brother. He's dying and he's alone." She ran to the door. Mary called out, "Hannah, they won't let you in. It's not visiting time."

The door closed violently behind Hannah. Louisa seated herself on the wooden chair near the stove and drew her shawl close around her. "Go on, Walt, read to us. The house is quiet now."

II

Swayne was impressed. He bit his unlighted cigar and waved at Walt. "Let's hear it again."

Walt read evenly:

> *"First O songs for a prelude,*
> *Lightly strike on the stretch'd tympanum pride*
>   *and joy in my city,*
> *How she led the rest to arms, how she gave the*
>   *cue,*
> *How at once with lithe limbs unwaiting a mo-*
>   *ment she sprang,*
> *(O superb! O Manhattan, my own, my peerless!*
> *O strongest you in the hour of danger, in crisis!*

O truer than steel!)
How you sprang—how you threw off the cos-
tumes of peace with indifferent hand,
How your soft opera-music changed, and the
drum and fife were heard in their stead,
How you led to the war, (that shall serve for
our prelude, songs of soldiers),
How Manhattan drum-taps led."

"Nice spirit to those lines. Like the song of De-
borah in the Bible." Swayne finally lighted his cigar
and settled back in his swivel chair luxuriously. "Let's
hear some more."

He watched the clouds of smoke drift upward with
the air of Olympian Zeus contemplating his stock of
thunderbolts. Walt read on:

"War! an arm'd race is advancing! the welcome for
battle, no turning away;
War! be it weeks, months, or years, an arm'd race
is advancing to welcome it.
Mannahatta a-march—and it's O to sing it well!
It's O for a manly life in the camp.
And the sturdy artillery,
The guns bright as gold, the work for giants, to
serve well the guns,
Unlimber them! (No more as the past forty-years
for salute or courtesies merely),
Put in something now besides powder and wadding.
And you lady of ships, you Mannahatta,
Old matron of this proud, friendly, turbulent city,
Often in peace and wealth you were pensive or
covertly frown'd amid all your children,
But now you smile with joy exulting old Manna-
hatta."

"Are they all in the same vein?" Swayne queried
approvingly.

"No, there are other scenes—the losses, the bloodshed, the grief." He began to recite from memory "Come up from the fields, father, here's a letter from our Pete."

As Walt read the lines descriptive of Pete's wound, Swayne frowned and straightened up severely in his chair. Walt sensed that all was not well but read calmly on:

> *"Grieve not so, dear mother, (the just-grown daugh-*
> *ter speaks through her sobs,*
> *The little sisters huddle around speechless and*
> *dismay'd),*
> *See, dearest mother, the letter says Pete will soon*
> *be better.*
> *Alas poor boy, he will never be better, (nor maybe*
> *needs to be better, that brave and simple soul),*
> *While they stand at home at the door he is dead*
> *already,*
> *The only son is dead.*
> *But the mother needs to be better,*
> *She with thin form presently drest in black,*
> *By day her meals untouch'd, then at night fitfully*
> *sleeping, often waking,*
> *In the midnight waking, weeping, longing with one*
> *deep longing,*
> *O that she might withdraw unnoticed, silent from*
> *life escape and withdraw,*
> *To follow, to seek, to be with her dear dead son."*

"Very sympathetic and even tragic," commented Swayne, "but most untimely."

"You mean Pete's death?" Walt knew better but the question was already out.

"No, of course not. The poem itself. It's a question of timing. Such writings would discourage enlistments. It would be a distinct disservice to our country to publish them at this time."

"You would withhold the truth? Shall the people

326

of our country be blind to what is happening? Let
them see every aspect of this conflict—the cause—and
the great suffering—not only the uniforms, the flag
and the braid."

"It would shock with its realism. And I repeat, sir,
that it would discourage enlistments."

"Do the tombstones or cemeteries discourage
births?"

"Not at all in point. After the war, perhaps. Not
now! We'll not publish these now. We've got a war
to win!"

III

Walt, in Brooklyn, found the same desolate masses
of sick and wounded as in Washington. Again he
loaded his bag with trinkets, confections, tobacco and
writing paper. Again he made his daily rounds.

Jeff came to him at the Military Hospital as he sat
writing a letter for an old veteran. He bore disturbing
tidings. "George is a prisoner in Virginia. They've got
him at Camp Petersburg."

"I'll go back to Washington. There may be something I can do. Sit on the edge of the bed, Jeff. I've
got to finish this letter. It won't take long."

"It will take long. I ain't half through!" protested
the old soldier, irascibly. "I ain't mentioned none of
my cousins yet, an' you can't leave out names without
hurtin' peoples' feelings."

Jeff volunteered to aid. "Go on, Walt, you'll have
to pack. You can cheer Mother up a bit. I'll finish
the letter."

The grizzled invalid was far from pleased. "Two
kinds of handwriting'll look mighty peculiar."

Jeff checked a violent oath with difficulty and

grinned up at his brother. "I'm learning, Walt. I've learned a little patience since New Orleans."

* * * *

Major Hapgood shook his head in a gesture of absolute finality. "It's no use arguing. I can't get you a pass, Walt. And there are no exchanges of prisoners for the present. Better wait. There may be a new policy in a month or two." Hapgood hesitated. "Walt, I've got some good news for you."

Walt looked at Hapgood curiously. "Has it got to do with my book?"

"Your book! Your book! Always your book! Why can't you be practical, Walt? Poets starve. Forget your damned book and smell the coffee—and it's mighty good coffee, if I do say it myself." He thrust a blank form in front of Walt's face. "Fill it out, man. It's twelve hundred a year to start with and sixteen hundred a year if they keep you on."

Walt read the brief statement. It was his appointment as clerk in the Indian Bureau of the Department of the Interior. He felt a sudden wave of great joy engulfing him completely and warming his heart within him. There would be money to send home to the family—to Nancy, to Jesse, to his mother, and money left over for the contents of his bag, for "the boys"— and there was that comfortable feeling of security, the strange sense of security and well being that a few extra dollars in the pocket always give.

"Thank you, Major Hapgood. This *is* good news."

"Don't thank me. It was that O'Connor friend of yours. A persistent Irishman if there ever was one. Now you'll be able to pull away from writing your nasty rhymes. What the hell do you know about Indians, Walt?"

"Nothing." Walt was curt.

"Fine. That qualifies you as an expert by government standards."

"Then by the same standard, allow me to congratulate you on your expert opinion of poetry, Major."

Major Hapgood was momentarily taken aback. He lifted his eyebrows angrily and then laughed. "Don't be offended, Walt. You're too sensitive."

"No one can offend me, Major. I can only offend myself. And that I haven't done thus far. You'll have to believe that, Major."

"I don't know what the hell you're talking about. And besides, there's a couple of hundred troopers to pay off. I'm busy. So good luck, Walt, and better get that form in before six o'clock or someone else might horn in on your job."

At the Indian Bureau Walt listened patiently to the many complaints invariably presented with great dignity by the chiefs of western tribes. The complaints were almost all of the same pattern—"Your agents rob and cheat us." "They move us from one place to another." "We are brave Lakota." "Mississippi our home." "No rest for us." "No game to hunt." "The white man mocks us."

Walt carefully noted the claims and, obedient to Ashton's counsel, filled out reports—many imposing reports. Then he watched the stolid groups dwindle and new delegations come.

Slowly, he orientated himself to his new duties. He studied the procedure of his fellow clerk, J. Hubley Ashton. Ashton was mild, extremely deferential to each complainant, and fond of making many notations as though the complaints of the Indians must be carefully scrutinized as a prelude to action. He always seemed cool and comfortable in spite of his tight collar and lace cravat.

"Just take them in your stride, Mr. Whitman. Give

them a full sympathetic hearing and stop them only when they begin repeating themselves."

The first week Walt reacted emotionally to each complaint. After that he grew absorbed mostly in the recording, filing and other ministerial acts.

He reproached himself. "Just like a surgeon who becomes hardened to the sight of another's pain and blood." But the surgeon operates—and perhaps saves a life or a limb. Whereas he, Walt Whitman—what on earth *did* happen to the complaints so carefully recorded? Was all this merely a safety valve so that the Indians could let off steam? What kind of America were we becoming if neither the black folk nor the red could obtain justice?

* * * *

The tall young chief of the Sioux did not want to wait for his interview with Mr. Ashton. He pushed his way angrily to the front of the line. "Talk and more talk. Another push—then more talk. White men always too busy, but not too busy to push us into setting sun. White Father too busy; only red man not busy. He sit quiet and wait to die."

Walt with difficulty persuaded the young chieftain to wait and he himself remained in the office while Ashton checked the list of complaints. Secretary of the Interior Harlan came in without knocking and peremptorily took over the questioning.

"Chief Gray Fox, why do you fight the White Father? He is a good father. He is now trying to free the black people. He is very busy."

"The White Father is always busy. When black people free as red man, what happen then? Him starve like red man starve?"

Harlan looked hastily at the report Walt had drawn up and again addressed himself to Chief Gray Fox.

"It's all here for Big White Father to read. White Father will take care of his red children."

The young chieftain arose sullenly and left the room without a word or nod of farewell. Harlan shrugged his shoulders, then with a frown he threw the Sioux report on Ashton's desk. "File it away. There's nothing can be done in the middle of a war." He brightened up after a moment. "You will be glad to hear, Mr. Whitman, that my predecessor, John Usher, had recommended an increase in your annual salary. The increase was approved and will take effect next month."

Ashton warmly shook hands with Walt. Harlan smiled. "I knew you'd be pleased."

"But the Sioux —" Walt felt a sense of guilt. The petition of Chief Gray Fox had been tabled. His own raise only intensified his discomfort. "What about them? They'll make trouble. They've got good reason to make trouble."

Ashton nodded gravely. "They'll make trouble all right—and with just cause. We're not doing very much to help them."

Harlan flung his great arms about and disagreed. "You're wrong, Ashton, and you too, Walt. The trouble is they won't help themselves. They're lazy. Face it. They're benighted savages—pagans, and I repeat, sir, they're lazy. Not a Christian in a wagonload. You take the Negroes—they at least accept the gospel, attend church, sing hymns. Many of them are deeply religious. But not the Indians. They're too blind—too stubborn! They belong with the ancient Egyptians. They wrap their dead in a blanket, sit him up in his grave and give him a bow and some arrows and corn for his trip to the Happy Hunting Ground. They're lazy! They don't want to work in this world or the next."

Ashton grinned. "Do white men want to work in the next world? That isn't my idea of Paradise. And so far as this world is concerned, why generalize? Most men are lazy unless they have a goal. What goal is there for the Indians?"

Walt suggested mildly, "You promised that the Great White Father would see the report. Perhaps if the President were to see it —"

Harlan grunted. "That's all he needs! You pick the right moment, Mr. Whitman."

"They're entitled to some immediate relief. Perhaps —"

Harlan's voice became brittle. "Perhaps! Perhaps! Perhaps you arrogate too much to yourself, Mr. Whitman."

"I don't see why you should be offended, Mr. Harlan. I merely suggested that his plea be heard by the President. That seems to me fair and democratic."

"But we're not a democracy, Mr. Whitman. Democracies are forever inefficient. True democracies exist only in the minds of poets. Democracy might work in a small community; but it's impossible in a great country. Let's be realistic. We're a republic. There *is* quite a difference, you know. Read your Plato more carefully. Not everyone's voice deserves equally to be heard. The electorate is a privilege for the qualified or the elect. Not every war whoop or jackal's howl is entitled to a vote."

Walt was indignant—outraged. "That concept isn't enough for the growing spirit of America."

"Enough? It's quite enough!" Harlan arose slowly from his chair. "More would lead to anarchy." He faced Ashton ironically. "I love these men with feet set firmly in the clouds."

Ashton strove to mollify Harlan. "Mr. Whitman is a poet. His book 'Leaves of Grass' has been favorably received by many great men. Emerson himself has praised it."

"Indeed?" Harlan asked quietly, "Have you a copy here, Mr. Whitman?"

Walt nodded and went at once to his desk. "It has some of my pencilled notes in the margins but I'm sure you won't mind them."

Harlan took the book into his hands without removing his eyes from Whitman. "I'll read it," he said slowly. "I'll read it. Not now. But I'll read it."

He surveyed Whitman as though he had never seen him before, then bowed slightly and left the office.

Ashton shook his head contritely. "I'm sorry now. I shouldn't have mentioned the book."

"I'm *glad* you did. It's the most important thing in my life. It *is* my life. I'm convinced of it now. Men like Harlan convince me my work is needed. I must complete it. I've tried to get a publisher for a series of war poems, but without success. If I could take a short leave—just a few weeks—and return to New York —"

"Go ahead, Walt. You're entitled to a rest. Those long hours in the hospitals have worn you out. Don't worry about a thing. I'll look after the routine reports. The rest can wait till you come back. Let me be the first to congratulate you on your second volume of verse."

"It's not really a second volume. It's the continuation of my work. It will all be one book. First I'll publish these war songs separately under the title 'Drum Taps.' Then I'll include them in 'Leaves of Grass'— for it's all one. Everything I write is all one —"

IV

Louisa welcomed Walt in trembling eager silence. She clung to him tightly, then hurried to heat water for his bath. She knew how her son liked to relax in the metal tub sometimes for more than an hour. As Walt luxuriously bathed he read the headlines of the several papers he had purchased at the station. It was all election news, with only the briefest bulletins telling of the conflict.

Lincoln's reelection now seemed confirmed. McClellan had piled up almost two million votes but had carried only three states, therefore in the electoral college he could hope for only twenty-one votes against two hundred and eleven for Lincoln.

So Lincoln had met the backwash—the bitter waves of man's worst qualities—envy and malice—and the waves had not quenched the flame of his faith—one man's faith among the bewildered, the apathetic, the frightened—the uncertain.

A few Union victories just before election and the lethargic doubt-weighted waters of the collective soul of America began to flow forward again.

When Walt had bathed and eaten it was late afternoon. Jeff came home just as Walt was leaving. They embraced affectionately. Walt told his brother about his hopes for "Drum Taps." "They're timely and they should appear now. I'll talk to Swayne once more and if he refuses to publish them, then I'll print them myself."

"Sure you will. Nothing ever stops you. You seem to drift, Walt, but you keep moving ahead. Your Will to Joy—I wish I had some of it." Jeff put his hand on Walt's shoulder admiringly. "You never get discouraged—really discouraged—do you? And once I thought you were too easy going. I can't forget New Orleans."

"I can't forget it either!"

"Anne?"

"Yes, Anne."

"I've often wondered why you don't marry."

Walt was silent and Jeff did not pursue that subject. Instead he said, "I wouldn't worry about the book. Great books and great men are not always recognized at once. You have to stand off at a distance to see the mightiest peaks. Don't worry, Walt. If a man like Emerson values your work —"

"No, Jeff, I'm not worried. I know my work is good. It may take a long while but there's holiness in my book and it takes people a while to recognize holiness when there are no painted wings and halos to ornament it, for holiness is a simple thing."

* * * *

Walt took his verses to six publishers. The answers were almost identical. "A rather gruesome picture to present to the public." "Perhaps after the war." "It will discourage enlistments."

"I can't wait! These poems must appear now! Sorry!"

So Walt took his beloved "Drum Taps" to a near-by print shop and began himself to set the poems in type as he had once done with "Leaves of Grass." He worked tenderly and tirelessly. It would make a slender volume—but then some day it would be the very heart of his "Leaves of Grass."

At the end of twelve days the book was ready to be bound.

"It's done, Ma," he told Louisa early one morning as she prepared a simple breakfast. "I've been up half the night, but it's done."

He sighed with a profound sense of relief and began to describe some of the poems to Louisa. Perhaps she understood—perhaps she didn't, but to her he poured out his sense of joy and of well-being at a task completed. He unfolded the morning paper. Gone was his joy as he stared with wide uncomprehending eyes at the heavy black type.

Letters are sledge hammers, Walt. They crush and stun!

Louisa turned a curious glance in his direction. Walt's face was gray. His hands trembled. He sat down at the table, the paper stretched out before him over the cups and saucers.

"What is it, Walt? What's happened?"

Walt did not move.

"Speak up, son, what's ailing you?" Louisa ran to him as she spoke.

Walt answered dully. "The President is dead. Lincoln's been murdered." Then all of a sudden his shoulders shook and he sobbed a dry convulsive weeping—a gasping of breath—with no tears as an outlet.

"Don't, Walt. I can't stand it. I've never heard you cry. Not since you were a baby." Louisa's fingers were touching his hair. Walt quieted himself almost at once.

"He was a great man, Mother."

"What's going to happen now?" Louisa clasped and unclasped her hands. "George is in the rebel prison and Jeff wondering if he'll be drafted—and the war dragging without any hope—and now with Lincoln dead —"

"No, Ma, the war is over. When Lee surrendered that was the end. Johnston can't hold out against Sherman. But Lincoln should have lived to see the new birth. He should have lived — he should have waited — a little while longer —"

And Walt went to his room and wrote, dipping his pen into the new and bitter ink of a great staggering personal loss, for now he knew that this man who had nodded to him once was bone of his bone and heart of his heart. And as he wrote one part of his brain wailed, "I thought I had solved Death. Of what am I afraid? All that there was of Lincoln is eternal;

why do I sorrow so deeply?" But Walt wept on—and could not be consoled.

V

Fred Banks' eyes looked distant and tiny through the thick lenses of his spectacles as he peered at Walt.

"You can't do that. You can't keep adding things!"

Banks was a book binder who never concerned himself with the contents of the books he bound. It was a craft and a living. With the gravity of an undertaker placing a corpse in a casket the busy little book binder glued and sewed. Now there were new pages to insert. He demurred; Walt was insistent.

"Shall I sew them in—or tip them in? It's a job and a half."

"Sew them in if you can."

Walt felt that the new verses must be included at all costs—Lincoln's death—Lincoln's death!

The binder nodded. "I'll do it with most. But some of the books are sewed and glued already. Some are in the presses. You don't want me to tear the bound copies apart."

"No. Let those go as they are."

Thus he added to his slender volume of "Drum Taps" the songs "When Lilacs Last in the Dooryard Bloom'd" and the rhymed ballad "O Captain, My Captain!"

Review copies were mailed at once. Then Walt himself distributed most of the copies to the book shops of Brooklyn and New York. A few he sent to Boston. Now he would wait for comment. It would take a while.

Black flags—Train of Sorrows—move across the land. Oh dearly beloved son of man —; beloved? No, they doubted you, maligned you while you lived. Great books and great men are not quickly recognized—but even the South is grieving. No—not genuine. Self interest—that's all. Lincoln would have made easier terms. Move on, black train of blacker sorrow—forlorn —forlorn. Let the weary ashes rest.

Death! Death, do I understand you at last? Are you then the final, loving all-embracing act of love of Him that fashioned me—enclosing and absorbing me and making me a part of Him forever?

And when the sightless cell that moved upon the dark breast of the deep swallowed the cell that floated near it—was that the first stirring of a final love?

And are they all—the opening jaws that rend and swallow and devour; are they the primal urge from which inevitably flowers the hungry heart that would contain, absorb, enfold, embrace the world?

Are hate and darkness and devouring, the deep, deep roots of love?

To own by slaying and consuming—to own by reaching and embracing—are they then kin—one song rising from plane to plane along the keyboard of the aeons until the finite world's embraced by Infinite Love?

Death! Death do I understand you at last?

* * * *

A few weeks after the death of Lincoln, Walt was back at his desk. Ashton looked ill and tired. "It'll take a better man than one tailor President to sew the Union together. There's been all hell to pay since Lincoln was murdered. Now they're murdering him all over again."

Walt understood Ashton's cutting reference to Johnson. "I'm out of touch with things political. Isn't Johnson continuing with Lincoln's policies?"

"Leaving the Negroes' right to the ballot up to their former owners! That's a laugh! Where's the freedom in that? Without the ballot as theirs by right you're trading chains of iron for chains of fear, prejudice and hate. Where's the liberty in that?"

"Give him a chance. Don't forget that he was the only senator from the South that refused to go with his state. That takes a lot of character—a lot of courage. His being from the South will act as a brake on any revenge plots of our radical Republicans."

"What revenge are you talking of?"

"The same faint-hearted Republicans who voted for McClellan in the hope of an armistice with the South on almost any terms the Confederate States might suggest, will be the first to demand harsh measures with the defeated South."

"Why so?"

"Because few men can be generous in victory. If Johnson shows the slightest mercy for the South he'll be pounced upon."

Ashton reflected, "The death of Lincoln may serve to calm the bitterness and hate of the Southern states. Is there a Providence in that?"

Walt did not answer. He did not know what to answer. God was forever Inscrutable, so why attempt to span the Infinite. The wide, wide Universe was quite enough. He settled at his desk and began to file away the reports that Ashton had filled out in his absence. Ashton walked over to him.

"Harlan's been around several times asking for you. By the way, here's your last check including the raise."

"Well, then, everything's all right, isn't it? You don't think Harlan carries a grudge because of our discussion?"

"I don't know."

"Well this raise sort of answers the question, doesn't it?"

"I hope so."

"Forget it, Ashton. Here's a copy of my new book.

There's one poem there at the end I want you to read carefully. It's called 'When Lilacs Last in the Dooryard Bloom'd.' "

Ashton turned the pages slowly till he reached the song, and read aloud. He read well and Walt felt the caressing quality of his voice almost like a friendly handclasp. Then Ashton paused, turned the page and read on silently, his face glowing.

"The rhythm and beat of it! Walt, you've done something! Walt, this is truly great!"

"O Captain! my Captain, our fearful trip is done,
The ship has weather'd every rack, the prize we
*   sought is won,*
The port is near, the bells I hear, the people all
*   exulting,*
While follow eyes the steady keel, the vessels grim
*   and daring;*
But O heart! Heart! Heart!
O the bleeding drops of red,
Where on the deck my Captain lies,
Fallen cold and dead.

O Captain! my Captain! rise up and hear the bells!
Rise up—for you the flag is flung—for you the bugle
*   trills,*
For you bouquets and ribbon'd wreaths—for you
*   the shores a-crowding,*
For you they call, the swaying mass, their eager
*   faces turning;*
*   Here Captain! dear Father!*
*   The arm beneath your head!*
*   It is some dream that on the deck,*
*   You've fallen cold and dead.*

My Captain does not answer, his lips are pale and
*   still,*
My father does not feel my arm, he has no pulse
*   nor will,*

The ship is anchor'd safe and sound, its voyage
closed and done,
From fearful trip the victor ship comes in with
object won:
  Exult O shores, and ring O bells!
  But I with mournful tread,
    Walk the deck my Captain lies,
    Fallen cold and dead."

Ashton sat staring radiantly at the page. "I don't care what anyone says—this is a great work!" Suddenly his eyes glistened with eagerness. He arose excitedly. "Please Walt! May I have this reprinted? Is it all right with you?" Without waiting for an answer he hurried out of the office.

Walt looked after him, a frown of irritation and wonder deepening between his brows. "So he's gotten as far as that! 'O Captain, my Captain!' he calls great. Then it will take centuries before they understand my real work—centuries! Patterns of habit! Heavy shackles of habit chaining the soul! Because it rhymes he likes it! And why *did I* write it in rhyme? Say that my grief stunned me into the accepted habits of mourning.

Come now, Walt, you too are man. The same frailties, fears, doubts and even habits persist in you. It is against them that you shout—your own conflict—and your own Will to Joy. It is against the whetstone of your sorrow that you sharpen your song. If you were truly and completely what you sing—you could not sing."

He thought of Jeff—of Anne—and of how such souls fit into brave dreams and not into the habit of well-ordered life, and then he thought of Anne again. She had been premature in the long road. So she had stepped back, her ears open to his song of a day that was too far ahead to be hers. She had understood. Anne had understood. He bowed his head and murmured very low, "I can be patient, too, I suppose. I can be patient too."

* * * *

Walt's second salary check alleviated his anxiety for the immediate future and gave him funds for "the boys." Now he was back in the old routine—office hours nine to four, often less, for he was his own master as to his goings and comings—then, with his bag loaded with gifts for the soldiers, he made his way to the hospitals, usually remaining with the wounded until past midnight.

All Washington knew Walt now. The comic sketches of him that appeared from time to time in the press made him a familiar figure to many who had not met him. His "Drum Taps" had awakened a group of critics to pen favorable reviews.

O'Connor's genuinely warm invitations to his small but friendly apartment were eagerly accepted and Walt began to feel more and more that Washington was home. If life were to move on just this way he would be content.

Then one morning, lounging on the pleasant island of a contented hour, he lazily opened a long, slender envelope. A brief note of yellow paper fluttered out:

"The Services of Walter Whitman of New York, as a clerk in the Indian Office, will be dispensed with from and after this date.

James Harlan."

Walt was startled and shocked. Suddenly firm props were knocked from under him. Anger, bitterness —a sense of insecurity assailed him. He stared at the note as though by re-reading it he could alter its meaning. Ashton, busy at his own desk, had not looked up. Walt walked over to him and without a word placed the brief message before his eyes.

Ashton gaped. "Harlan! Damn it! But why?"

Walt smiled and shrugged his shoulders. He picked up the note and read it again. Ashton arose and, putting on his hat, walked quickly to the door.

"Where are you going, Hubley?"

"I'm going to talk to Harlan. This is ridiculous. He gave you no warning."

"You're a good friend but your being angry won't do any good. If you're bound to go, let me go with you. It's my fight."

VI

They both walked to Harlan's home in silence. The Negro servant asked them into the parlor and took their hats. In a short while Harlan entered and nodded slightly and formally in their direction. He seemed irritated with them.

"I would appreciate it, gentlemen, if these matters could wait until I got down to the office."

Ashton half arose to go.

"No, never mind. You're here, so tell me what's on your mind." He offered a slender cigar first to Walt and, upon his refusal, to Ashton, who accepted it and lit it at once.

Walt waited for Ashton to begin, but after a while, embarrassed by his friend's silence, he held out the note he had received.

"Never mind, Whitman, I know what it is. Sorry, but there are hundreds of veterans and dependents of veterans that have to be placed in government jobs. They come first."

Walt spoke gently, telling himself to be calm and courteous for the sake of his own self respect. "In a sense I too am a veteran. The medical men will tell you of the service I have rendered and am rendering in the hospitals."

Harlan frowned. "I seriously question the value of that service. We have had complaints from men of the cloth about the type of conversation that you indulge in. Atheism of the rankest sort. The one comfort a wounded man has you take away from him."

"So that's it!"

"Not entirely."

"What else?"

"Your book—obscene, filthy, indecent —"

Walt arose to go. Ashton finally spoke up. "You've misjudged him, sir. Frankness isn't indecency."

"Come now. I'm not a child. I recognize perversion when I see it. Have you read his Calamus? What other conclusion can a reader arrive at? Sodomy and buggery lurk there to poison the minds of the young. What kind of a defense is it to say 'He's frank about it?' "

He turned to Walt who was looking at him with mildly puzzled eyes. "Explain what you mean in Calamus—any other way if you can. The hair on your chest becomes in your poetic words 'scented herbage.' What else than semen can you mean by 'Take the white tears of my blood if that is what you are after?' Wait a moment!" Harlan left the room and returned a moment later with the copy of "Leaves of Grass" that Walt had loaned him. He flipped the pages to a marker and read aloud:

*"When I saw the full moon in the west grow pale
and disappear in the morning light,
When I wander'd alone over the beach, and un-
dressing bathed, laughing with the cool waters,
and saw the sun rise,
And when I thought how my dear friend my lover
was on his way coming, O then I was happy,
O then each breath tasted sweeter, and all that day*

*my food nourish'd me more, and the beautiful
day pass'd well,*

*And the next came with equal joy, and with the
next at evening came my friend,*

*And that night while all was still I heard the waters
roll slowly continually up the shores,*

*I heard the hissing rustle of the liquid and sands as
directed to me whispering to congratulate me,*

*For the one I love most lay sleeping by me under the
same cover in the cool night,*

*In the stillness in the autumn moonbeams his face
was inclined toward me,*

*And his arm lay lightly around by breast—and that
night I was happy."*

Harlan lifted his head triumphantly. "Explain that
if you can!"

Walt met his glance wearily. "This is a strange star
chamber proceeding! I am first condemned and sen-
tenced then asked to defend myself. You ask me to
explain. I could explain it if I knew the answer myself, if I could truly distinguish between the sun's warm
playing with the womb of the earth and a man's caress."

"You see!" Harlan exclaimed turning to Ashton.
"It's obvious! He's sex mad. It's a sickness—a perversion. And do you expect me to give a people's trust
into the hands of such a one!"

Walt regarded him curiously and without anger.
"My songs of comradeship seem to you sex madness?"

"Your description of man's love for man is vile.
You express it in gross physical terms."

"Is not the 'Song of Songs' expressed in physical
terms?"

"This is pure sophistry. You descriptions are erotic.
Man does not love man in the same way as man loves
a woman. And if he does, it's a gross perversion—condemned in the Bible—a mortal sin."

Ashton broke in. "You surely realize that Mr. Whitman sees sex as a universal force—sublimating itself—the love of Jonathan for David 'more wonderful than the love of woman.' Isn't that the explanation, Walt?"

Walt arose white-faced. He looked from one to the other. "No, I don't think so. I don't know. I told you I can't explain it and I can't. It's there and I won't change a word of it."

"You don't seem to make any distinction between a man's love for a woman and a man's love for a man."

"Perhaps in the chemistry of my body there is no difference."

"But that would make you—"

"What?"

"A homosexual—a Sodomite."

Walt's face grew very white, nevertheless his eyes held Harlan's steadily. "You make things very simple, Mr. Harlan, like being a Democrat or a Republican."

"A moral life *is* simple."

"You are very fortunate, Mr. Harlan. All the various feelings, driving forces and mysterious yearnings in the brain and blood of man become quite easy of explanation to you. And if you condemn for the thought or the emotion as for the deed then almost every man that walks this earth is a rapist or a murderer."

Harlan snorted impatiently. "But when you set down thoughts like these in print, *that* becomes a vile deed—and I draw my own conclusions as to your conduct."

"Mr. Harlan, you could not possibly understand my verse."

"Why, because my thoughts refuse to flow in gutters or because your verse is too difficult for my understanding?"

"No, because your mind sees everything as black or white—God or the Devil—hero and villain—evil and good—guilt and innocence. Supposing you were correct in your insinuations—supposing that in the glands of my body there were a chemistry that made me yearn for a man's physical embrace—am I then a criminal—am I then evil?"

"Evil if you yield to it!"

"Tragic if I yield to it, but beautiful if I sublimate it in acts of kindness."

"Not to be trusted."

"Myself or my verse?"

"Both. They are one."

"In that you are right."

Harlan held the book out to Whitman, who did not notice the gesture. Ashton asked dutifully, almost humbly, "Would you reconsider, sir?"

"No. Not if it meant my own dismissal! Good day!"

Ashton, walking uncomfortably at Walt's side, tried to break the awkward silence. "Let me talk to James Speed in your behalf. He'll get you on in the Treasury Department."

"If you wish."

"Leave your personal papers in the desk. I'll take care of them until you get your new post."

"Are you that confident?"

"More than that—I'm certain. Are you coming up?"

"No, I'll visit O'Connor."

"Don't let him stir you up. That sputtering firebrand will make an issue of it."

"Let it be an issue!"

"You can't afford it. There are too many Harlans in the world."

"All the more reason for a Whitman!"

"All right, you damned Lucifer, be stubborn. Make it hard for me."

"My Latin is sparse, but doesn't Lucifer mean 'the light bringer?'" Walt smiled. "No, Ashton, I'm no rebel against God unless Harlan is God. I am nothing without God. The Father is in me and I am in the Father!"

"You live by the Scriptures and yet you say you're not a Christian! You deny that Jesus is the Son of God?"

"No, on the contrary I affirm it. He was and so are you and so am I—all of us, the Hottentot, the southern Negro, the northern Eskimo—Chief Gray Fox whom we turned away—all, all alike the sons of God—and Jesus not one whit the holier—and I no holier than Jesus or the Zulu, the Eskimo or the Mongol."

Ashton's expression was woebegone. "You're a long way from being a Christian by Harlan's definition and by mine too."

"I can't help that."

"But if it could be proved to you that Jesus was immaculately conceived, God's own spirit —"

"I resent the word 'immaculate,' and so do Emerson and Thoreau, for if you say his birth was unspotted and unblemished then you imply that all others are. I refuse to be an imperfect thing."

"But if it could be *proved* to you! I'm only asking you to suppose. Why be as stubborn as Harlan?"

Walt paused in his brisk stride and faced Ashton. "If it were true I'd resent it for all eternity, for loving God as I do, I would shrink at the knowledge that He loved one other of His sons more than He loved me."

"Are you that selfish?"

"No, only democratic—even in my religion."

"You don't believe in Perdition or Hell?"

"A Loving God, Divinely Merciful, could not create one."

"What *is* your creed anyway? You don't believe in Satan?"

"If God's love fills the Universe there's no room for devils."

"And miracles? Don't you believe in miracles?"

Walt recited softly lines he had written long ago, —

> *"Why, who makes much of a miracle?*
> *As to me, I know of nothing else but miracles,*
> *Whether I walk the streets of Manhattan*
> *Or dart my sight over the roofs of the houses*
>   *toward the sky,*
> *Or wade with naked feet along the beach just*
>   *in the edge of the water,*
> *Or stand under trees in the woods —"*

Walt paused, trying to remember the rest, then added, "To me every hour of the light and dark is a miracle."

"And Eternal Life?"

"I think *all* things are good and are eternal."

"And personal resurrection?"

"I don't know and it makes no difference. I believe life is Eternal. To love the All is enough. To believe in the comradeship of man on earth is enough."

"Calamus?"

"Yes, leaves of grass, one leaning upon the other lovingly. And you?"

Ashton frowned thoughtfully. "I need faith in eternal life—in personal resurrection. I couldn't live without it. I'm a Christian, Walt."

"But this clinging to *personal* resurrection, *personal* salvation—isn't there something of the fear of death in it?"

"No, the hope of God's Eternal Love. Why do you speak of fear?"

"Because when I was a child one thought terrified me above all others. It whispered to me, 'You're going to die, Walt. You're going to cease to exist. There will

349

come a moment when you won't *be* any more, and even if there's a Heaven it can't be forever. After a million years or more it will have to end and you won't be there or anywhere, and the planets will move about the great emptiness of space and you won't be there or anywhere.' "

"Well, that has never troubled me. I know my Saviour liveth and is Eternal—even though my mind cannot grasp eternity. Neither can it grasp infinite space, and yet —"

"Does personal salvation mean so much to you?"

Ashton nodded. "More than anything else in the world."

VII

O'Connor raved. He shouted and banged his fist. "What a reason for dismissal! A witch hunt! Light your fires, kindle the faggots, you fanatics, but I'll have my say about it. Get out, Walt! Get out and let me write. We'll lance this festering carbuncle before it poisons the body politic."

"Ashton said you'd flare up."

"And Ashton was only half right. I'll do much more than flare!"

While O'Connor wrote angrily, Ashton interviewed Attorney General James Speed. Speed was most agreeable.

"I'll take him on, but where'll I put him, Hubley? There's only the library."

"Put him in the library. He can work there as well as any place."

And so quite suddenly Walt had a job again—a better job, and books to his heart's content. He loved the very smell of the old volumes.

In January O'Connor's pamphlet flooded the book

shops. Here were bold, clear clanging phrases like mighty trumpets: —

"I have had the honor, which I esteem a very high one, to know Walt Whitman intimately for several years, and am conversant with the details of his life and history. Scores and scores of persons, who know him well, can confirm my own report of him, and I have therefore no hesitation in saying that the scandalous assertions of Mr. Harlan, derived from whom I know not, as to his being a bad man, a free lover, etc., belong to the category of those calumnies at which, as Napoleon said, innocence itself is confounded. A better man in all respects, or one more irreproachable in his relations to the other sex, lives not upon this earth. His is the great goodness, the great chastity of spiritual strength and sanity. I do not believe that from the hour of his infancy, when Lafayette held him in his arms, to the present hour, in which he bends over the last wounded and dying of the war, any one can say aught of him, which does not consort with the largest and truest manliness. I am perfectly aware of the miserable lies which have been put into circulation respecting him, of which the story of his dishonoring an invitation to dine with Emerson, by appearing at the table of the Astor House in a red shirt, and with the manners of a rowdy, is a mild specimen. I know too the inferences drawn by wretched fools, who, because they have seen him riding upon the top of an omnibus; or at Pfaff's restaurant; or dressed in rough clothes suitable for his purposes, and only remarkable because the wearer was a man of genius; or mixing freely and lovingly, like Lucretius, like Rabelais, like Francis Bacon, like Rembrandt, like all great students of the world, with low and equivocal and dissolute persons, as well as with those of a different character, must needs set him down as a brute, a scallawag, and a criminal. Mr. Harlan's allegations are of a piece with these. If I could associate the title with a really great person, or if the name of man were not radically superior, I should say that for solid nobleness of character, for native elegance and delicacy of soul, for a courtesy which is the very passion of thoughtful kindness and forbearance, for his tender and paternal respect and manly honor for woman, for love and heroism carried into the pettiest details of life, and for a large and homely beauty of manners, which makes the civilities of parlors fantastic and puerile in comparison, Walt Whitman deserves to be considered the grandest gentleman that treads this continent.——"

"At most, our best books were but struggling beams; behold in 'Leaves of Grass' the immense and absolute sunrise! It is all our own! The nation is in it! In form a series of chants, in substance it is an epic of America. It is distinctively and utterly American. Without model, without imitation, without reminiscence, it is evolved entirely from our own polity and popular life. Look at what it celebrates and contains! hardly to be enumerated without sometimes using the powerful, wondrous phrases of its author, so indissoluble are they with the things described. The essences, the events, the objects of America; the myriad varied landscapes; the teeming and giant cities; the generous and turbulent populations; the prairie solitudes, the vast pastoral plateaus; the Mississippi; the land dense with villages and farms; the habits, manners, customs; the enormous diversity of temperatures; the immense geography; the red aborigines passing away, 'charging the water and the land with names'; the early settlements; the sudden uprising and defiance of the Revolution; the august figure of Washington; the formation and sacredness of the Constitution; the pouring in of the emigrants; the million-masted harbors; the general opulence and comfort; the fisheries, and whaling, and gold-digging, and manufactures, and agriculture; the dazzling movement of new States, rushing to be great; Nevada rising, Da-Kota rising, Colorado rising; the tumultuous civilization around and beyond the Rocky Mountains, thundering and spreading; the Union impregnable; feudalism in all its forms forever tracked and assaulted; liberty deathless on these shores; the noble and free character of the people; the equality of male and female; the ardor, the fierceness, the friendship, the dignity, the enterprise, the affection, the courage, the love of music, the passion for personal freedom; the mercy and justice and compassion of the people; —"

"Perpetual hymns break from him in praise of the divineness of the universe; he sees a halo around every shape, however low; and life in all its forms inspires a rapture of worship.

How some persons can think a book of this sort bad, is clearer to me than it used to be. Swedenborg says that to the devils, perfumes are stinks. I happen to know that some of the vilest abuse 'Leaves of Grass' has received, has come from men of the lowest possible moral life. It is not so easy to understand how some persons of culture and judgment can fail to perceive its literary greatness. —"

"Nothing that America had before in literature rose above construction; this is a creation. Idle, and worse than idle, is any attempt to place this author either among or below the poets of the day. They are but singers; he is a bard. In him you have one of that mighty brotherhood who, more than statesmen, mold the future; who, as Fletcher of Saltoun said, when they make the songs of a nation, it matters not who makes the laws. I class him boldly, and the future will confirm my judgment, among the great creative minds of the world. By a quality almost incommunicable, which makes its possessor, no matter what his diversity or imperfections, equal with the Supremes of art, and by the very structure of his mind, he belongs there. His place is beside Shakespeare, Aeschylus, Cervantes, Dante, Homer, Isaiah—the bards of the last ascent, the brothers of the radiant summit. And if any man think this estimate extravagant, I leave him, as Lord Bacon says, to the gravity of that judgment, and pass on. Enough for me to pronounce this book grandly good and supremely great. Clamor, on the score of its morality, is nothing but a form of turpitude; denial of its greatness is nothing but an insanity; and the roar of Sodom and the laughter of Bedlam shall not, by a hair's breadth, swerve my verdict. —"

Walt read the autographed copy that O'Connor gave him and was pleased. "I can be silent. My friends defend me."

There was one phrase in O'Connor's pamphlet that caught on from the beginning—it was the very title of his letter—"the good gray poet." Newspapers seized upon it and it became in a short time the very synonym for Whitman. The Calamus issue was for the moment muted. The haunting phrase "good gray poet" had been a fortunate one and displaced all other word pictures of the bard.

On such small things do men's repute depend.

O'Connor fairly gleamed and glistened with the joy of battle. "You like what I wrote, don't you? This isn't all, Walt. I'm writing a story called 'The Carpenter.' Does it suggest anything to you?"

Walt looked at O'Connor oddly. "You mean to cast me in *that* role?"

"Does it astound you?"

"No, it just seems odd. I'm not worthy." Then he added softly, "Call it coincidence and nothing more.

I *did* work at a carpenter's trade, you know."

* * * *

The young soldier sat on the edge of the cot and bowed his head. Walt looked down at him and asked the routine questions.

"Stomach?"

"No!"

"What seems to be wrong?"

"Nothing."

"Why did you come to the infirmary?"

"I don't know. I feel like killing myself."

Walt sat down on the solitary camp chair. His mind prodded the unknown, the dull opaque cloud that overwhelmed the youth. Abruptly he remembered a chance item in the newspaper—"Farm Boy Amputates His Hand." The short account had stated laconically that when the farm boy had been asked the reason for his act he had answered, quoting the verse incorrectly, "The hand that sinneth against you shall be cut off."

Walt ventured a shot in the dark. "Do you masturbate?"

The dejected soldier lifted his head and looked at Walt with an amazed incredulous expression not unmixed with guilt. His lips formed the word "Yes."

Walt spoke casually, "And you've been told or taught that you're bound to go insane or die or be everlastingly damned. Is that it?"

The youth did not answer but stared at Walt with eager hungry eyes.

"Well, that's a lot of foolishness. You're not going to die and you're not going to go insane. It's a stupid thing you're doing, pouring out the strength of you, when it should be stored up for manhood and the one you'll meet some day."

The soldier arose slowly to his feet. "I don't know

how to thank you, mister. I can't begin —"

His relief was a joy to behold. Walt knew he had stripped away the dark concentration of guilt. "Bring a thing out into the sunlight, my boy. There's nothing to fear except ignorance."

In the days that followed soldiers and civilians gathered around Walt to hear him speak of the things he had written. Young students of the classics found his iconoclasm challenging.

"Ah, Socrates," smiled O'Connor, "You'll be charged with corrupting the youth of America—and then the Hemlock."

"Be consistent, Bill. Yesterday I was The Carpenter; today I am Socrates. Who *am* I?"

"What difference is there? A Moses threatened with stoning by his own people, a Prometheus crucified to Mount Caucasus by an angry Zeus, a Jesus impaled by mocking Romans—thus the fate of teachers through the ages!"

"Prophet of ill omen," laughed Walt, "can my fate be averted?"

"Yes, if you change your song."

"How?"

"Make it palatable to the powerful. Make it palatable to Zeus. Steal none of their fire from the Sun Chariot of their special privilege to bring down to the caves and slums of mere man."

"I'll not do that."

"Not even take a little sting out of your song?"

"No."

"They'll bribe you if they can't crush you. Oh I don't mean a bribe of money alone. Flattery, even adulation."

"No."

"The bribe of flattery is more effective than persecution."

"Why are you telling me these things?"

"There's talk of lectures to be given by you. You're quite popular with the young students."

* * * *

Walt received an austere and impressive note from Dartmouth College:

"Will you be good enough to appear at our Commencement Exercises and read to us selections of your songs? We would be greatly honored by your acceptance. Please note the time and place on the enclosed announcement."

Walt felt a great triumphant joy like a mighty tide in his heart. *This* was recognition! *This* was arrival! In the halls of learning—*his* verse! How could he know that three of the graduating students had slyly conspired to shock the conservative members of the faculty by encouraging the student body to request Walt's appearance?

Emerson would hear of this honor. Thoreau, Eldridge, Swayne, Harlan—faces—upraised eyebrows—Louisa. Anne, loving, proud, sharing —

Take your pen, Walt. Dip it in flame. Write! Write! No more doubting your gift. No more wrestling with mighty phrases. *All* that you say is holy—inspired—exalted —

What will it be like to stand before a vast throng of the famed? Sons of the rich and the mighty go to Dartmouth.

* * * *

It was an imposing audience, a most impressive array of the literary. They were all there, a stiffly silent challenge of austere, intent faces. Walt wore a flowing black tie especially purchased for the occasion, and his demeanor was spirited—proud. Ashton was there, of course, eager to share his friend's triumph.

"Ashton, I've dreamed of this moment."

357

Walt was confident, assured. He had often envisioned himself on a scholarly lecture platform. But his dream had not attained to this. This was the moment! These were new poems—new songs hastily written, perhaps too hastily written but carrying a message—perhaps too obvious a message. These would not offend. Here he would take no chances on being misunderstood. These songs would be good counsel to youth everywhere. These verses were eloquent sermons. No one will reproach you, Walt! Here you will win general approval. Listen—your name! This is the moment! They are introducing you.

Faces turned to him. Faces turned to him. Mouths parted as though to drink. Eyes wide surveying him. He began to read:

> *"You just maturing youth! You male or female!*
> *Remember the organic compact of These States,*
> *Remember the pledge of the Old Thirteen thence-*
> *   forward to the rights, life, liberty, equality of*
> *   man,*
> *Remember what was promulged by the founders,*
> *   ratified by The States, signed in black and white*
> *   by the Commissioners, and read by Washington*
> *   at the head of the army,*
> *Remember the purposes of the founders,—Remem-*
> *   ber Washington;*
> *Remember the copious humanity streaming from*
> *   every direction toward America;*
> *Remember the hospitality that belongs to nations*
> *   and men; (Cursed be nation, woman, man,*
> *   without hospitality!)*
> *Remember, government is to subserve individuals,*
> *Not any, not the President, is to have one joy more*
> *   than you or me."*

Someone in the audience laughed and was quickly hushed. Walt was undisturbed.

*"Anticipate when the thirty or fifty millions, are to
become the hundred or two hundred millions,
of equal freemen and freewomen, amicably
joined.*

*Recall ages—One age is but a part—ages are but
a part;*

Recall the angers, bickerings, delusions, superstitions, of the idea of caste,

Recall the bloody cruelties and crimes.

Anticipate the best women;

*I say an unnumbered new race of hardy and well-defined women are to spread through all these
States,"*

There were whispers in the audience that mercifully he could not hear in their entirety. "Is this poetry?"
"Horn book philosophy!" "What gibberish!"

Walt sensed the mood of the audience, felt a sudden
cold sickening of the heart, but plunged on.

*"I say a girl fit for these States must be free, capable,
dauntless, just the same as a boy."*

There were a few murmurs. Some very few applauded. Walt began his next selection:

"Great are the myths—I too delight in them;

*Great are Adam and Eve—I too look back and
accept them;*

*Great the risen and fallen nations, and their poets,
women, sages, inventors, rulers, warriors, and
priests.*

Great is Liberty! great is Equality! I am their follower;

*Helmsmen of nations, choose your craft! where you
sail, I sail,*

I weather it out with you, or sink with you.

*Great is Youth—equally great is Old Age—great
are the Day and Night;*

Great is Wealth—great is Poverty—great is

Expression—great is silence."

"Very great indeed, and in this instance much to be desired," boomed a deep voice from the rear of the hall. This time they all laughed and no one hushed them.

One bald-headed man with flabby throat-skin, held his head back and crowed his laughter like a frenzied rooster.

Laughter—laughter—mean laughter—cruel laughter—scratching, clawing laughter.

Walt, cut to the heart, plunged on:

> *"Youth, large, lusty, loving—Youth, full of grace, force, fascination!*
> *Do you know that Old Age may come after you, with equal grace, force, fascination!*
> *Day, full-blown and splendid—Day of the immense sun, action, ambition, laughter,*
> *The Night follows close, with millions of suns, and sleep, and restoring darkness.*
> *Wealth, with the flush hand, fine clothes, hospitality;*
> *But when the Soul's wealth, which is candor, knowledge, pride, enfolding love;*
> *(Who goes for men and women showing Poverty richer than wealth?)*
> *Expression of speech! in which is written on said, forget not that Silence is also expressive,*
> *That anguish as hot as the hottest, and contempt as cold as the coldest, may be without words."*

Now the audience sat impatient, stiff and cold, almost hostile.

> *"Great is Life, real and mystical, wherever and whoever;*

Great is Death—sure as life holds all parts to-
*   gether,*
Death holds all parts together.
Has Life much purport?— Ah, Death has the
*   greatest purport."*

"Death would be a blessing," whispered a robed student, and again there was a burble of laughter.

Walt, dazed at his failure and yet desperately persisting, was about to read another poem. The chairman, his benevolent face framed in ruddy sideburns, hastened forward with as much tact as he could summon for the emergency.

"We are indeed grateful to our guest poet who has so graciously read from his hitherto unpublished works. And now our graduates will receive those testimonies to their labors for which they have so long waited."

Walt sat down, a cold horrifying frost tide sweeping through him. He had bored and wearied them. He had failed O'Connor and Ashton. He had too hastily phrased. Why had he not read instead from "Drum Taps" or "Myself I Sing?"

People were dispersing. "Good Night! Good Night!" They were ignoring him. He was forgotten or remembered as a jest. Follow the flow of people. There are the doors and outside the chill night air. Look about you and hope you are not seen. Shrink, Walt—shrink!

Ashton found him at last and placed his hand on Walt's shoulder as though to comfort him. Walt looked at him in the dim light of the gas lamp.

"Tonight I failed. Tonight I offended myself."

VIII

Walt lay awake in his dark room, his eyes open, but unable to see one object on the walls or near his bed. The darkness engulfed him—pressed upon him—

shrouded him—and he stared hard trying to pierce it
—stared until the tears flowed over—and he could see
nothing.

But Melville was there—and Foster too—and Nellie
with her bruised throat—and Jesse with the spittle on
his beard—and Eddie with his hollow stare—and there
were bleeding legs and arms heaped near his bed—for
he could smell the stench of rotting flesh.

Now will you yield?

Curse life and cease to be!

What made you think you heard a song?

Walt flung his arms towards the darkness above
him—his blood chilling and burning—his tense nerves
straining and quivering.

"If there is no Singer and no song—I'll still sing
on, sculpturing chaos with my Will to Joy—giving it
light and form and warmth and pattern."

Walt—are you then a God?

No! No! But He is there—He must be—*must be*—
and He who flung chaos into the awesome void gave
me, His partner in Creation, — my song, — where else
could I have gotten it—gave me my song to shape that
chaos, and will it into form.

> "O, I am sure they really came from Thee,
> The urge, the ardor, the unconquerable will,
> ·The potent, felt, interior command, stronger than
>   words,
> A message from the heavens whispering to me, even
>   in sleep;
> These sped me on.
> One effort more, my altar this bleak sand:
> That Thou, O God, my life hast lighted
> With ray of light, steady, ineffable, vouchsafed of
>   Thee,
> Light rare, untellable, lighting the very light,
> Beyond all signs, descriptions, languages;

For that, O God, be it my latest word, here on my
   knees,
Old, poor and paralyzed, I thank Thee.
My terminus near,
The clouds already closing in upon me,
The voyage balked, the course disputed, lost,
I yield my ships to Thee.
My hands, my limbs grow nerveless,
My brain feels rack'd, bewilder'd;
Let the old timbers part, I will not part,
I will cling fast to Thee, O God, though the waves
   buffet me,
Thee, Thee at least I know."

Part Eight

THE GOAL

The Treasury Building was deserted. In the glow of the astral lamp Whitman's face was haloed in silver. O'Connor's friendly visit had lengthened into hours.

"There is much that I would like to write about you, Walt, and I know so little of the mainsprings of your life."

"And I know less."

O'Connor was insistent. "America needs your voice. It must read you and understand you as it is beginning to understand Lincoln. These songs of yours are mighty, but I must know more about you—little personal things that will bring you close to people. Why do you make such a mystery of yourself?"

"I'm no mystery at all. There is nothing of me that is not in my songs. I *am* Leaves of Grass. It is myself I sing. The rest is unimportant."

"No, Walt. The little things, little weaknesses, the human things that give you dimension and shape."

"They're not important."

"Let's not quibble. I need notes for a biography. Give me any information you can."

"You know all about my family—my mother, my brothers, my sisters. What else can I tell you?"

"Walt, just who is Anne Sedley?"

Walt stared at O'Connor, not a muscle of his face working. There are no secrets! Secrets will out! Open floodgates! Rush you frothing waters! Sweep over rock, and flood the shores!

365

"Who is Anne Sedley? Tell me about her." O'Connor loosened a rapid explanatory stream of words. "I called for your books and papers at your old office. There were some of your notes, a letter and a picture. Ashton told me you had left them there when you moved into the Attorney General's office."

Walt was only half listening to O'Connor. All of a sudden he felt the clutch of panic. He was thinking, "Anne, Anne, I should have burnt your letter. He'll tell Nellie and she'll tell her neighbors. Then the cruel lips will buzz through the city and the land. They'll condemn me, my darling, and cast me out. *I* don't matter—but my Book—my Song!

Walt and a Negress! Walt and a Negress! My Book will be scorned, marred. It is far too far in advance of the time. Only you and I understand. My own flesh and blood will cast me out."

"Give me the letter and the picture!" Walt tried to rise. A frightful dizziness overpowered him. He fell back into his chair. His arm seemed frozen, numb.

O'Connor, alarmed, moved to him quickly. "What's wrong, Walt? Let me help you."

Walt sat staring at him. "Bill, forget about what you read in the letter. It can bring no good to anyone. My arm seems numb. It will pass. Bill, give me the letter and the picture."

"Don't worry about a thing, Walt. If you're not well let me take you to my home. I feel guilty and ashamed at reading the letter, but why didn't you tell me that you have a wife and son? What was there to hide?"

Walt stared at O'Connor, trying to read his mind. "But you read the letter. You know, then. Don't pretend you don't know."

"Walt, why don't you send for her? Why don't you send for them both?"

"I don't dare. It would be cruel to them."

"I don't understand."

Strange that O'Connor was not shocked. His voice was just as gentle as before. "When did you last see your son?"

"I have never seen him."

O'Connor shook his head. "Why do I have to ask these questions? Can't you *tell* me? Why do you keep these things secret?"

"You read the letter; you know the answer. Why do you torture me?"

"You're torturing yourself. Send for your wife and son."

"You can't mean what you're saying. Anne's a quadroon. The child may be altogether black. I don't know —"

"But you said she's a quadroon."

"She's still a Negress in the eyes of the world."

"But she's your wife. I'm not suggesting that whites or Negroes should go out of their way to intermarry. Chances are that people prefer those with whom they have a lot in common. But where such a marriage *does* exist don't let fear or prejudice break it up."

"I have no alternative."

O'Connor looked at Walt as though he had been slapped across the lips. "Hold on there, Walt. What's that you're saying? Let me understand you. You mean you're ashamed of them—ashamed of their color—ashamed of admitting they're yours?"

"Shame has nothing to do with it, neither fear nor shame. I'm facing realities. Bill, try to understand that I love Anne. All my songs of love were inspired by her and when I could not pour that love out on her I spilled it all the more lavishly on everyone and everything around me. I'm not ashamed of anything—but there are realities of time and temporary circumstance.

It would be cruel to them—most cruel to them, but worse than that—it would destroy my Song."

O'Connor's lip curled in perplexed disdain. "You mean that after all the blood that's been shed Anne is still a slave? You mean that all your songs about the brotherhood of man are only words? Not you too! Walt, I believed in you as my sainted mother believed in miracles. I beheld you as a Samson destroying the pillars of prejudice, and now I admit I don't understand you at all."

Walt made no comment and O'Connor continued furiously. "Why did we fight this war? It's far more difficult to wed the plantation South to the industrialized North than it is to maintain your marriage with Anne—and yet we're going to do it! We're going to make that Union stick!"

Walt spoke softly as though to calm O'Connor and not enrage him more. "If I take Anne and my son into my arms I destroy my song and I destroy them. It's too premature. Give me the letter and the picture, Bill."

O'Connor's eyes grew dull. "Here, take them. I've got no more use for them."

"And for me either?" As Walt reached for the small packet and held it with both trembling hands a great pity touched the heart of the man who had worshipped him. He bent toward him pleading,

"Be the symbol of what you proclaim. Seal your song with your deed, as Lincoln sealed his faith with his life. This is the moment for a complete victory. The Negro has been liberated! Accept your wife and son before the world. Walt, Walt, the world will be the better for it."

Walt tried to rise. Now his whole side was paralyzed. Even his speech seemed labored and thick. He *must* make O'Connor understand. He must! He must!

"Bill, listen to me while I can still speak! Listen

to me! I have set before America its true shining goal
—the complete—the utter freedom of Man. We're
climbing—climbing steadily. One rash act and we fall
to our death. The bloody wound between the North
and the South must heal. That takes time, Bill. That
takes time!"

"What has this to do with you and Anne?"

"Everything! You've got to understand the fears of
the whites of the South. To them equality of the Negro
conjures up visions of sex let loose on a rampage between black and white. Let them learn by degrees that
the freedom of the Negro does not necessarily mean
sharing their bed with him. I, the singer of the song,
must proceed slowly or I claw the wound.

Anne herself would not want it. She told me so.
Bill, why don't you see the task and all the obstacles
clearly? Have you ever been South? Have you seen
the Negro in the South—the depths of his pit? All I
ask for is patience and effort — one generation — two
generations, perhaps a little longer, and he is raised
from the pit. Why must you hasten the end before its
time?"

O'Connor did not answer. He clasped his hands
tightly across his knees and sat with his head bowed
down as one surveys dying embers. Finally he muttered
tonelessly, "Singing the things you haven't got the guts
to do. We take it all out in talk, don't we? We wrap
all our rottenness and our greed in the bright colors of
ideals and go out to fight and die because we're vicious
animals who want an excuse for plundering and killing."

"The boys I took care of in the hospitals weren't
vicious."

"So they were stupid, arrogant, quarrelsome, ad-
venturous, if you want it that way. Sick of the plow
and the farm. Drawn by the glamor of gold braid,

anxious to draw a bead on something else besides squirrels and rabbits. One learning to swagger from the other—the whole pattern of salute—march—hero worship—cock-of-the-walk—uniforms—glory! And as for the rest—the ideals of brotherhood, the breaking of the bonds of slavery—just a balm to conscience."

"No, that's not true. What they felt was a true spark of the flame ahead. Under pressure sparks fly. It takes a while before they catch."

O'Connor did not speak.

"O'Connor, you've got to believe that I've been true to myself. I believe absolutely in the equality of man but we're not ready. We haven't cleansed *ourselves* of fear and prejudice. The Negroes aren't ready for real equality yet. We must help them prepare for it, and, what is more important, prepare ourselves to receive them. My songs are ahead of the times by a hundred or several hundred years. They're the advance scouts that point the future. There's a truth for every age. My age isn't here yet—but it will surely come."

"There's a contradiction in your speech and actions. You say you love Anne —"

"I know. I know, but they're not all Annes—not yet. It will take time."

O'Connor waved his hand impatiently. "A new environment—real liberty—and in one generation the Negroes will prove that only our chains of prejudice and enforced ignorance have held them back."

"Individuals, yes—but it takes longer for a whole people. And besides it will take much longer for the whites to tear out and weed out the deep roots of *their* bigotry. The clansmen are on the march and the burned and mutilated bodies of Negroes are hanging from trees. We must teach—educate—calm and appeal. Hurry the process and you have an anarchy of emotions that will have a dangerous reaction—and all our gains will be lost. We must proceed slowly—slowly, with devotion and patience."

O'Connor walked towards the door. "Impatient in song and patient in deed, and to me you were the Second Coming." He whirled about and faced Walt, "But an act of Marriage would not shock. Show me one logical reason, just one, not based on prejudice or fear, that should stand between you and Anne. Is there a religion on earth that would condemn you?"

"They'd find a way."

"So you yield out of cowardice!"

"No, out of careful deliberation. I'm sorry if I've disappointed you. But you've got to be patient."

"That was Harlan's line of talk. 'Wait, noble Red Man. Soon salvation cometh. Be patient!' The future promise that kills the present deed. No, Walt, the future changes nothing except the metal of the shackles, and poets sell us out by substituting words for deeds. I thought you and Harlan were as far apart as the poles, but you talk like the prophet Amos and act like the bigot Harlan."

"No." Walt spoke gently, trying to calm his friend. "*He* doesn't want it to ever be different—and I *do!* I believe in America. I believe that it will become the perfect democracy, but it must take time."

O'Connor stared at Walt and slowly shook his head. "No, if a thing is right it's right now, was right yesterday and will be right tomorrow. If the Negroes are citizens of America then they must have every right that I have—*every* right!"

"I repeat, they're not ready for it yet."

"Not ready for the ballot either?"

"No. They must first learn to use it intelligently. Moses could not lead his own generation of the Children of Israel into the Promised Land. They were not ready. They died in the desert, but their children —.

Bill, in spite of what you wrote I'm not the Carpenter. I can't promise to build a Temple in three days."

O'Connor's face was livid. He tried to speak but words did not come. At last they tore themselves from his lips. "That's not fair! Now you're mocking me and my worship of you. For the drug of words you gave Nellie, accept my gratitude. Narcotics are helpful, but as for the rest—Walt, you and your lying songs be damned!" He strode from the room with no word of farewell.

Walt felt a stabbing pain over his eyes. "O'Connor's impatient—too impatient. Things grow. They don't explode into being."

But Walt, *you* are responsible for his anger and disappointment. You yourself gave him the architect's plan and now you say, "Don't build the house!"

I didn't say that. I said, "Build slowly. Let the green lumber season itself. Lay a firm foundation. First preserve the Union and then strike shackles off; then heal bruises; then take them by the arm and show them the way—and that, Walt, is what you're singing. It's the song of the long road you're singing—the long path to follow. You've got to sing out now so people will see the goal ahead. Slow? Yes, Walt, that's the trouble with songs like yours—they're so far ahead of people."

* * * *

The chill winter rain came down out of a dreary nowhere. Walt's arm felt inert—dead, and the right side of his face seemed as heavy as lead. He walked with difficulty.

"I'll ask the doctor at the hospital what's wrong."

Now the rain was muted to a fine mist. This was much better. There was comfort and solace in the moist caress of the twilight.

The young soldier who stood on the curb tipped his

hat as he leaned on his crutch. One empty trouser leg was folded up at the knee, but the jaunty smile of the crippled man made his loss seem like a medal for valor.

"I beg your pardon, sir; you're Walt Whitman, aren't you?"

Walt nodded. His tongue seemed swollen and he could not speak. He was thinking, "I'd better hurry on to the hospital. Something is very strange. The arm is paralyzed. My cheek—my face—but I mustn't offend this young soldier!"

"May I shake your hand, Mr. Whitman? I've wanted to for a long time. I've learned your songs by heart—almost all of them. You see, at the hospital there were weeks when they thought they could save my leg, so they waited. The boy in the next bed to mine gave me your book. It's like the sound of trumpets—clear trumpets—and every word sings. I know them by heart. Yes sir, I'll prove it to you:

"*I hear America singing, the varied carols I hear,*
Those of mechanics, each one singing his as it
   should be blithe and strong,
The carpenter singing his as he measures his plank
   or beam,
The mason singing his as he makes ready for work,
   or leaves off work,
The boatman singing what belongs to him in his
   boat, the deck-hand singing on the steamboat
   deck,
The shoemaker singing as he sits on his bench, the
   hatter singing as he stands.
The wood-cutter's song, the ploughboy's on his way
   in the morning, or at noon intermission or at
   sundown,
The delicious singing of the mother, or of the young
   wife at work, or of the girl sewing or washing,

*Each singing what belongs to him or her and to
none else."*

The young man paused. "That's not exactly true,
Mr. Whitman. You sing for me. I can't put words together that way and make them sound like organ
music."

Walt grasped the outstretched hand and turned
away. He was not far from the hospital. It was hard to
see through the mist but now it didn't matter, for all
around him there was mighty music—and the music
held him under the arms and moved him forward—
firmly—steadily—steadily—

A NOTE ON THE TYPE USED IN THIS BOOK

The text of this book has been set on the Linotype in a type-face called "Baskerville." The face is a facsimile reproduction of types cast from molds made for John Baskerville (1706-1775) from his designs. The punches for the revived Linotype Baskerville were cut under the supervision of the English printer George W. Jones.

John Baskerville's original face was one of the forerunners of the type-style known as "modern-face" to printers.